TIME FLYZ

TUNNEL TWIST-UP

ZONDERVAN®

Tunnel Twist-up
Copyright © 2008 by Ben Avery
Illustrations copyright © 2008 by Adi Darda Gaudiamo

Library of Congress Cataloging-in-Publication Data: Applied for
ISBN 978-0-310-71364-7

Requests for information should be addressed to:

Zondervan, *Grand Rapids, Michigan 49530*

Series Editor: Bud Rogers
Managing Art Director: Merit Alderink

Printed in the United States of America

08 09 10 11 12 13 •10 9 8 7 6 5 4 3 2 1

GRAPHIC NOVELS

TUNNEL TWIST-UP

SERIES EDITOR:
BUD ROGERS

STORY BY BEN AVERY
ART BY ADI DARDA GAUDIAMO

ZONDERVAN®

ZONDERVAN.com/
AUTHORTRACKER
follow your favorite authors

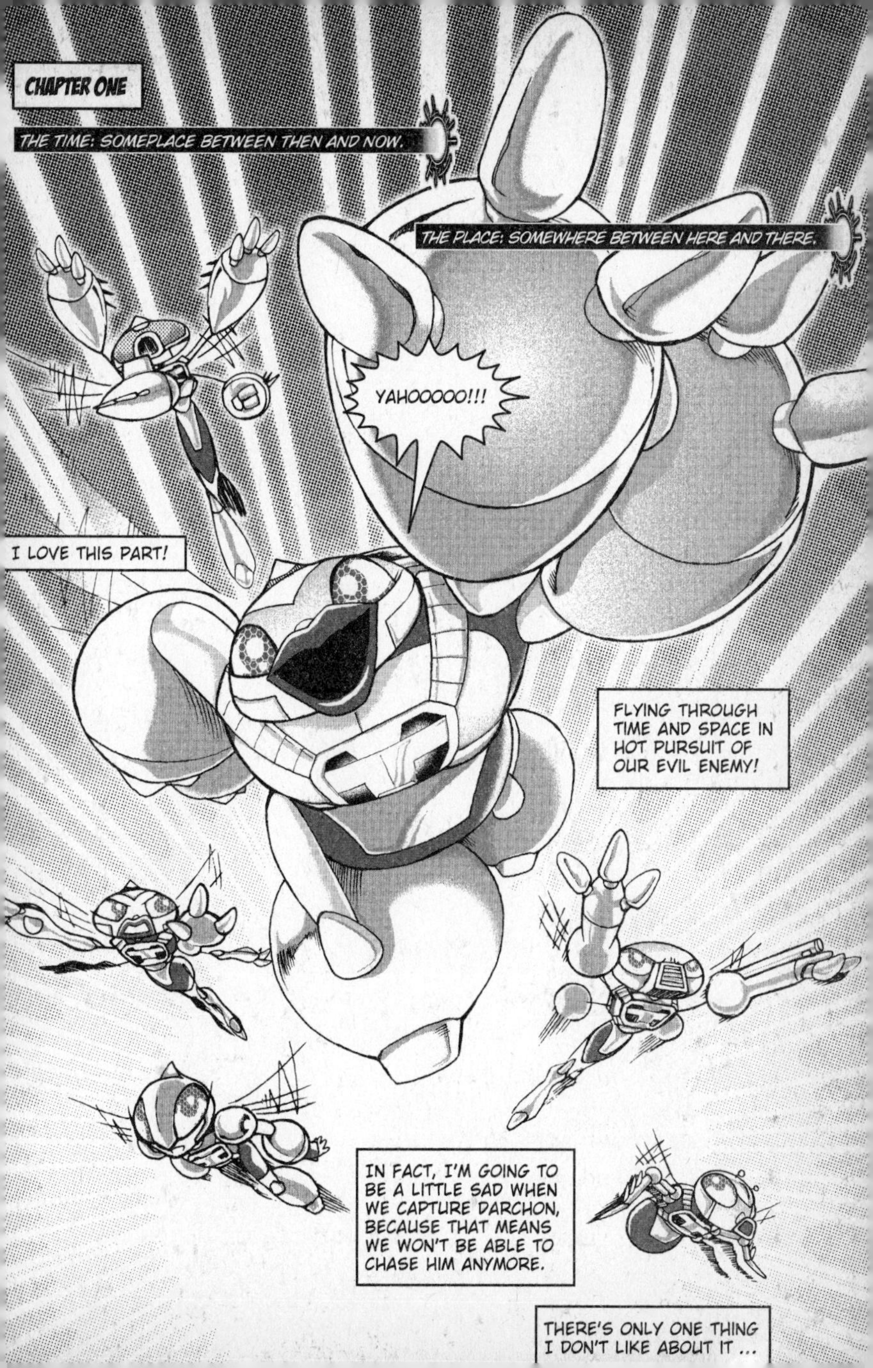
CHAPTER ONE
THE TIME: SOMEPLACE BETWEEN THEN AND NOW.
THE PLACE: SOMEWHERE BETWEEN HERE AND THERE.
YAHOOOOO!!!
I LOVE THIS PART!
FLYING THROUGH TIME AND SPACE IN HOT PURSUIT OF OUR EVIL ENEMY!
IN FACT, I'M GOING TO BE A LITTLE SAD WHEN WE CAPTURE DARCHON, BECAUSE THAT MEANS WE WON'T BE ABLE TO CHASE HIM ANYMORE.
THERE'S ONLY ONE THING I DON'T LIKE ABOUT IT ...

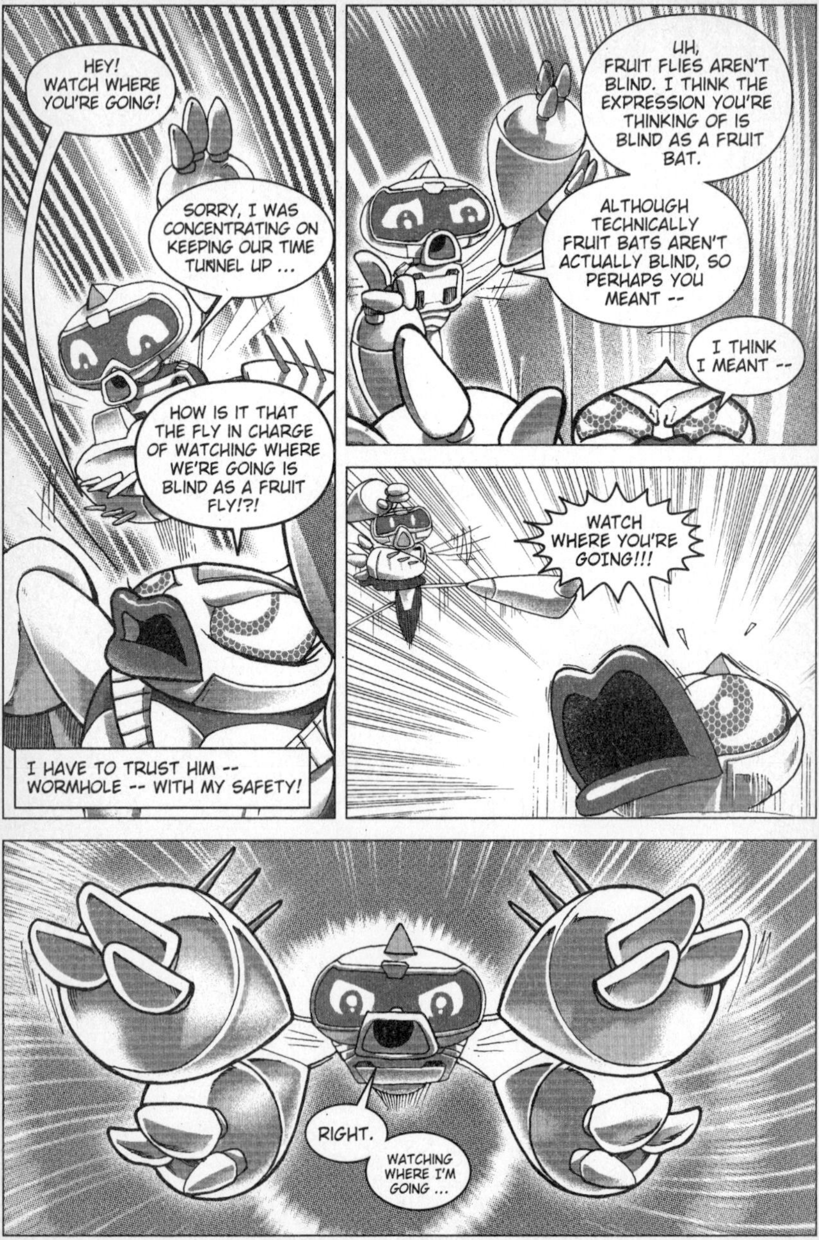
HEY! WATCH WHERE YOU'RE GOING!
SORRY, I WAS CONCENTRATING ON KEEPING OUR TIME TUNNEL UP ...
HOW IS IT THAT THE FLY IN CHARGE OF WATCHING WHERE WE'RE GOING IS BLIND AS A FRUIT FLY!?!
I HAVE TO TRUST HIM -- WORMHOLE -- WITH MY SAFETY!
UH, FRUIT FLIES AREN'T BLIND. I THINK THE EXPRESSION YOU'RE THINKING OF IS BLIND AS A FRUIT BAT.
ALTHOUGH TECHNICALLY FRUIT BATS AREN'T ACTUALLY BLIND, SO PERHAPS YOU MEANT --
I THINK I MEANT --
WATCH WHERE YOU'RE GOING!!!
RIGHT.
WATCHING WHERE I'M GOING ...

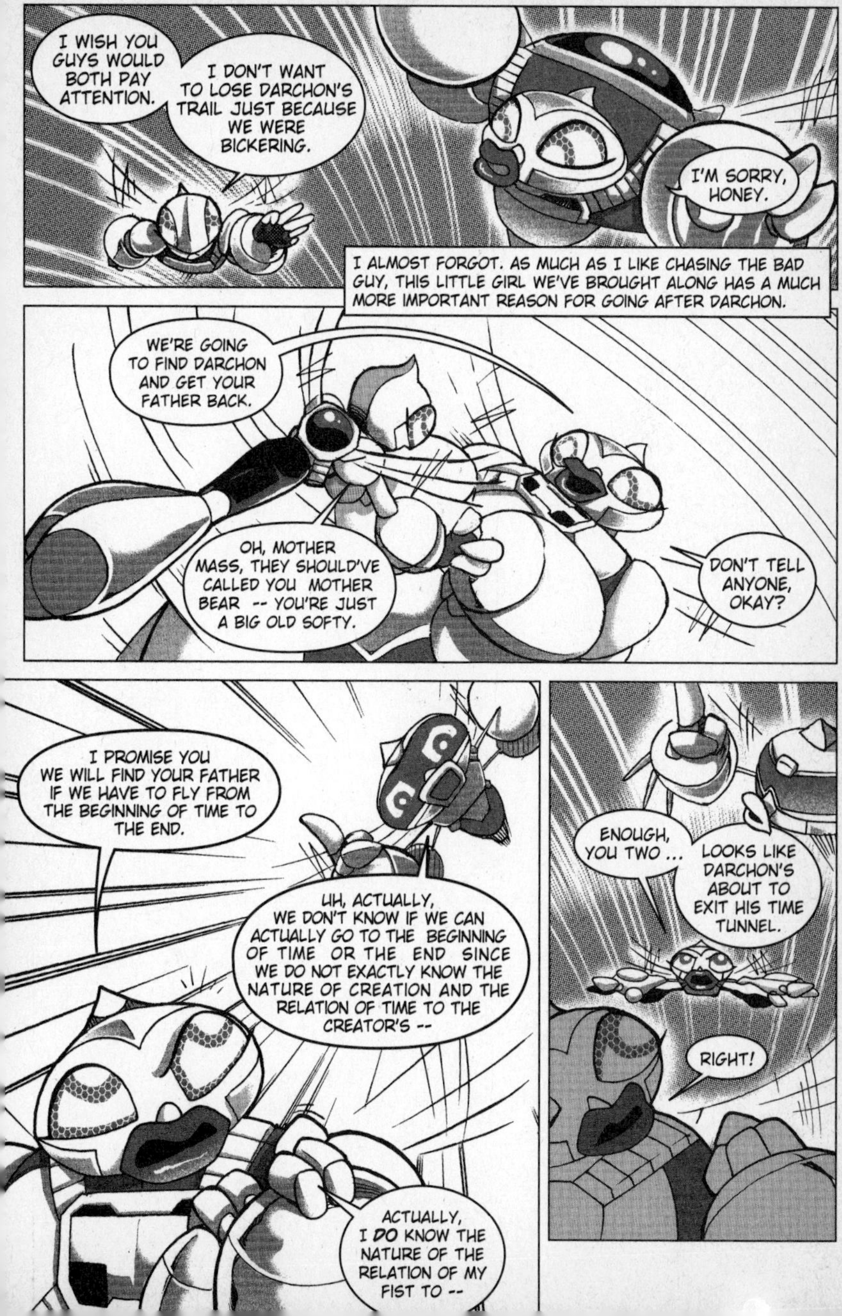
I WISH YOU GUYS WOULD BOTH PAY ATTENTION.
I DON'T WANT TO LOSE DARCHON'S TRAIL JUST BECAUSE WE WERE BICKERING.
I'M SORRY, HONEY.
I ALMOST FORGOT. AS MUCH AS I LIKE CHASING THE BAD GUY, THIS LITTLE GIRL WE'VE BROUGHT ALONG HAS A MUCH MORE IMPORTANT REASON FOR GOING AFTER DARCHON.
WE'RE GOING TO FIND DARCHON AND GET YOUR FATHER BACK.
OH, MOTHER MASS, THEY SHOULD'VE CALLED YOU MOTHER BEAR -- YOU'RE JUST A BIG OLD SOFTY.
DON'T TELL ANYONE, OKAY?
I PROMISE YOU WE WILL FIND YOUR FATHER IF WE HAVE TO FLY FROM THE BEGINNING OF TIME TO THE END.
UH, ACTUALLY, WE DON'T KNOW IF WE CAN ACTUALLY GO TO THE BEGINNING OF TIME OR THE END SINCE WE DO NOT EXACTLY KNOW THE NATURE OF CREATION AND THE RELATION OF TIME TO THE CREATOR'S --
ACTUALLY, I *DO* KNOW THE NATURE OF THE RELATION OF MY FIST TO --
ENOUGH, YOU TWO ...
LOOKS LIKE DARCHON'S ABOUT TO EXIT HIS TIME TUNNEL.
RIGHT!

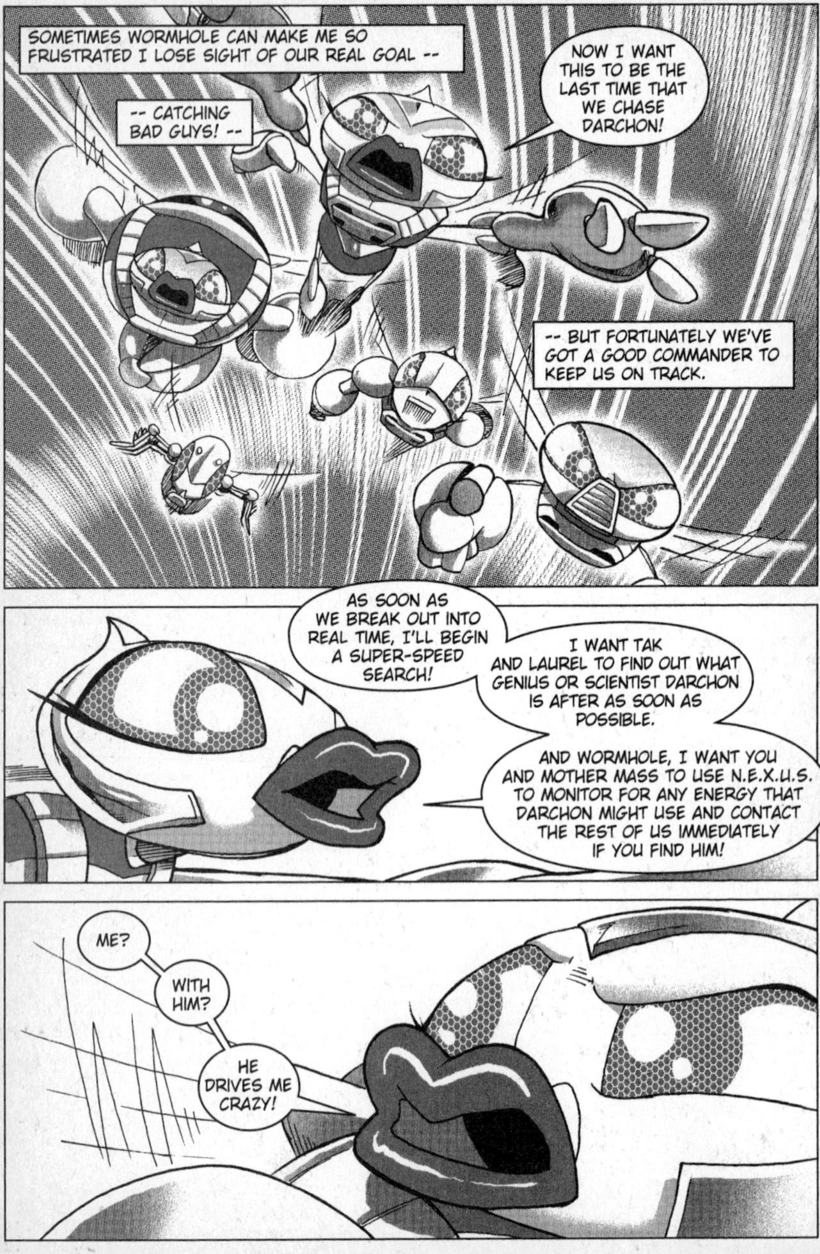
SOMETIMES WORMHOLE CAN MAKE ME SO FRUSTRATED I LOSE SIGHT OF OUR REAL GOAL --
-- CATCHING BAD GUYS! --
NOW I WANT THIS TO BE THE LAST TIME THAT WE CHASE DARCHON!
-- BUT FORTUNATELY WE'VE GOT A GOOD COMMANDER TO KEEP US ON TRACK.
AS SOON AS WE BREAK OUT INTO REAL TIME, I'LL BEGIN A SUPER-SPEED SEARCH!
I WANT TAK AND LAUREL TO FIND OUT WHAT GENIUS OR SCIENTIST DARCHON IS AFTER AS SOON AS POSSIBLE.
AND WORMHOLE, I WANT YOU AND MOTHER MASS TO USE N.E.X.U.S. TO MONITOR FOR ANY ENERGY THAT DARCHON MIGHT USE AND CONTACT THE REST OF US IMMEDIATELY IF YOU FIND HIM!
ME?
WITH HIM?
HE DRIVES ME CRAZY!

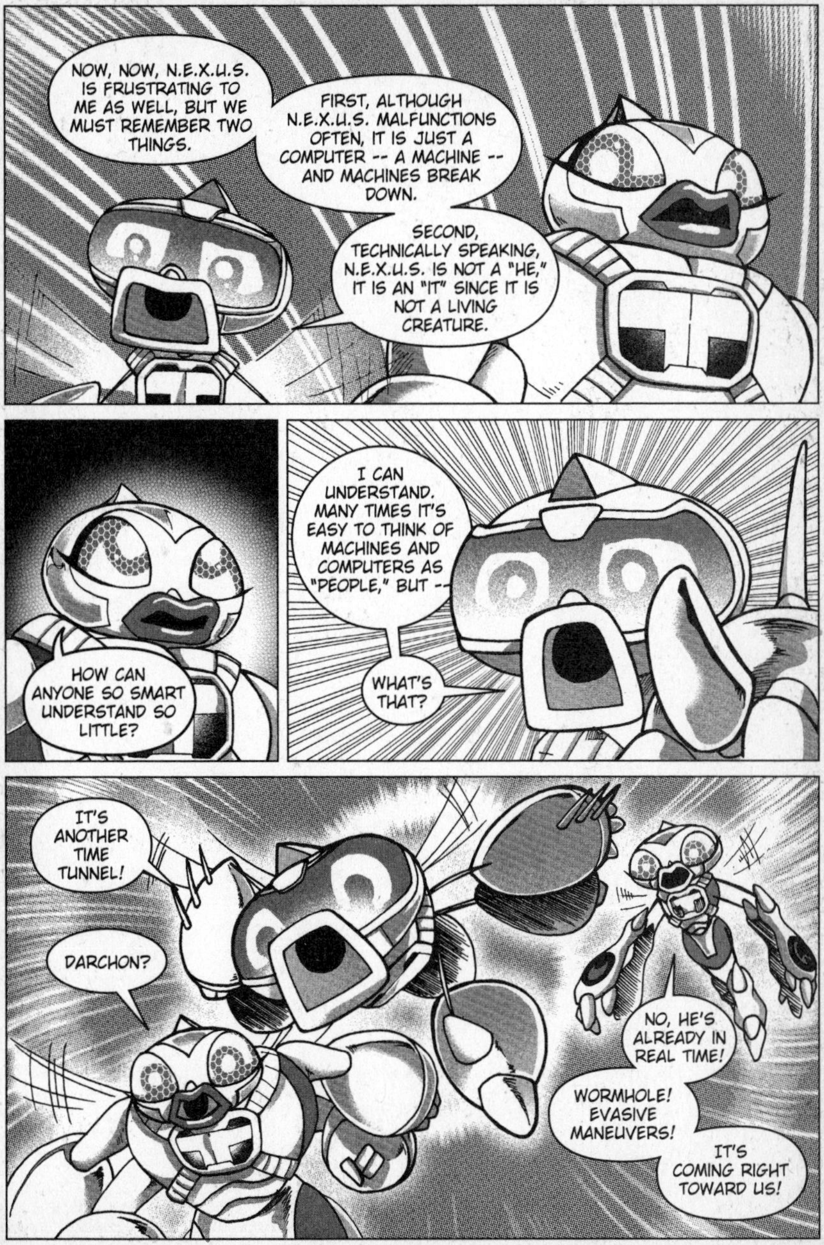
NOW, NOW, N.E.X.U.S. IS FRUSTRATING TO ME AS WELL, BUT WE MUST REMEMBER TWO THINGS.
FIRST, ALTHOUGH N.E.X.U.S. MALFUNCTIONS OFTEN, IT IS JUST A COMPUTER -- A MACHINE -- AND MACHINES BREAK DOWN.
SECOND, TECHNICALLY SPEAKING, N.E.X.U.S. IS NOT A "HE," IT IS AN "IT" SINCE IT IS NOT A LIVING CREATURE.
HOW CAN ANYONE SO SMART UNDERSTAND SO LITTLE?
I CAN UNDERSTAND. MANY TIMES IT'S EASY TO THINK OF MACHINES AND COMPUTERS AS "PEOPLE," BUT --
WHAT'S THAT?
IT'S ANOTHER TIME TUNNEL!
DARCHON?
NO, HE'S ALREADY IN REAL TIME!
WORMHOLE! EVASIVE MANEUVERS!
IT'S COMING RIGHT TOWARD US!

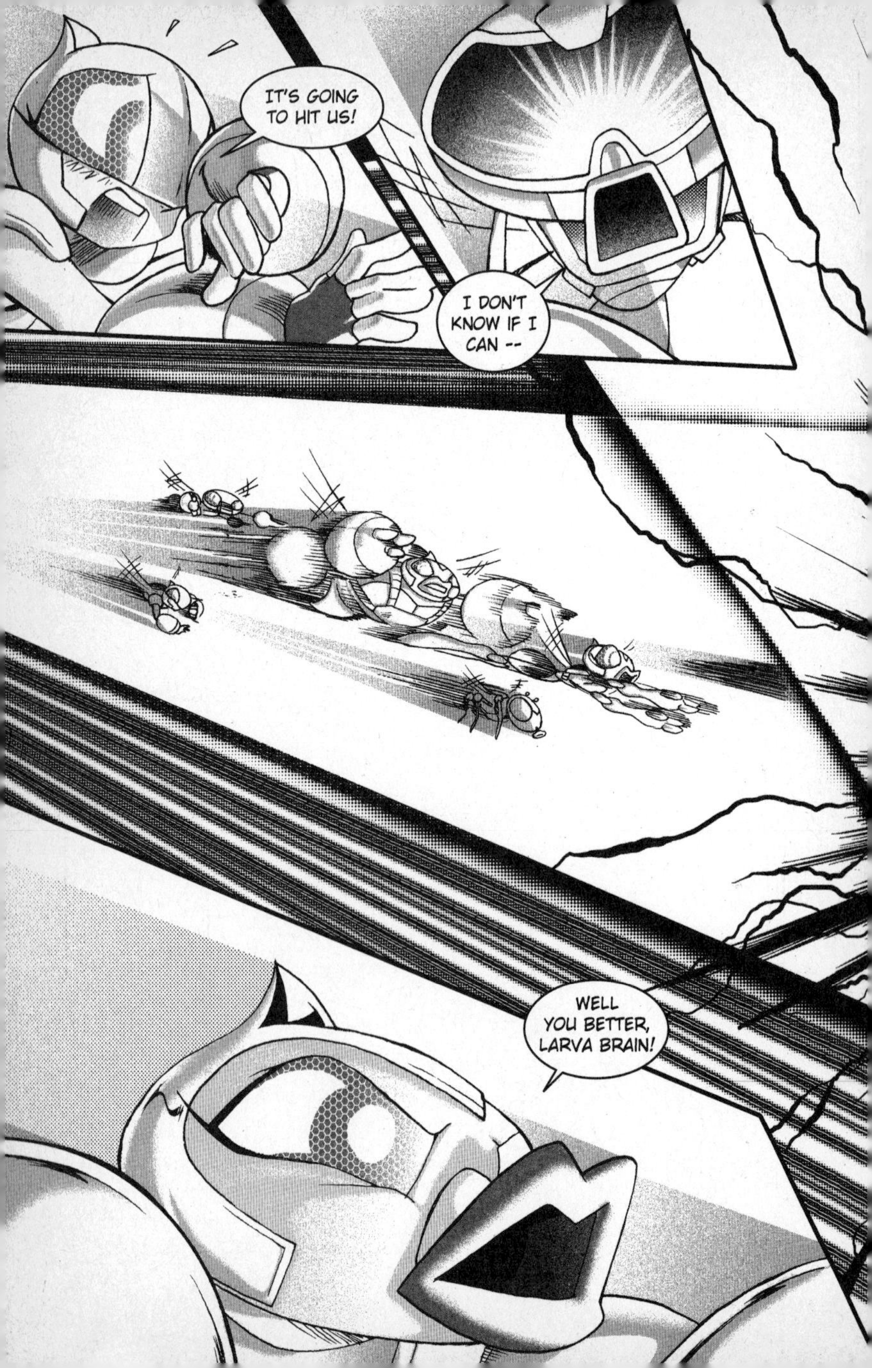
IT'S GOING TO HIT US!
I DON'T KNOW IF I CAN --
WELL YOU BETTER, LARVA BRAIN!

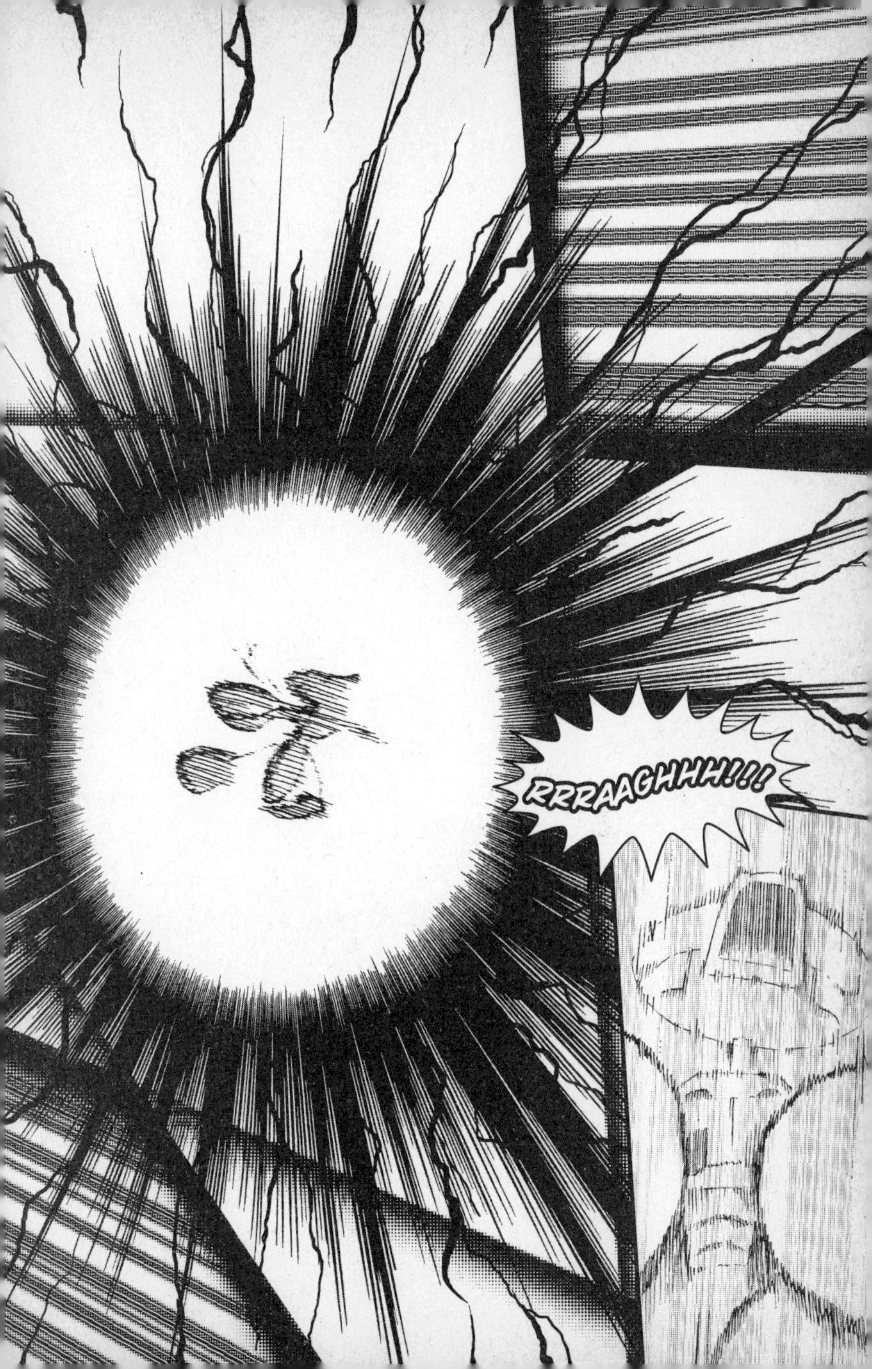
RRRAAGHHH!!!

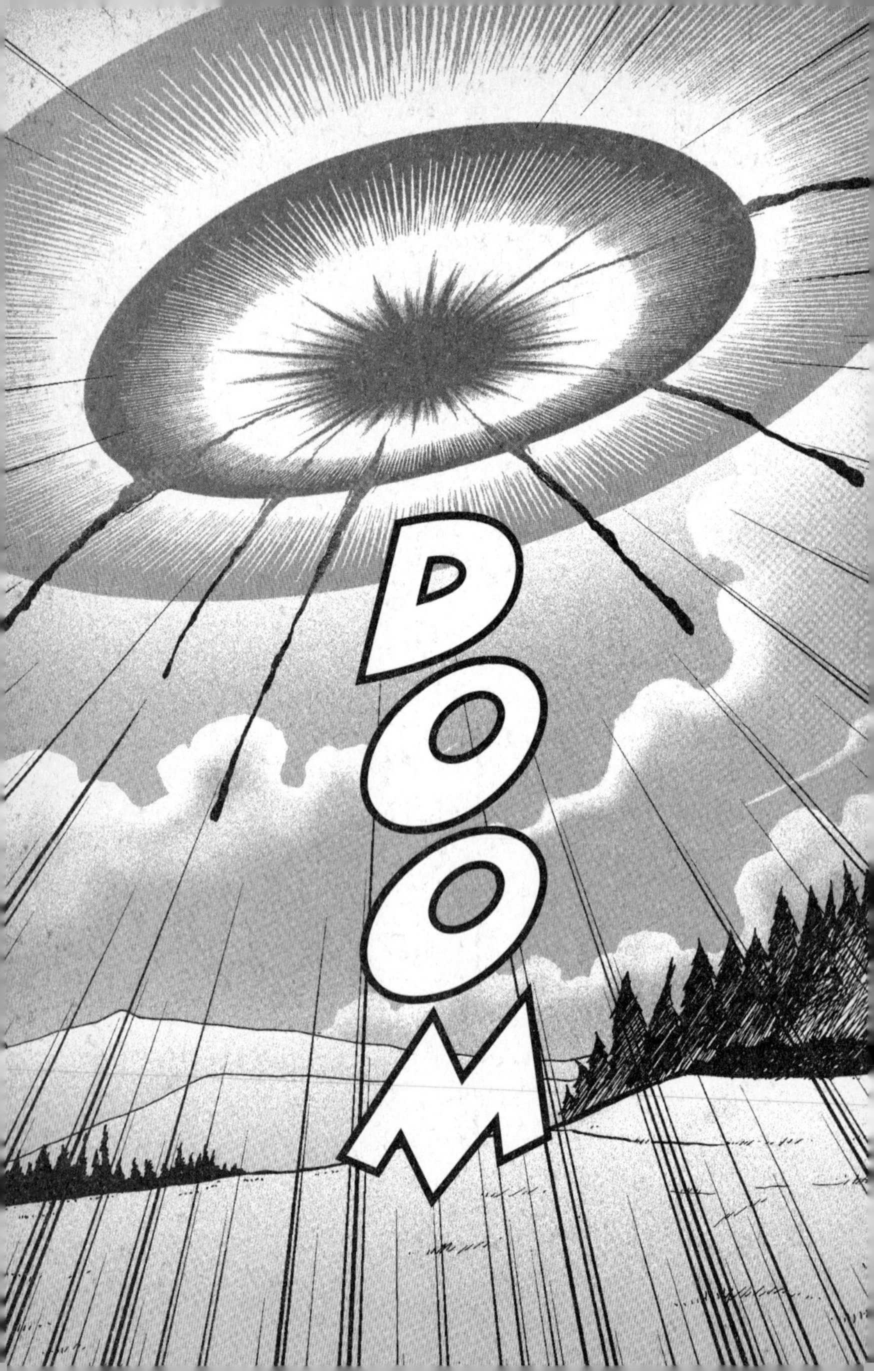
DOOM

AAAAAAAAAAAAHHHH!

AAAAAAAAAAAAAAAAAA!!!

AAHHHH!

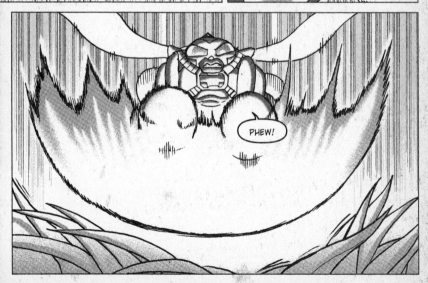

PHEW!

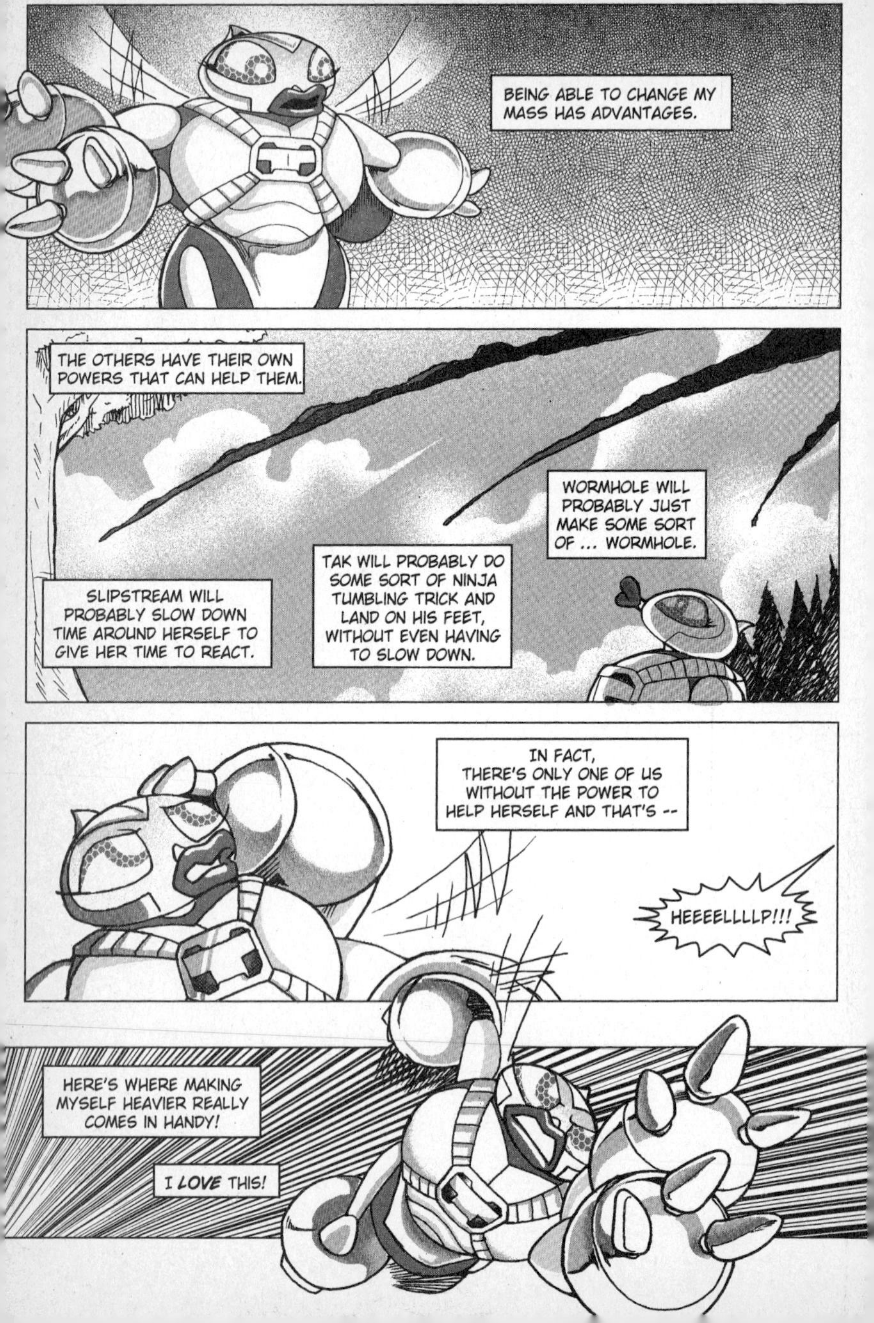

BEING ABLE TO CHANGE MY MASS HAS ADVANTAGES.
THE OTHERS HAVE THEIR OWN POWERS THAT CAN HELP THEM.
SLIPSTREAM WILL PROBABLY SLOW DOWN TIME AROUND HERSELF TO GIVE HER TIME TO REACT.
TAK WILL PROBABLY DO SOME SORT OF NINJA TUMBLING TRICK AND LAND ON HIS FEET, WITHOUT EVEN HAVING TO SLOW DOWN.
WORMHOLE WILL PROBABLY JUST MAKE SOME SORT OF ... WORMHOLE.
IN FACT, THERE'S ONLY ONE OF US WITHOUT THE POWER TO HELP HERSELF AND THAT'S --
HEEEELLLLP!!!
HERE'S WHERE MAKING MYSELF HEAVIER REALLY COMES IN HANDY!
I *LOVE* THIS!

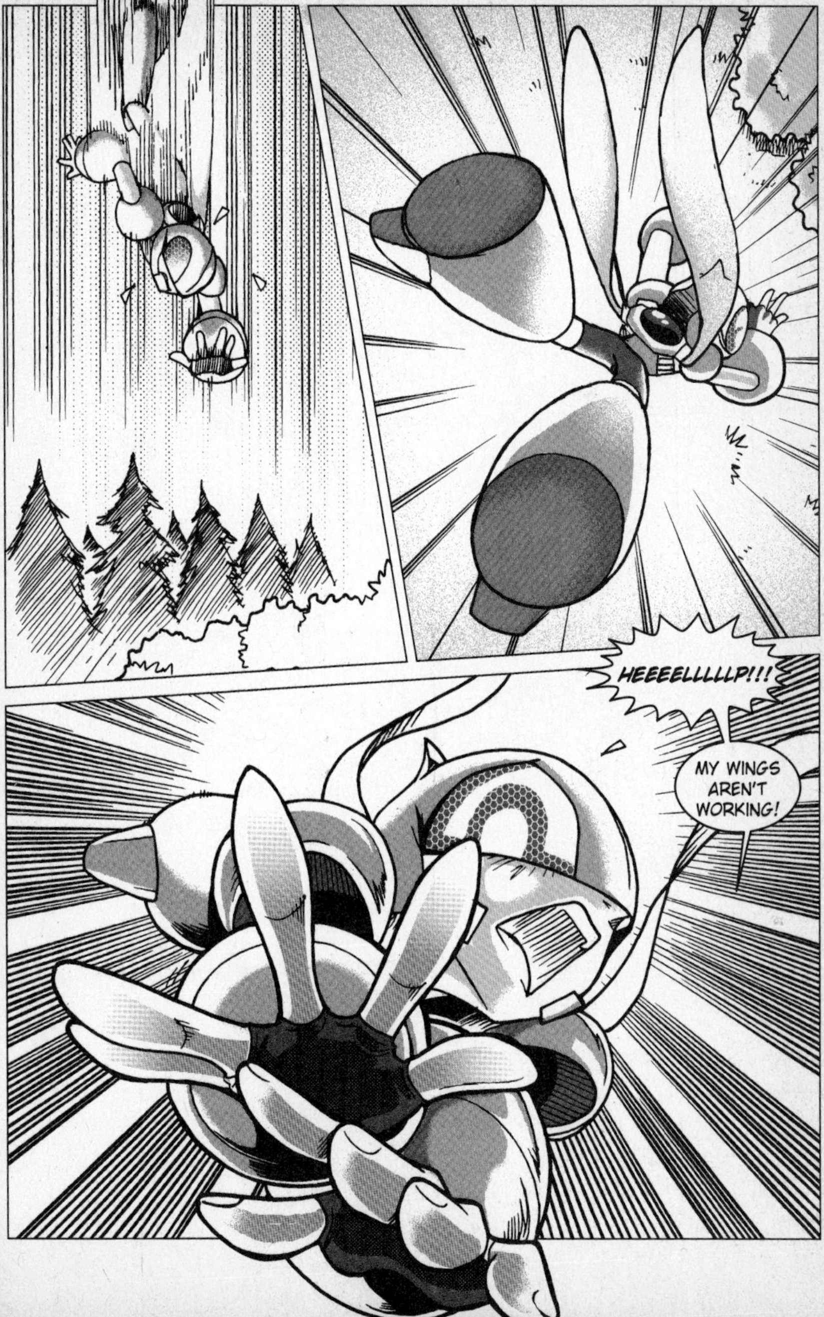
HEEEELLLLLLP!!!
MY WINGS AREN'T WORKING!

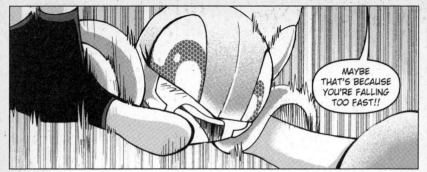

MAYBE THAT'S BECAUSE YOU'RE FALLING TOO FAST!!

MOTHER MASS?

YOU'VE SPENT TOO MUCH TIME WITH WORMHOLE! THAT SOUNDED LIKE SOMETHING HE'D --

YOU WANT ME TO RESCUE YOU OR NOT?

RIGHT! SORRY!

YOU CAN RESCUE ME ANY TIME NOW!

I'M REALLY VERY, VERY SORRY!

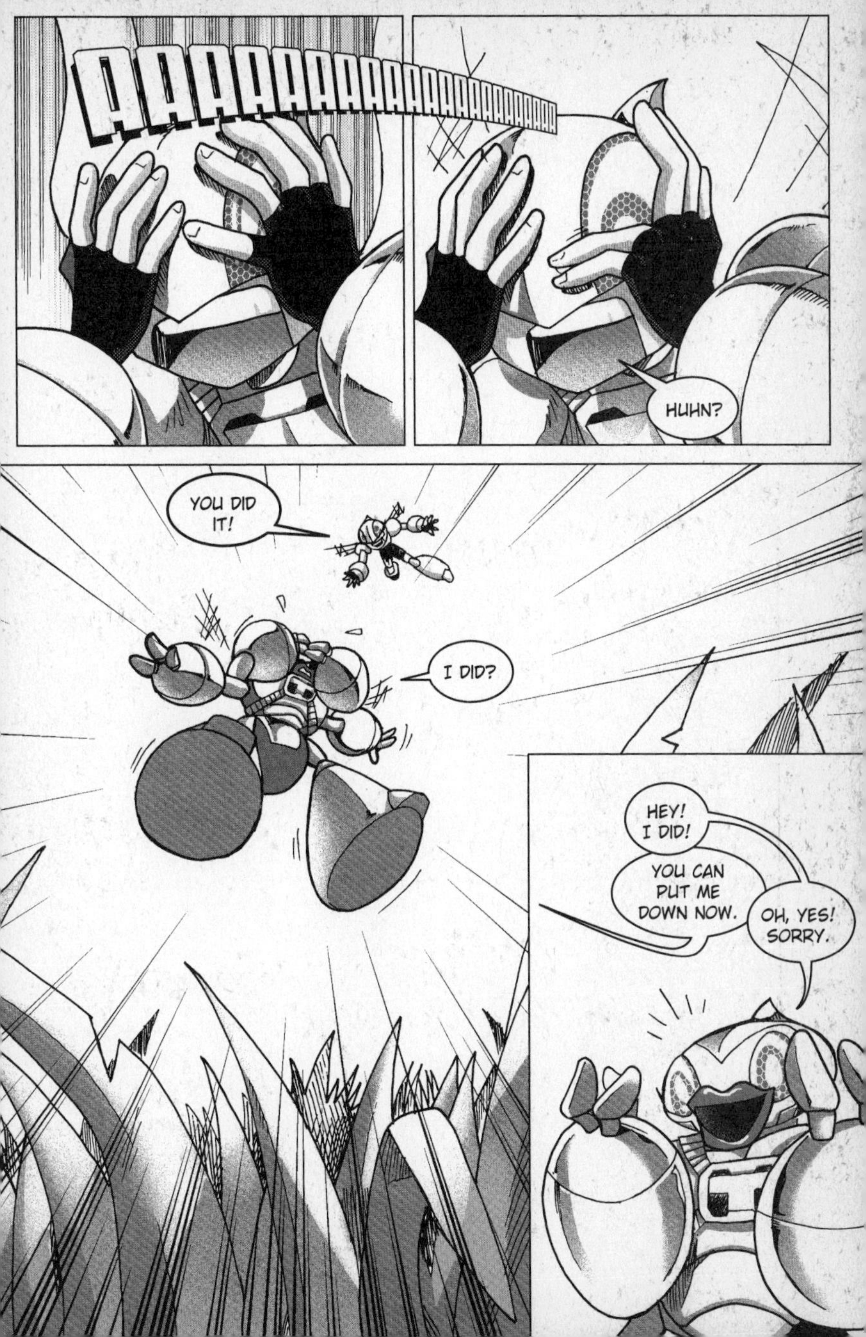
AAAAAAAAAAAAAAAAAAAAAAA
HUHN?
YOU DID IT!
I DID?
HEY! I DID!
YOU CAN PUT ME DOWN NOW.
OH, YES! SORRY.

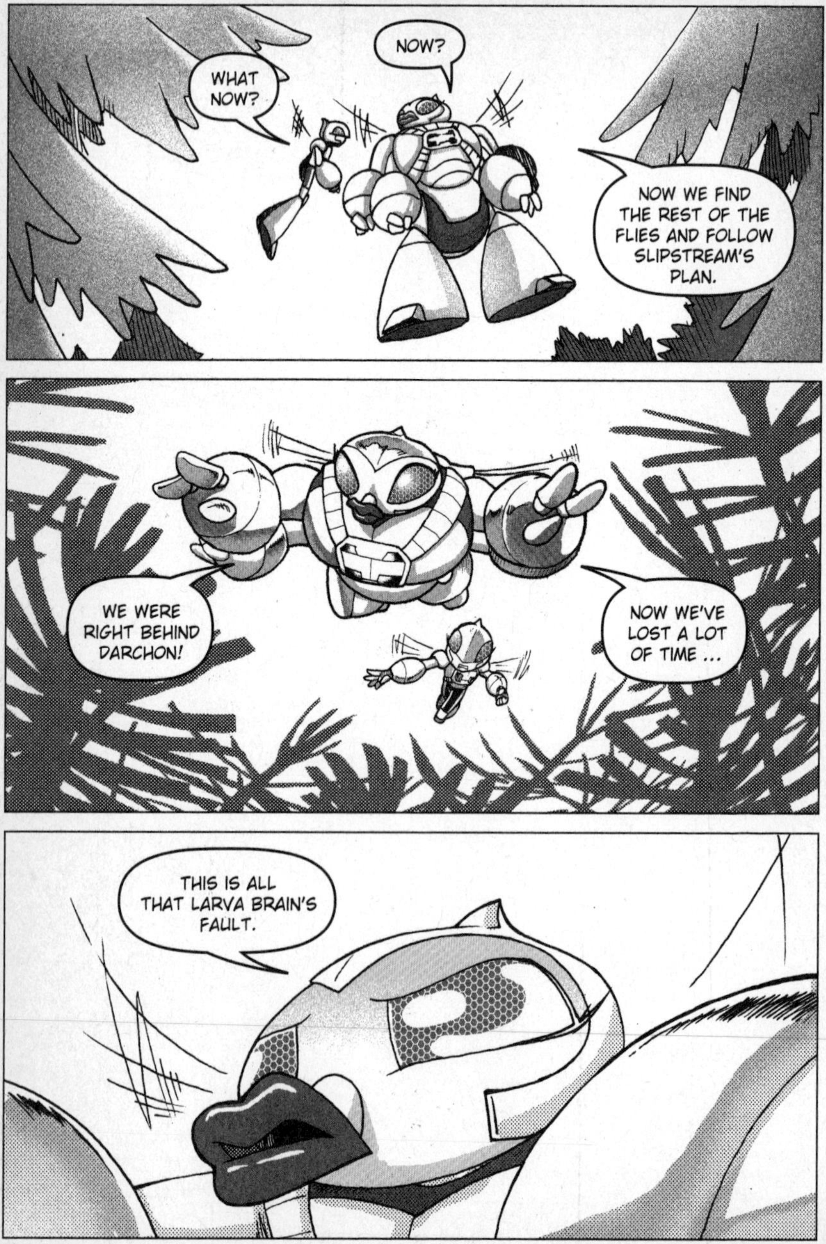
WHAT NOW?
NOW?
NOW WE FIND THE REST OF THE FLIES AND FOLLOW SLIPSTREAM'S PLAN.
WE WERE RIGHT BEHIND DARCHON!
NOW WE'VE LOST A LOT OF TIME ...
THIS IS ALL THAT LARVA BRAIN'S FAULT.

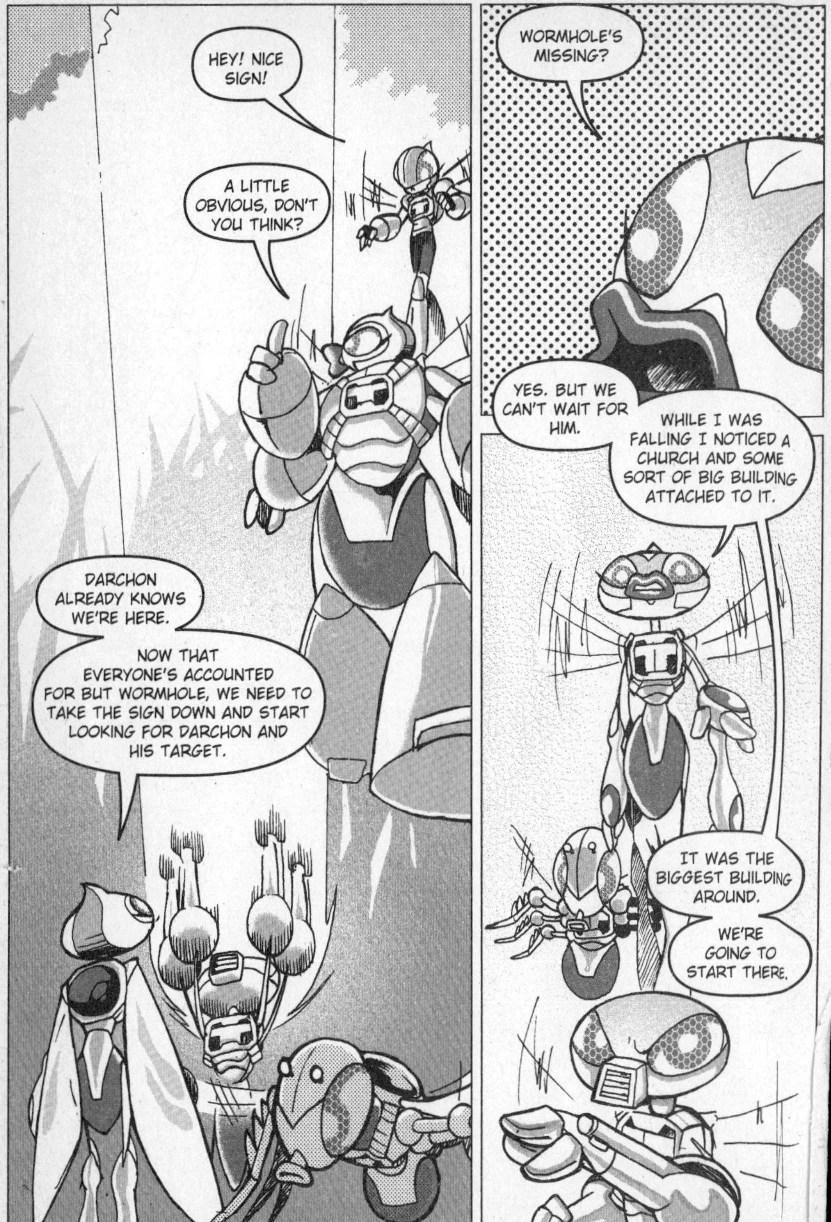
HEY! NICE SIGN!
A LITTLE OBVIOUS, DON'T YOU THINK?
DARCHON ALREADY KNOWS WE'RE HERE.
NOW THAT EVERYONE'S ACCOUNTED FOR BUT WORMHOLE, WE NEED TO TAKE THE SIGN DOWN AND START LOOKING FOR DARCHON AND HIS TARGET.
WORMHOLE'S MISSING?
YES. BUT WE CAN'T WAIT FOR HIM.
WHILE I WAS FALLING I NOTICED A CHURCH AND SOME SORT OF BIG BUILDING ATTACHED TO IT.
IT WAS THE BIGGEST BUILDING AROUND.
WE'RE GOING TO START THERE.

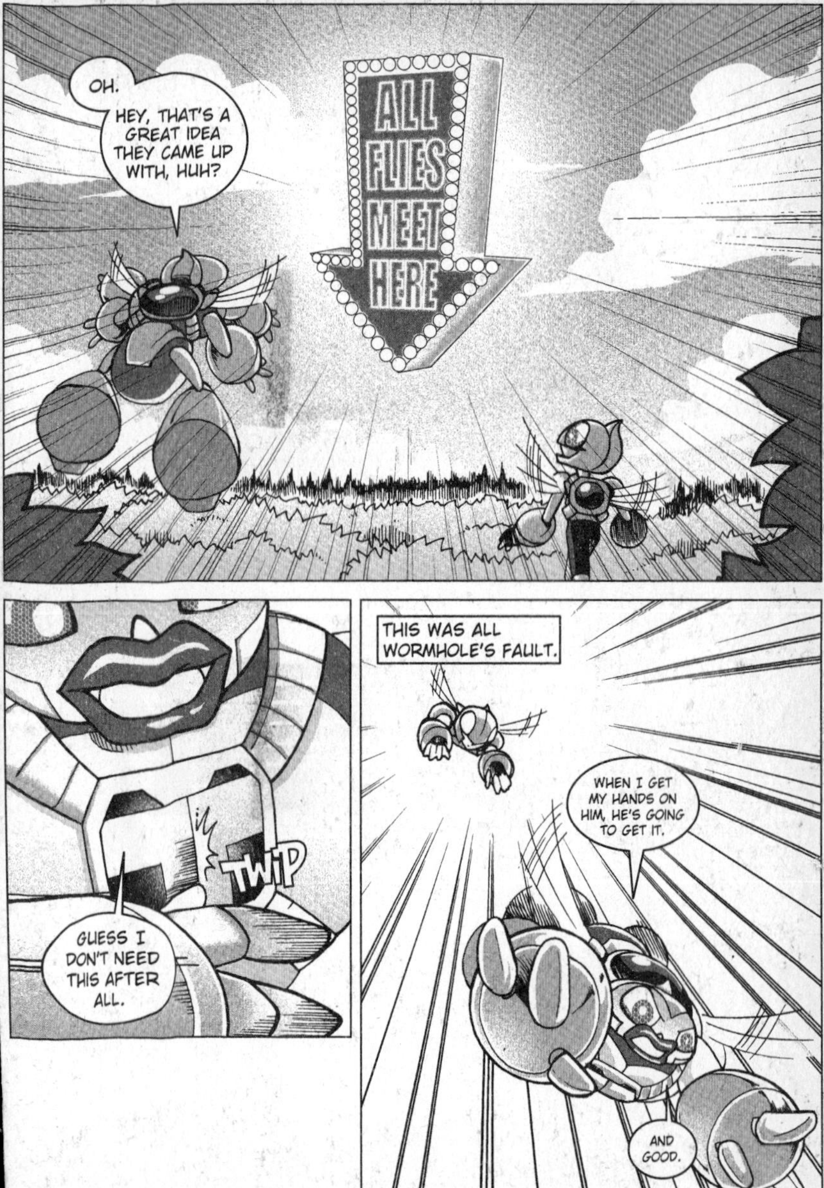
OH.
HEY, THAT'S A GREAT IDEA THEY CAME UP WITH, HUH?
ALL FLIES MEET HERE
TWIP
GUESS I DON'T NEED THIS AFTER ALL.
THIS WAS ALL WORMHOLE'S FAULT.
WHEN I GET MY HANDS ON HIM, HE'S GOING TO GET IT.
AND GOOD.

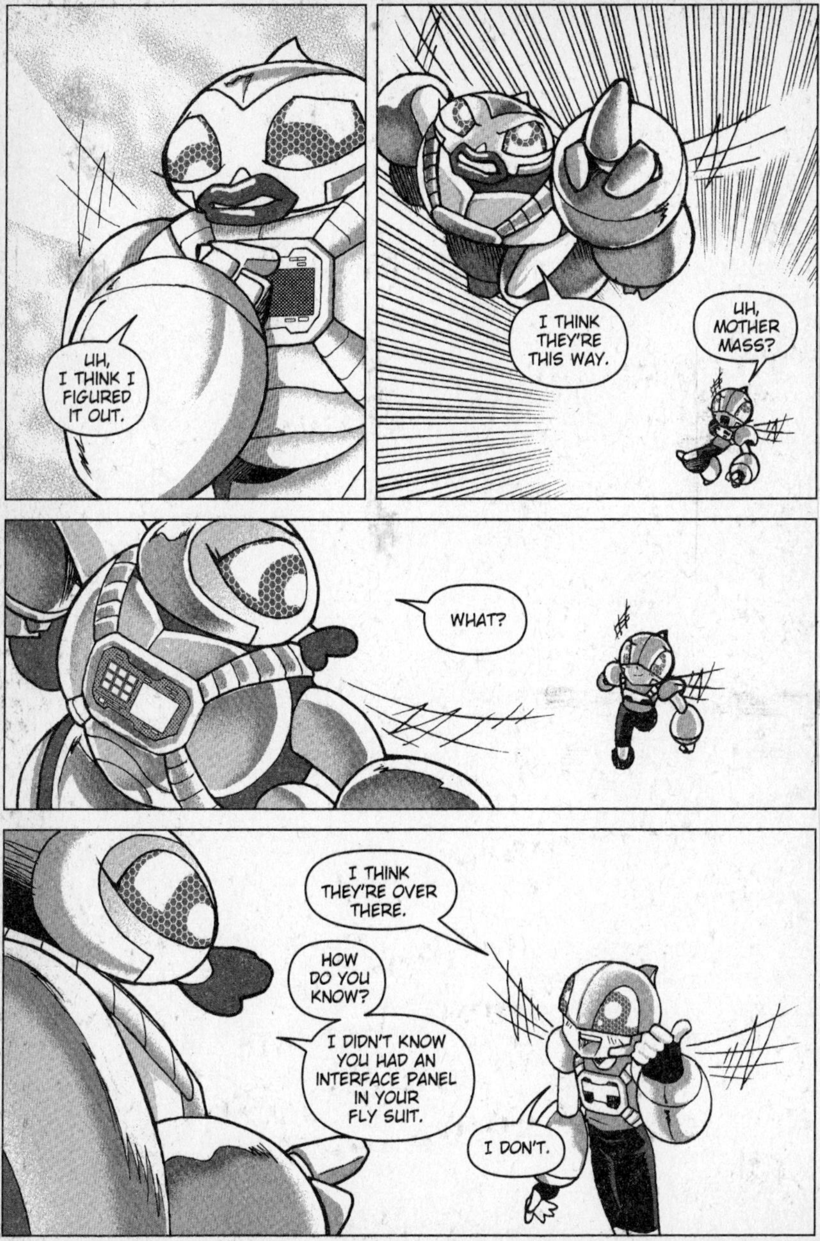
UH, I THINK I FIGURED IT OUT.
I THINK THEY'RE THIS WAY.
UH, MOTHER MASS?
WHAT?
I THINK THEY'RE OVER THERE.
HOW DO YOU KNOW?
I DIDN'T KNOW YOU HAD AN INTERFACE PANEL IN YOUR FLY SUIT.
I DON'T.

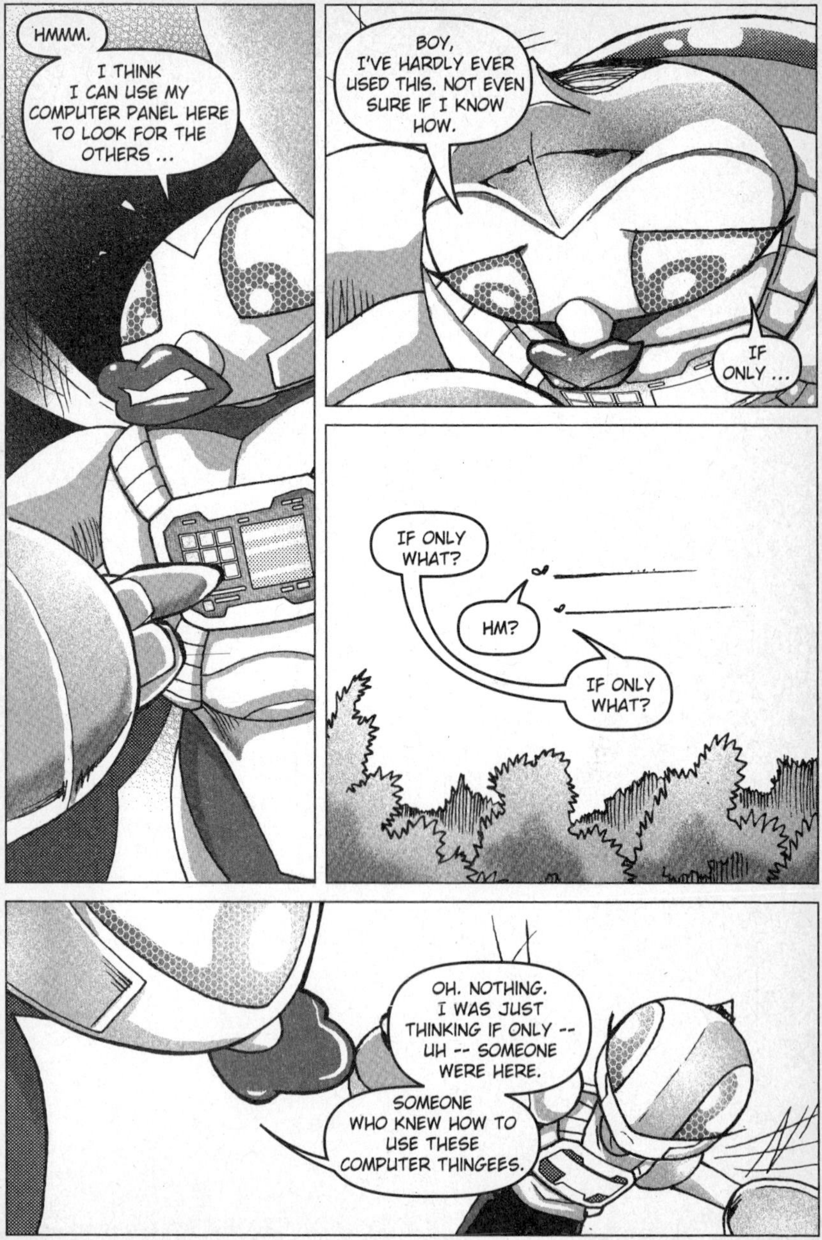

HMMM.
I THINK I CAN USE MY COMPUTER PANEL HERE TO LOOK FOR THE OTHERS ...
BOY, I'VE HARDLY EVER USED THIS. NOT EVEN SURE IF I KNOW HOW.
IF ONLY ...
IF ONLY WHAT?
HM?
IF ONLY WHAT?
OH. NOTHING. I WAS JUST THINKING IF ONLY -- UH -- SOMEONE WERE HERE.
SOMEONE WHO KNEW HOW TO USE THESE COMPUTER THINGEES.

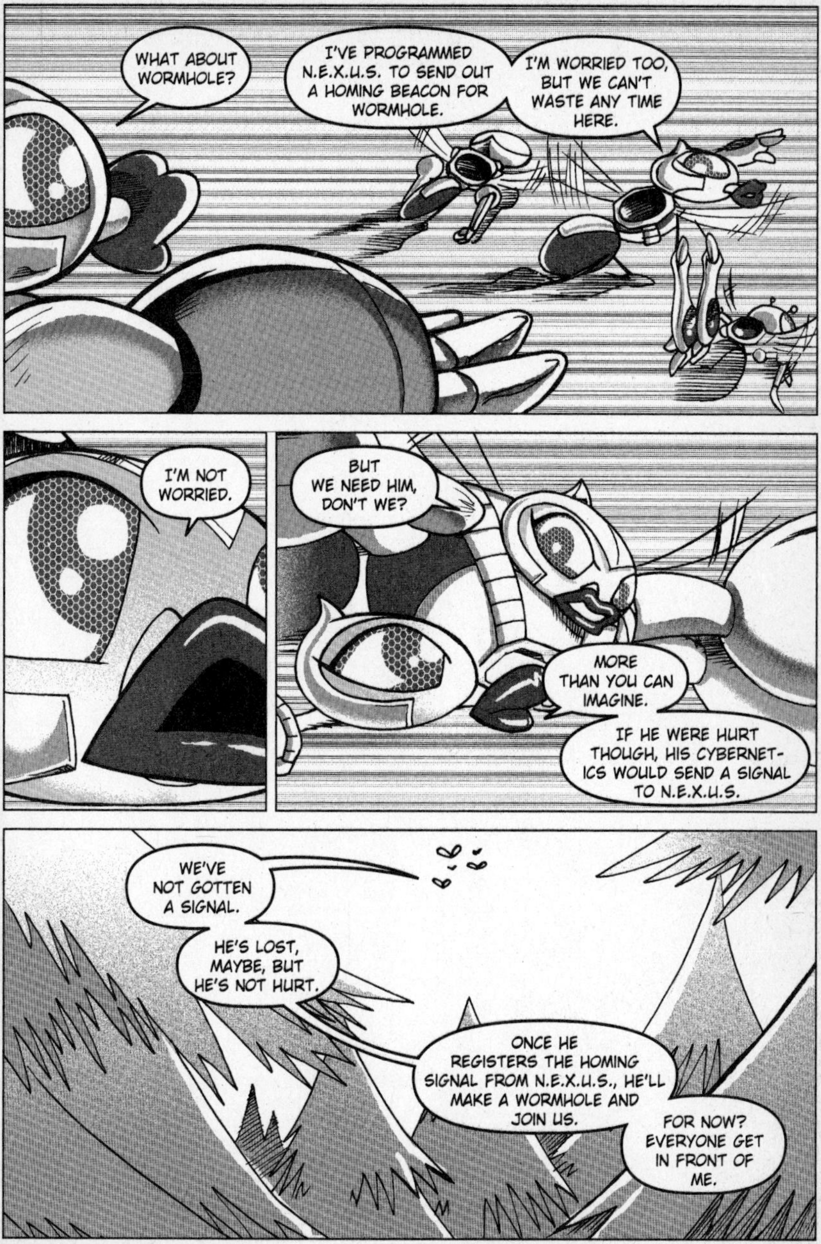
WHAT ABOUT WORMHOLE?
I'VE PROGRAMMED N.E.X.U.S. TO SEND OUT A HOMING BEACON FOR WORMHOLE.
I'M WORRIED TOO, BUT WE CAN'T WASTE ANY TIME HERE.
I'M NOT WORRIED.
BUT WE NEED HIM, DON'T WE?
MORE THAN YOU CAN IMAGINE.
IF HE WERE HURT THOUGH, HIS CYBERNET-ICS WOULD SEND A SIGNAL TO N.E.X.U.S.
WE'VE NOT GOTTEN A SIGNAL.
HE'S LOST, MAYBE, BUT HE'S NOT HURT.
ONCE HE REGISTERS THE HOMING SIGNAL FROM N.E.X.U.S., HE'LL MAKE A WORMHOLE AND JOIN US.
FOR NOW? EVERYONE GET IN FRONT OF ME.

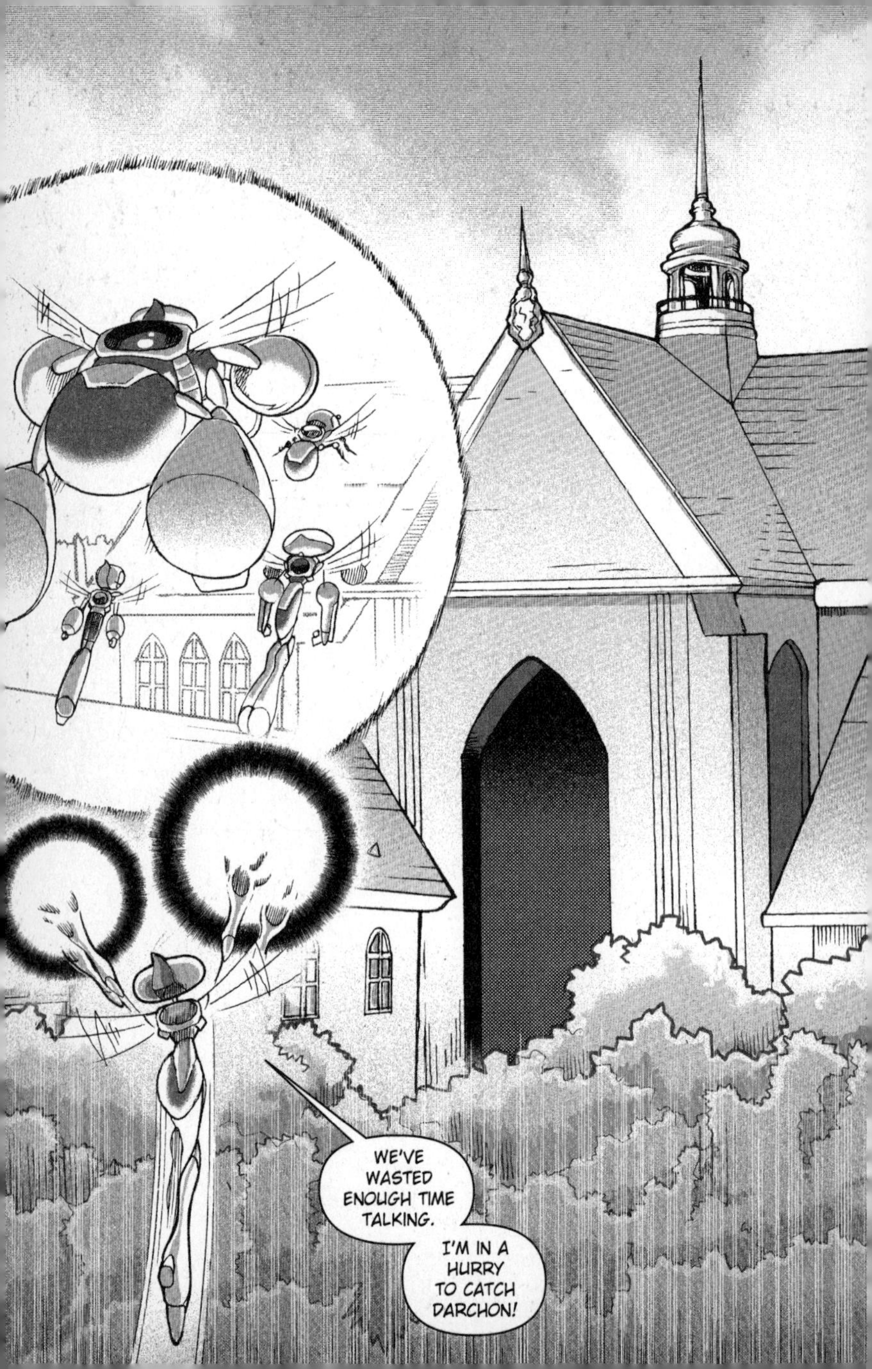
WE'VE WASTED ENOUGH TIME TALKING.
I'M IN A HURRY TO CATCH DARCHON!

CHAPTER TWO

I CAN UNDERSTAND EVERYTHING THEY'RE SAYING.

WELL, YOU ALREADY HAVE THE LANGUAGE, GUYS. CZECH.

ANY IDEAS WHERE TO START?

LAUREL MAY NOT HAVE ANY POWERS TO SPEAK OF, BUT SOMETIMES IT'S REALLY NICE TO HAVE AN ACTUAL HUMAN ON OUR SIDE.

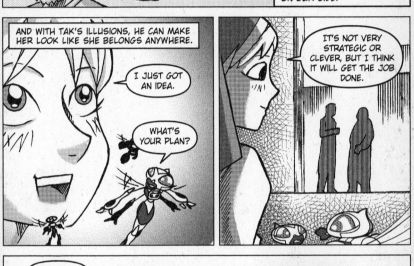

AND WITH TAK'S ILLUSIONS, HE CAN MAKE HER LOOK LIKE SHE BELONGS ANYWHERE.

I JUST GOT AN IDEA.

WHAT'S YOUR PLAN?

IT'S NOT VERY STRATEGIC OR CLEVER, BUT I THINK IT WILL GET THE JOB DONE.

EXCUSE ME ...

... I'M LOOKING FOR A VERY IMPORTANT MAN. A BRILLIANT SCIENTIST.

"BRILLIANT SCIENTIST"?

SOMETIMES SHE DOES THINGS DIFFERENTLY THAN WE FLIES WOULD.

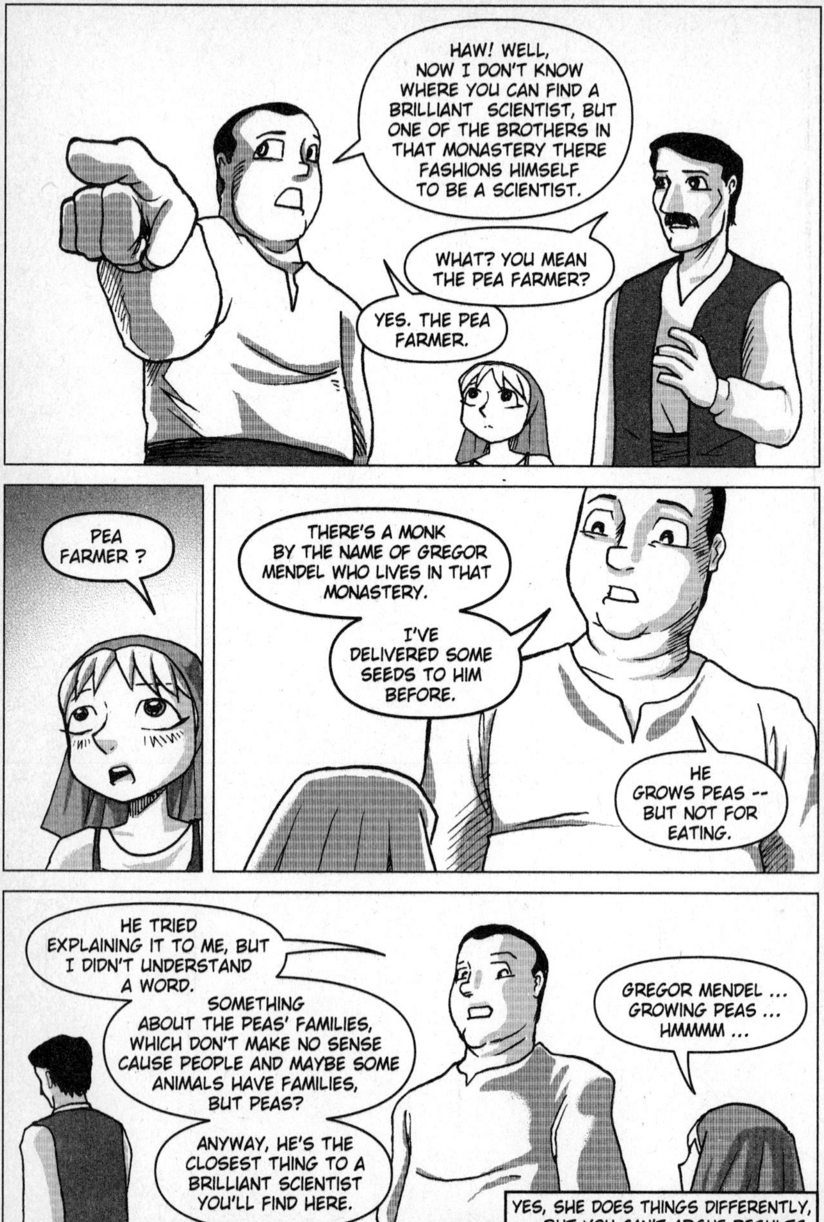
HAW! WELL, NOW I DON'T KNOW WHERE YOU CAN FIND A BRILLIANT SCIENTIST, BUT ONE OF THE BROTHERS IN THAT MONASTERY THERE FASHIONS HIMSELF TO BE A SCIENTIST.
WHAT? YOU MEAN THE PEA FARMER?
YES. THE PEA FARMER.
PEA FARMER ?
THERE'S A MONK BY THE NAME OF GREGOR MENDEL WHO LIVES IN THAT MONASTERY.
I'VE DELIVERED SOME SEEDS TO HIM BEFORE.
HE GROWS PEAS -- BUT NOT FOR EATING.
HE TRIED EXPLAINING IT TO ME, BUT I DIDN'T UNDERSTAND A WORD.
SOMETHING ABOUT THE PEAS' FAMILIES, WHICH DON'T MAKE NO SENSE CAUSE PEOPLE AND MAYBE SOME ANIMALS HAVE FAMILIES, BUT PEAS?
ANYWAY, HE'S THE CLOSEST THING TO A BRILLIANT SCIENTIST YOU'LL FIND HERE.
GREGOR MENDEL ... GROWING PEAS ... HMMMM ...
YES, SHE DOES THINGS DIFFERENTLY, BUT YOU CAN'T ARGUE RESULTS.

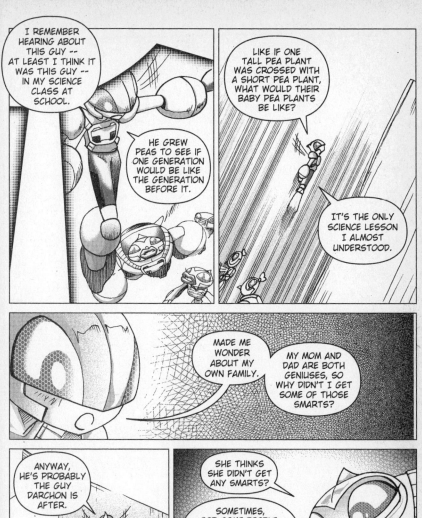

I REMEMBER HEARING ABOUT THIS GUY -- AT LEAST I THINK IT WAS THIS GUY -- IN MY SCIENCE CLASS AT SCHOOL.

HE GREW PEAS TO SEE IF ONE GENERATION WOULD BE LIKE THE GENERATION BEFORE IT.

LIKE IF ONE TALL PEA PLANT WAS CROSSED WITH A SHORT PEA PLANT, WHAT WOULD THEIR BABY PEA PLANTS BE LIKE?

IT'S THE ONLY SCIENCE LESSON I ALMOST UNDERSTOOD.

MADE ME WONDER ABOUT MY OWN FAMILY.

MY MOM AND DAD ARE BOTH GENIUSES, SO WHY DIDN'T I GET SOME OF THOSE SMARTS?

ANYWAY, HE'S PROBABLY THE GUY DARCHON IS AFTER.

SHE THINKS SHE DIDN'T GET ANY SMARTS?

SOMETIMES, FOR SOME PEOPLE, IT'S EASY FOR THEM TO SEE THE GOOD IN OTHERS, BUT HARD FOR THEM TO SEE THE GOOD IN THEMSELVES.

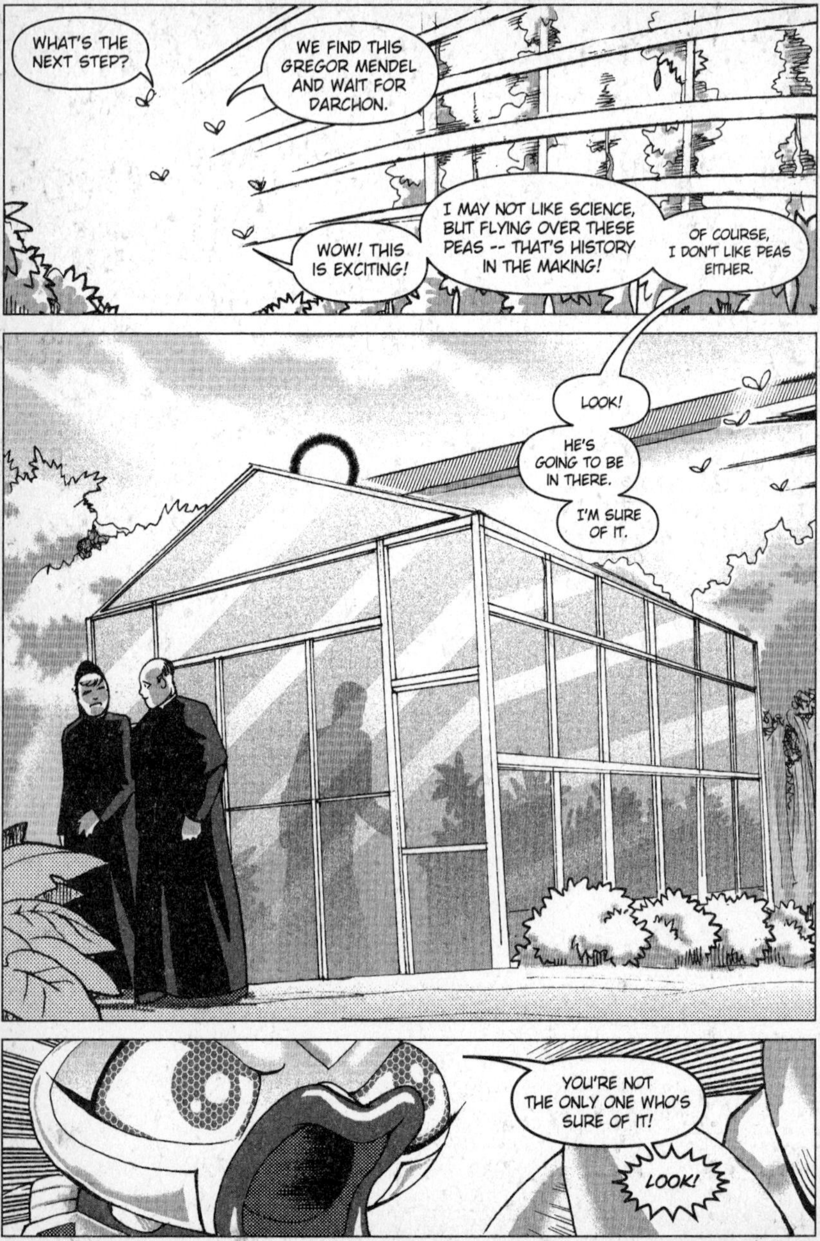
WHAT'S THE NEXT STEP?
WE FIND THIS GREGOR MENDEL AND WAIT FOR DARCHON.
WOW! THIS IS EXCITING!
I MAY NOT LIKE SCIENCE, BUT FLYING OVER THESE PEAS -- THAT'S HISTORY IN THE MAKING!
OF COURSE, I DON'T LIKE PEAS EITHER.
LOOK!
HE'S GOING TO BE IN THERE.
I'M SURE OF IT.
YOU'RE NOT THE ONLY ONE WHO'S SURE OF IT!
LOOK!

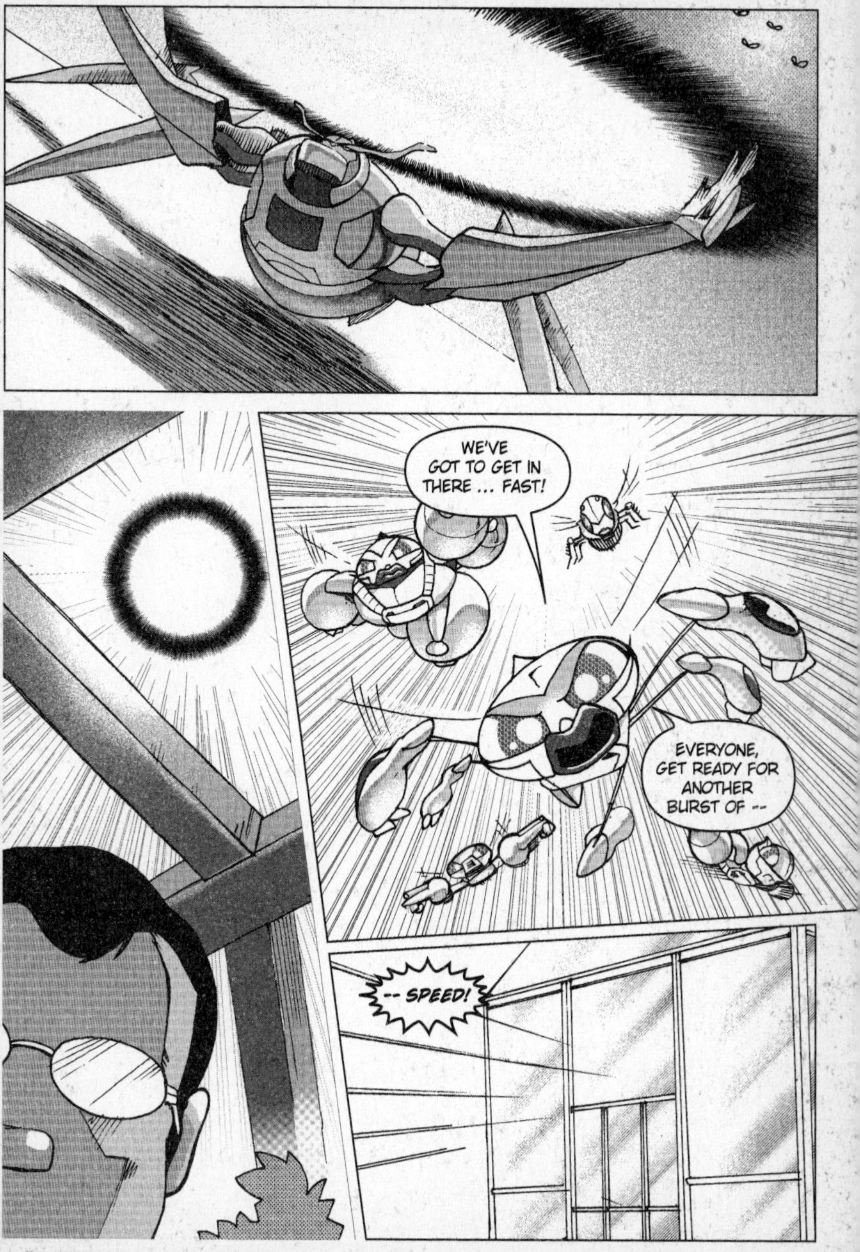
WE'VE GOT TO GET IN THERE ... FAST!
EVERYONE, GET READY FOR ANOTHER BURST OF --
-- SPEED!

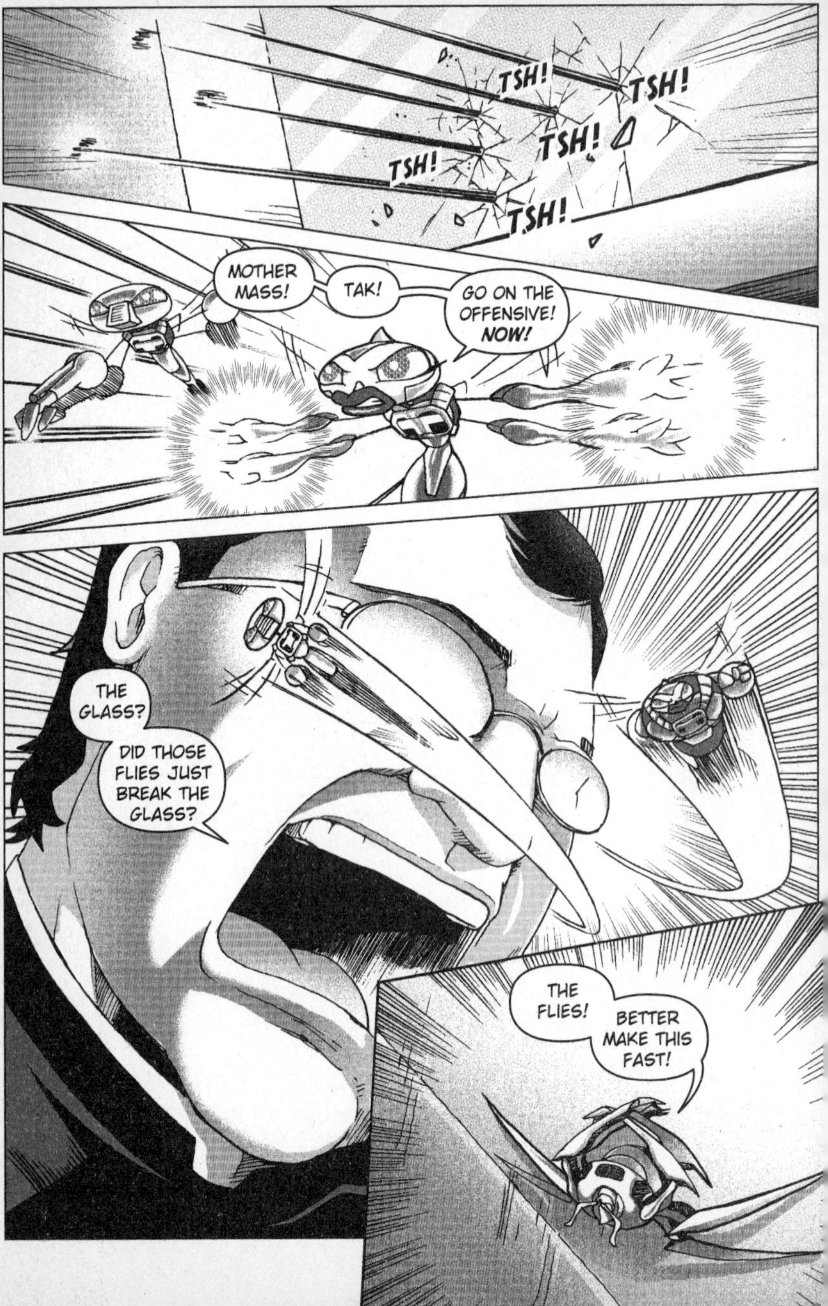

TSH!
TSH!
TSH!
TSH!
TSH!
MOTHER MASS!
TAK!
GO ON THE OFFENSIVE! NOW!
THE GLASS?
DID THOSE FLIES JUST BREAK THE GLASS?
THE FLIES!
BETTER MAKE THIS FAST!

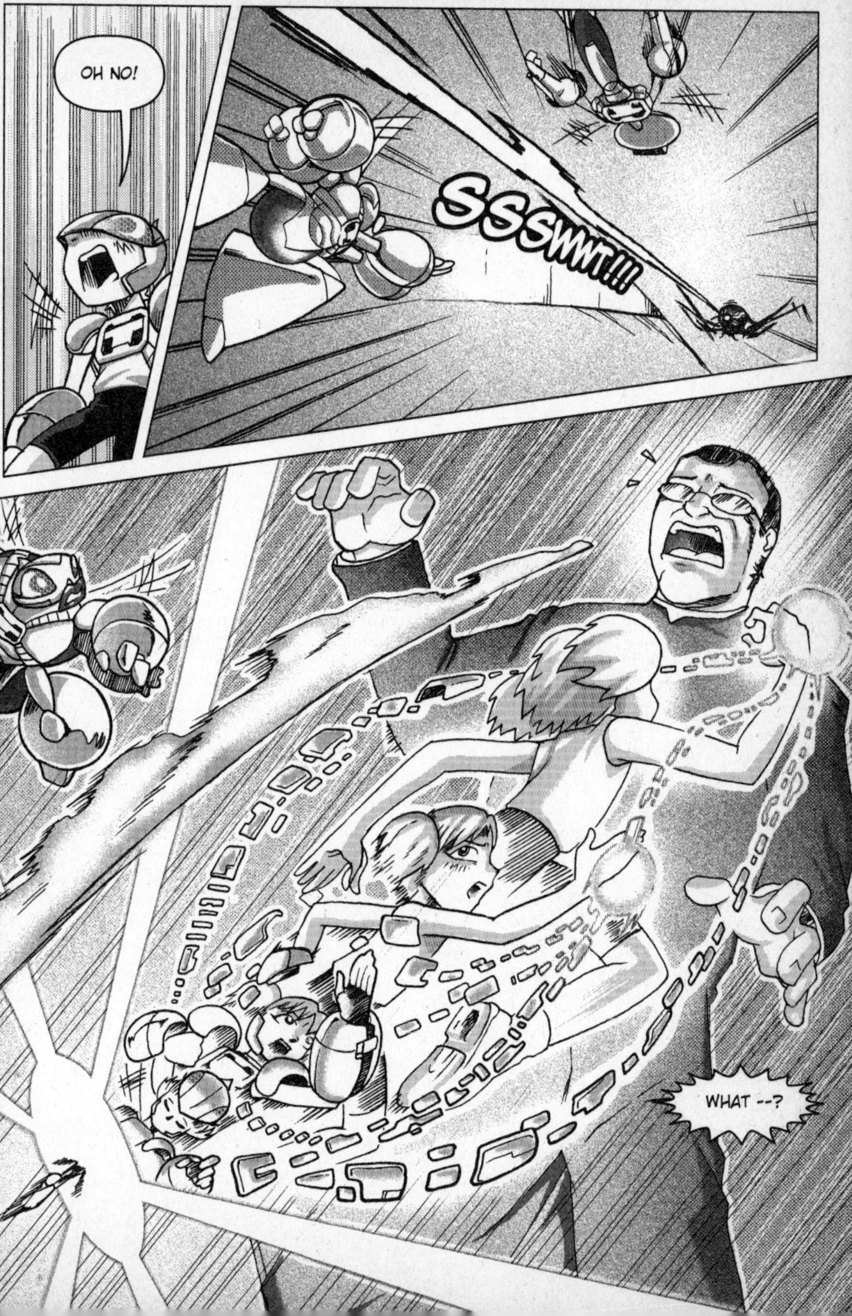
OH NO!
SSSWWT!!!
WHAT --?

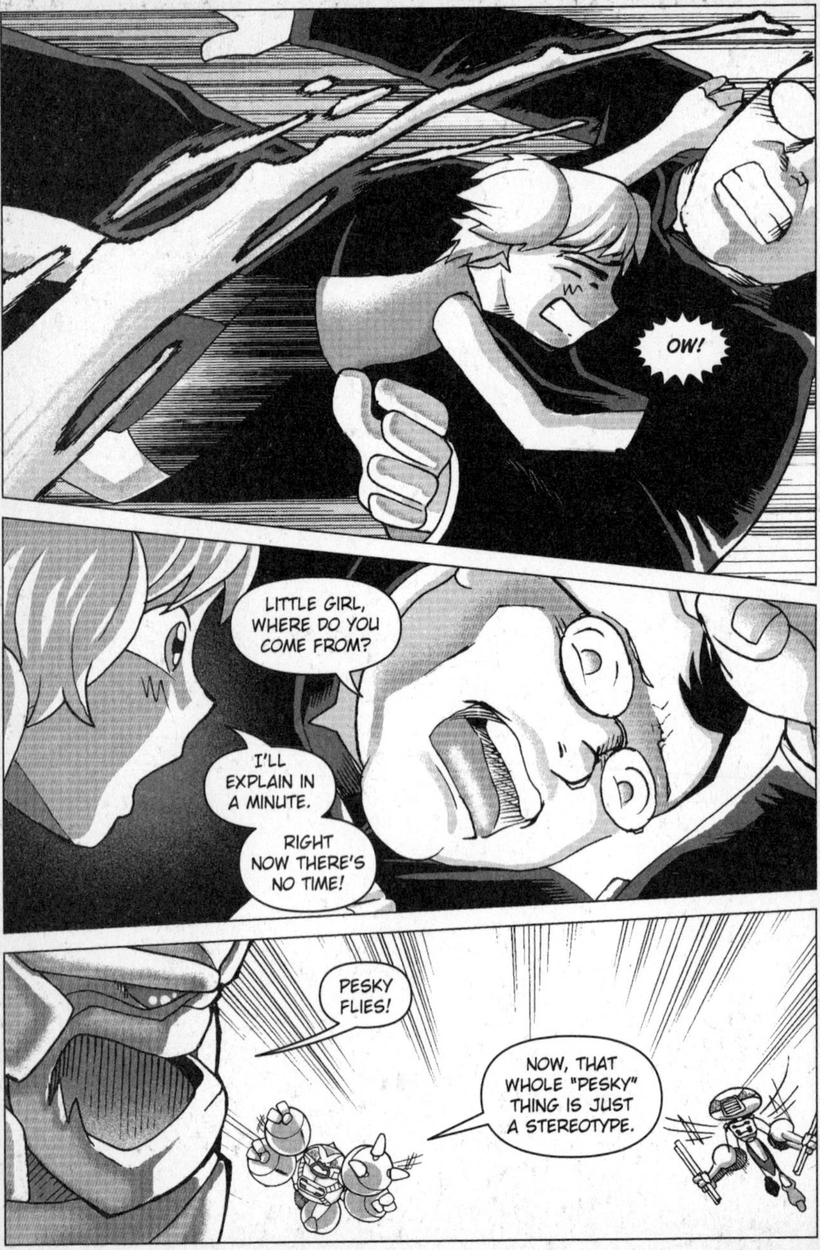
OW!
LITTLE GIRL, WHERE DO YOU COME FROM?
I'LL EXPLAIN IN A MINUTE.
RIGHT NOW THERE'S NO TIME!
PESKY FLIES!
NOW, THAT WHOLE "PESKY" THING IS JUST A STEREOTYPE.

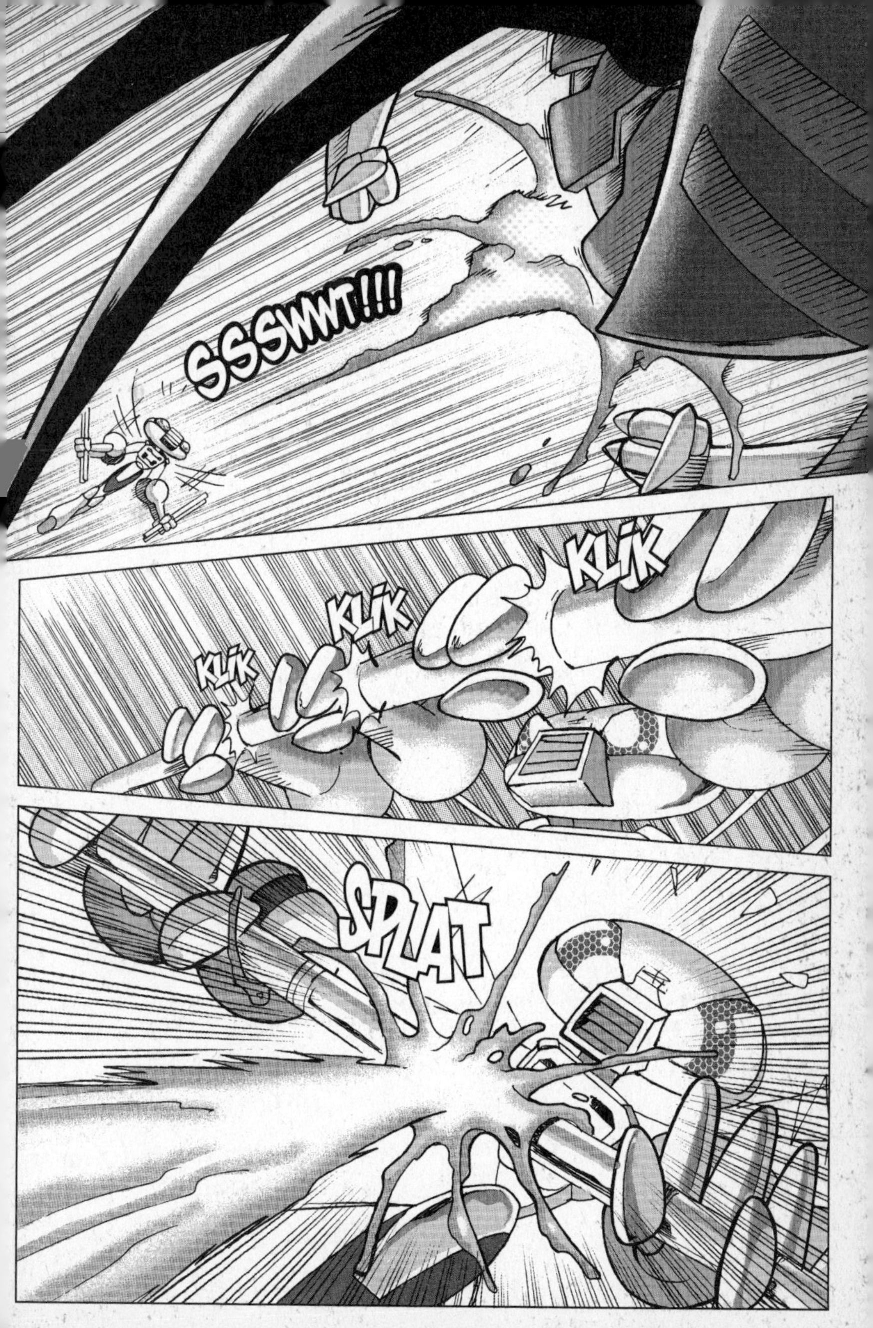
SSSWWT!!!
KLIK
KLIK
KLIK
SPLAT

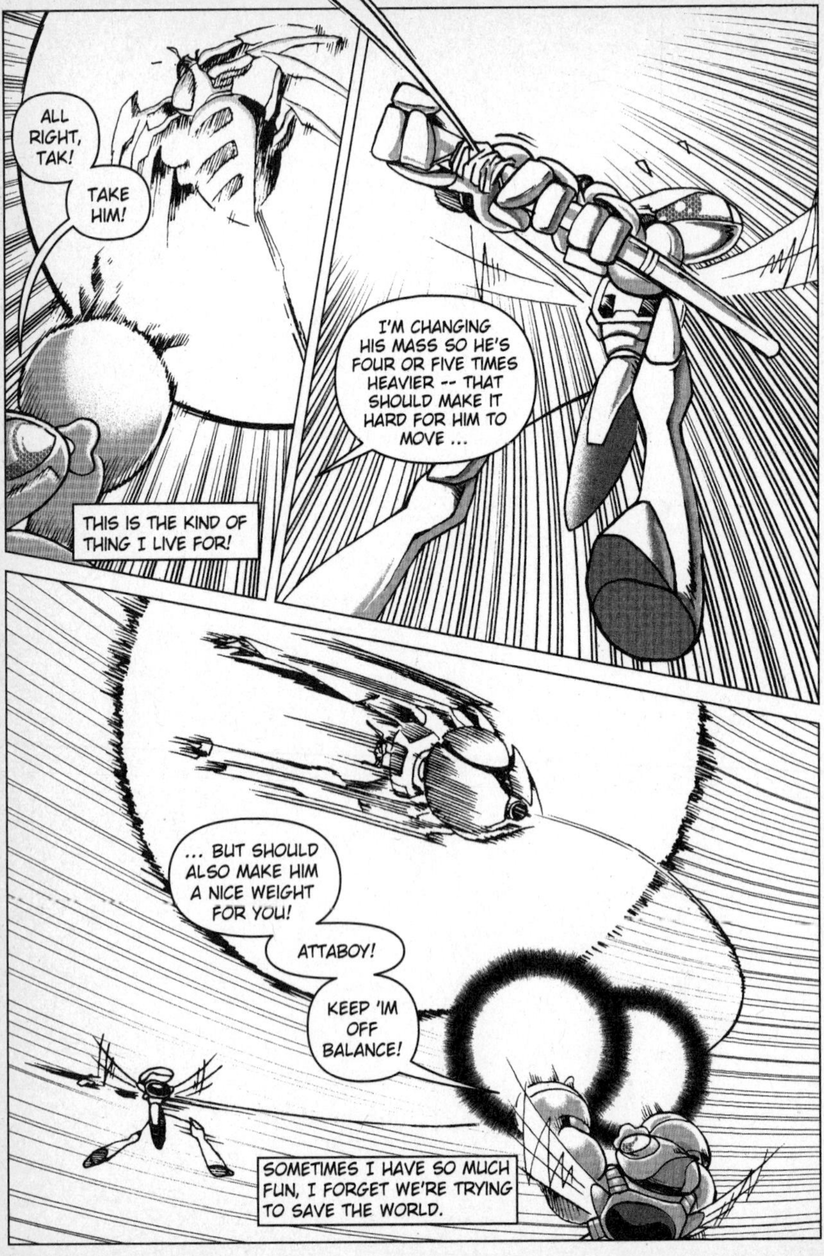
ALL RIGHT, TAK!
TAKE HIM!
THIS IS THE KIND OF THING I LIVE FOR!
I'M CHANGING HIS MASS SO HE'S FOUR OR FIVE TIMES HEAVIER -- THAT SHOULD MAKE IT HARD FOR HIM TO MOVE ...
... BUT SHOULD ALSO MAKE HIM A NICE WEIGHT FOR YOU!
ATTABOY!
KEEP 'IM OFF BALANCE!
SOMETIMES I HAVE SO MUCH FUN, I FORGET WE'RE TRYING TO SAVE THE WORLD.

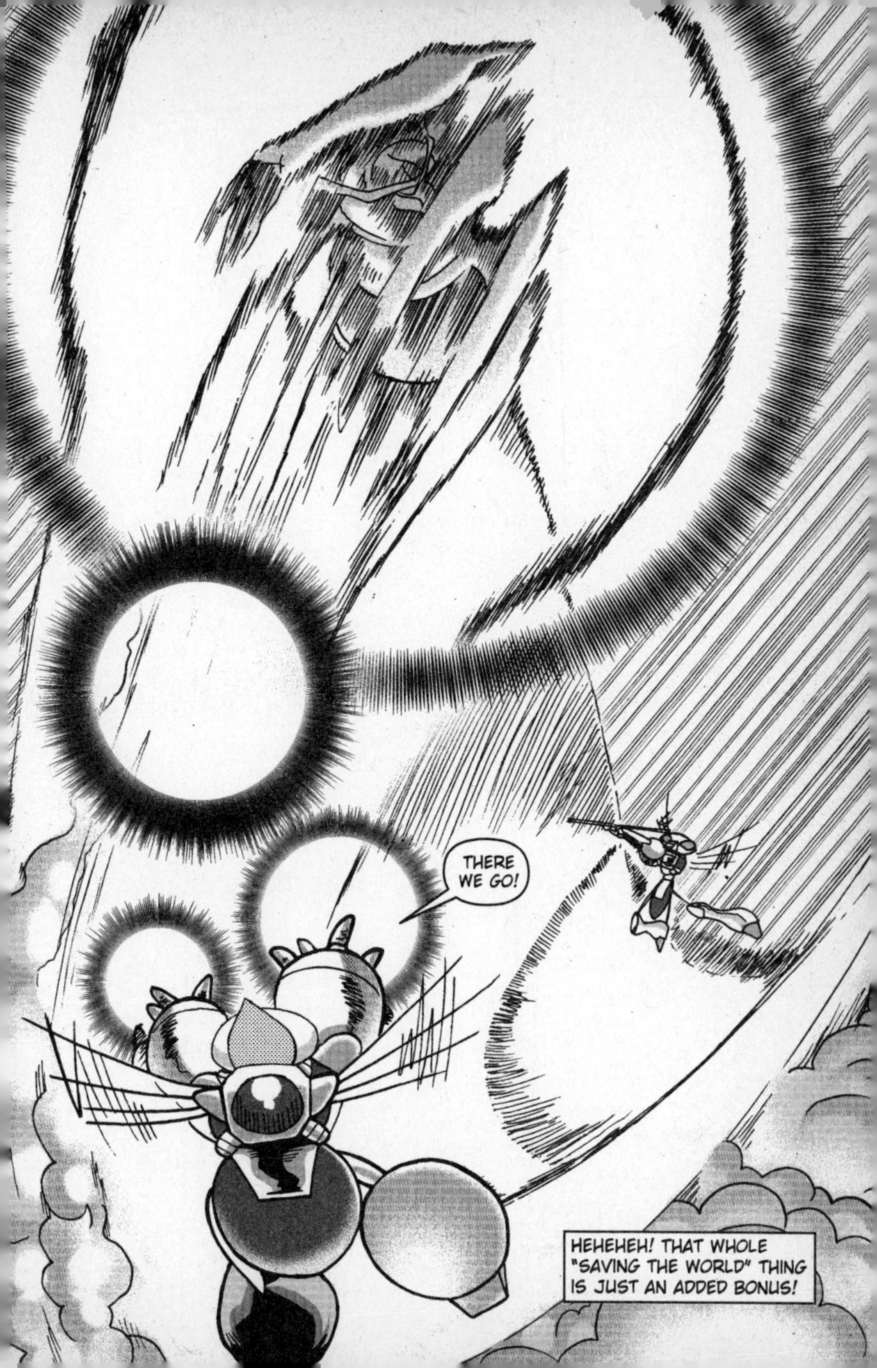
THERE WE GO!
HEHEHEH! THAT WHOLE "SAVING THE WORLD" THING IS JUST AN ADDED BONUS!

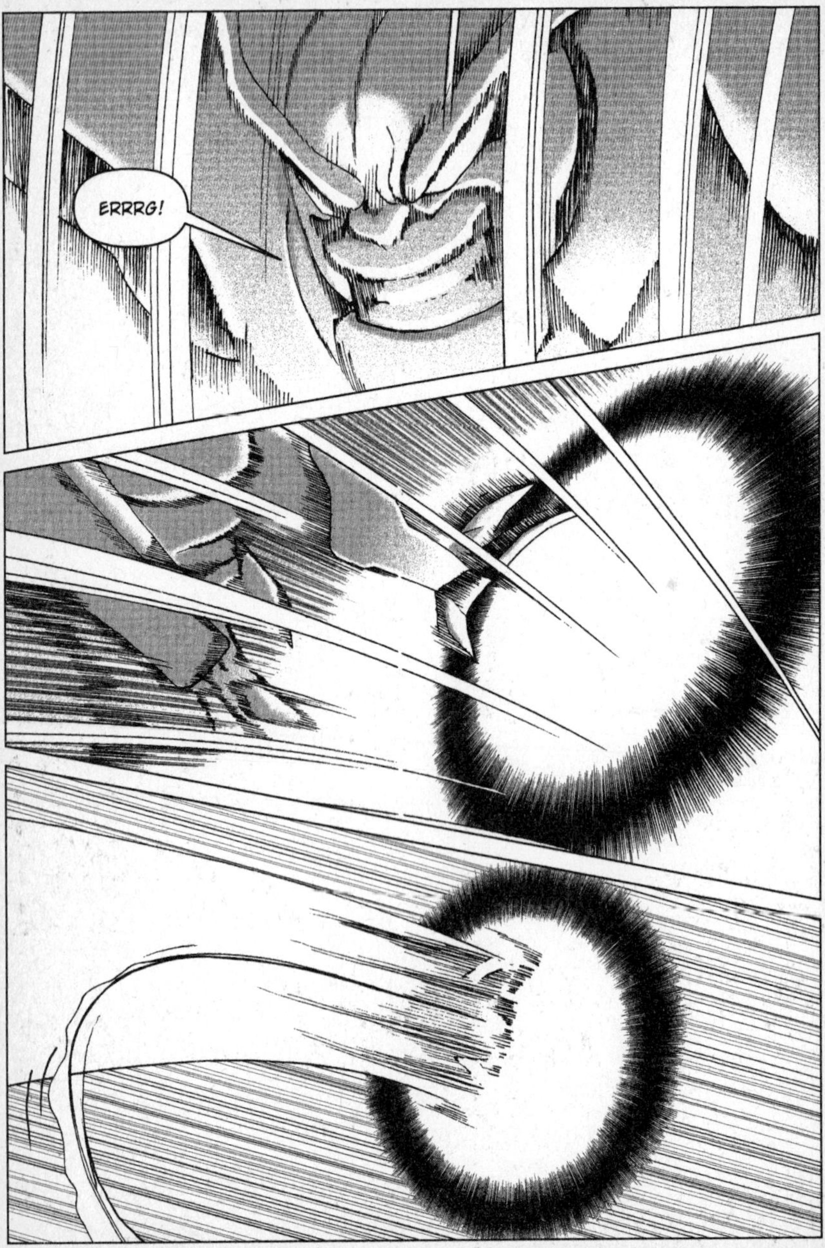
ERRRG!

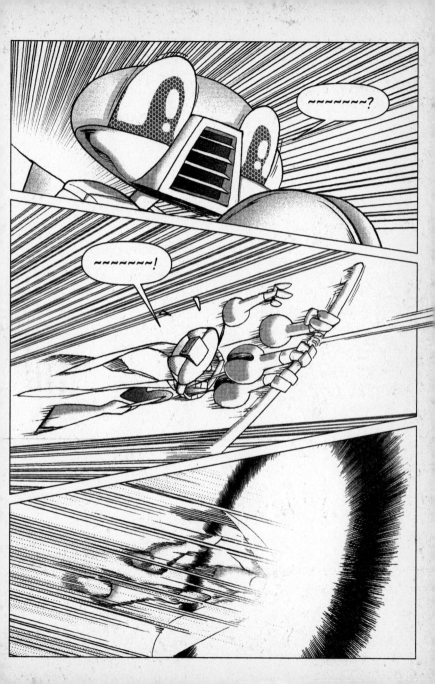

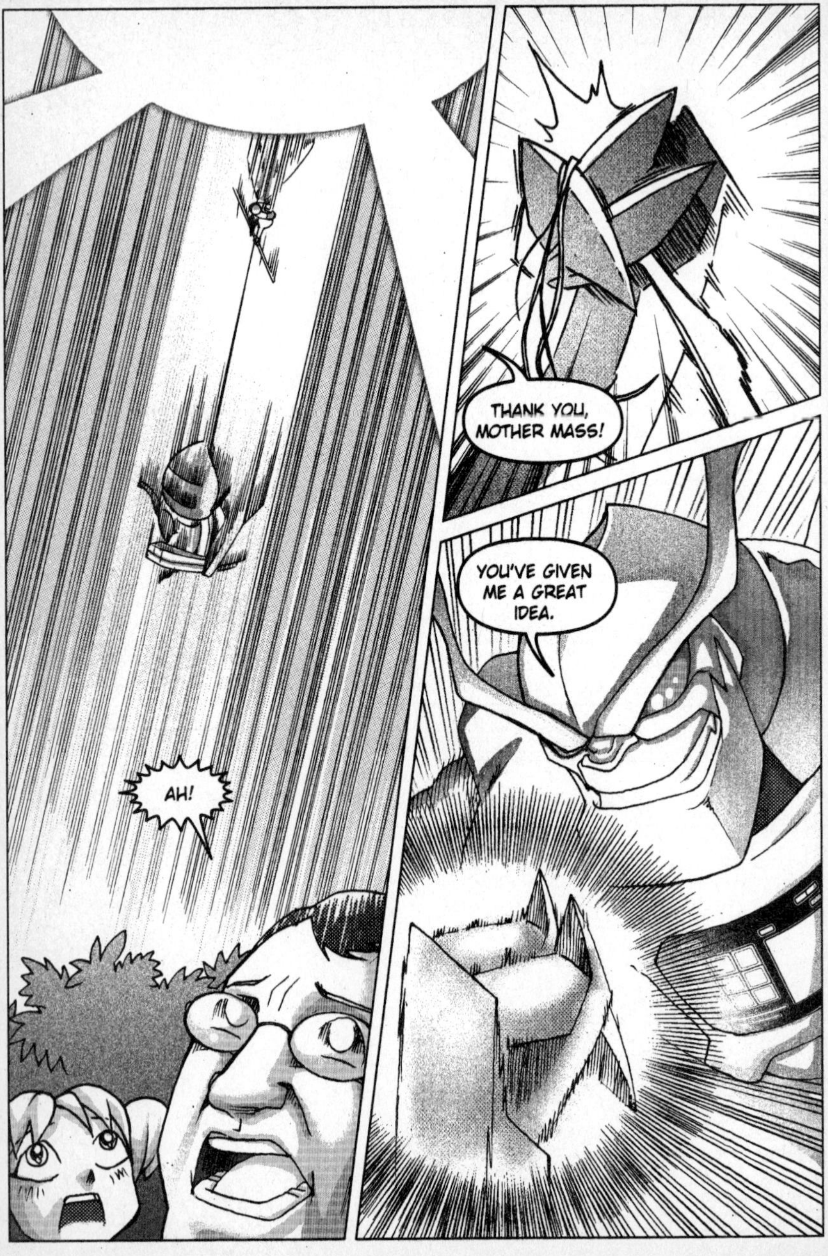
AH!
THANK YOU, MOTHER MASS!
YOU'VE GIVEN ME A GREAT IDEA.

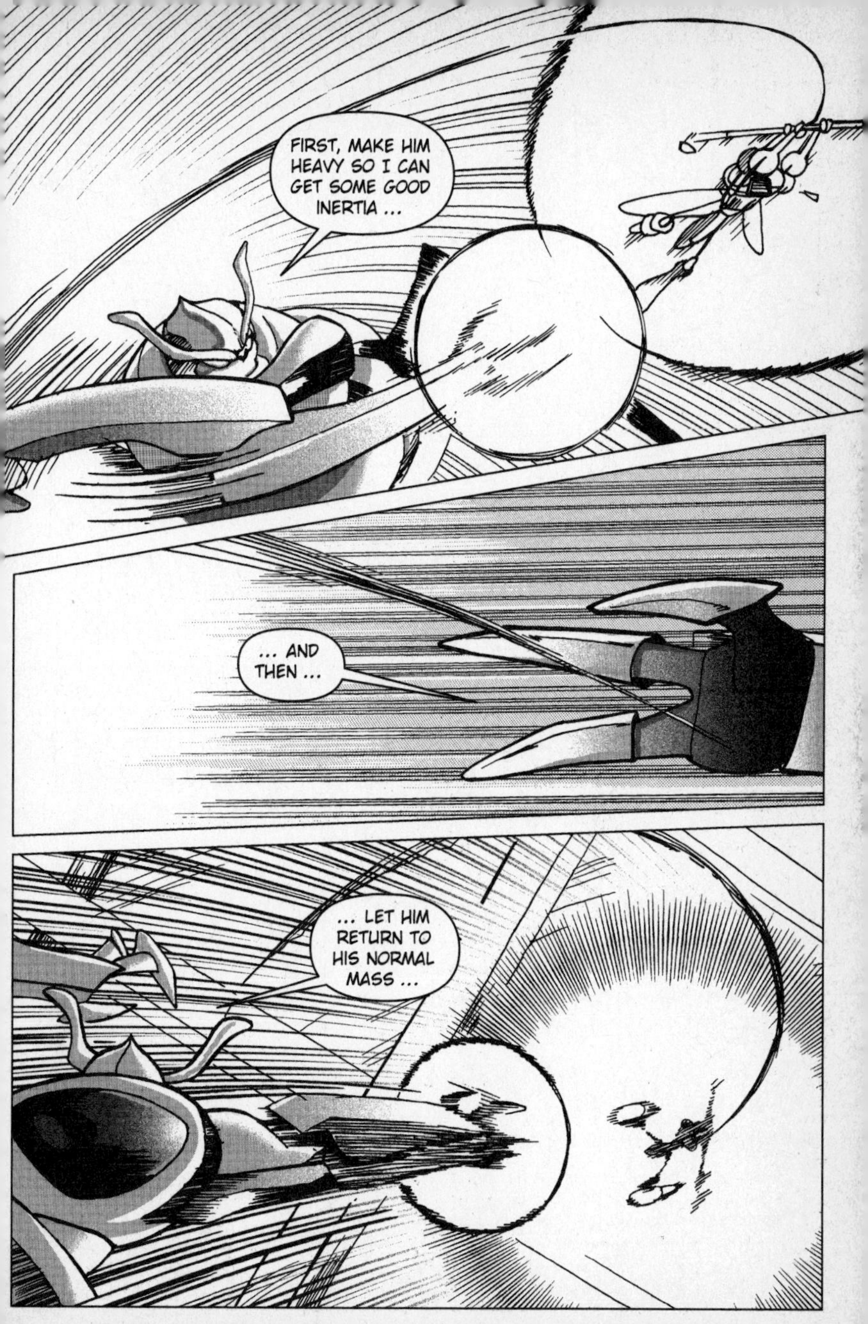
FIRST, MAKE HIM HEAVY SO I CAN GET SOME GOOD INERTIA ...
... AND THEN ...
... LET HIM RETURN TO HIS NORMAL MASS ...

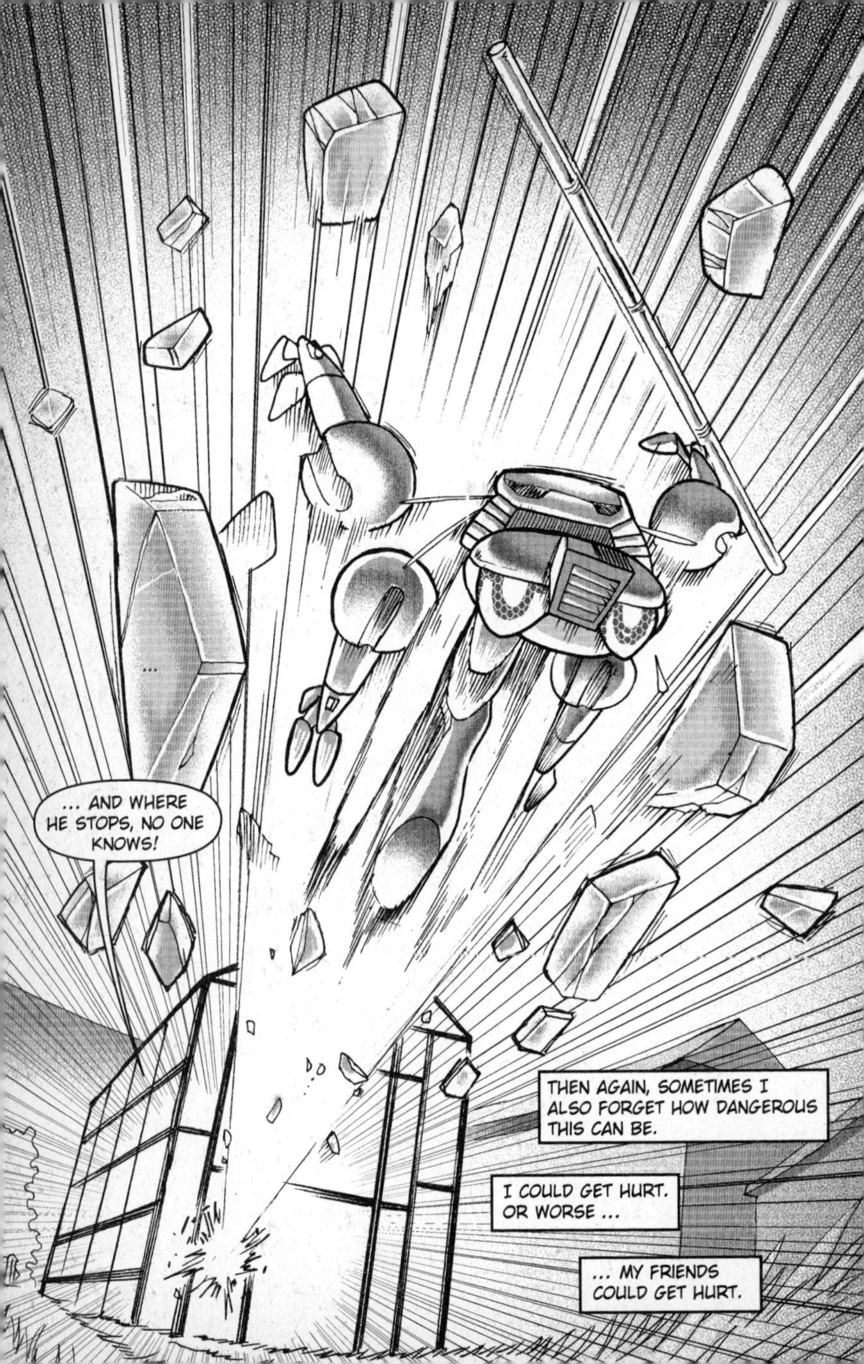
...
... AND WHERE HE STOPS, NO ONE KNOWS!
THEN AGAIN, SOMETIMES I ALSO FORGET HOW DANGEROUS THIS CAN BE.
I COULD GET HURT. OR WORSE ...
... MY FRIENDS COULD GET HURT.

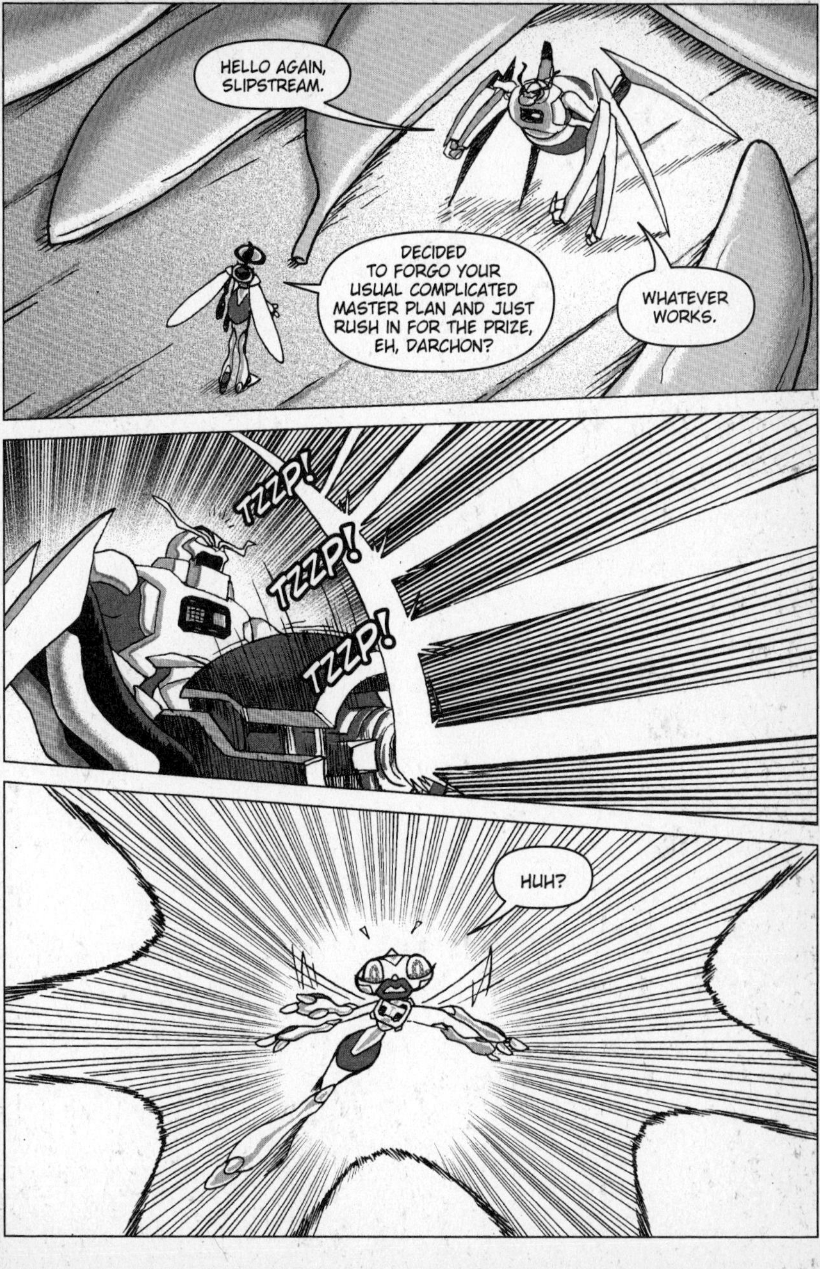
HELLO AGAIN, SLIPSTREAM.
DECIDED TO FORGO YOUR USUAL COMPLICATED MASTER PLAN AND JUST RUSH IN FOR THE PRIZE, EH, DARCHON?
WHATEVER WORKS.
TZZP!
TZZP!
TZZP!
HUH?

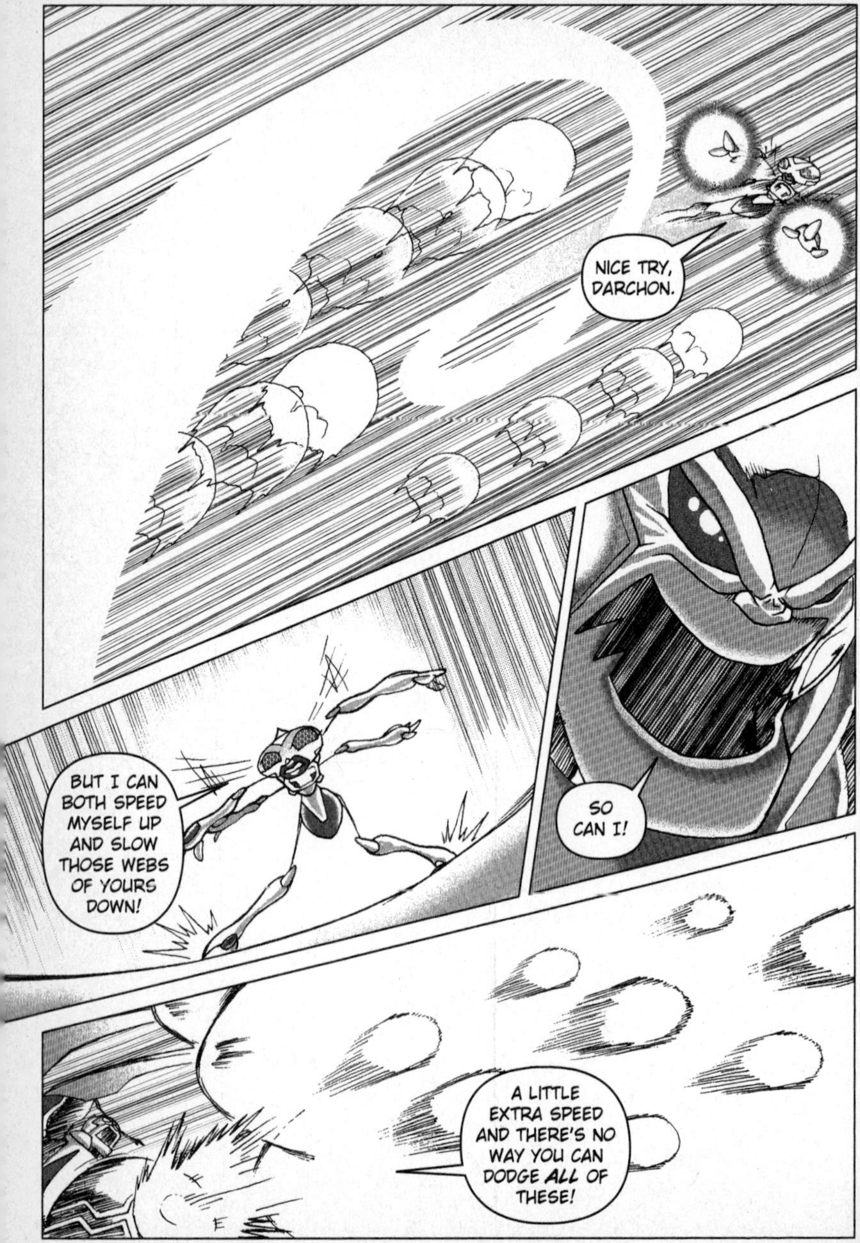
NICE TRY, DARCHON.
BUT I CAN BOTH SPEED MYSELF UP AND SLOW THOSE WEBS OF YOURS DOWN!
SO CAN I!
A LITTLE EXTRA SPEED AND THERE'S NO WAY YOU CAN DODGE ALL OF THESE!

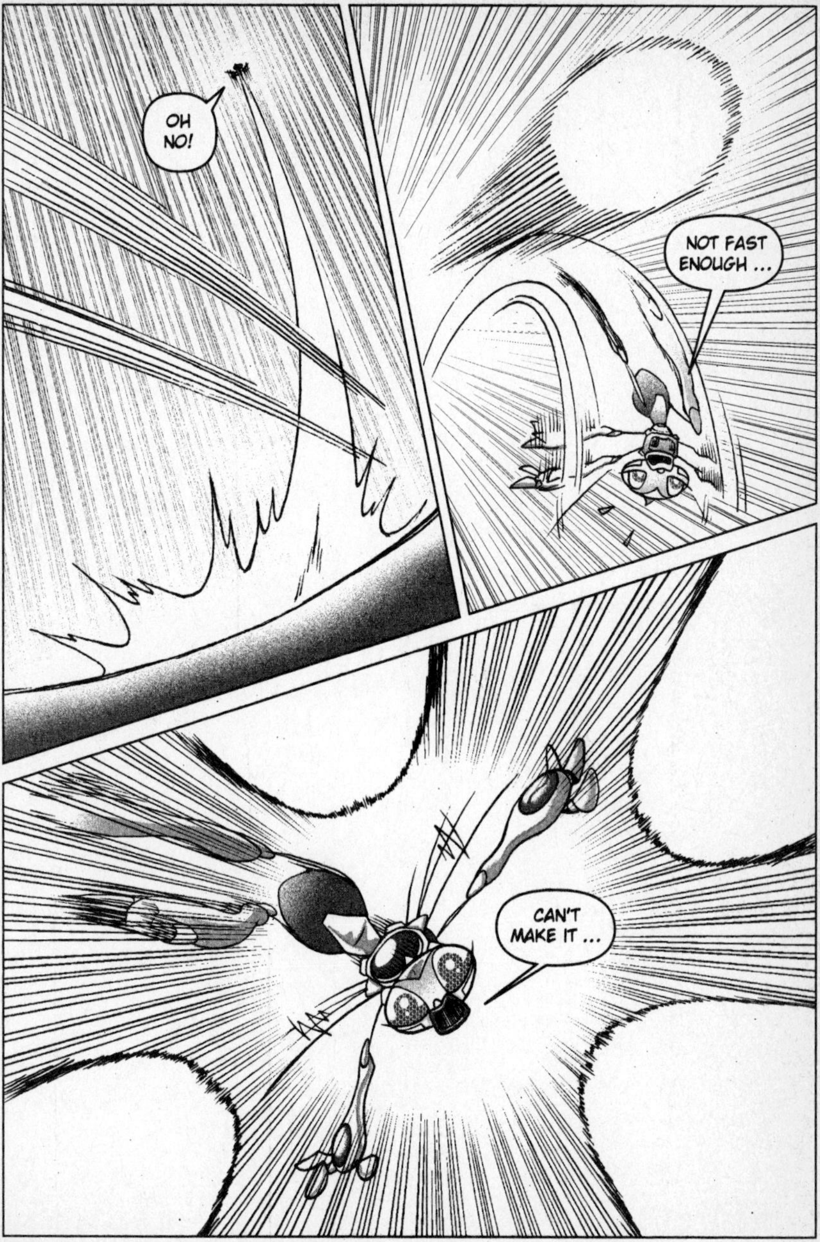
OH NO!
NOT FAST ENOUGH ...
CAN'T MAKE IT ...

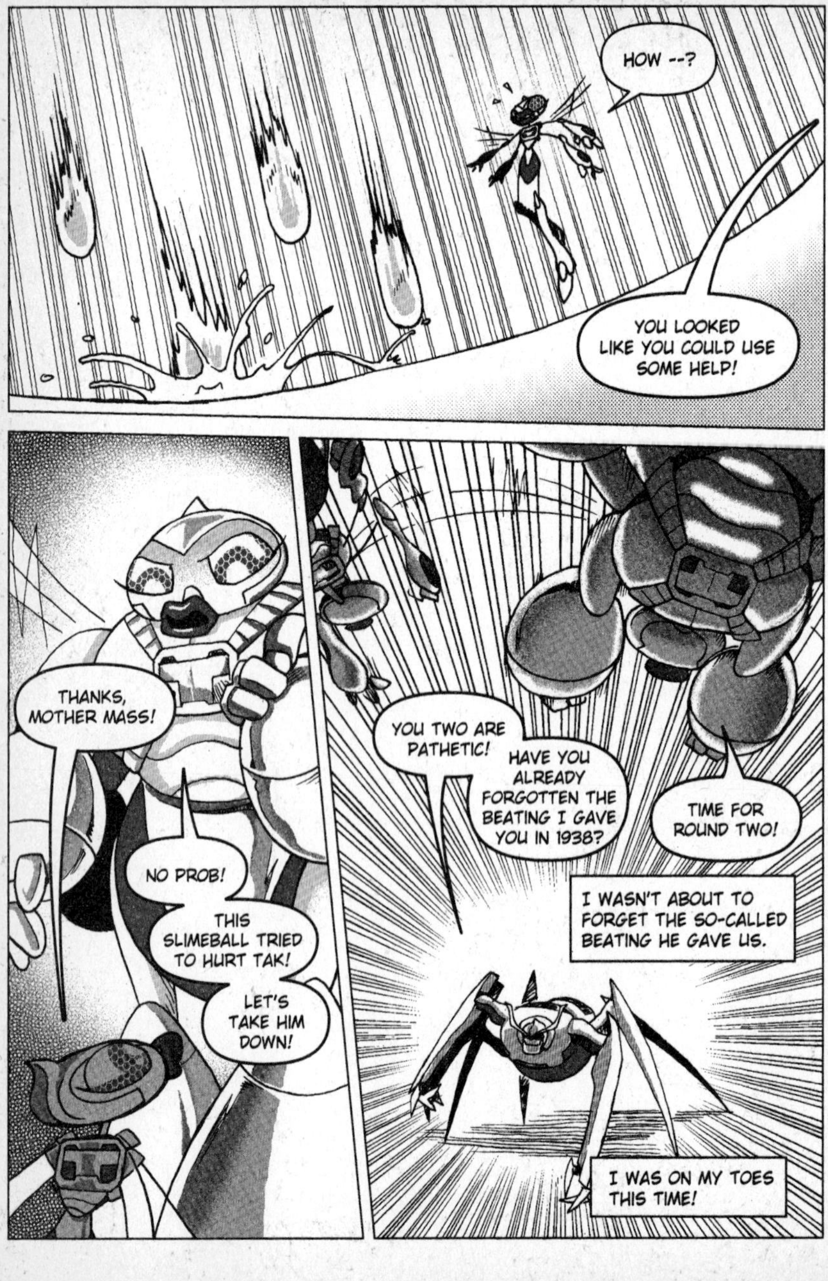
HOW --?
YOU LOOKED LIKE YOU COULD USE SOME HELP!
THANKS, MOTHER MASS!
NO PROB!
THIS SLIMEBALL TRIED TO HURT TAK!
LET'S TAKE HIM DOWN!
YOU TWO ARE PATHETIC!
HAVE YOU ALREADY FORGOTTEN THE BEATING I GAVE YOU IN 1938?
TIME FOR ROUND TWO!
I WASN'T ABOUT TO FORGET THE SO-CALLED BEATING HE GAVE US.
I WAS ON MY TOES THIS TIME!

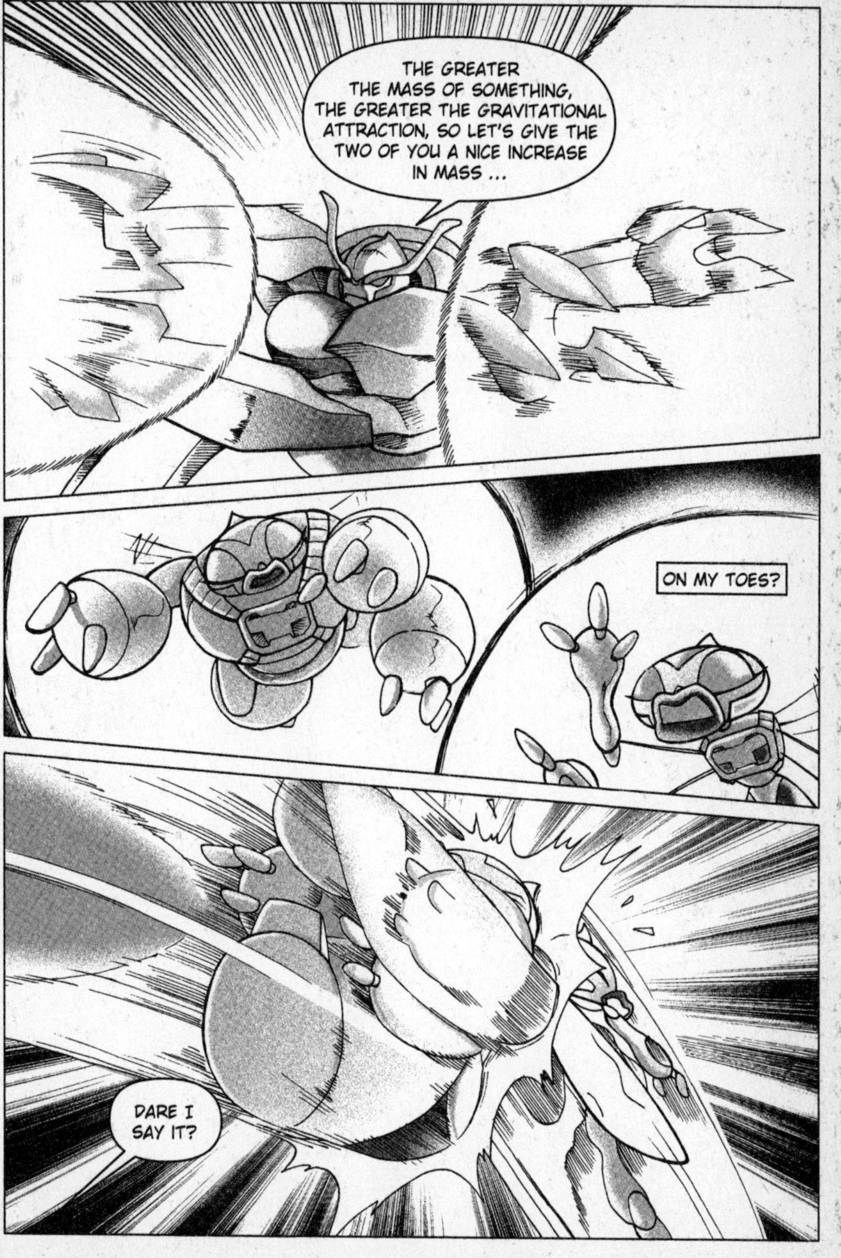
THE GREATER THE MASS OF SOMETHING, THE GREATER THE GRAVITATIONAL ATTRACTION, SO LET'S GIVE THE TWO OF YOU A NICE INCREASE IN MASS ...
ON MY TOES?
DARE I SAY IT?

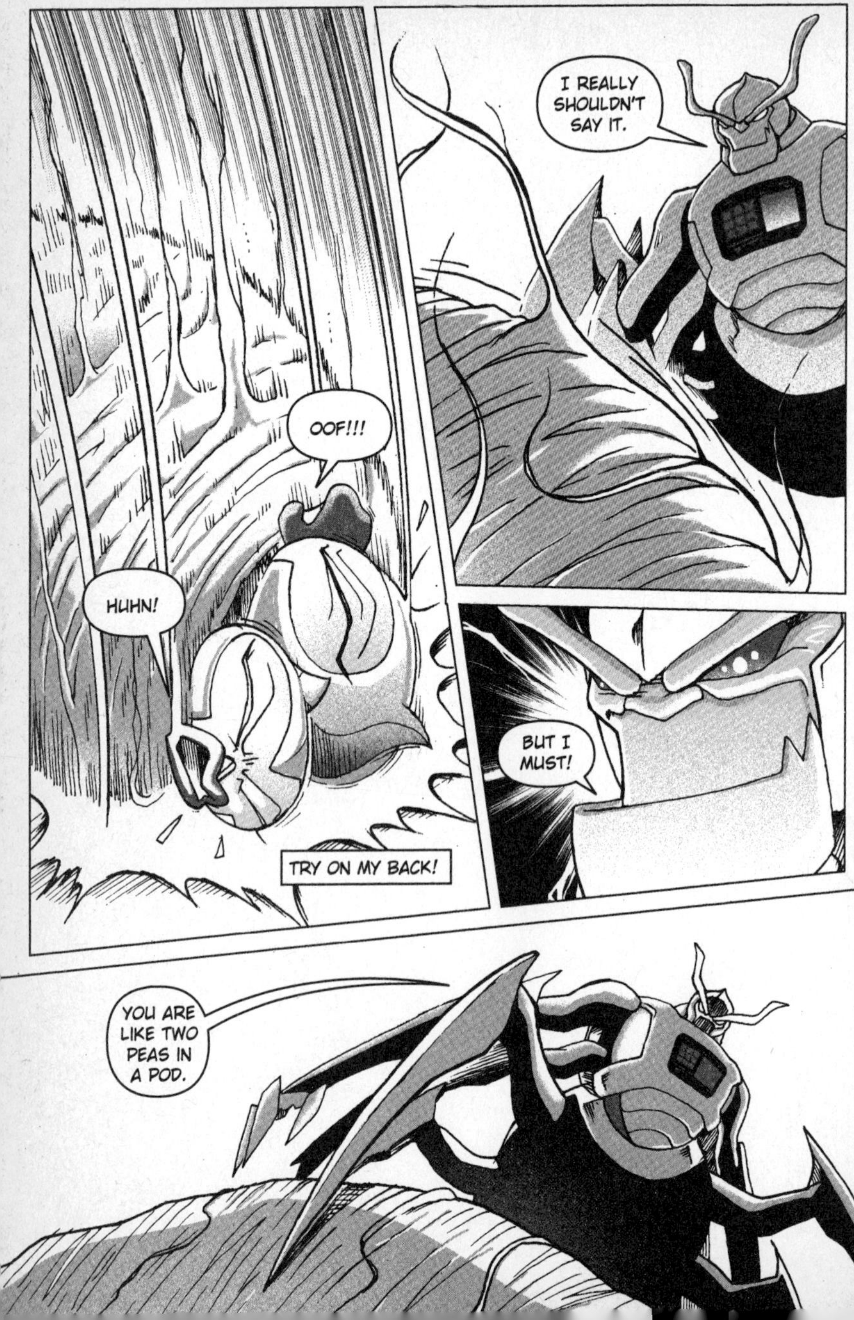
OOF!!!
HUHN!
TRY ON MY BACK!
I REALLY SHOULDN'T SAY IT.
BUT I MUST!
YOU ARE LIKE TWO PEAS IN A POD.

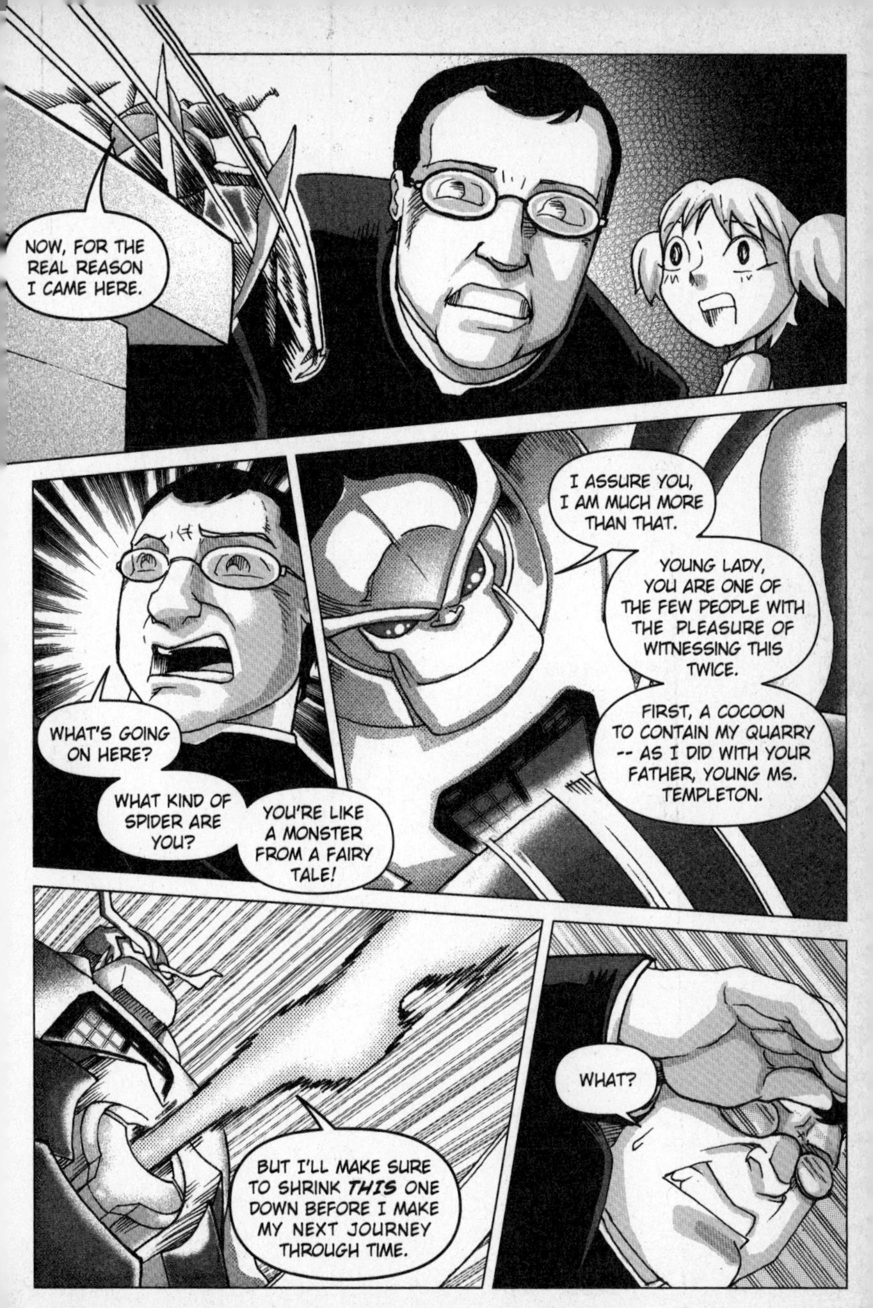
NOW, FOR THE REAL REASON I CAME HERE.
WHAT'S GOING ON HERE?
WHAT KIND OF SPIDER ARE YOU?
YOU'RE LIKE A MONSTER FROM A FAIRY TALE!
I ASSURE YOU, I AM MUCH MORE THAN THAT.
YOUNG LADY, YOU ARE ONE OF THE FEW PEOPLE WITH THE PLEASURE OF WITNESSING THIS TWICE.
FIRST, A COCOON TO CONTAIN MY QUARRY -- AS I DID WITH YOUR FATHER, YOUNG MS. TEMPLETON.
BUT I'LL MAKE SURE TO SHRINK *THIS* ONE DOWN BEFORE I MAKE MY NEXT JOURNEY THROUGH TIME.
WHAT?

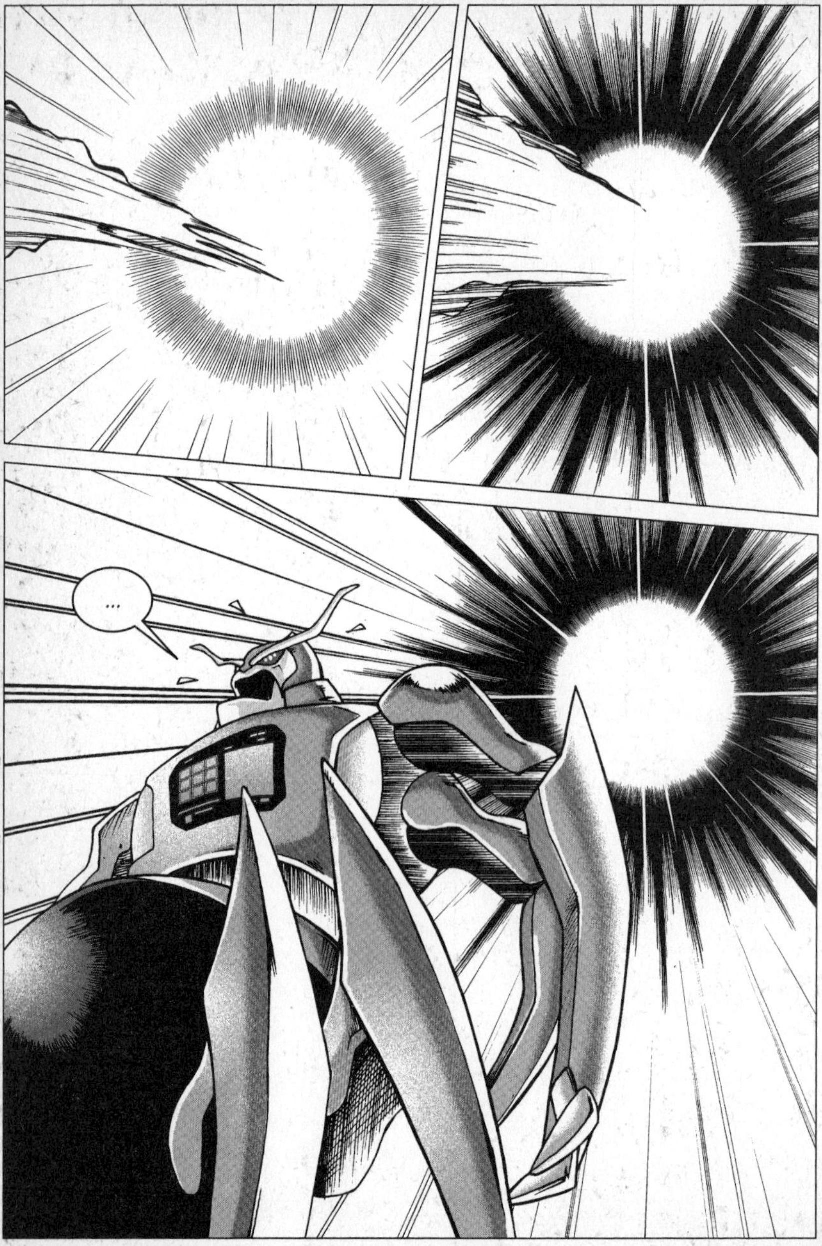
...

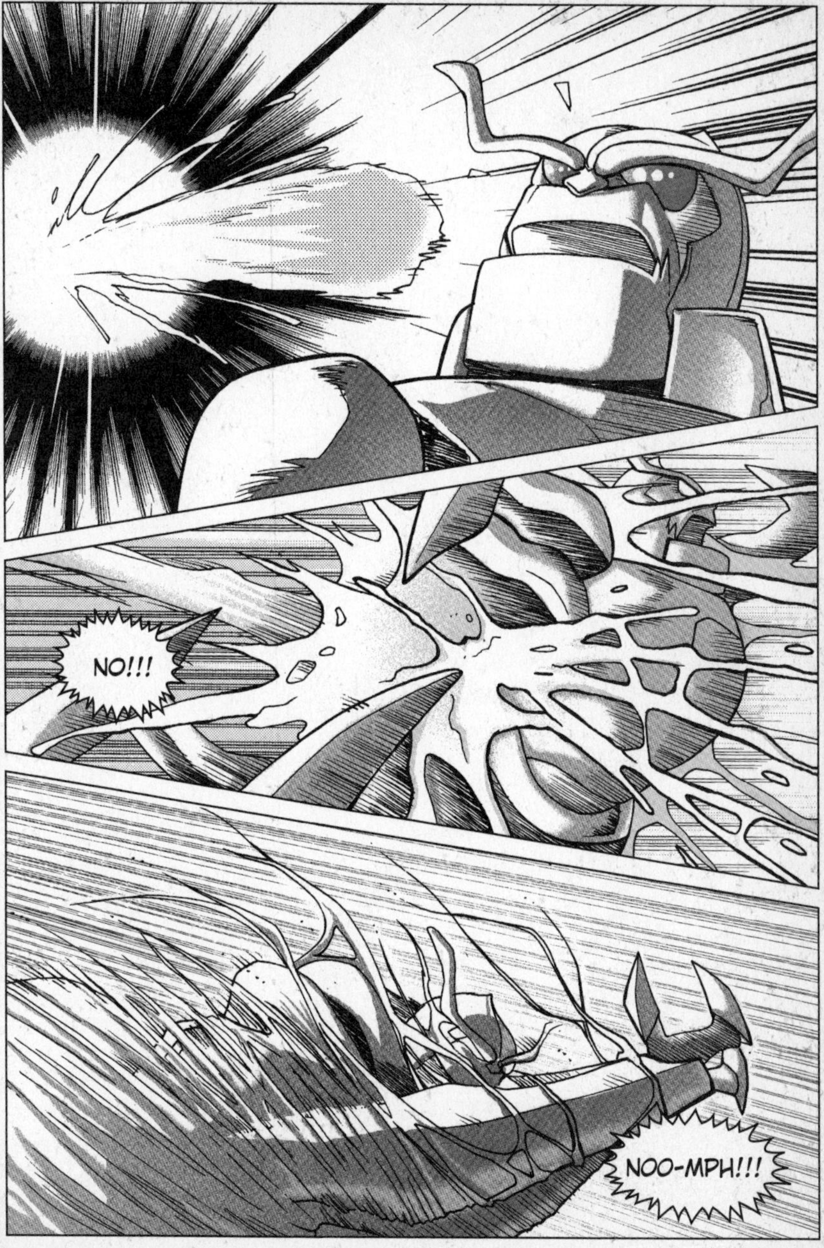
NO!!!
NOO-MPH!!!

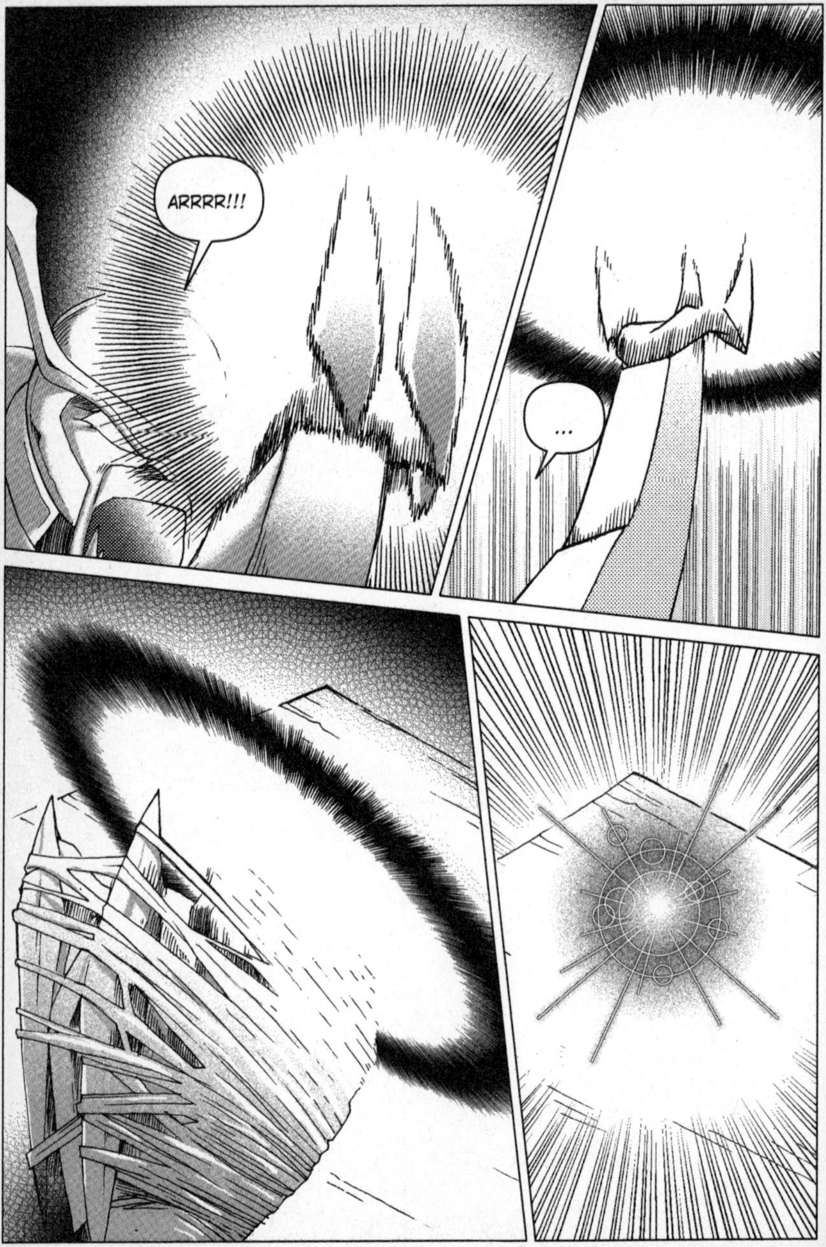
ARRRR!!!
...

WHAT WAS THAT?

I THINK IT WAS WORMHOLE!

SPIDERS, FLIES, AND WORMS?

I'M SORRY, SIR.

I KNOW IT'S CONFUSING, BUT I'LL EXPLAIN EVERYTHING IN A MOMENT. AFTER I HELP MY FRIENDS.

THE FLIES?

RIGHT!

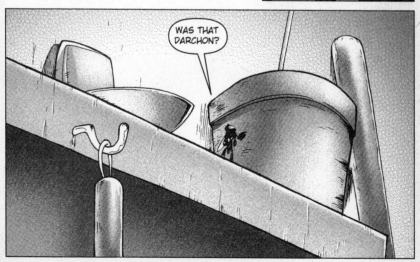

WAS THAT DARCHON?

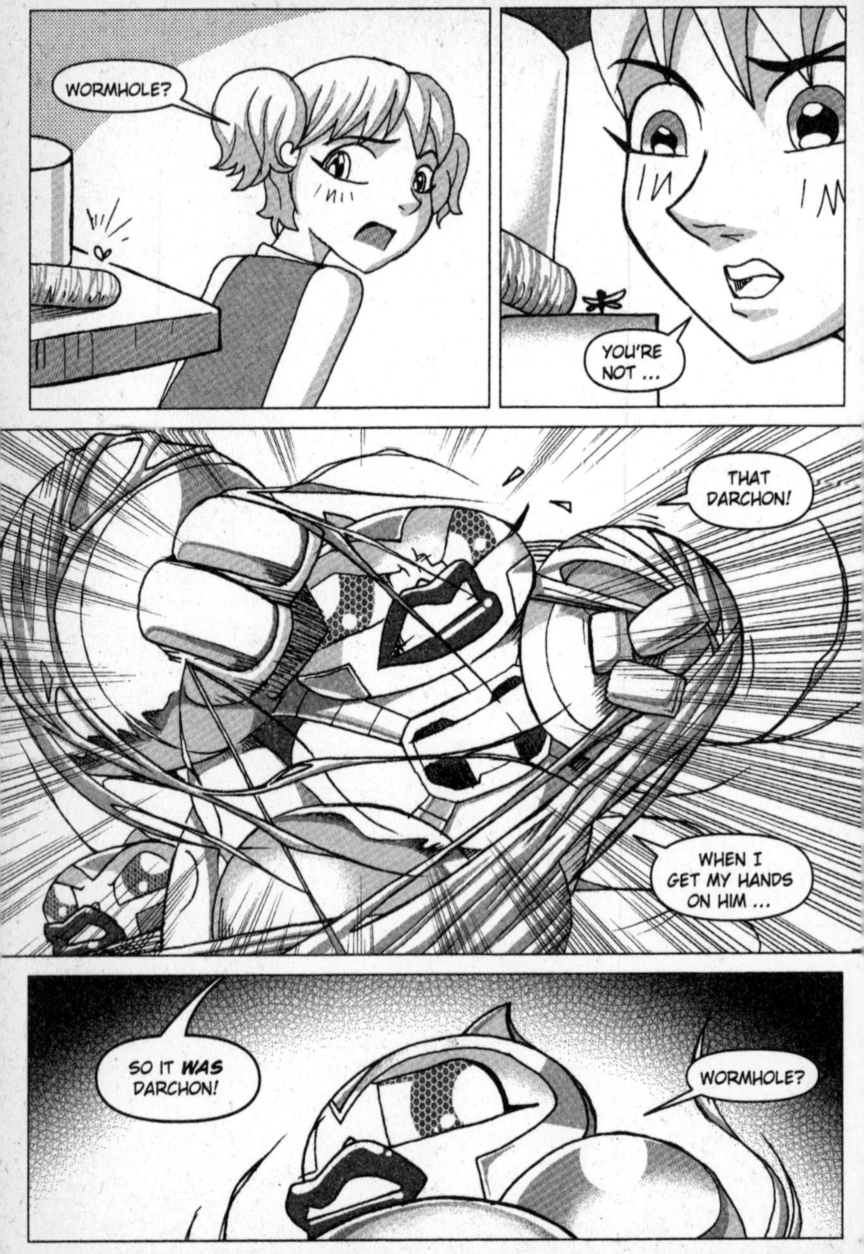
WORMHOLE?
YOU'RE NOT ...
THAT DARCHON!
WHEN I GET MY HANDS ON HIM ...
SO IT **WAS** DARCHON!
WORMHOLE?

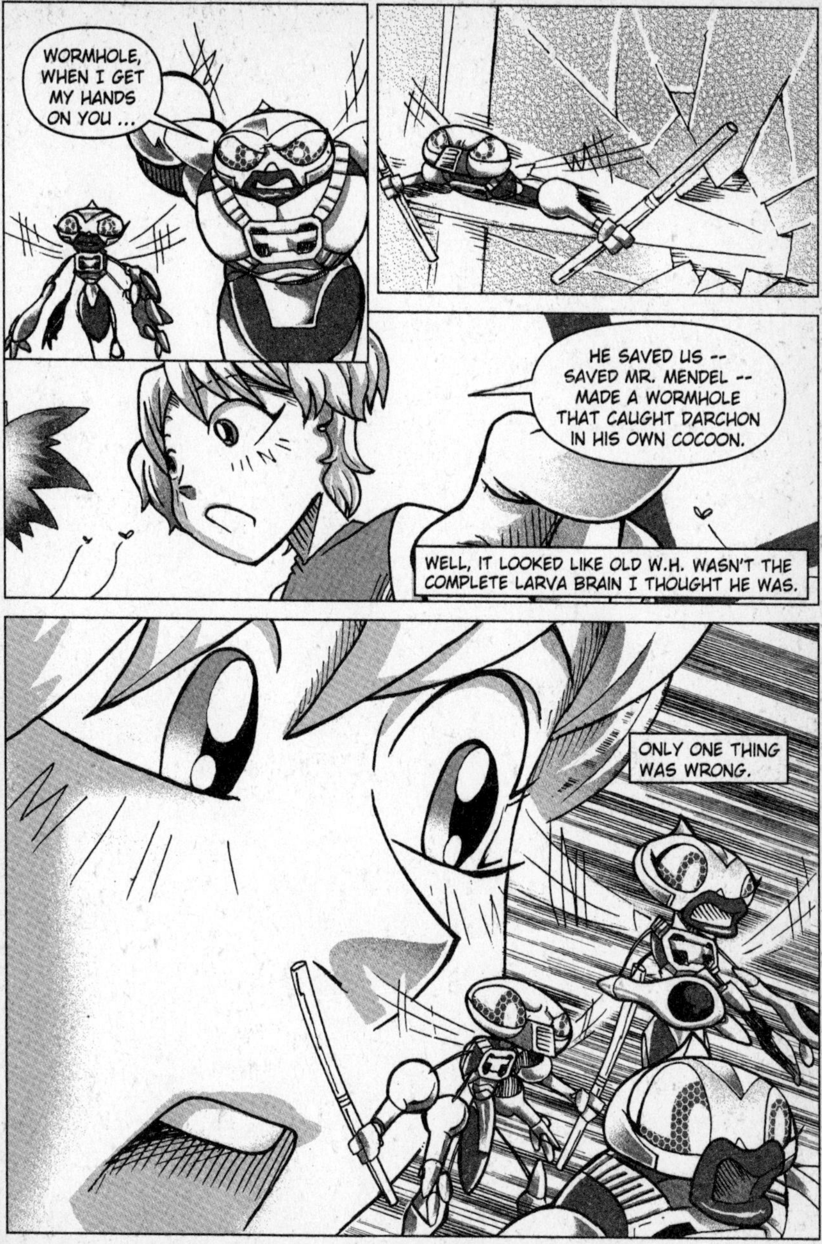
WORMHOLE, WHEN I GET MY HANDS ON YOU ...
HE SAVED US -- SAVED MR. MENDEL -- MADE A WORMHOLE THAT CAUGHT DARCHON IN HIS OWN COCOON.
WELL, IT LOOKED LIKE OLD W.H. WASN'T THE COMPLETE LARVA BRAIN I THOUGHT HE WAS.
ONLY ONE THING WAS WRONG.

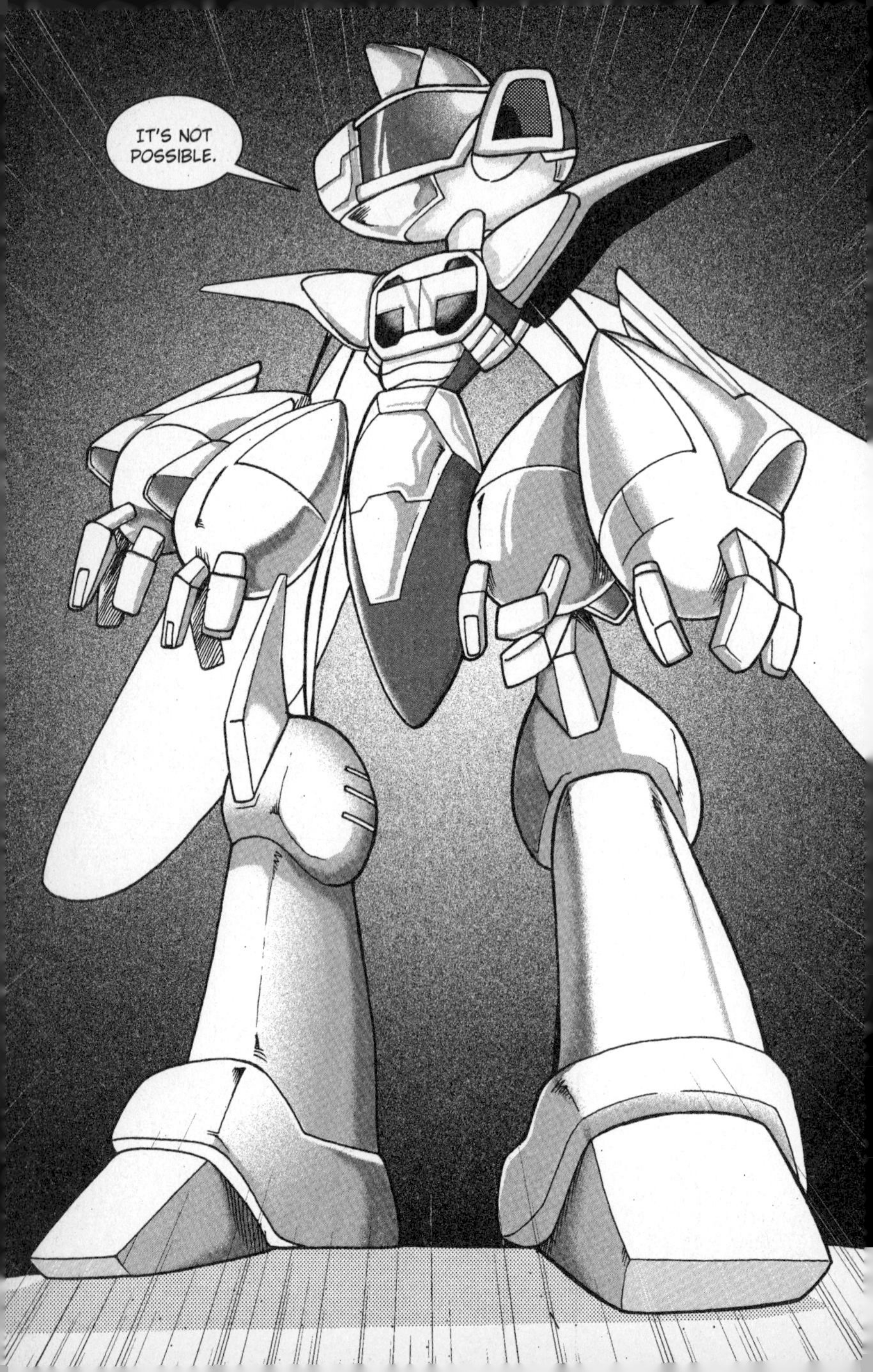
IT'S NOT POSSIBLE.

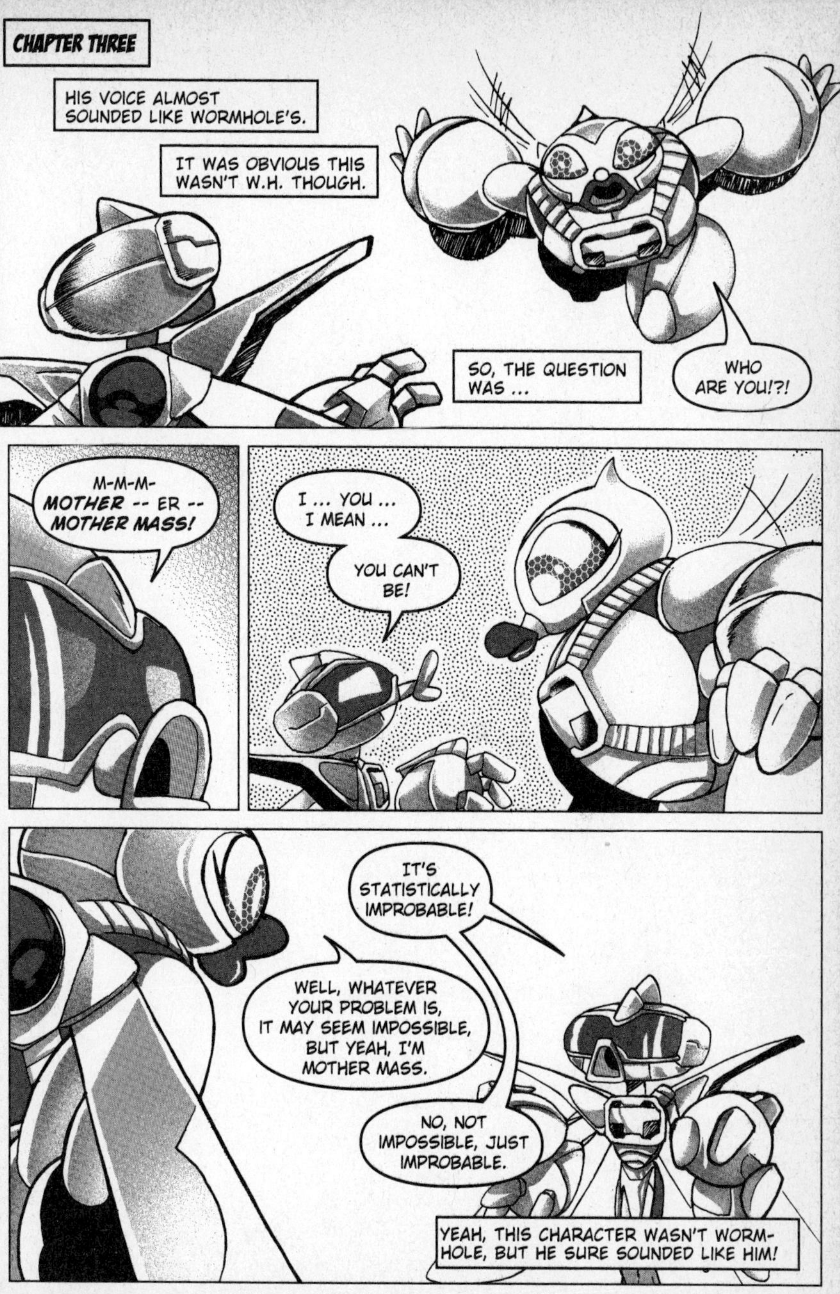
CHAPTER THREE
HIS VOICE ALMOST SOUNDED LIKE WORMHOLE'S.
IT WAS OBVIOUS THIS WASN'T W.H. THOUGH.
SO, THE QUESTION WAS ...
WHO ARE YOU!?!
M-M-M- *MOTHER* -- ER -- *MOTHER MASS!*
I ... YOU ... I MEAN ...
YOU CAN'T BE!
IT'S STATISTICALLY IMPROBABLE!
WELL, WHATEVER YOUR PROBLEM IS, IT MAY SEEM IMPOSSIBLE, BUT YEAH, I'M MOTHER MASS.
NO, NOT IMPOSSIBLE, JUST IMPROBABLE.
YEAH, THIS CHARACTER WASN'T WORM-HOLE, BUT HE SURE SOUNDED LIKE HIM!

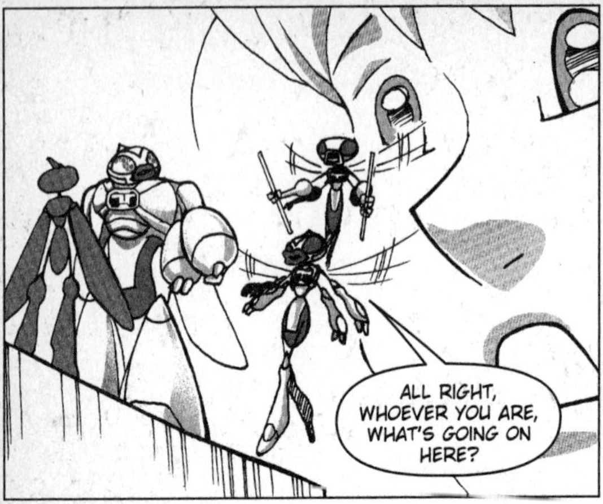
ALL RIGHT, WHOEVER YOU ARE, WHAT'S GOING ON HERE?
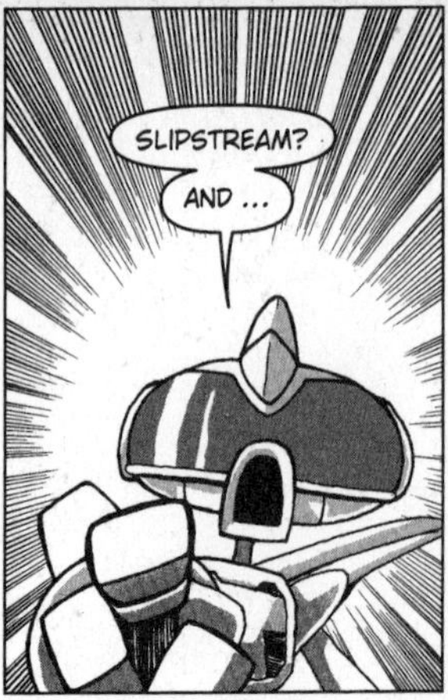
SLIPSTREAM?
AND ...
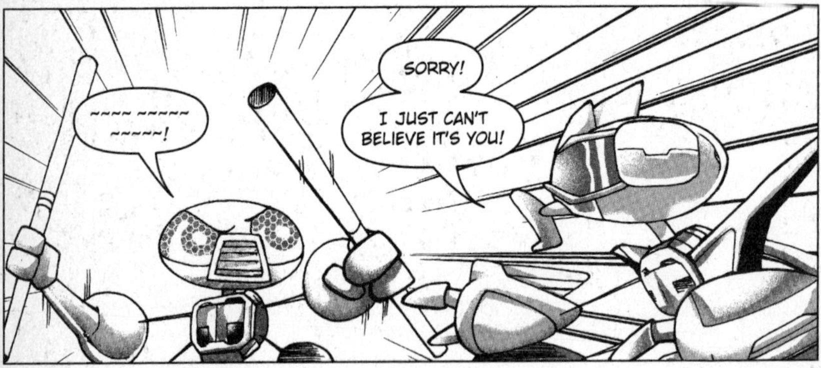

SORRY!
I JUST CAN'T BELIEVE IT'S YOU!
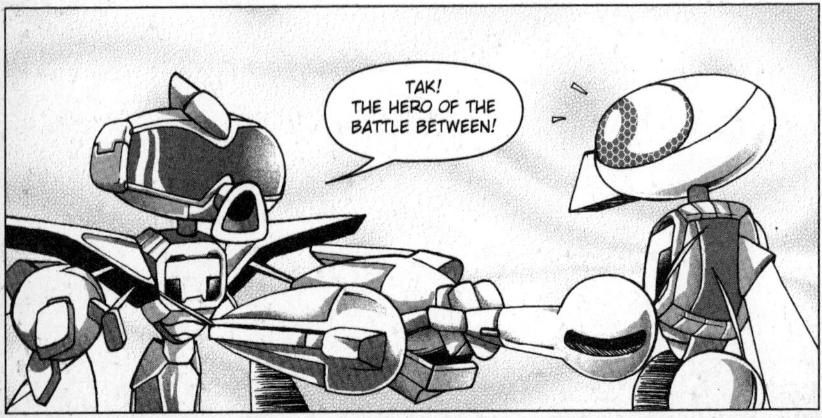
TAK!
THE HERO OF THE BATTLE BETWEEN!

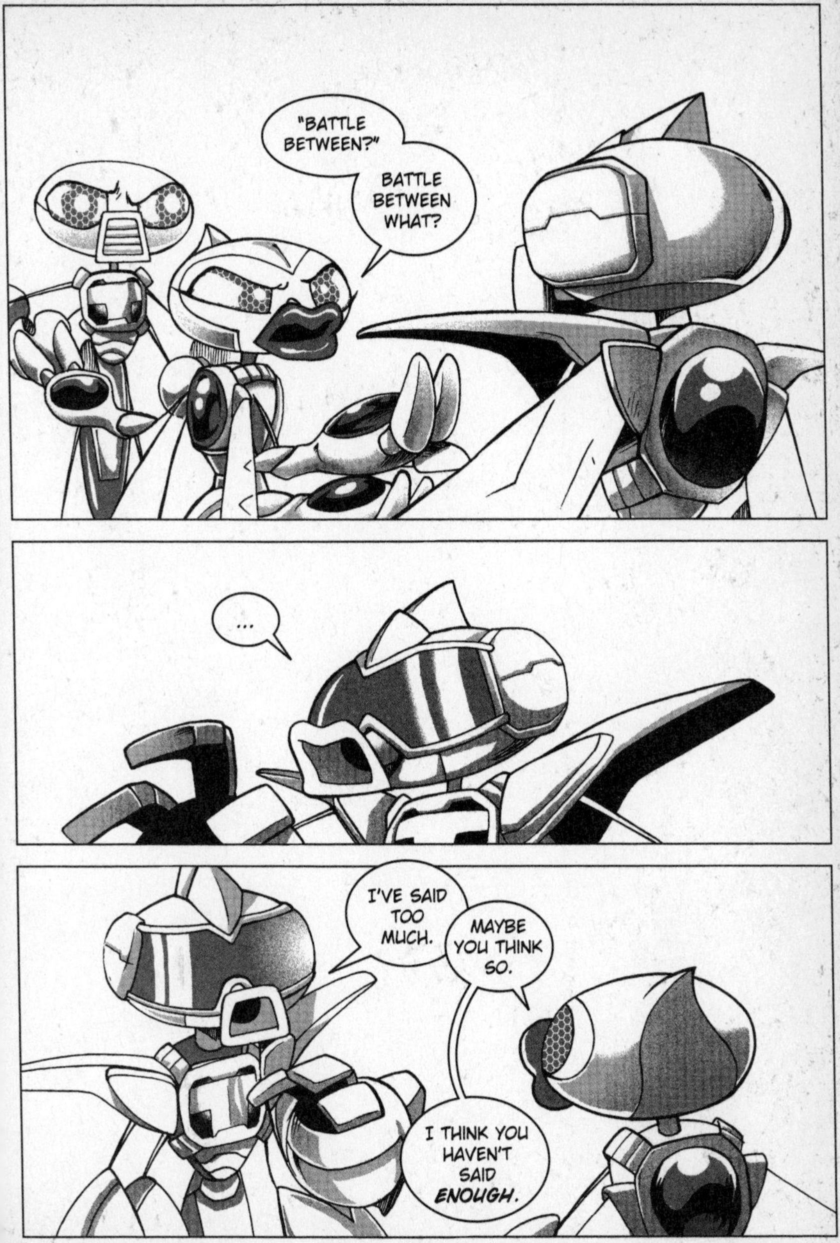
"BATTLE BETWEEN?"
BATTLE BETWEEN WHAT?
...
I'VE SAID TOO MUCH.
MAYBE YOU THINK SO.
I THINK YOU HAVEN'T SAID *ENOUGH*.

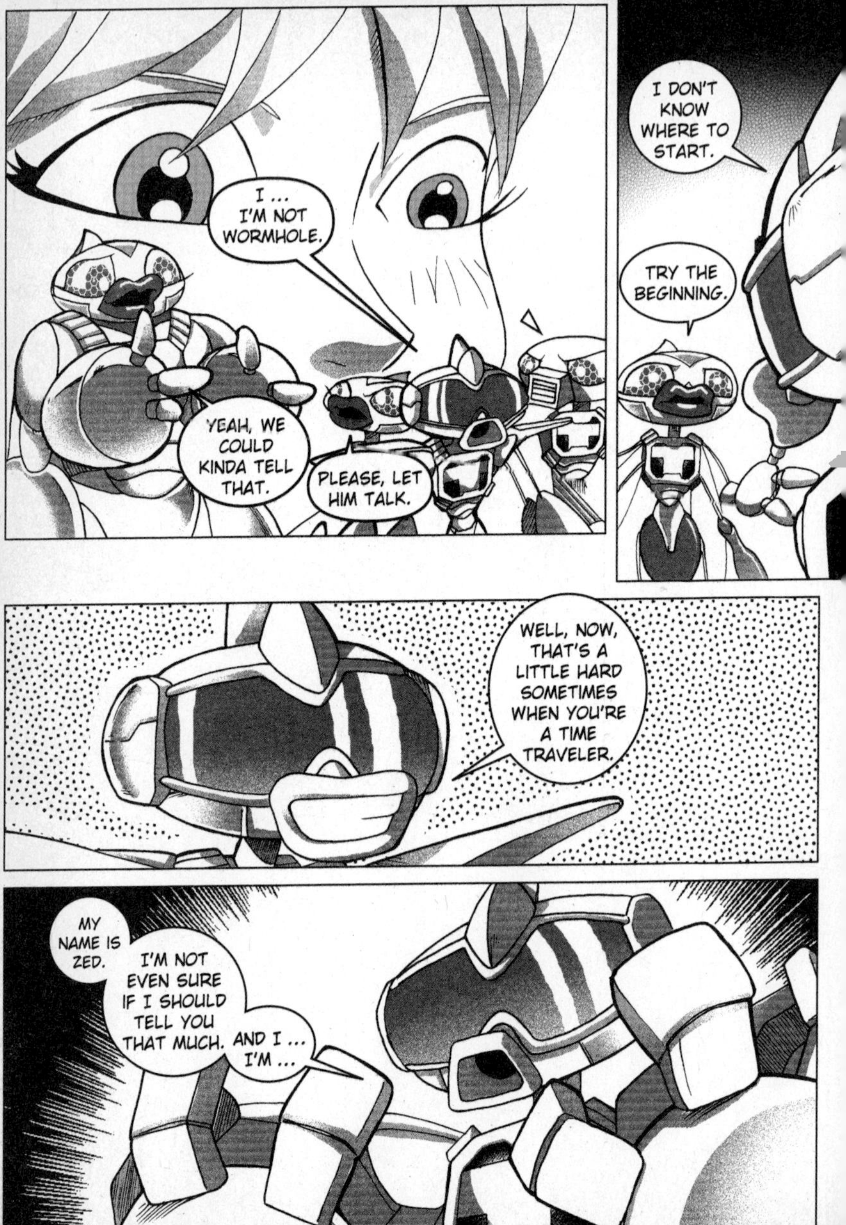
I ... I'M NOT WORMHOLE.
YEAH, WE COULD KINDA TELL THAT.
PLEASE, LET HIM TALK.
I DON'T KNOW WHERE TO START.
TRY THE BEGINNING.
WELL, NOW, THAT'S A LITTLE HARD SOMETIMES WHEN YOU'RE A TIME TRAVELER.
MY NAME IS ZED.
I'M NOT EVEN SURE IF I SHOULD TELL YOU THAT MUCH.
AND I ... I'M ...

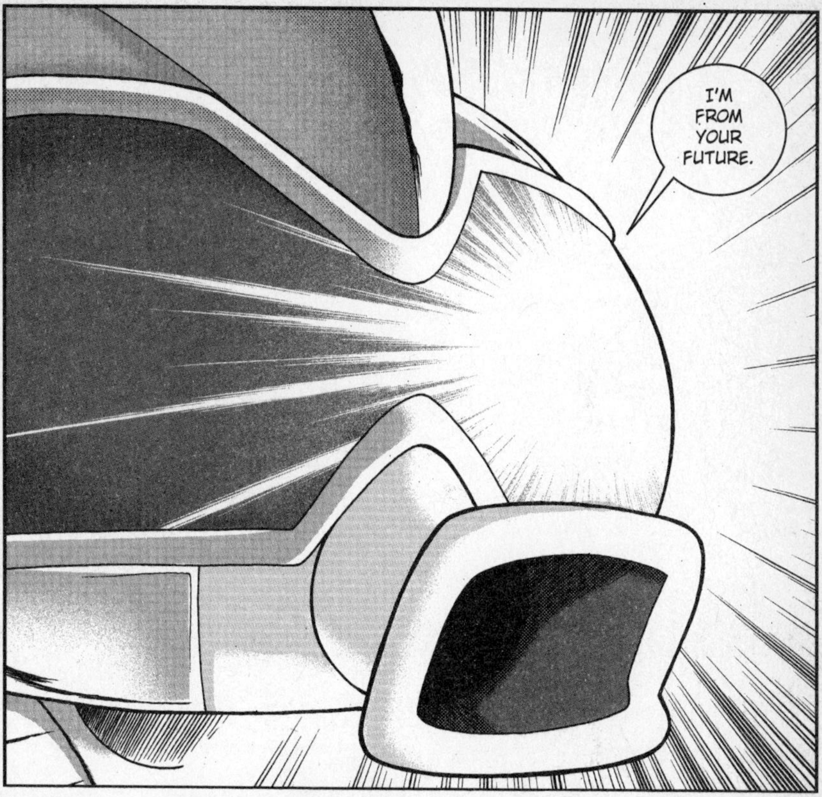
I'M FROM YOUR FUTURE.

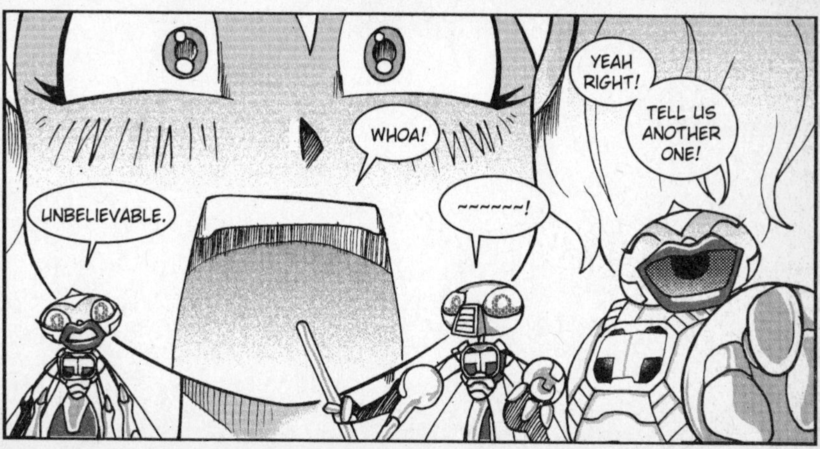
UNBELIEVABLE.
WHOA!
~~~~~~!
YEAH RIGHT!
TELL US ANOTHER ONE!
~~~~~~

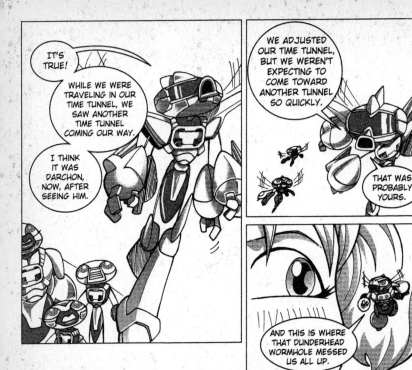

IT'S TRUE!

WHILE WE WERE TRAVELING IN OUR TIME TUNNEL, WE SAW ANOTHER TIME TUNNEL COMING OUR WAY.

I THINK IT WAS DARCHON, NOW, AFTER SEEING HIM.

WE ADJUSTED OUR TIME TUNNEL, BUT WE WEREN'T EXPECTING TO COME TOWARD ANOTHER TUNNEL SO QUICKLY.

THAT WAS PROBABLY YOURS.

AND THIS IS WHERE THAT DUNDERHEAD WORMHOLE MESSED US ALL UP.

WHOEVER WAS CONTROLLING YOUR TIME TUNNEL, THOUGH, DID AN AMAZING JOB OF DODGING US.

OUR TIME TUNNELS COULD HAVE SLAMMED INTO EACH OTHER, WHICH WOULD HAVE BEEN DISASTROUS.

WHOEVER IT WAS SAVED *ALL* OUR LIVES!

"DUNDERHEAD?"

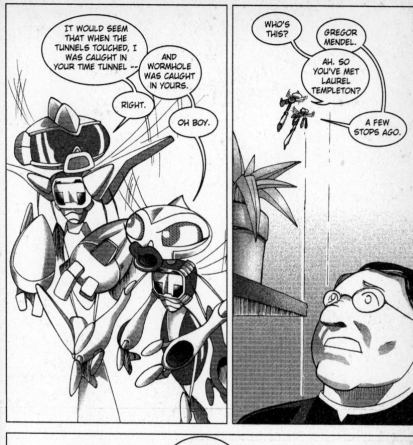

IT WOULD SEEM THAT WHEN THE TUNNELS TOUCHED, I WAS CAUGHT IN YOUR TIME TUNNEL --

AND WORMHOLE WAS CAUGHT IN YOURS.

RIGHT.

OH BOY.

WHO'S THIS?

GREGOR MENDEL.

AH. SO YOU'VE MET LAUREL TEMPLETON?

A FEW STOPS AGO.

SO DARCHON HAS CAPTURED IMHOTEP, NEWTON, FRANKLIN, TEMPLETON, WEI BOYANG, AND DA VINCI?

YES. AND A FEW MORE.

BUT SINCE WE PICKED UP LAUREL, WE WERE ABLE TO PROTECT --

BANNEKER AND MEITNER.

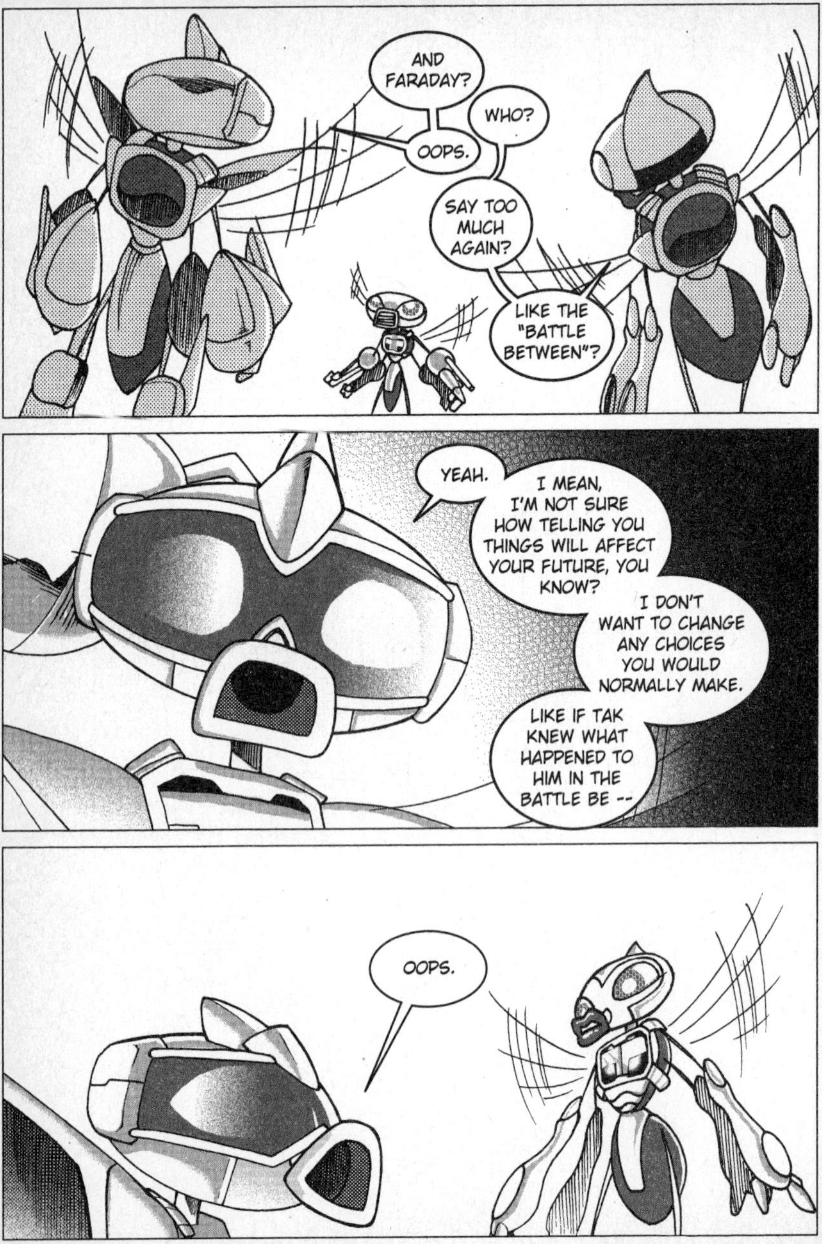
AND FARADAY?
OOPS.
WHO?
SAY TOO MUCH AGAIN?
LIKE THE "BATTLE BETWEEN"?
YEAH.
I MEAN, I'M NOT SURE HOW TELLING YOU THINGS WILL AFFECT YOUR FUTURE, YOU KNOW?
I DON'T WANT TO CHANGE ANY CHOICES YOU WOULD NORMALLY MAKE.
LIKE IF TAK KNEW WHAT HAPPENED TO HIM IN THE BATTLE BE --
OOPS.

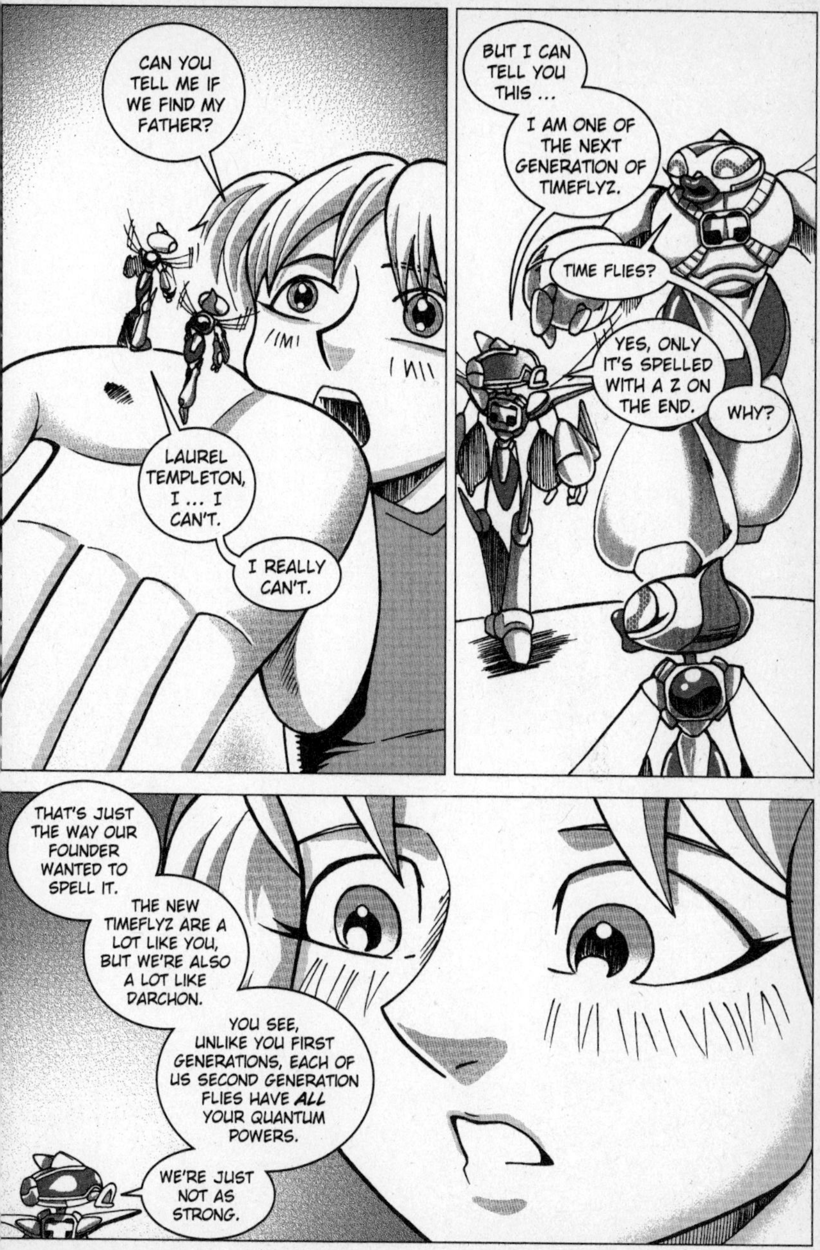
CAN YOU TELL ME IF WE FIND MY FATHER?
LAUREL TEMPLETON, I ... I CAN'T.
I REALLY CAN'T.
BUT I CAN TELL YOU THIS ...
I AM ONE OF THE NEXT GENERATION OF TIMEFLYZ.
TIME FLIES?
YES, ONLY IT'S SPELLED WITH A Z ON THE END.
WHY?
THAT'S JUST THE WAY OUR FOUNDER WANTED TO SPELL IT.
THE NEW TIMEFLYZ ARE A LOT LIKE YOU, BUT WE'RE ALSO A LOT LIKE DARCHON.
YOU SEE, UNLIKE YOU FIRST GENERATIONS, EACH OF US SECOND GENERATION FLIES HAVE *ALL* YOUR QUANTUM POWERS.
WE'RE JUST NOT AS STRONG.

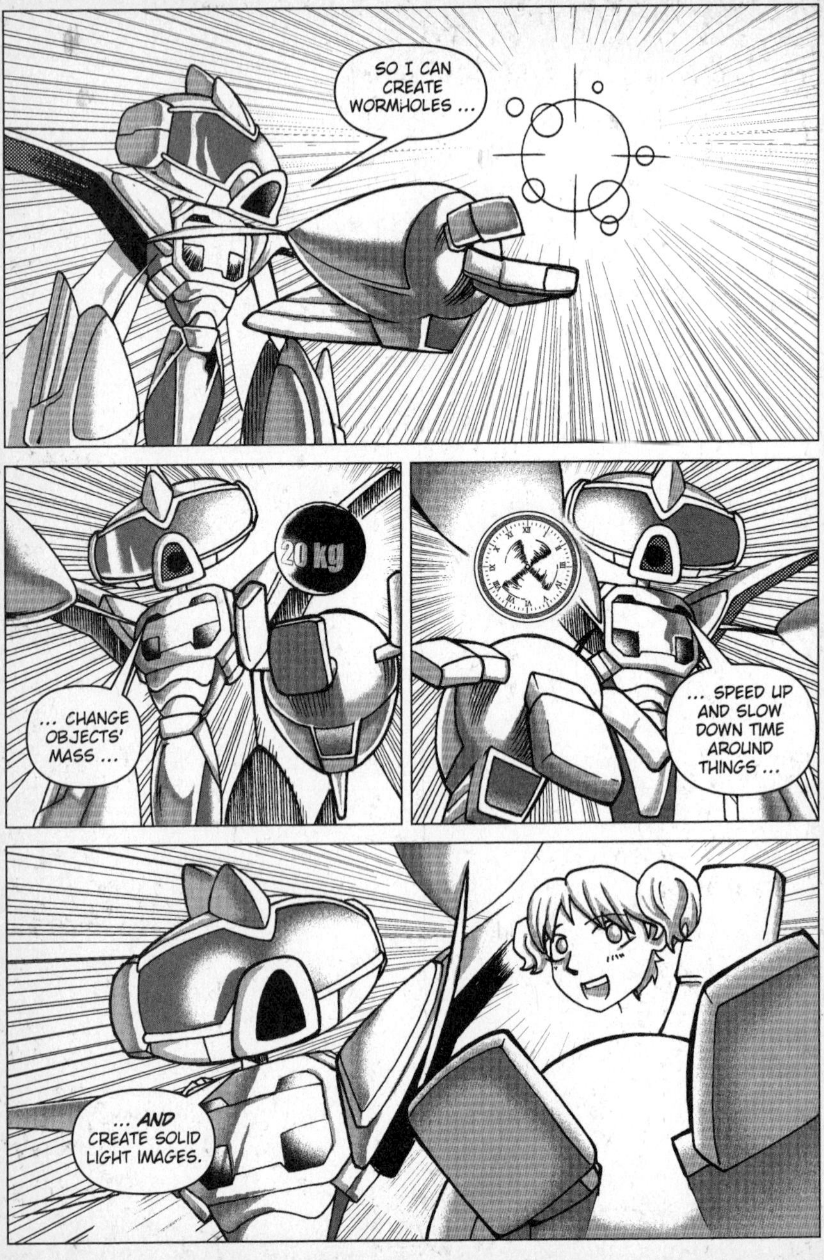
SO I CAN CREATE WORMHOLES ...
20 kg
... CHANGE OBJECTS' MASS ...
... SPEED UP AND SLOW DOWN TIME AROUND THINGS ...
... *AND* CREATE SOLID LIGHT IMAGES.

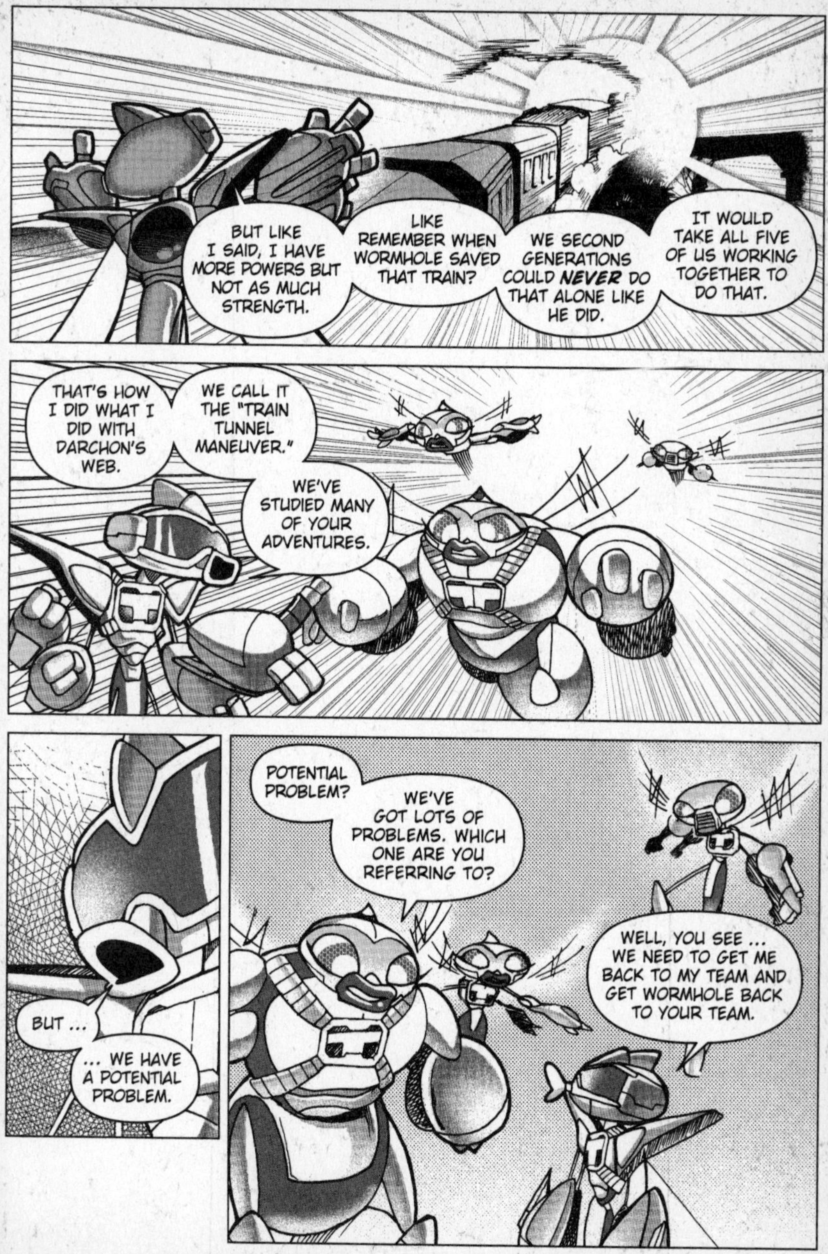
BUT LIKE I SAID, I HAVE MORE POWERS BUT NOT AS MUCH STRENGTH.
LIKE REMEMBER WHEN WORMHOLE SAVED THAT TRAIN?
WE SECOND GENERATIONS COULD **NEVER** DO THAT ALONE LIKE HE DID.
IT WOULD TAKE ALL FIVE OF US WORKING TOGETHER TO DO THAT.
THAT'S HOW I DID WHAT I DID WITH DARCHON'S WEB.
WE CALL IT THE "TRAIN TUNNEL MANEUVER."
WE'VE STUDIED MANY OF YOUR ADVENTURES.
BUT ...
... WE HAVE A POTENTIAL PROBLEM.
POTENTIAL PROBLEM?
WE'VE GOT LOTS OF PROBLEMS. WHICH ONE ARE YOU REFERRING TO?
WELL, YOU SEE ... WE NEED TO GET ME BACK TO MY TEAM AND GET WORMHOLE BACK TO YOUR TEAM.

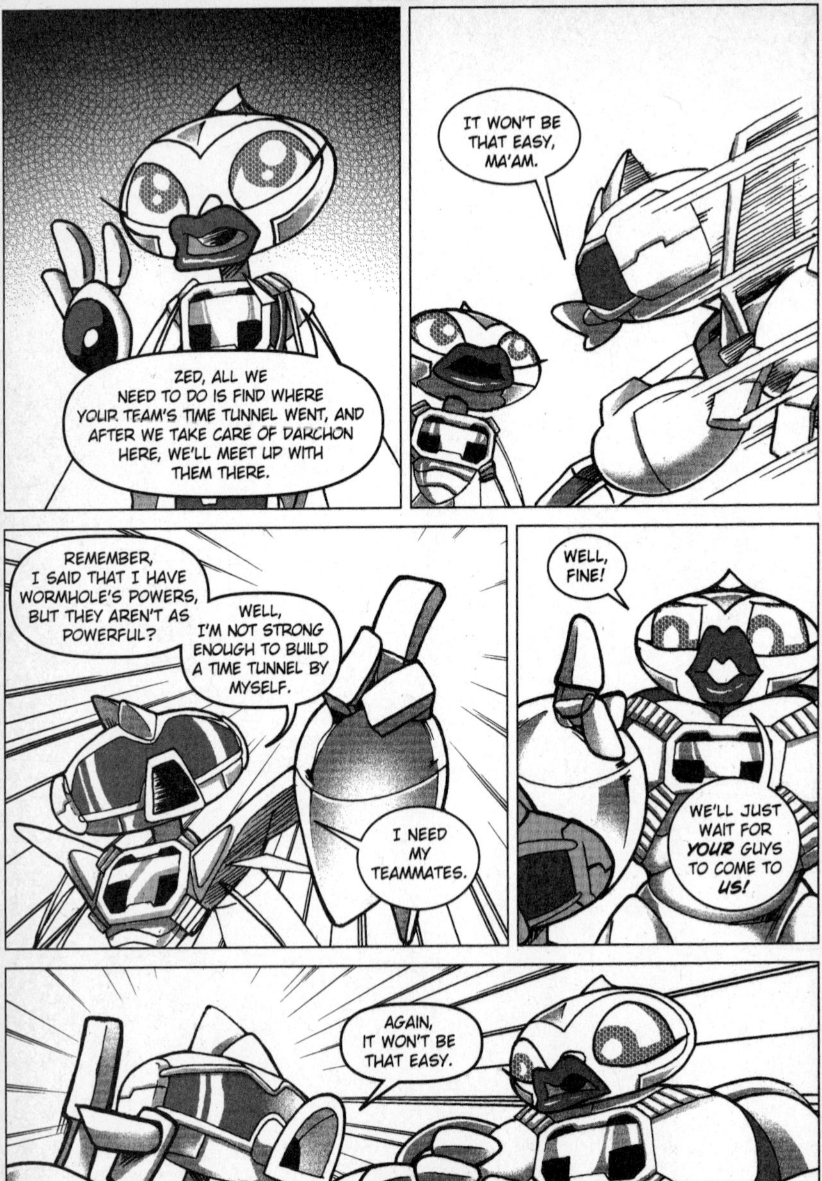
ZED, ALL WE NEED TO DO IS FIND WHERE YOUR TEAM'S TIME TUNNEL WENT, AND AFTER WE TAKE CARE OF DARCHON HERE, WE'LL MEET UP WITH THEM THERE.
IT WON'T BE THAT EASY, MA'AM.
REMEMBER, I SAID THAT I HAVE WORMHOLE'S POWERS, BUT THEY AREN'T AS POWERFUL?
WELL, I'M NOT STRONG ENOUGH TO BUILD A TIME TUNNEL BY MYSELF.
I NEED MY TEAMMATES.
WELL, FINE!
WE'LL JUST WAIT FOR ***YOUR*** GUYS TO COME TO ***US!***
AGAIN, IT WON'T BE THAT EASY.

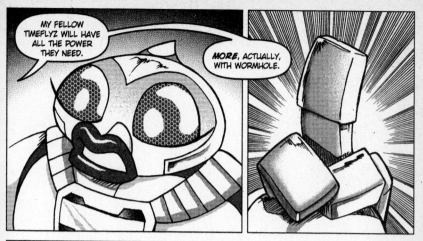

MY FELLOW TIMEFLYZ WILL HAVE ALL THE POWER THEY NEED.

MORE, ACTUALLY, WITH WORMHOLE.

BUT THEY WON'T BE STRONG ENOUGH TO KEEP IT STABLE WITHOUT ME.

WORMHOLE CAN CREATE IT, BUT WITHOUT THE OTHER POWERS, HE CAN'T HELP THEM KEEP IT STABLE ENOUGH FOR TIME TRAVEL.

THAT'S SOMETHING WE CAN WORRY ABOUT LATER.

FOR NOW, WE HAVE A MISSION TO DO.

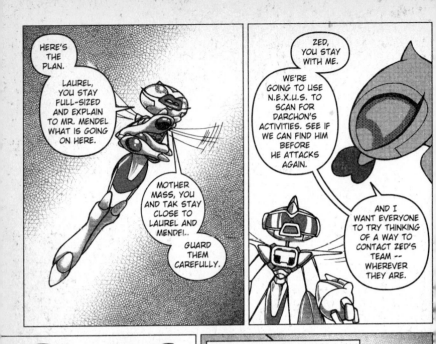

HERE'S THE PLAN.

LAUREL, YOU STAY FULL-SIZED AND EXPLAIN TO MR. MENDEL WHAT IS GOING ON HERE.

MOTHER MASS, YOU AND TAK STAY CLOSE TO LAUREL AND MENDEL.

GUARD THEM CAREFULLY.

ZED, YOU STAY WITH ME.

WE'RE GOING TO USE N.E.X.U.S. TO SCAN FOR DARCHON'S ACTIVITIES. SEE IF WE CAN FIND HIM BEFORE HE ATTACKS AGAIN.

AND I WANT EVERYONE TO TRY THINKING OF A WAY TO CONTACT ZED'S TEAM -- WHEREVER THEY ARE.

OH, THIS IS SO EXCITING!

I NEVER THOUGHT I'D GET TO GO ON A MISSION WITH YOU, SLIPSTREAM, BECAUSE YOU'RE SO OLD.

I MEAN, YOU'VE TAUGHT ME SO MUCH ABOUT ... I MEAN, I'VE LEARNED SO MUCH FROM YOUR EXPERIENCES THAT I ... NEVERMIND.

HMMM. TRY TO COME UP WITH A WAY TO COMMUNICATE WITH ZED'S TEAM AND WORMHOLE.

THAT WAS SOMETHING THAT WE'D NORMALLY ASK ...

WORMHOLE.

WHEN I GET MY HANDS ON HIM ...

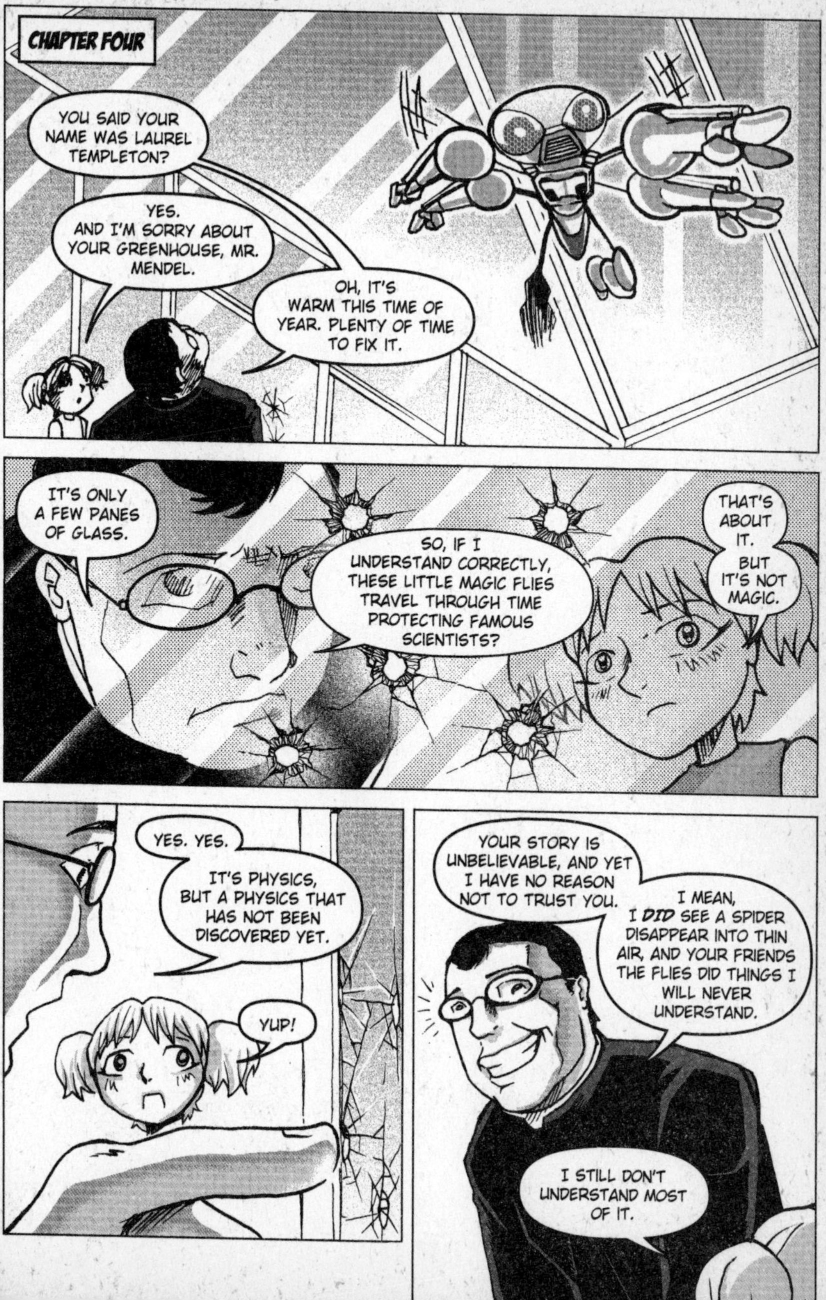
CHAPTER FOUR
YOU SAID YOUR NAME WAS LAUREL TEMPLETON?
YES. AND I'M SORRY ABOUT YOUR GREENHOUSE, MR. MENDEL.
OH, IT'S WARM THIS TIME OF YEAR. PLENTY OF TIME TO FIX IT.
IT'S ONLY A FEW PANES OF GLASS.
SO, IF I UNDERSTAND CORRECTLY, THESE LITTLE MAGIC FLIES TRAVEL THROUGH TIME PROTECTING FAMOUS SCIENTISTS?
THAT'S ABOUT IT.
BUT IT'S NOT MAGIC.
YES. YES.
IT'S PHYSICS, BUT A PHYSICS THAT HAS NOT BEEN DISCOVERED YET.
YUP!
YOUR STORY IS UNBELIEVABLE, AND YET I HAVE NO REASON NOT TO TRUST YOU.
I MEAN, I DID SEE A SPIDER DISAPPEAR INTO THIN AIR, AND YOUR FRIENDS THE FLIES DID THINGS I WILL NEVER UNDERSTAND.
I STILL DON'T UNDERSTAND MOST OF IT.

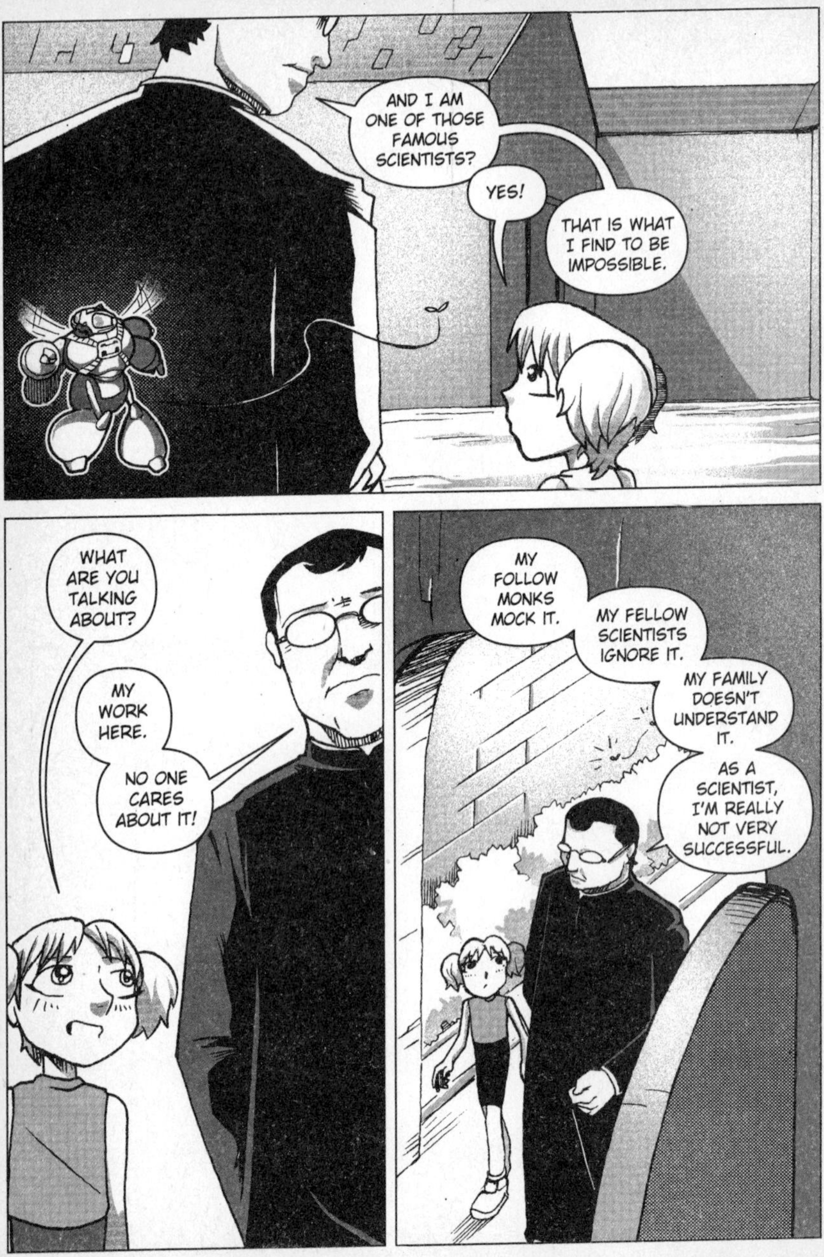
AND I AM ONE OF THOSE FAMOUS SCIENTISTS?
YES!
THAT IS WHAT I FIND TO BE IMPOSSIBLE.
WHAT ARE YOU TALKING ABOUT?
MY WORK HERE.
NO ONE CARES ABOUT IT!
MY FOLLOW MONKS MOCK IT.
MY FELLOW SCIENTISTS IGNORE IT.
MY FAMILY DOESN'T UNDERSTAND IT.
AS A SCIENTIST, I'M REALLY NOT VERY SUCCESSFUL.

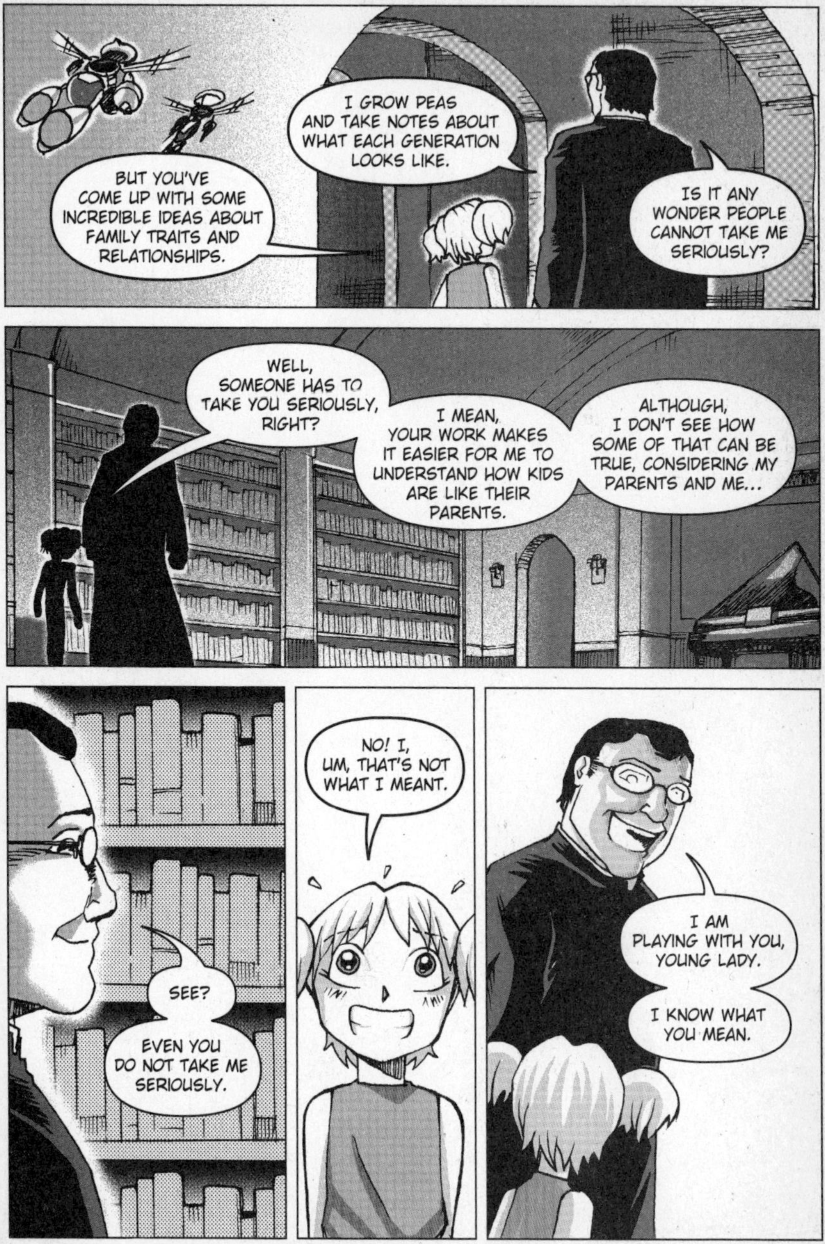
I GROW PEAS AND TAKE NOTES ABOUT WHAT EACH GENERATION LOOKS LIKE.
BUT YOU'VE COME UP WITH SOME INCREDIBLE IDEAS ABOUT FAMILY TRAITS AND RELATIONSHIPS.
IS IT ANY WONDER PEOPLE CANNOT TAKE ME SERIOUSLY?
WELL, SOMEONE HAS TO TAKE YOU SERIOUSLY, RIGHT?
I MEAN, YOUR WORK MAKES IT EASIER FOR ME TO UNDERSTAND HOW KIDS ARE LIKE THEIR PARENTS.
ALTHOUGH, I DON'T SEE HOW SOME OF THAT CAN BE TRUE, CONSIDERING MY PARENTS AND ME...
SEE?
EVEN YOU DO NOT TAKE ME SERIOUSLY.
NO! I, UM, THAT'S NOT WHAT I MEANT.
I AM PLAYING WITH YOU, YOUNG LADY.
I KNOW WHAT YOU MEAN.

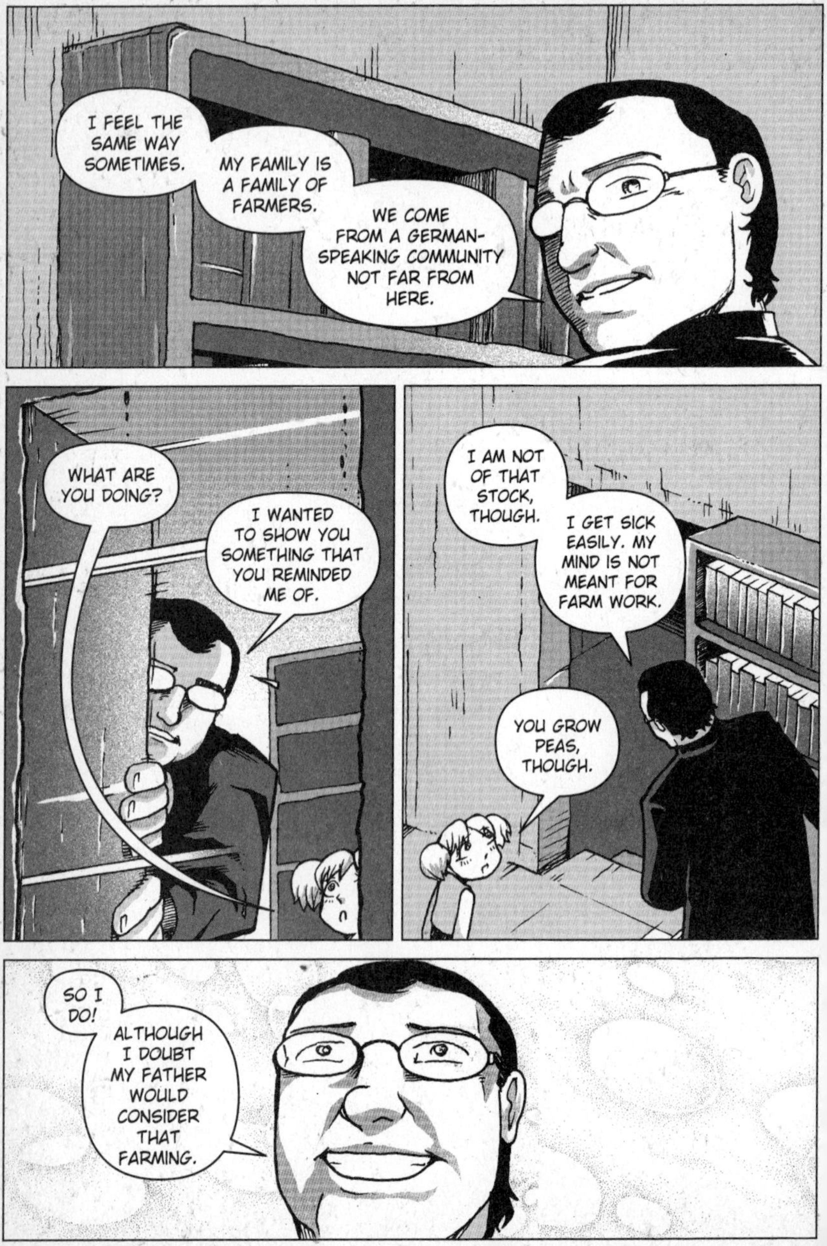
I FEEL THE SAME WAY SOMETIMES.
MY FAMILY IS A FAMILY OF FARMERS.
WE COME FROM A GERMAN-SPEAKING COMMUNITY NOT FAR FROM HERE.
WHAT ARE YOU DOING?
I WANTED TO SHOW YOU SOMETHING THAT YOU REMINDED ME OF.
I AM NOT OF THAT STOCK, THOUGH.
I GET SICK EASILY. MY MIND IS NOT MEANT FOR FARM WORK.
YOU GROW PEAS, THOUGH.
SO I DO!
ALTHOUGH I DOUBT MY FATHER WOULD CONSIDER THAT FARMING.

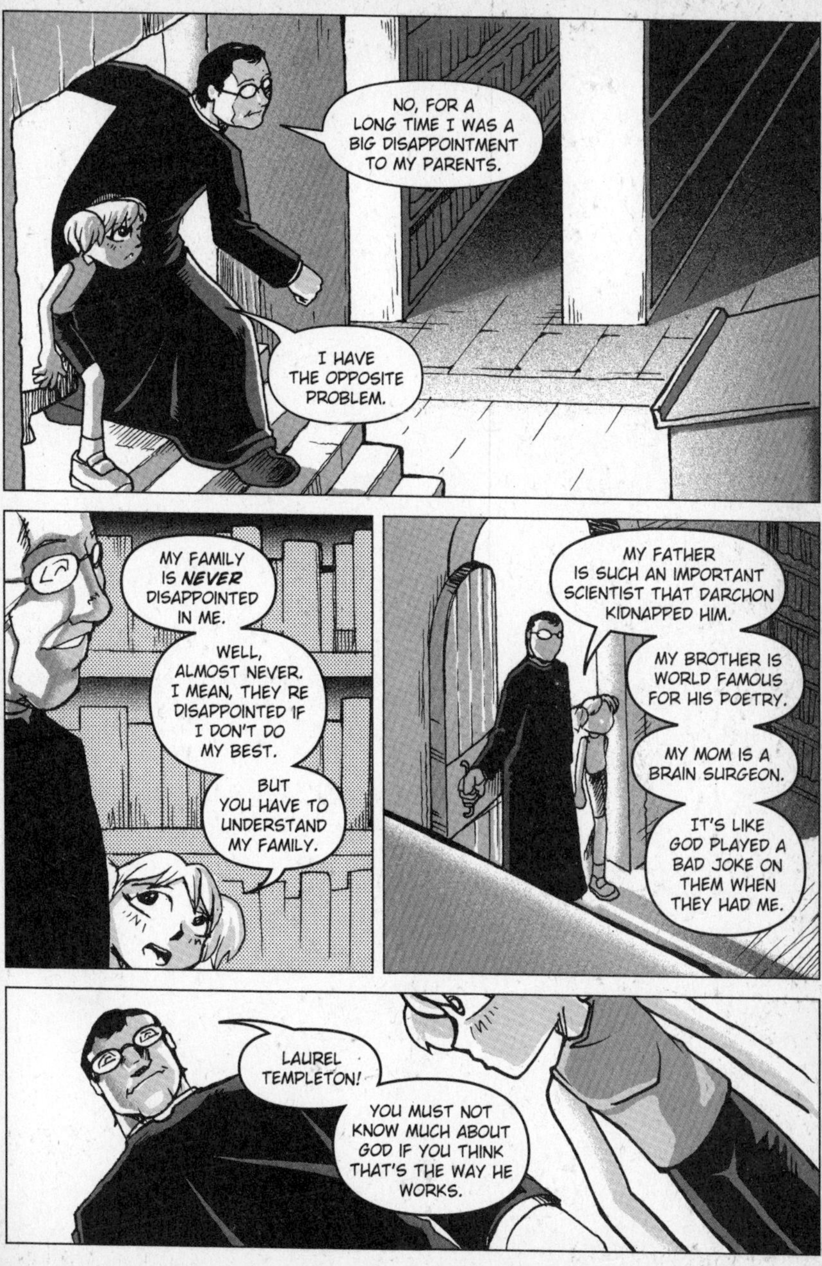
NO, FOR A LONG TIME I WAS A BIG DISAPPOINTMENT TO MY PARENTS.
I HAVE THE OPPOSITE PROBLEM.
MY FAMILY IS ***NEVER*** DISAPPOINTED IN ME.
WELL, ALMOST NEVER. I MEAN, THEY RE DISAPPOINTED IF I DON'T DO MY BEST.
BUT YOU HAVE TO UNDERSTAND MY FAMILY.
MY FATHER IS SUCH AN IMPORTANT SCIENTIST THAT DARCHON KIDNAPPED HIM.
MY BROTHER IS WORLD FAMOUS FOR HIS POETRY.
MY MOM IS A BRAIN SURGEON.
IT'S LIKE GOD PLAYED A BAD JOKE ON THEM WHEN THEY HAD ME.
LAUREL TEMPLETON!
YOU MUST NOT KNOW MUCH ABOUT GOD IF YOU THINK THAT'S THE WAY HE WORKS.

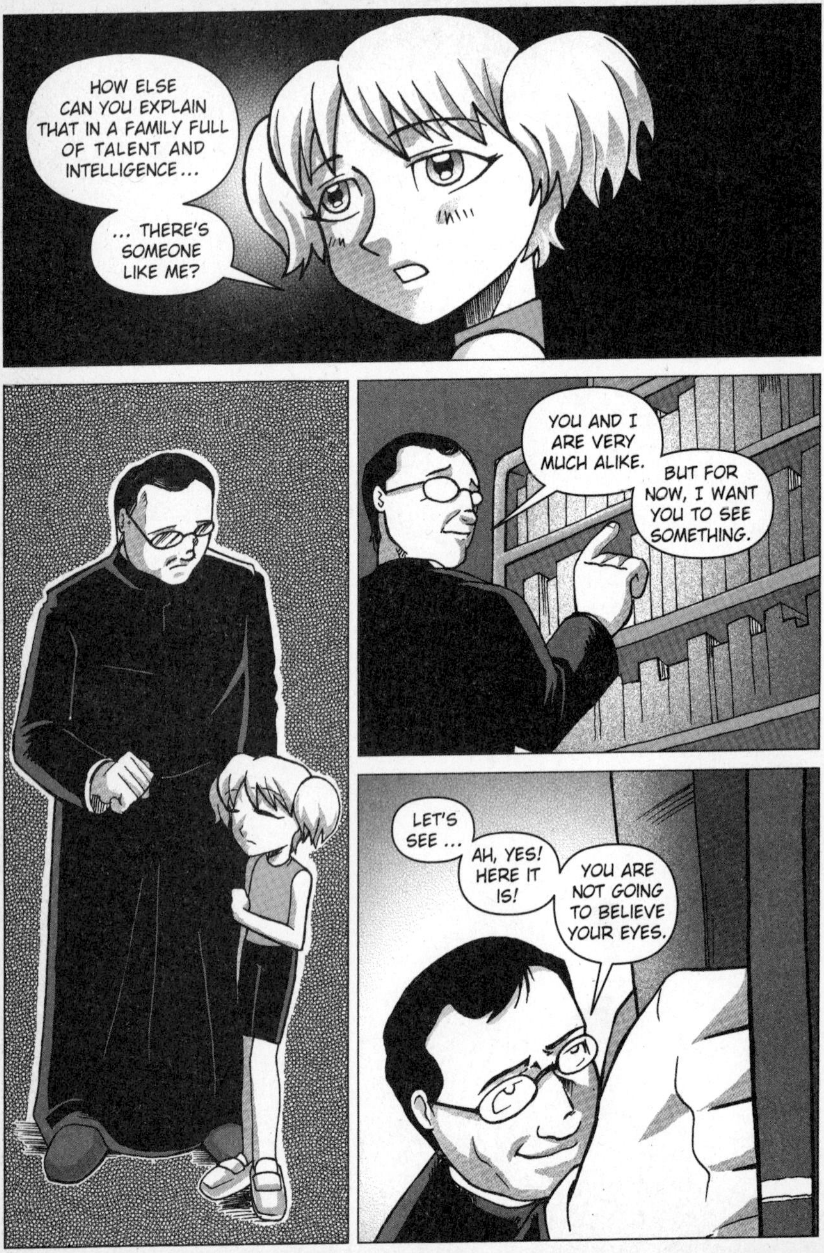
HOW ELSE CAN YOU EXPLAIN THAT IN A FAMILY FULL OF TALENT AND INTELLIGENCE ...
... THERE'S SOMEONE LIKE ME?
YOU AND I ARE VERY MUCH ALIKE.
BUT FOR NOW, I WANT YOU TO SEE SOMETHING.
LET'S SEE ...
AH, YES! HERE IT IS!
YOU ARE NOT GOING TO BELIEVE YOUR EYES.

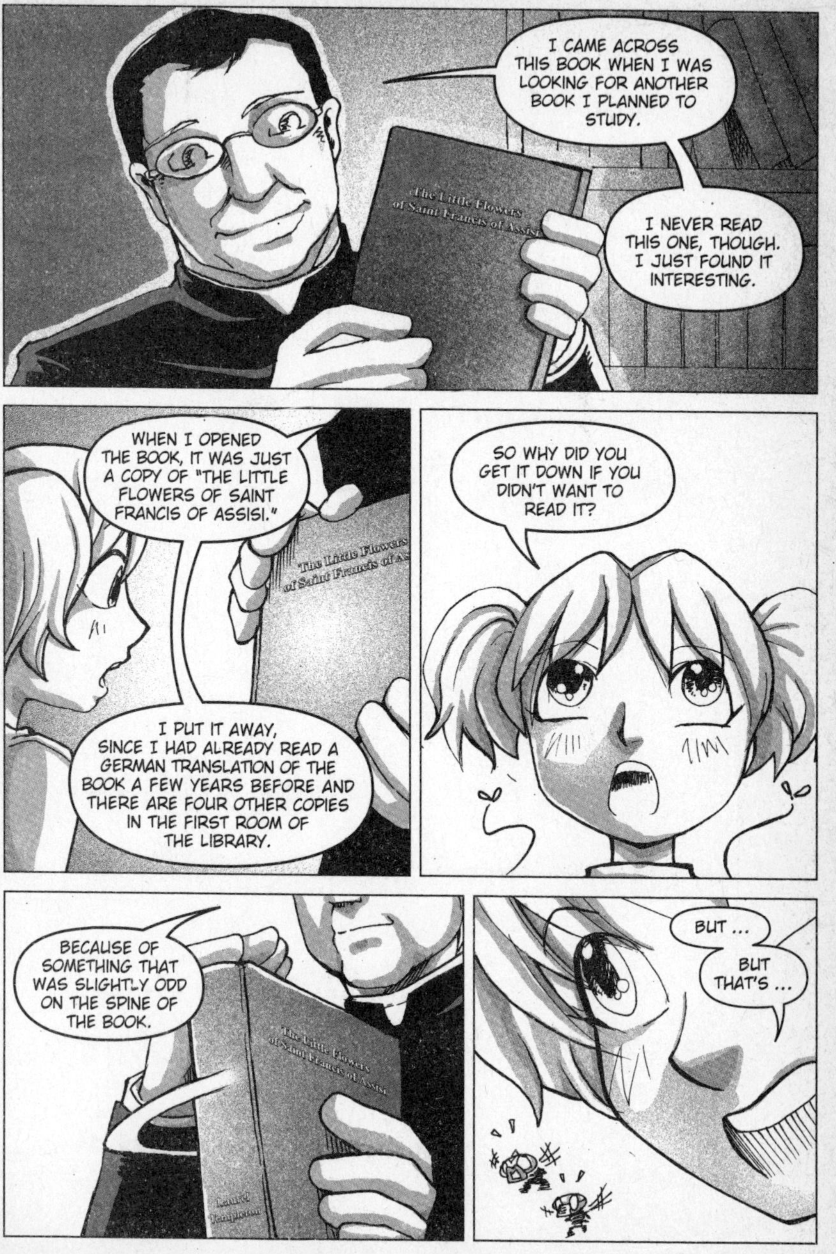
I CAME ACROSS THIS BOOK WHEN I WAS LOOKING FOR ANOTHER BOOK I PLANNED TO STUDY.
The Little Flowers of Saint Francis of Assisi
I NEVER READ THIS ONE, THOUGH. I JUST FOUND IT INTERESTING.
WHEN I OPENED THE BOOK, IT WAS JUST A COPY OF "THE LITTLE FLOWERS OF SAINT FRANCIS OF ASSISI."
I PUT IT AWAY, SINCE I HAD ALREADY READ A GERMAN TRANSLATION OF THE BOOK A FEW YEARS BEFORE AND THERE ARE FOUR OTHER COPIES IN THE FIRST ROOM OF THE LIBRARY.
SO WHY DID YOU GET IT DOWN IF YOU DIDN'T WANT TO READ IT?
BECAUSE OF SOMETHING THAT WAS SLIGHTLY ODD ON THE SPINE OF THE BOOK.
The Little Flowers of Saint Francis of Assisi
Laurel Templeton
BUT ...
BUT THAT'S ...

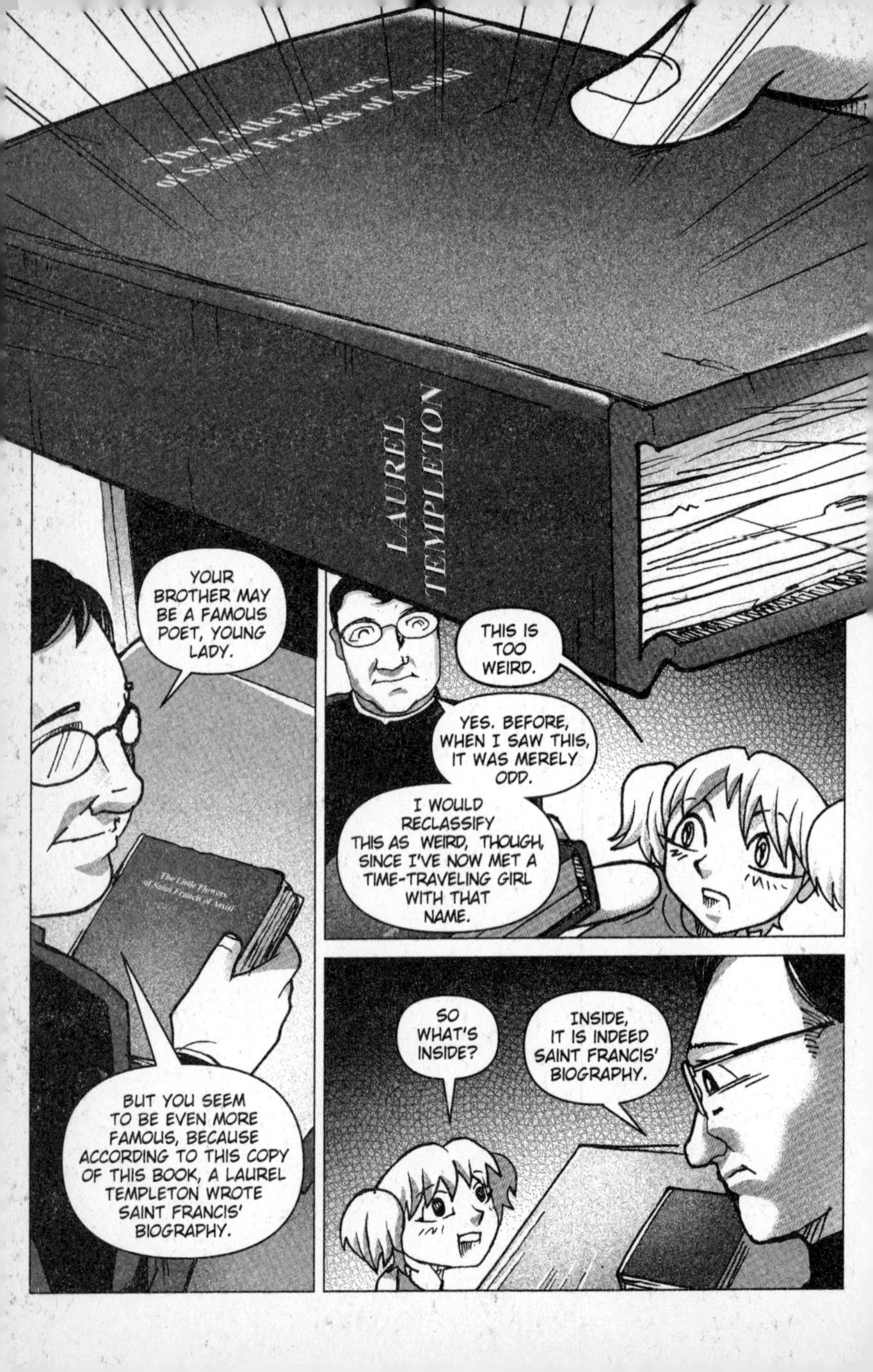
The Little Flowers of Saint Francis of Assisi
LAUREL TEMPLETON
YOUR BROTHER MAY BE A FAMOUS POET, YOUNG LADY.
The Little Flowers of Saint Francis of Assisi
BUT YOU SEEM TO BE EVEN MORE FAMOUS, BECAUSE ACCORDING TO THIS COPY OF THIS BOOK, A LAUREL TEMPLETON WROTE SAINT FRANCIS' BIOGRAPHY.
THIS IS TOO WEIRD.
YES. BEFORE, WHEN I SAW THIS, IT WAS MERELY ODD.
I WOULD RECLASSIFY THIS AS WEIRD, THOUGH, SINCE I'VE NOW MET A TIME-TRAVELING GIRL WITH THAT NAME.
SO WHAT'S INSIDE?
INSIDE, IT IS INDEED SAINT FRANCIS' BIOGRAPHY.

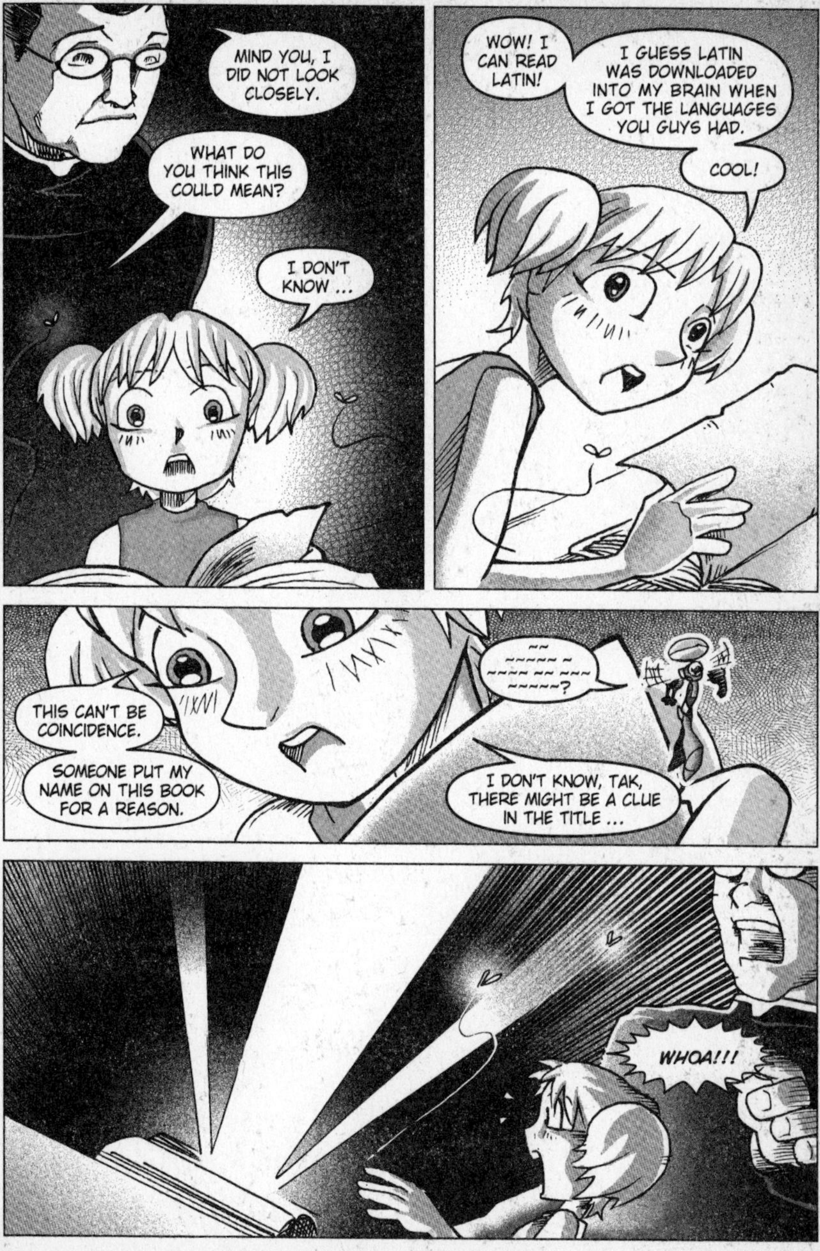
MIND YOU, I DID NOT LOOK CLOSELY.
WHAT DO YOU THINK THIS COULD MEAN?
I DON'T KNOW ...
WOW! I CAN READ LATIN!
I GUESS LATIN WAS DOWNLOADED INTO MY BRAIN WHEN I GOT THE LANGUAGES YOU GUYS HAD.
COOL!
THIS CAN'T BE COINCIDENCE.
SOMEONE PUT MY NAME ON THIS BOOK FOR A REASON.
~~ ~~~~~ ~ ~~~~ ~~ ~~~ ~~~~~?
I DON'T KNOW, TAK, THERE MIGHT BE A CLUE IN THE TITLE ...
WHOA!!!

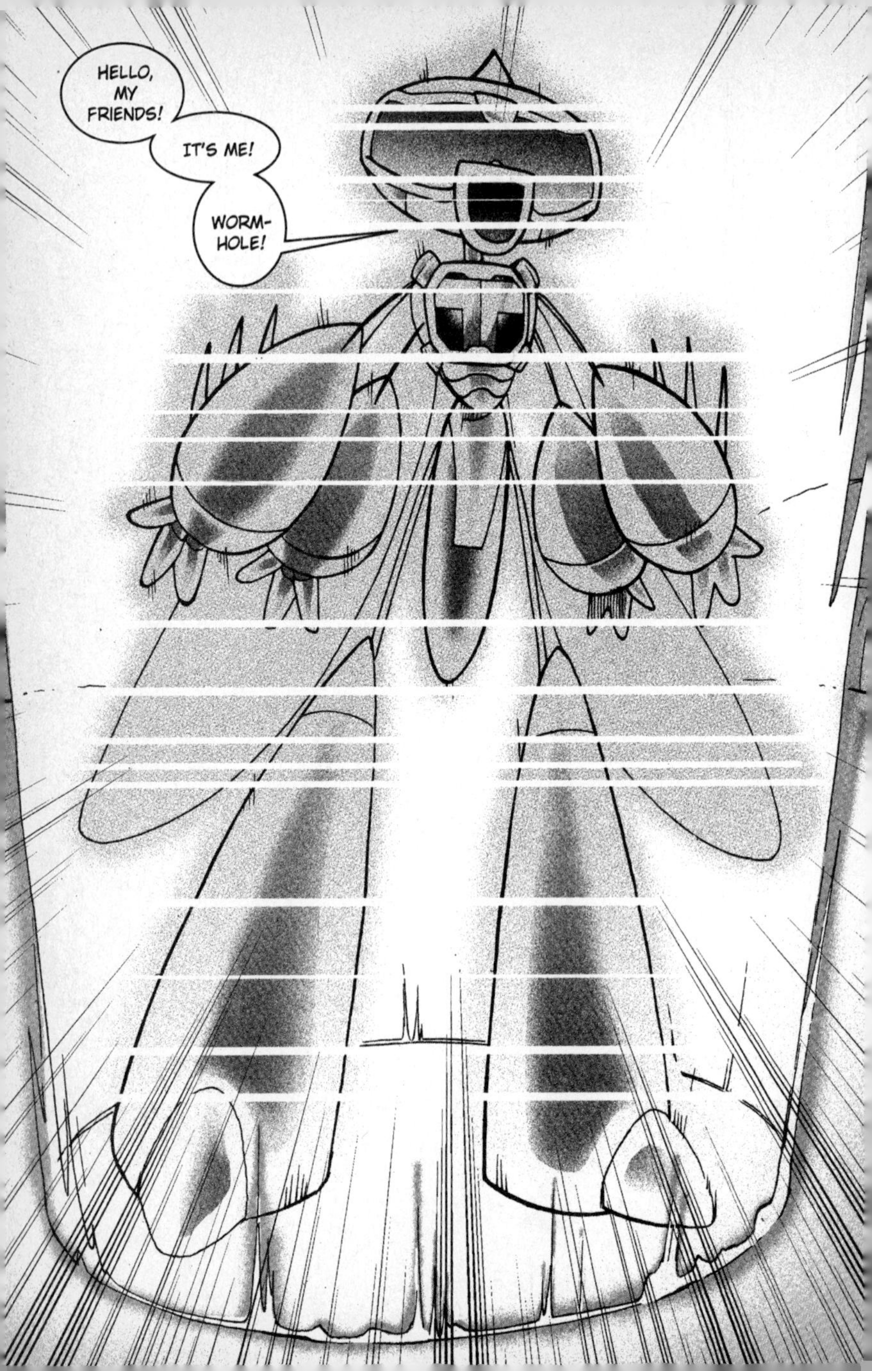
HELLO, MY FRIENDS!
IT'S ME!
WORM-HOLE!

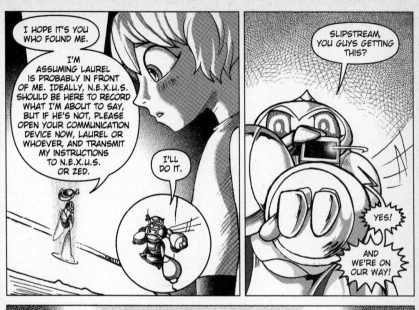

I HOPE IT'S YOU WHO FOUND ME.

I'M ASSUMING LAUREL IS PROBABLY IN FRONT OF ME. IDEALLY, N.E.X.U.S. SHOULD BE HERE TO RECORD WHAT I'M ABOUT TO SAY, BUT IF HE'S NOT, PLEASE OPEN YOUR COMMUNICATION DEVICE NOW, LAUREL OR WHOEVER, AND TRANSMIT MY INSTRUCTIONS TO N.E.X.U.S. OR ZED.

I'LL DO IT.

SLIPSTREAM, YOU GUYS GETTING THIS?

YES!

AND WE'RE ON OUR WAY!

EVEN THOUGH I'M NOT WITH YOU, YOU'VE PROBABLY FIGURED OUT THAT ZED AND I HAVE SWITCHED PLACES.

AND YOU'VE ALSO FIGURED OUT THAT ZED AND I NEED TO GET BACK.

AND YOU'VE ALSO FIGURED OUT THAT WE *CAN'T* GET BACK AND TRAVEL THROUGH TIME BECAUSE WE EACH NEED OUR FULL TEAM TO DO IT.

YES, YES, YES!

GET ON WITH IT!

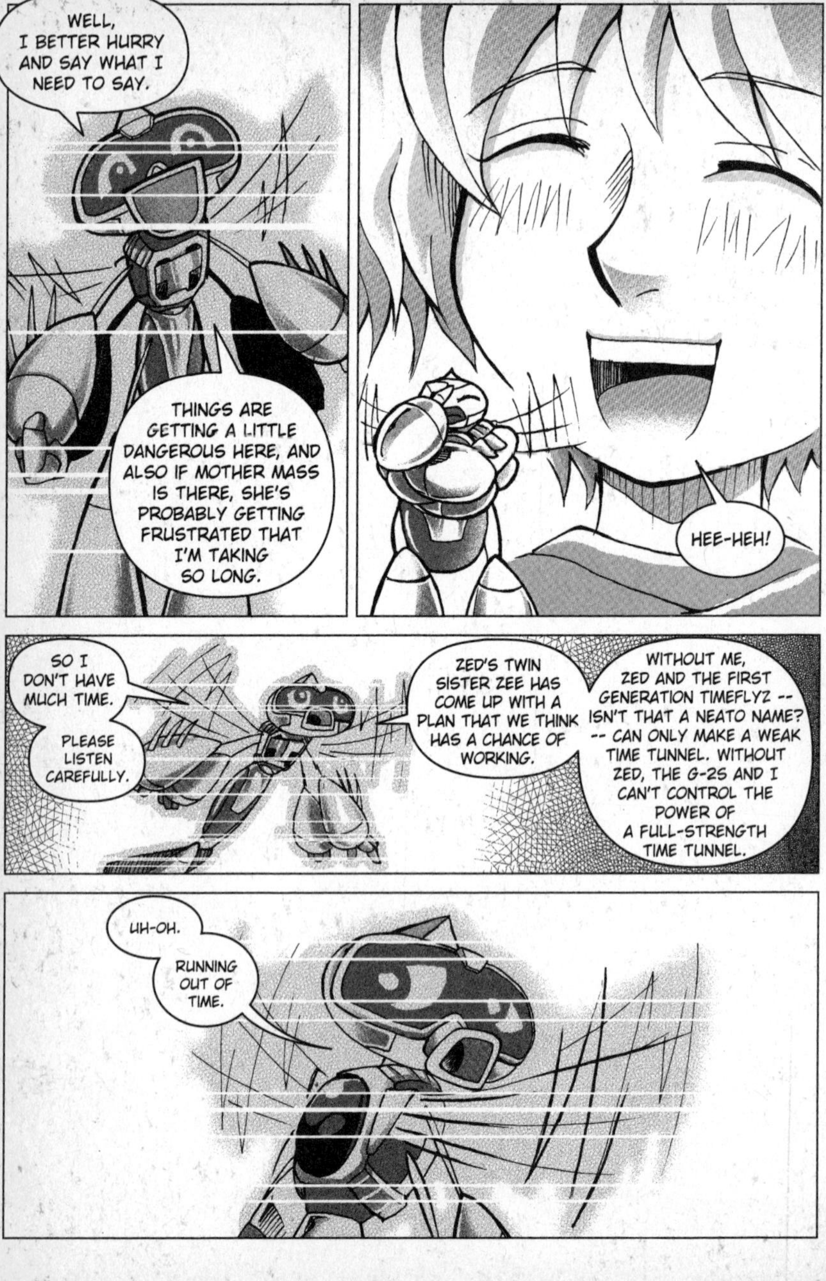
WELL, I BETTER HURRY AND SAY WHAT I NEED TO SAY.
THINGS ARE GETTING A LITTLE DANGEROUS HERE, AND ALSO IF MOTHER MASS IS THERE, SHE'S PROBABLY GETTING FRUSTRATED THAT I'M TAKING SO LONG.
HEE-HEH!
SO I DON'T HAVE MUCH TIME.
PLEASE LISTEN CAREFULLY.
ZED'S TWIN SISTER ZEE HAS COME UP WITH A PLAN THAT WE THINK HAS A CHANCE OF WORKING.
WITHOUT ME, ZED AND THE FIRST GENERATION TIMEFLYZ -- ISN'T THAT A NEATO NAME? -- CAN ONLY MAKE A WEAK TIME TUNNEL. WITHOUT ZED, THE G-2S AND I CAN'T CONTROL THE POWER OF A FULL-STRENGTH TIME TUNNEL.
UH-OH.
RUNNING OUT OF TIME.

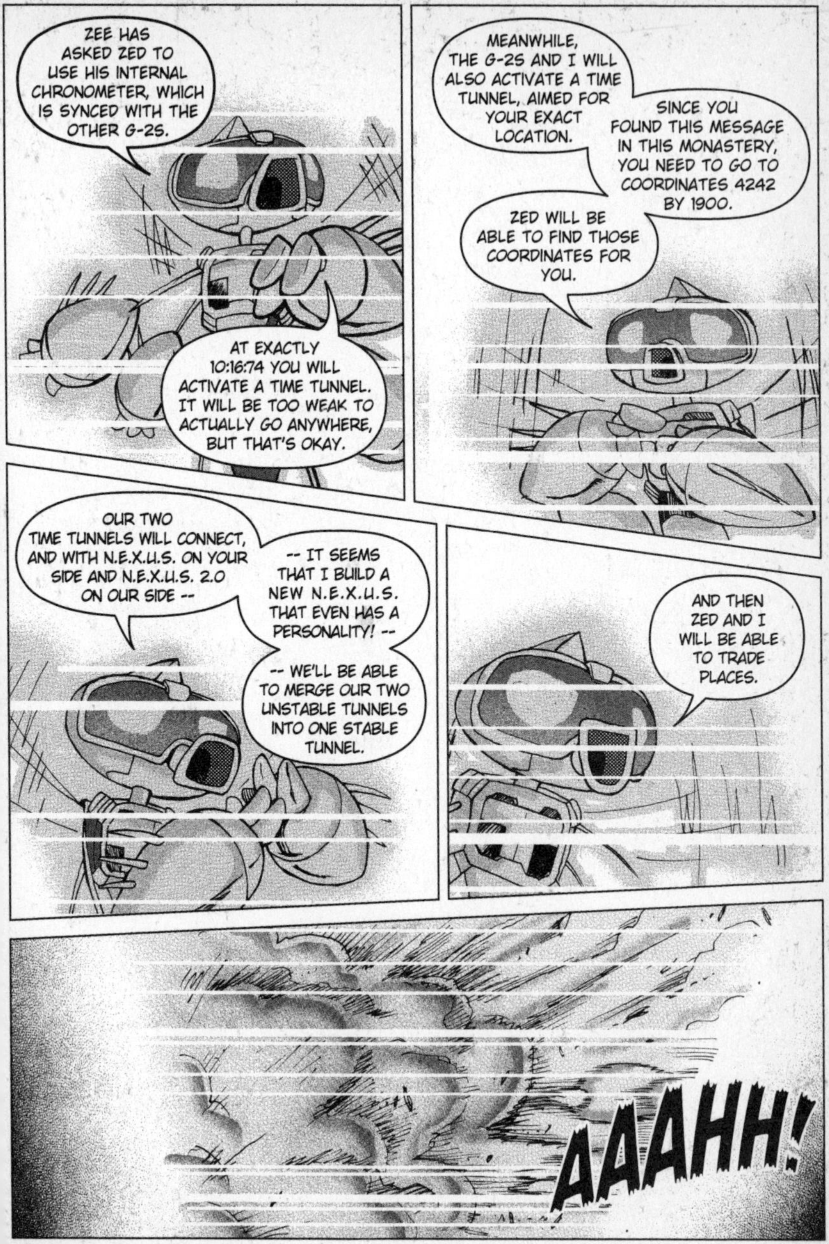
ZEE HAS ASKED ZED TO USE HIS INTERNAL CHRONOMETER, WHICH IS SYNCED WITH THE OTHER G-2S.
AT EXACTLY 10:16:74 YOU WILL ACTIVATE A TIME TUNNEL. IT WILL BE TOO WEAK TO ACTUALLY GO ANYWHERE, BUT THAT'S OKAY.
MEANWHILE, THE G-2S AND I WILL ALSO ACTIVATE A TIME TUNNEL, AIMED FOR YOUR EXACT LOCATION.
SINCE YOU FOUND THIS MESSAGE IN THIS MONASTERY, YOU NEED TO GO TO COORDINATES 4242 BY 1900.
ZED WILL BE ABLE TO FIND THOSE COORDINATES FOR YOU.
OUR TWO TIME TUNNELS WILL CONNECT, AND WITH N.E.X.U.S. ON YOUR SIDE AND N.E.X.U.S. 2.0 ON OUR SIDE --
-- IT SEEMS THAT I BUILD A NEW N.E.X.U.S. THAT EVEN HAS A PERSONALITY! --
-- WE'LL BE ABLE TO MERGE OUR TWO UNSTABLE TUNNELS INTO ONE STABLE TUNNEL.
AND THEN ZED AND I WILL BE ABLE TO TRADE PLACES.
AAAHH!

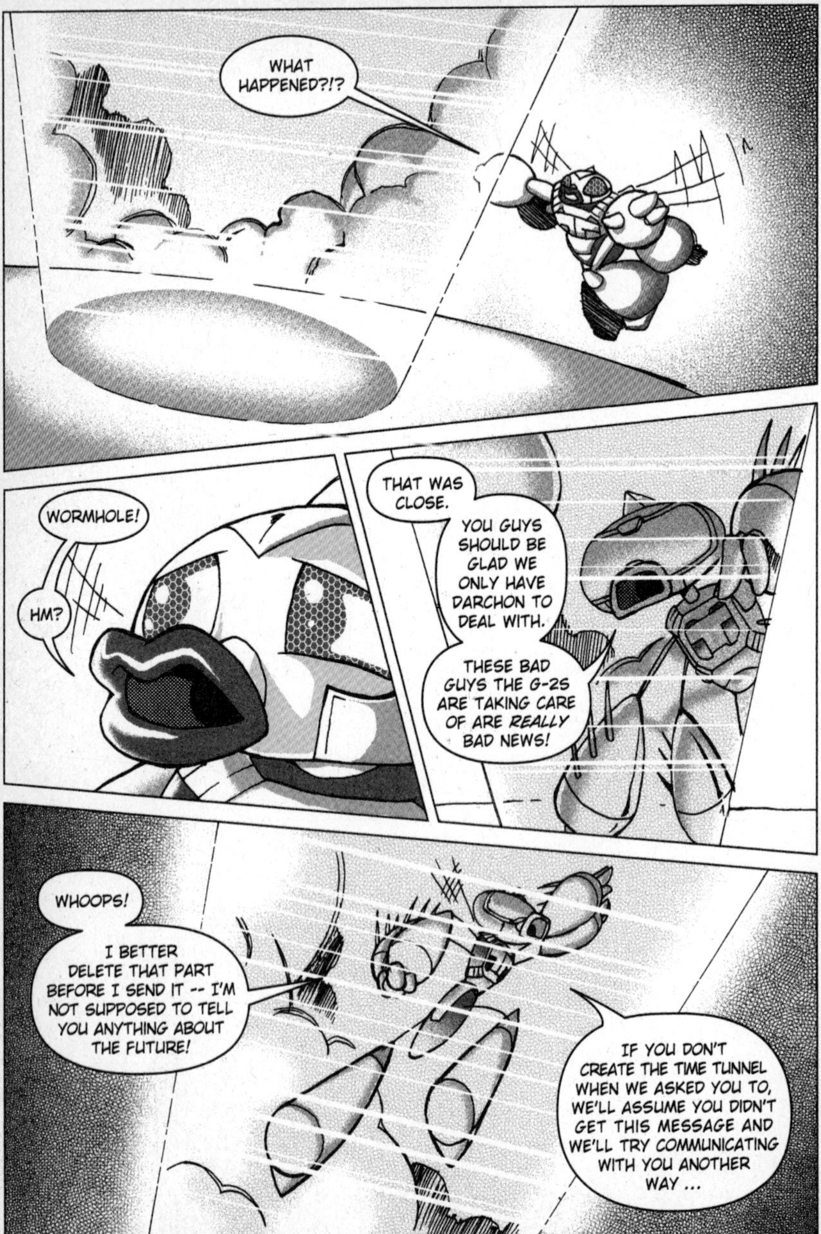
WHAT HAPPENED?!?
WORMHOLE!
HM?
THAT WAS CLOSE.
YOU GUYS SHOULD BE GLAD WE ONLY HAVE DARCHON TO DEAL WITH.
THESE BAD GUYS THE G-2S ARE TAKING CARE OF ARE *REALLY* BAD NEWS!
WHOOPS!
I BETTER DELETE THAT PART BEFORE I SEND IT -- I'M NOT SUPPOSED TO TELL YOU ANYTHING ABOUT THE FUTURE!
IF YOU DON'T CREATE THE TIME TUNNEL WHEN WE ASKED YOU TO, WE'LL ASSUME YOU DIDN'T GET THIS MESSAGE AND WE'LL TRY COMMUNICATING WITH YOU ANOTHER WAY ...

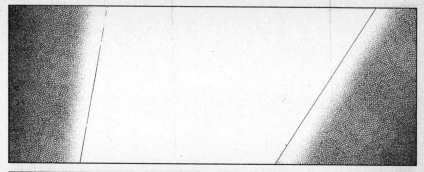

WOW.

I HOPE ...

I HOPE ...

UH ...

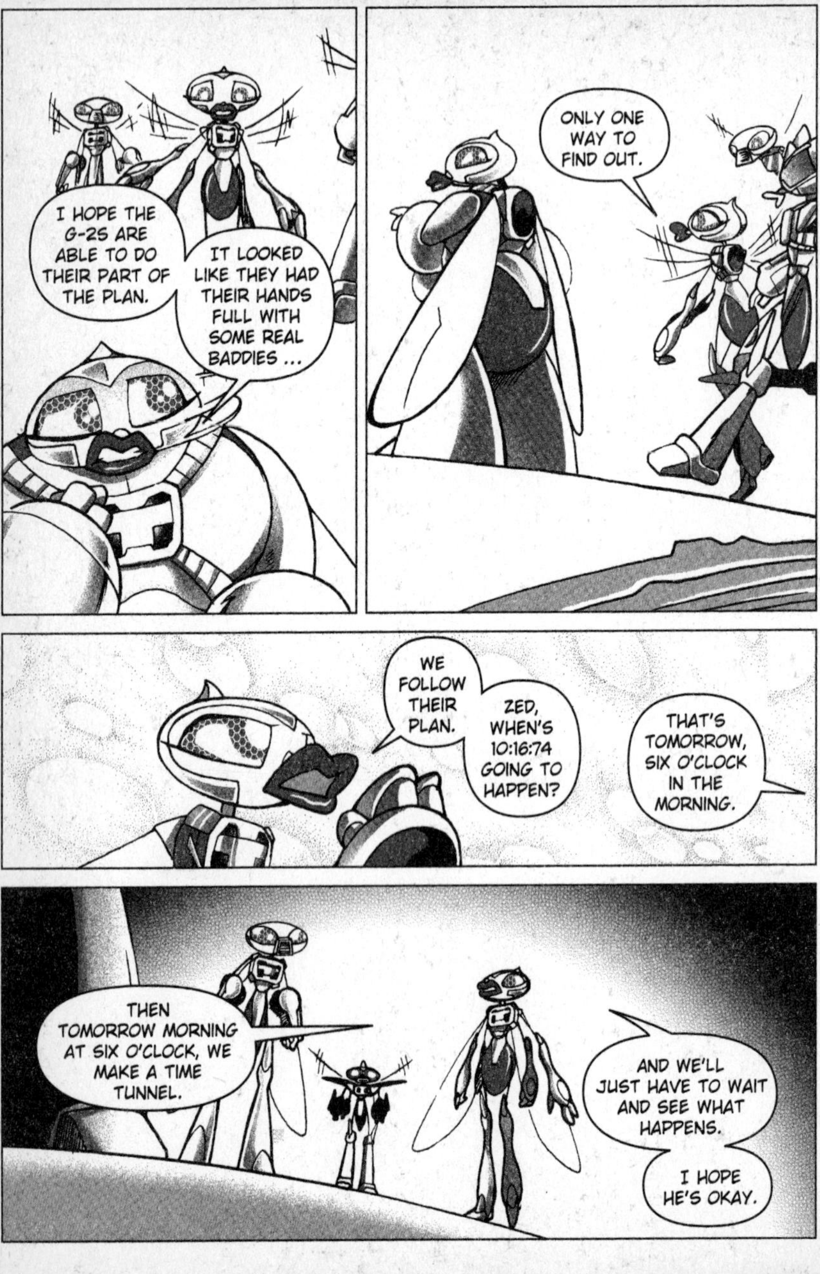
I HOPE THE G-2S ARE ABLE TO DO THEIR PART OF THE PLAN.
IT LOOKED LIKE THEY HAD THEIR HANDS FULL WITH SOME REAL BADDIES ...
ONLY ONE WAY TO FIND OUT.
WE FOLLOW THEIR PLAN.
ZED, WHEN'S 10:16:74 GOING TO HAPPEN?
THAT'S TOMORROW, SIX O'CLOCK IN THE MORNING.
THEN TOMORROW MORNING AT SIX O'CLOCK, WE MAKE A TIME TUNNEL.
AND WE'LL JUST HAVE TO WAIT AND SEE WHAT HAPPENS.
I HOPE HE'S OKAY.

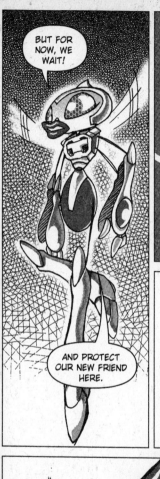

BUT FOR NOW, WE WAIT!

AND PROTECT OUR NEW FRIEND HERE.

ZED, LET'S PUT THE INFORMATION INTO OUR N.E.X.U.S.'S COMPUTER SO WE CAN BE AS PRECISE AS POSSIBLE ABOUT WHEN AND WHERE WE NEED TO CREATE OUR TIME TUNNEL.

RIGHT!

WOW! MR. MENDEL!

WE CAME HERE TO SAVE YOU, BUT IT LOOKS LIKE YOU SAVED US!

YES. WOW IS RIGHT.

YOU BETTER BE OKAY, LARVA BRAIN.

IF YOU AREN'T CAREFUL, I'M GONNA ... I'M GONNA ...

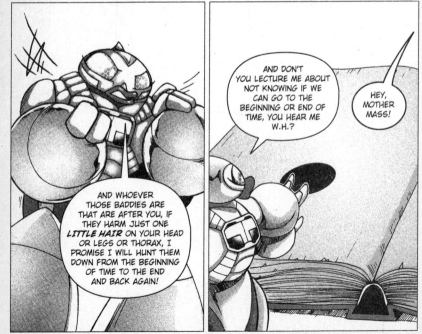

AND WHOEVER THOSE BADDIES ARE THAT ARE AFTER YOU, IF THEY HARM JUST ONE *LITTLE HAIR* ON YOUR HEAD OR LEGS OR THORAX, I PROMISE I WILL HUNT THEM DOWN FROM THE BEGINNING OF TIME TO THE END AND BACK AGAIN!

AND DON'T YOU LECTURE ME ABOUT NOT KNOWING IF WE CAN GO TO THE BEGINNING OR END OF TIME, YOU HEAR ME W.H.?

HEY, MOTHER MASS!

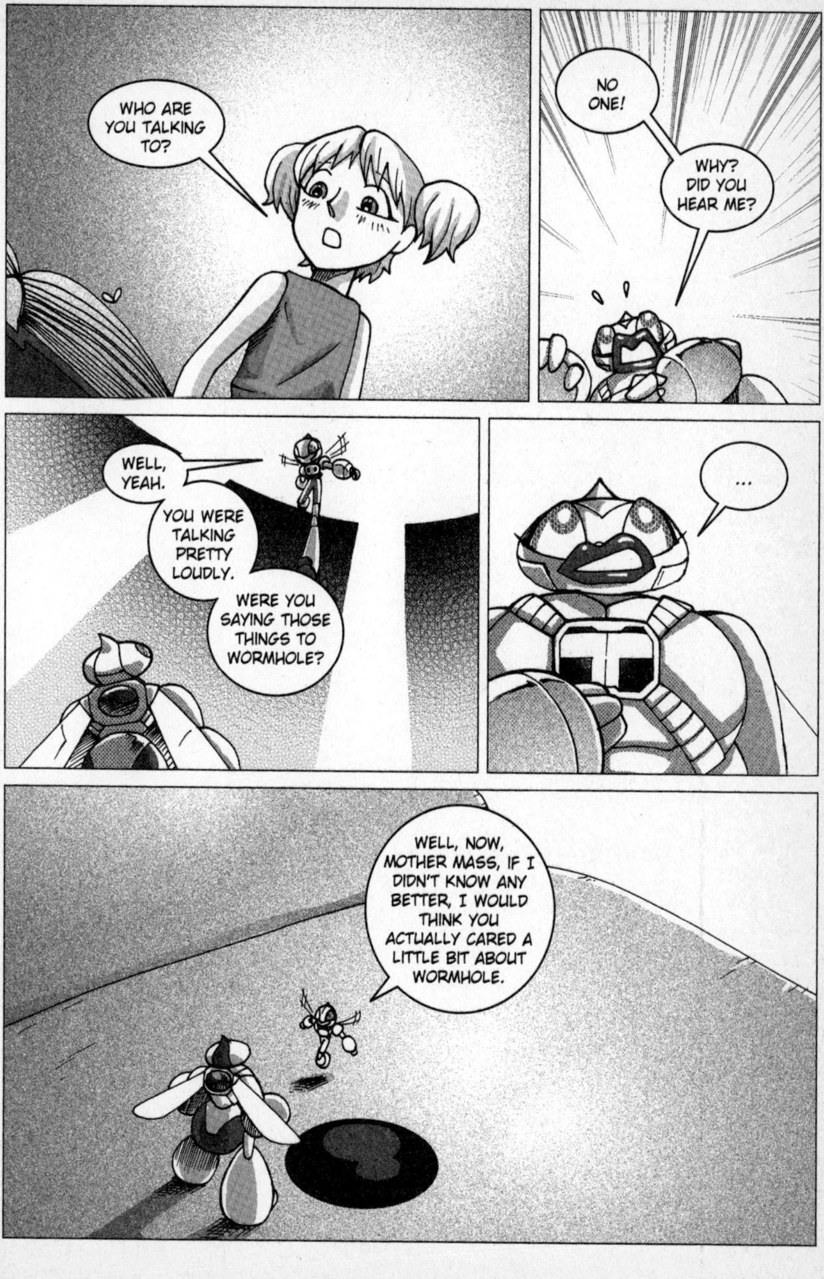
WHO ARE YOU TALKING TO?
NO ONE!
WHY? DID YOU HEAR ME?
WELL, YEAH.
YOU WERE TALKING PRETTY LOUDLY.
WERE YOU SAYING THOSE THINGS TO WORMHOLE?
...
WELL, NOW, MOTHER MASS, IF I DIDN'T KNOW ANY BETTER, I WOULD THINK YOU ACTUALLY CARED A LITTLE BIT ABOUT WORMHOLE.

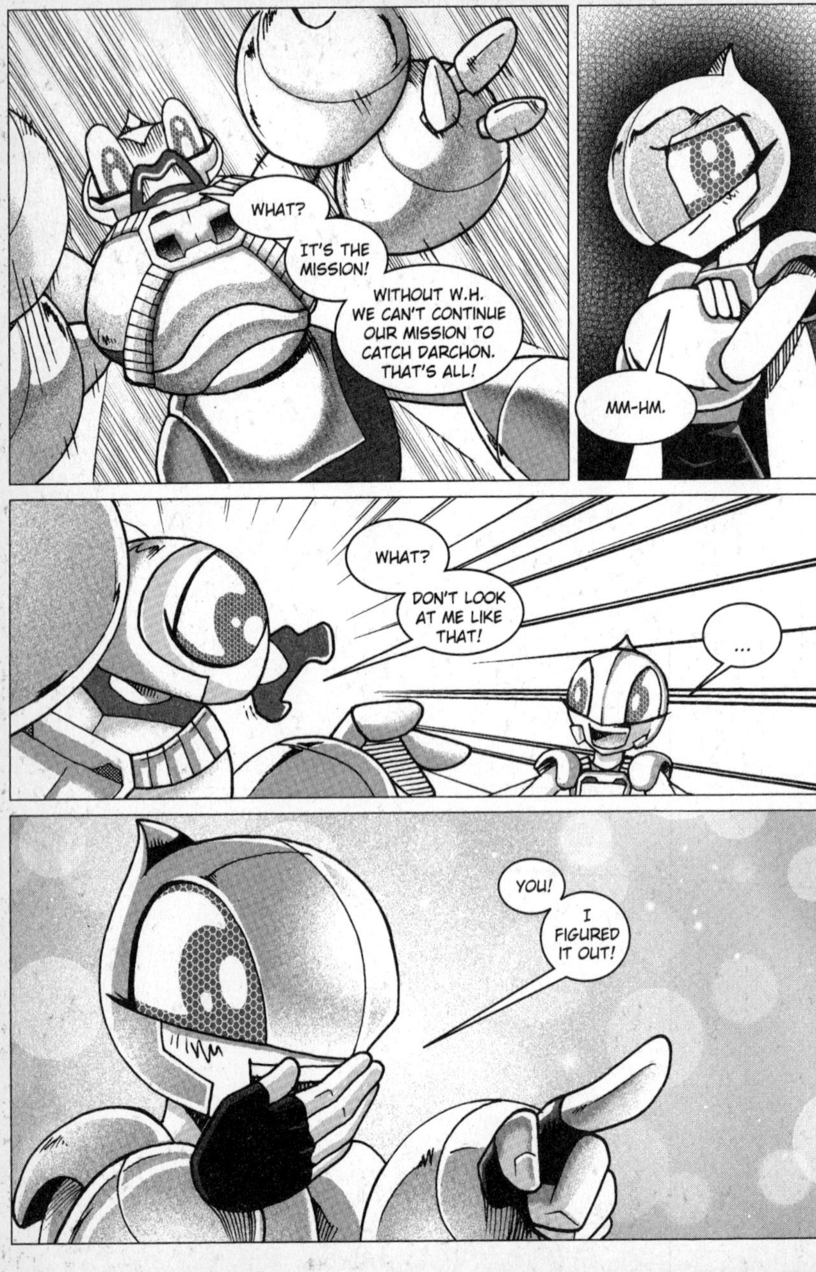
WHAT?
IT'S THE MISSION!
WITHOUT W.H. WE CAN'T CONTINUE OUR MISSION TO CATCH DARCHON. THAT'S ALL!
MM-HM.
WHAT?
DON'T LOOK AT ME LIKE THAT!
...
YOU!
I FIGURED IT OUT!

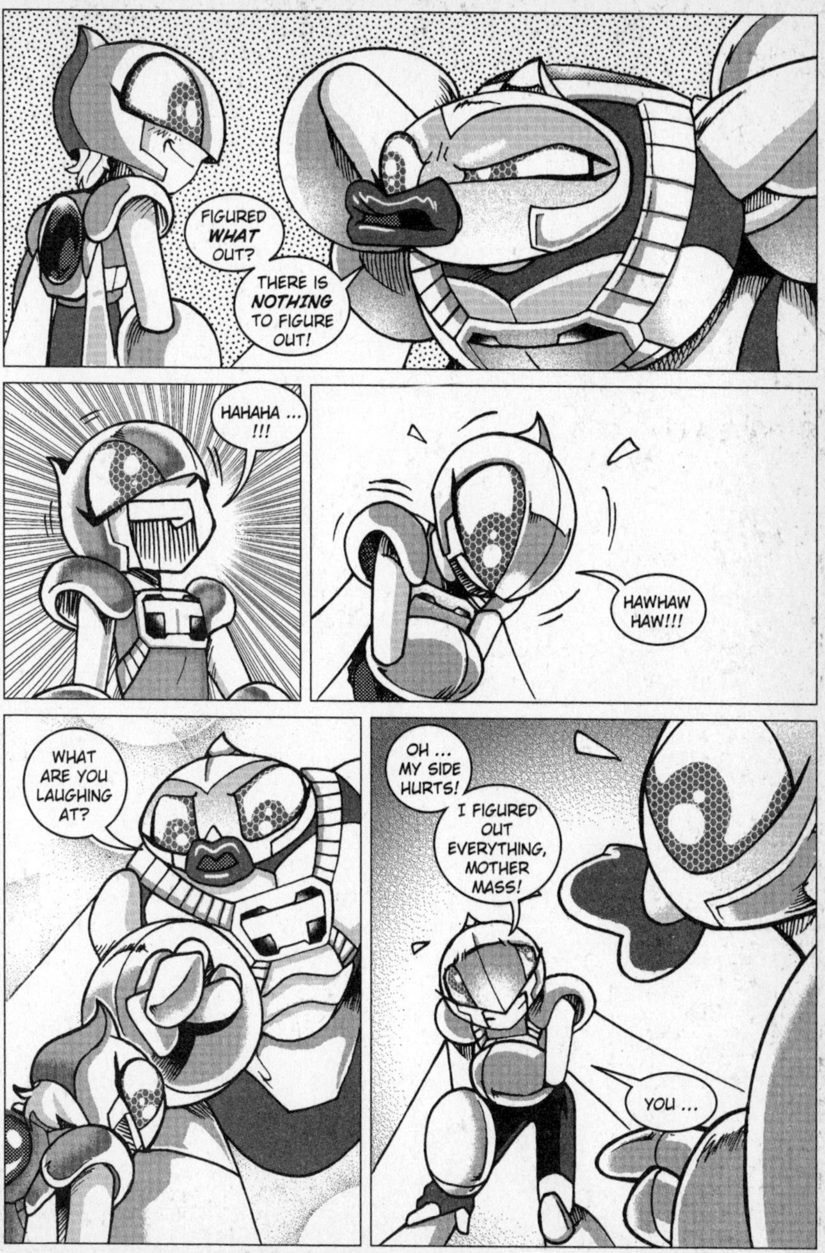
FIGURED **WHAT** OUT?
THERE IS **NOTHING** TO FIGURE OUT!
HAHAHA ... !!!
HAWHAW HAW!!!
WHAT ARE YOU LAUGHING AT?
OH ... MY SIDE HURTS!
I FIGURED OUT EVERYTHING, MOTHER MASS!
YOU ...

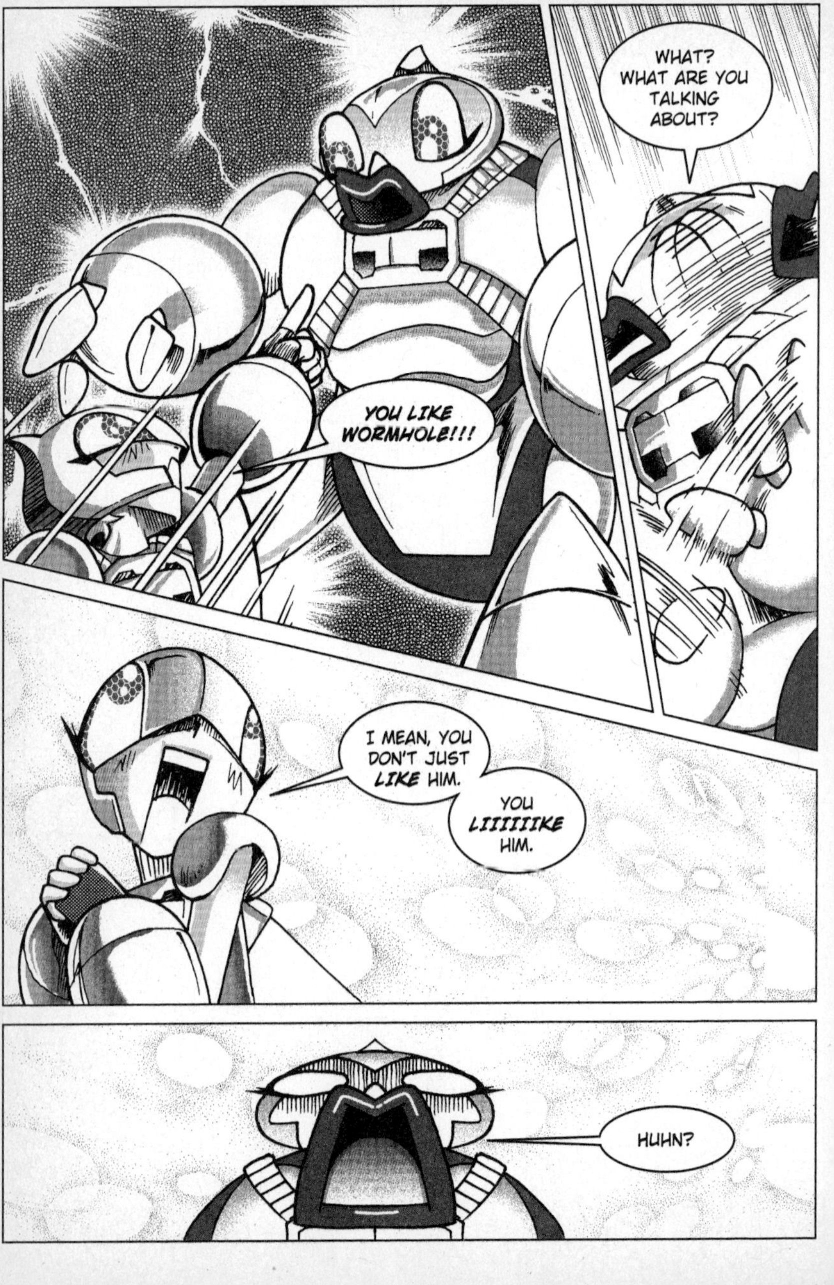
YOU LIKE WORMHOLE!!!
WHAT? WHAT ARE YOU TALKING ABOUT?
I MEAN, YOU DON'T JUST *LIKE* HIM.
YOU *LIIIIIIKE* HIM.
HUHN?

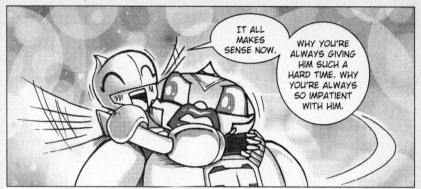

IT ALL MAKES SENSE NOW.

WHY YOU'RE ALWAYS GIVING HIM SUCH A HARD TIME. WHY YOU'RE ALWAYS SO IMPATIENT WITH HIM.

THAT DOESN'T MAKE ANY SENSE.

WHY WOULD I BE MEAN IF I LIKED HIM LIKE THAT?

OH, IT'S JUST YOUR WAY OF EXPRESSING YOUR FEELINGS.

SINCE YOU DON'T KNOW HOW TO DEAL WITH IT, IT JUST COMES OUT MEAN.

OH, I'M SO HAPPY!

ALL THIS TIME, I THOUGHT YOU WERE JUST A BIG BULLY.

BUT IT TURNS OUT YOU'RE JUST IN LOVE.

IN LOVE?

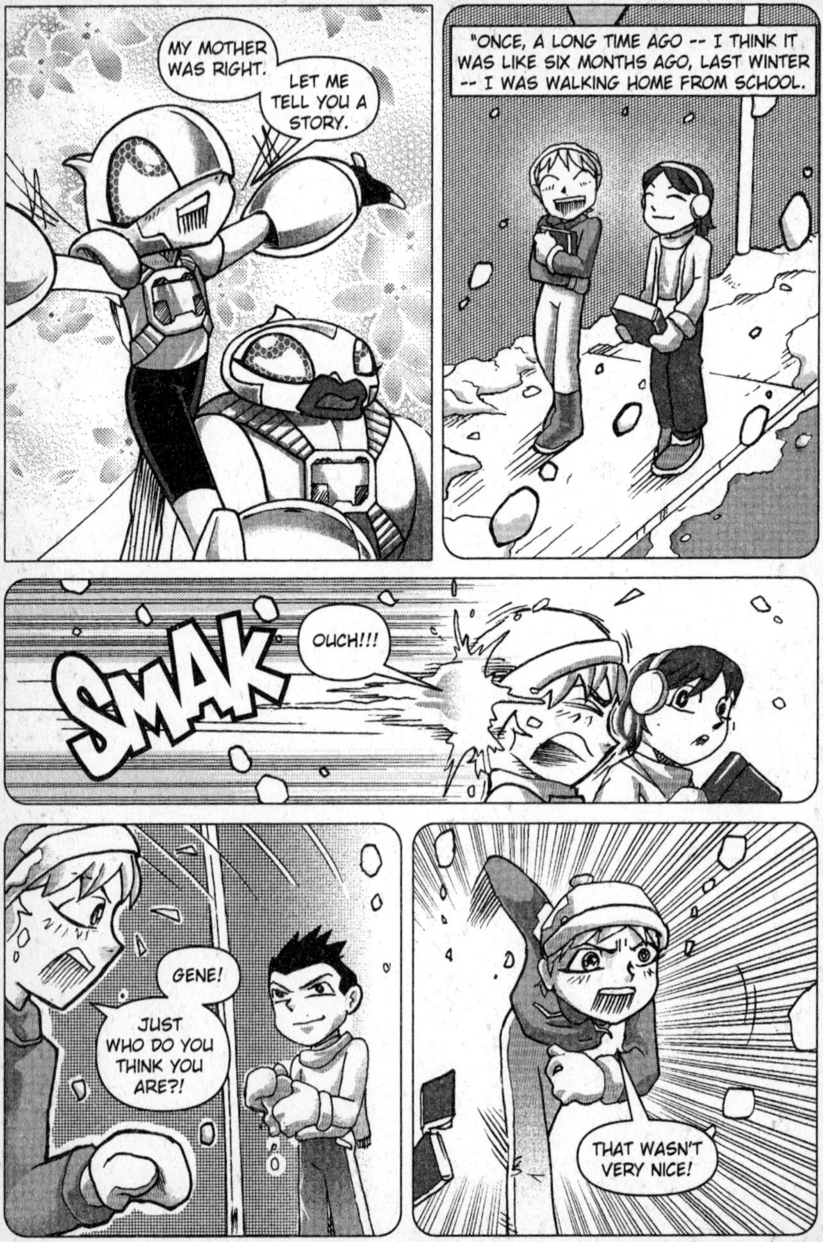
MY MOTHER WAS RIGHT.
LET ME TELL YOU A STORY.
"ONCE, A LONG TIME AGO -- I THINK IT WAS LIKE SIX MONTHS AGO, LAST WINTER -- I WAS WALKING HOME FROM SCHOOL.
SMAK
OUCH!!!
GENE!
JUST WHO DO YOU THINK YOU ARE?!
THAT WASN'T VERY NICE!

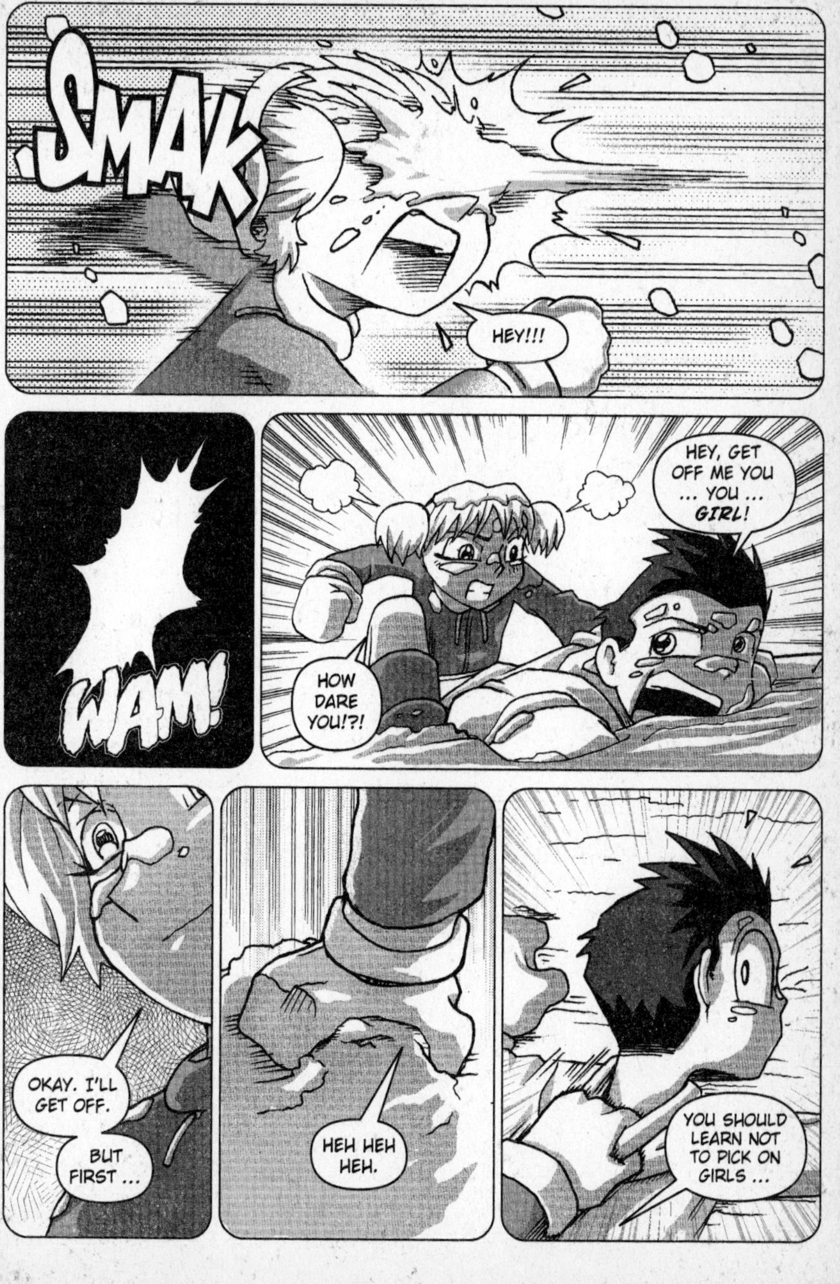
SMAK
HEY!!!
WAM!
HEY, GET OFF ME YOU ... YOU ... GIRL!
HOW DARE YOU!?!
OKAY. I'LL GET OFF.
BUT FIRST ...
HEH HEH HEH.
YOU SHOULD LEARN NOT TO PICK ON GIRLS ...

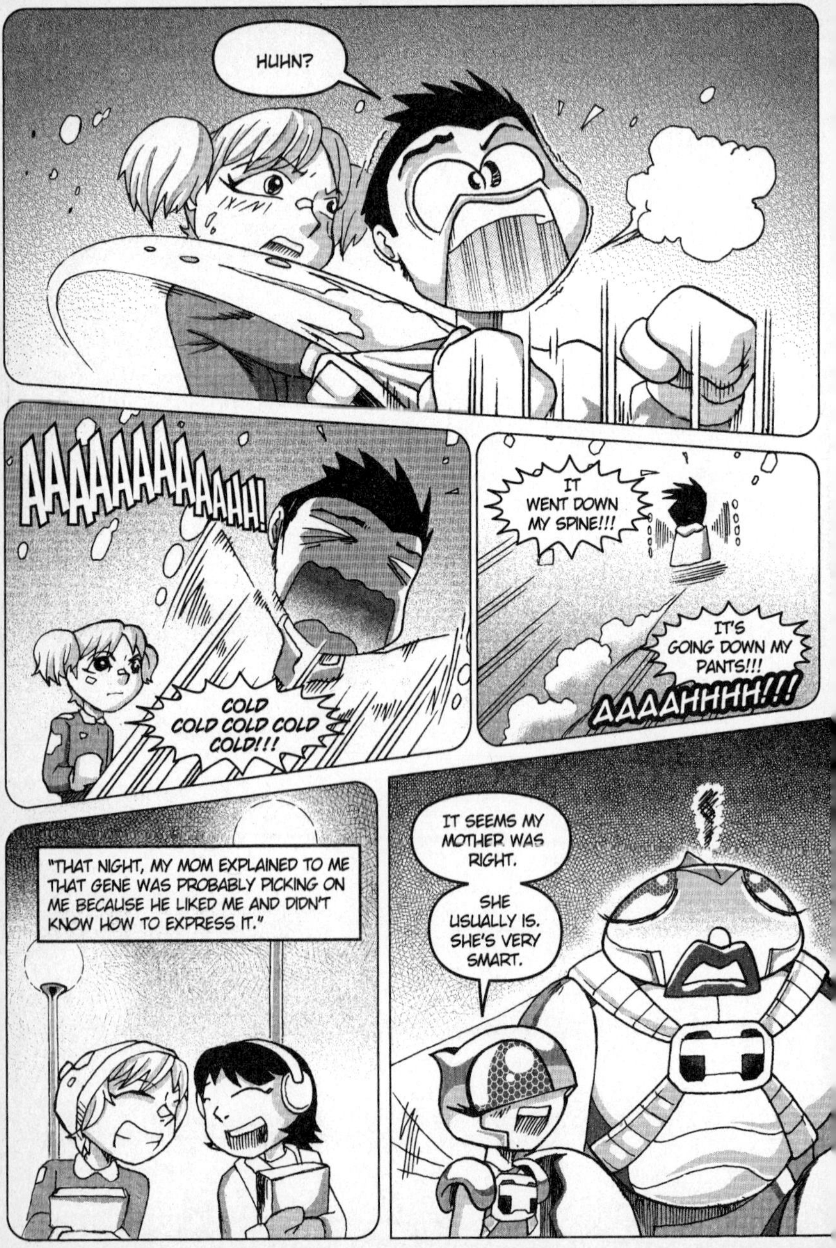
HUHN?
AAAAAAAAAAAAHH!
COLD COLD COLD COLD COLD!!!
IT WENT DOWN MY SPINE!!!
IT'S GOING DOWN MY PANTS!!!
AAAAHHHH!!!
"THAT NIGHT, MY MOM EXPLAINED TO ME THAT GENE WAS PROBABLY PICKING ON ME BECAUSE HE LIKED ME AND DIDN'T KNOW HOW TO EXPRESS IT."
IT SEEMS MY MOTHER WAS RIGHT.
SHE USUALLY IS. SHE'S VERY SMART.

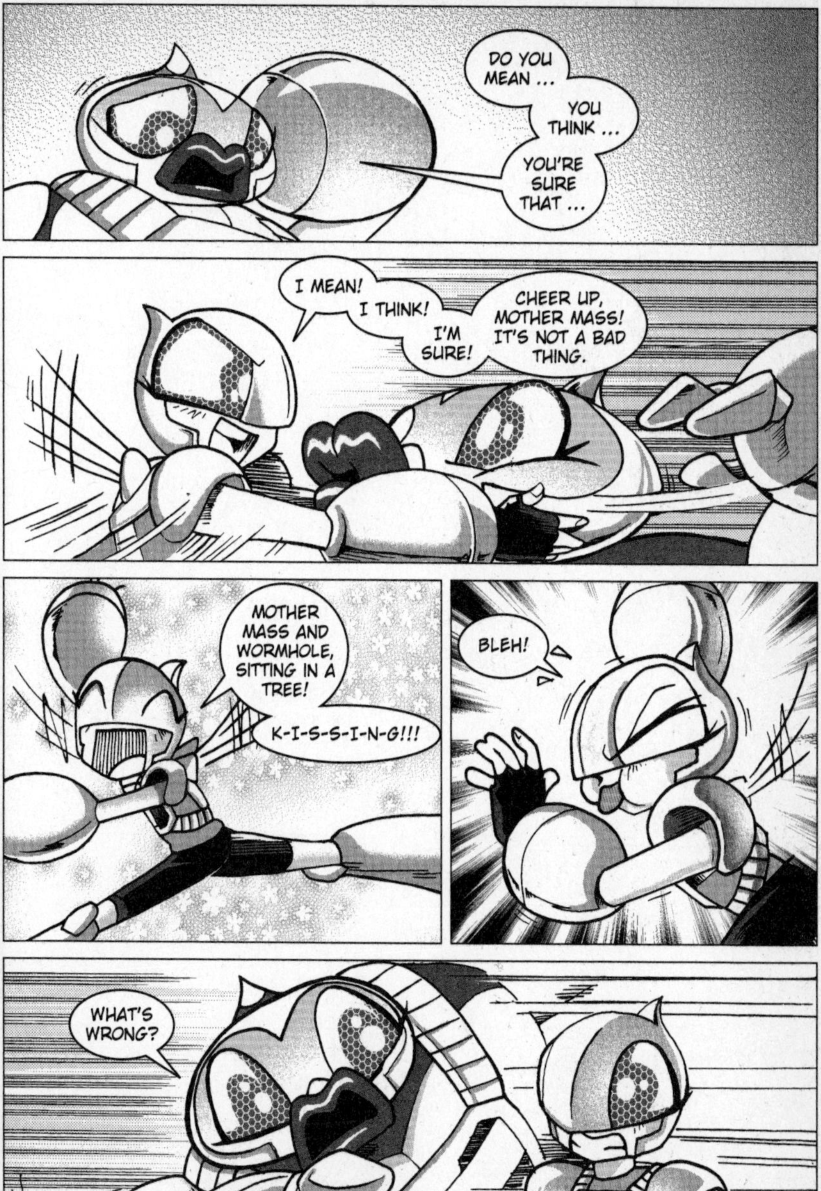
DO YOU MEAN ...
YOU THINK ...
YOU'RE SURE THAT ...
I MEAN!
I THINK!
I'M SURE!
CHEER UP, MOTHER MASS! IT'S NOT A BAD THING.
MOTHER MASS AND WORMHOLE, SITTING IN A TREE!
K-I-S-S-I-N-G!!!
BLEH!
WHAT'S WRONG?

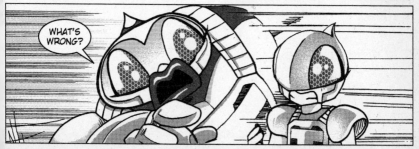

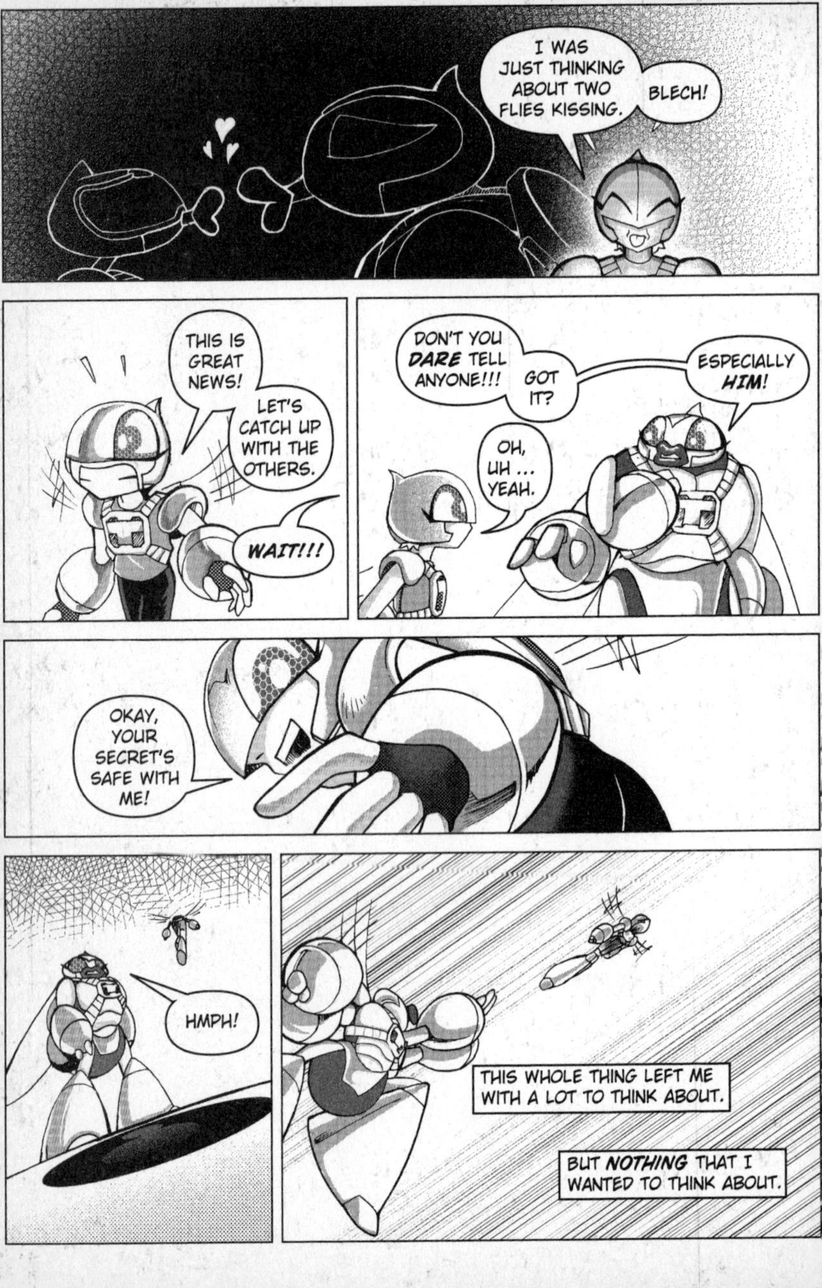
I WAS JUST THINKING ABOUT TWO FLIES KISSING.
BLECH!
THIS IS GREAT NEWS!
LET'S CATCH UP WITH THE OTHERS.
WAIT!!!
DON'T YOU DARE TELL ANYONE!!!
GOT IT?
ESPECIALLY HIM!
OH, UH ... YEAH.
OKAY, YOUR SECRET'S SAFE WITH ME!
HMPH!
THIS WHOLE THING LEFT ME WITH A LOT TO THINK ABOUT.
BUT NOTHING THAT I WANTED TO THINK ABOUT.

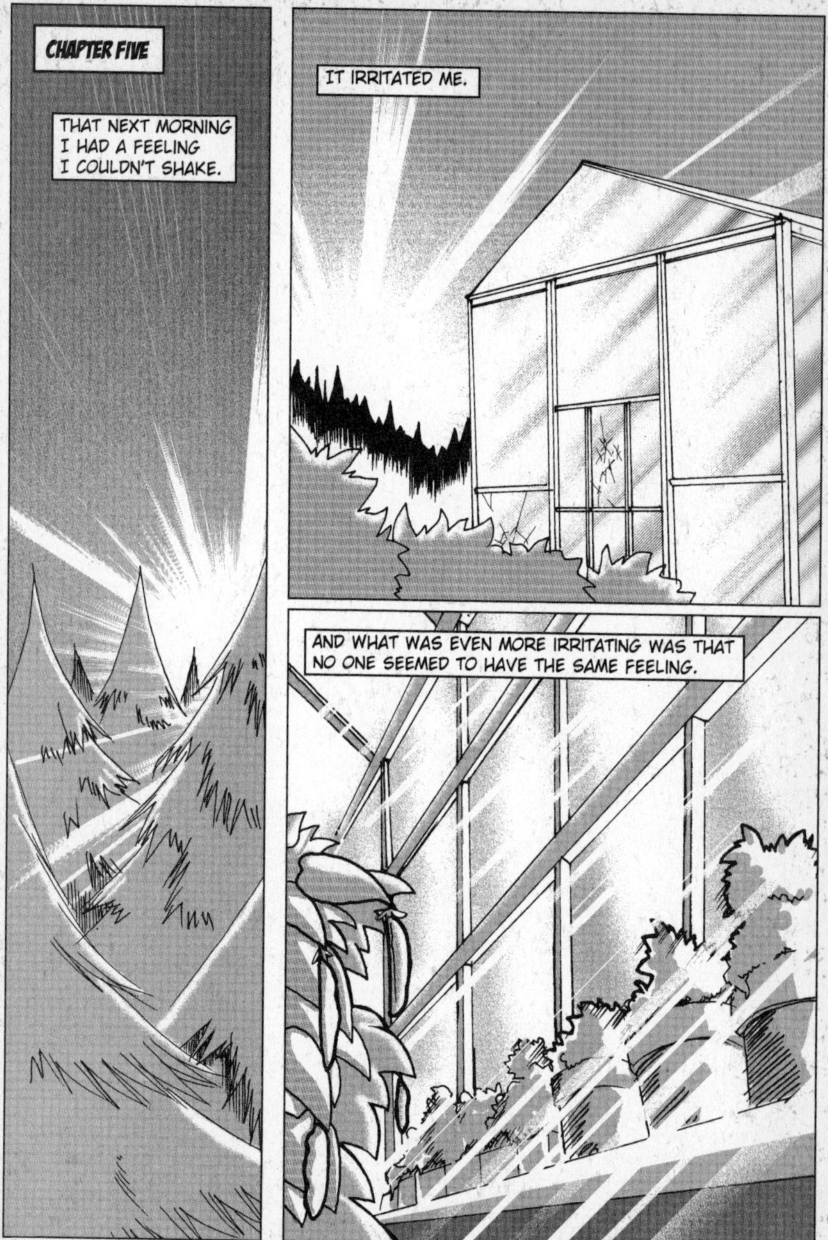
CHAPTER FIVE
THAT NEXT MORNING I HAD A FEELING I COULDN'T SHAKE.
IT IRRITATED ME.
AND WHAT WAS EVEN MORE IRRITATING WAS THAT NO ONE SEEMED TO HAVE THE SAME FEELING.

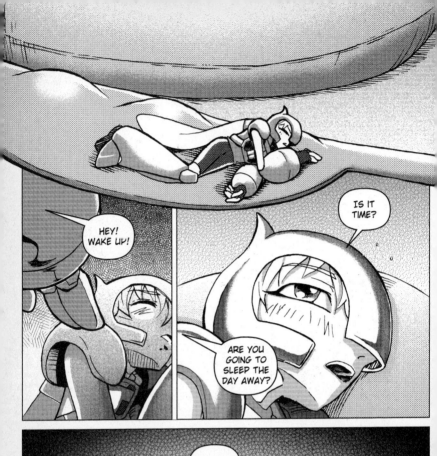

HEY! WAKE UP!

IS IT TIME?

ARE YOU GOING TO SLEEP THE DAY AWAY?

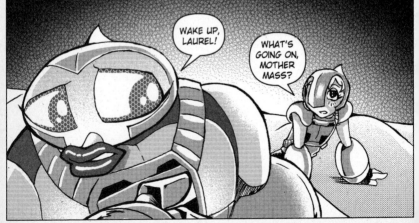

WAKE UP, LAUREL!

WHAT'S GOING ON, MOTHER MASS?

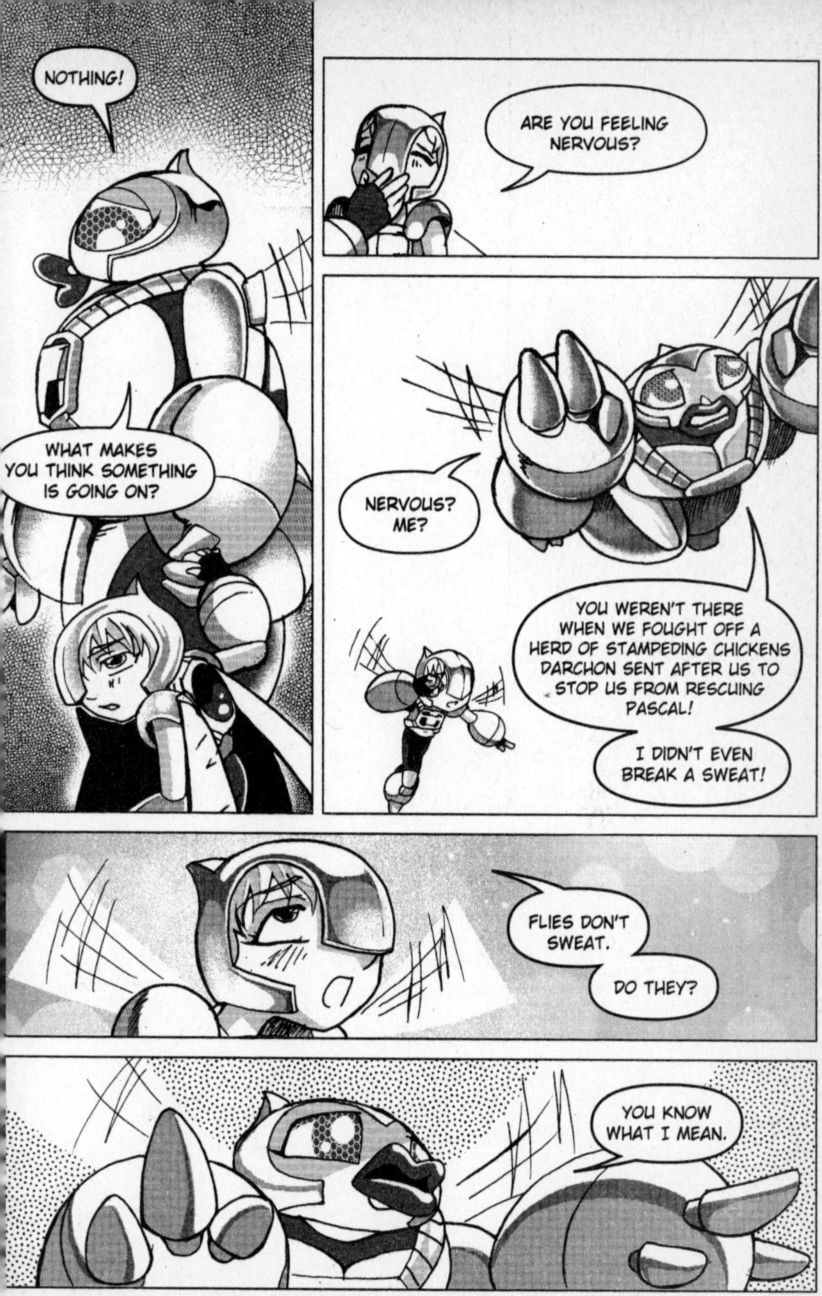
NOTHING!
WHAT MAKES YOU THINK SOMETHING IS GOING ON?
ARE YOU FEELING NERVOUS?
NERVOUS? ME?
YOU WEREN'T THERE WHEN WE FOUGHT OFF A HERD OF STAMPEDING CHICKENS DARCHON SENT AFTER US TO STOP US FROM RESCUING PASCAL!
I DIDN'T EVEN BREAK A SWEAT!
FLIES DON'T SWEAT.
DO THEY?
YOU KNOW WHAT I MEAN.

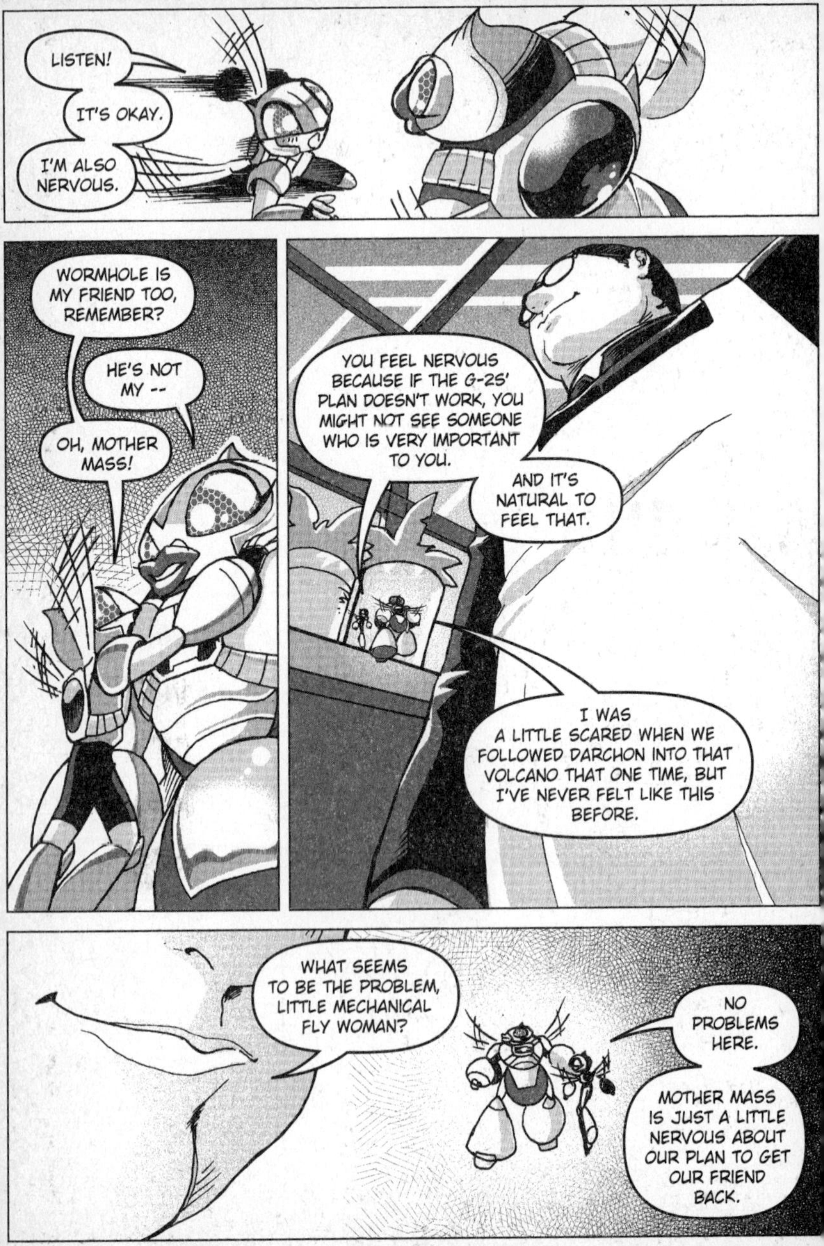
LISTEN!
IT'S OKAY.
I'M ALSO NERVOUS.
WORMHOLE IS MY FRIEND TOO, REMEMBER?
HE'S NOT MY --
OH, MOTHER MASS!
YOU FEEL NERVOUS BECAUSE IF THE G-25' PLAN DOESN'T WORK, YOU MIGHT NOT SEE SOMEONE WHO IS VERY IMPORTANT TO YOU.
AND IT'S NATURAL TO FEEL THAT.
I WAS A LITTLE SCARED WHEN WE FOLLOWED DARCHON INTO THAT VOLCANO THAT ONE TIME, BUT I'VE NEVER FELT LIKE THIS BEFORE.
WHAT SEEMS TO BE THE PROBLEM, LITTLE MECHANICAL FLY WOMAN?
NO PROBLEMS HERE.
MOTHER MASS IS JUST A LITTLE NERVOUS ABOUT OUR PLAN TO GET OUR FRIEND BACK.

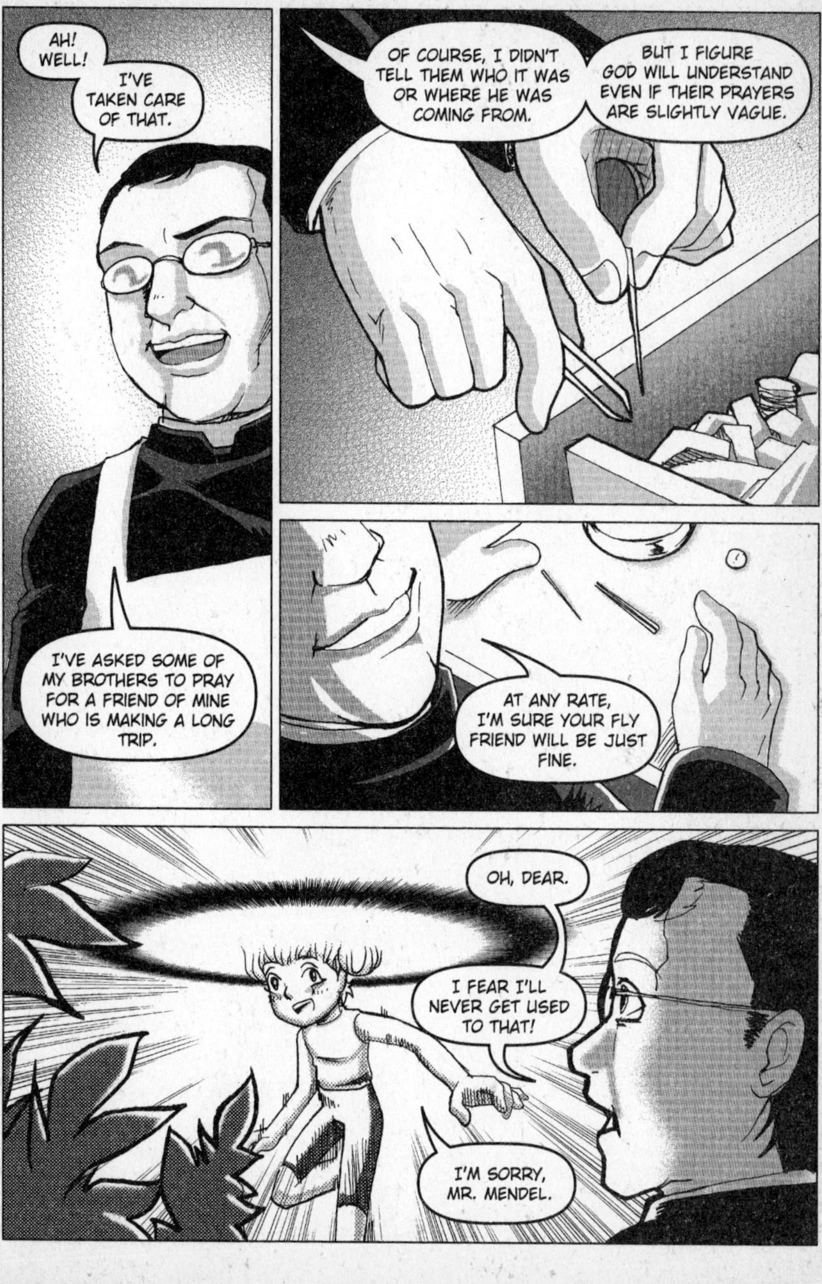
AH! WELL!
I'VE TAKEN CARE OF THAT.
I'VE ASKED SOME OF MY BROTHERS TO PRAY FOR A FRIEND OF MINE WHO IS MAKING A LONG TRIP.
OF COURSE, I DIDN'T TELL THEM WHO IT WAS OR WHERE HE WAS COMING FROM.
BUT I FIGURE GOD WILL UNDERSTAND EVEN IF THEIR PRAYERS ARE SLIGHTLY VAGUE.
AT ANY RATE, I'M SURE YOUR FLY FRIEND WILL BE JUST FINE.
OH, DEAR.
I FEAR I'LL NEVER GET USED TO THAT!
I'M SORRY, MR. MENDEL.

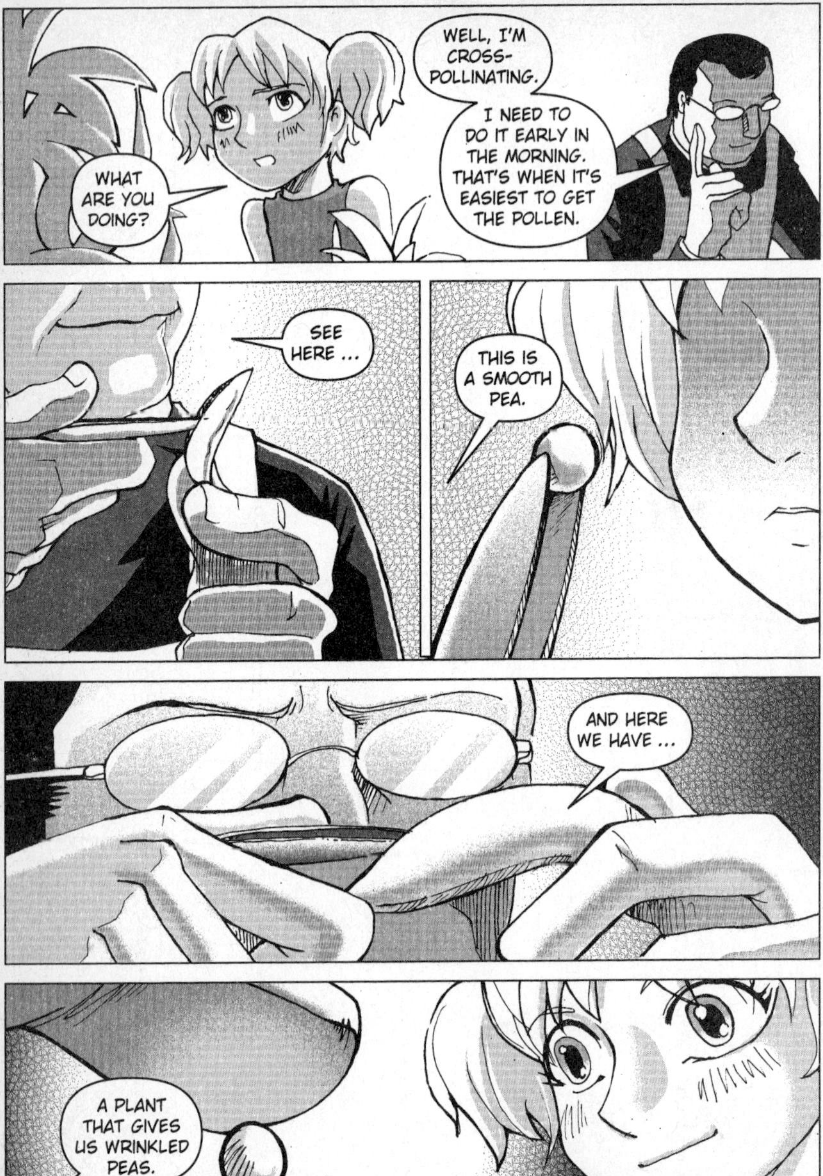
WHAT ARE YOU DOING?
WELL, I'M CROSS-POLLINATING.
I NEED TO DO IT EARLY IN THE MORNING. THAT'S WHEN IT'S EASIEST TO GET THE POLLEN.
SEE HERE ...
THIS IS A SMOOTH PEA.
AND HERE WE HAVE ...
A PLANT THAT GIVES US WRINKLED PEAS.

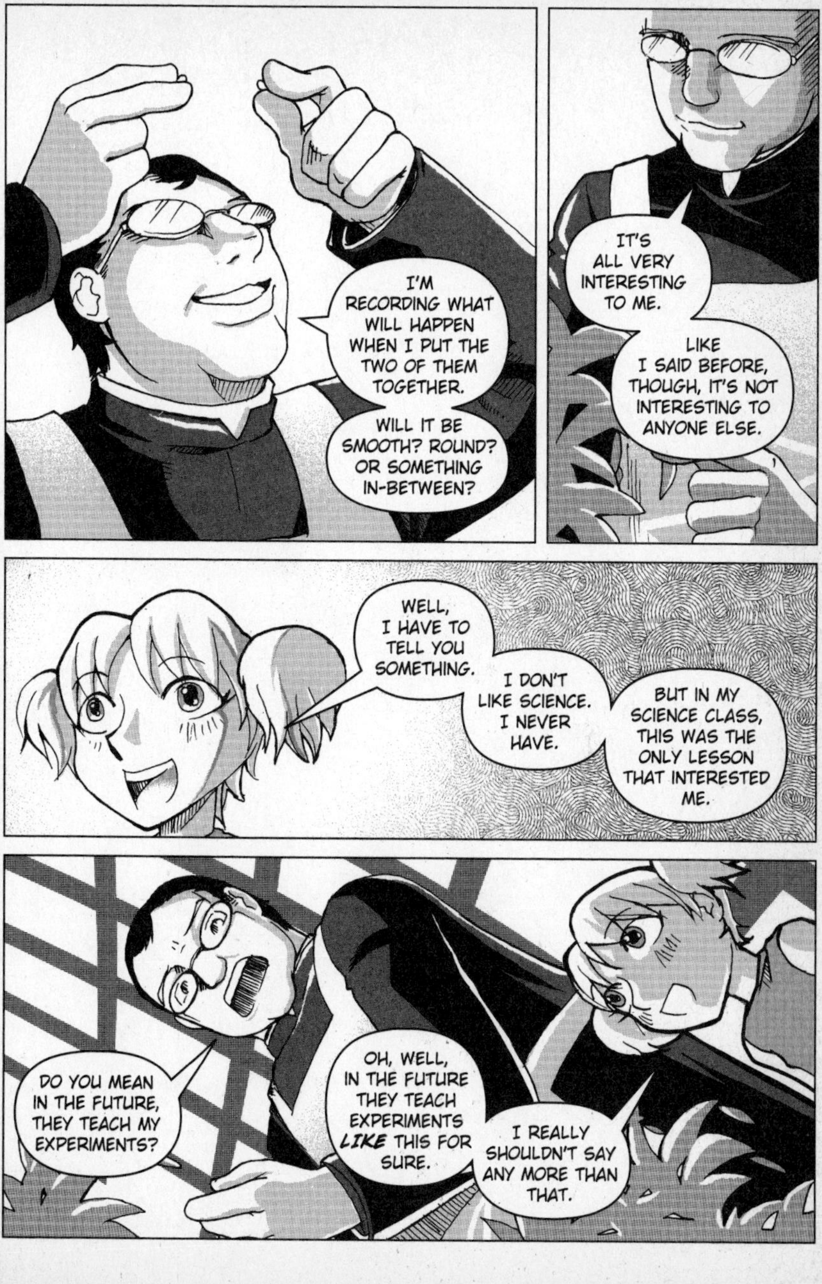
I'M RECORDING WHAT WILL HAPPEN WHEN I PUT THE TWO OF THEM TOGETHER.
WILL IT BE SMOOTH? ROUND? OR SOMETHING IN-BETWEEN?
IT'S ALL VERY INTERESTING TO ME.
LIKE I SAID BEFORE, THOUGH, IT'S NOT INTERESTING TO ANYONE ELSE.
WELL, I HAVE TO TELL YOU SOMETHING.
I DON'T LIKE SCIENCE. I NEVER HAVE.
BUT IN MY SCIENCE CLASS, THIS WAS THE ONLY LESSON THAT INTERESTED ME.
DO YOU MEAN IN THE FUTURE, THEY TEACH MY EXPERIMENTS?
OH, WELL, IN THE FUTURE THEY TEACH EXPERIMENTS *LIKE* THIS FOR SURE.
I REALLY SHOULDN'T SAY ANY MORE THAN THAT.

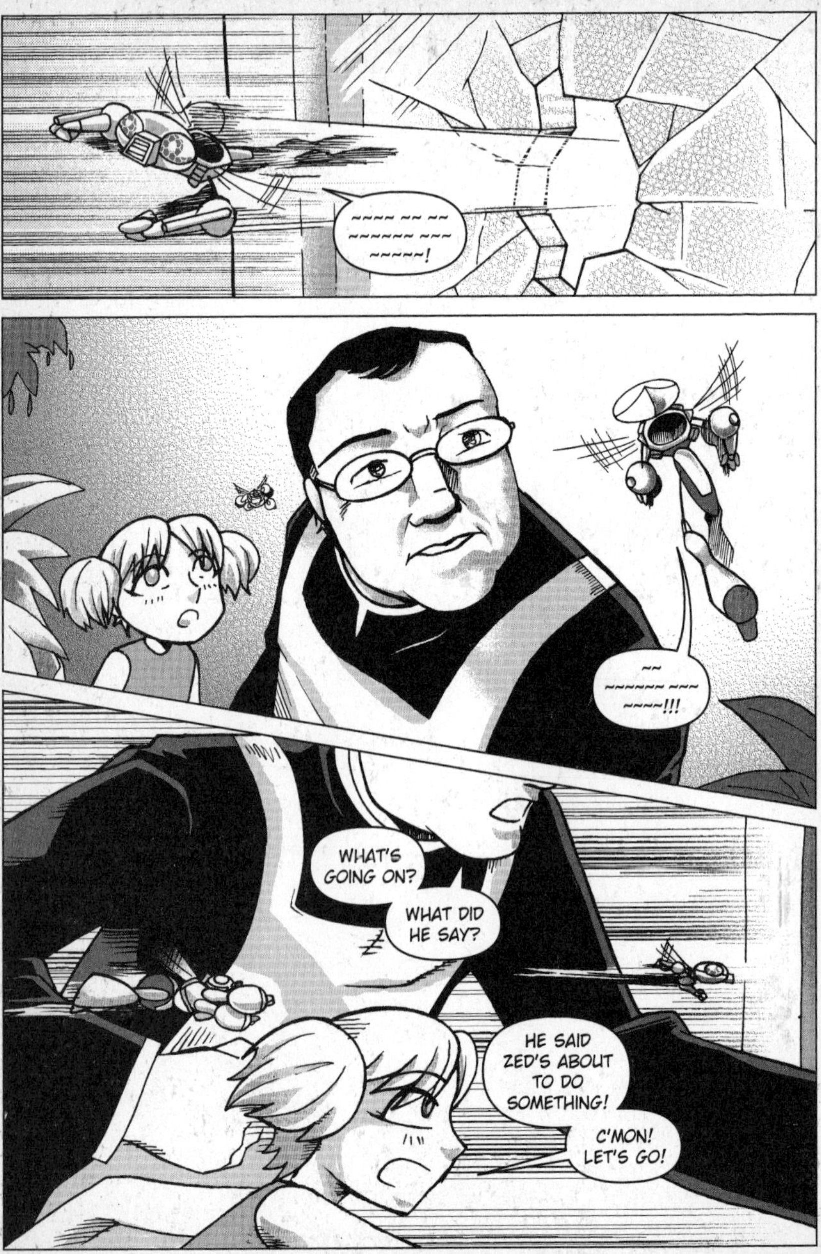
~~~~ ~~ ~~
~~~~~~ ~~~
~~~~~!
~~
~~~~~~ ~~~
~~~~!!!
WHAT'S GOING ON?
WHAT DID HE SAY?
HE SAID ZED'S ABOUT TO DO SOMETHING!
C'MON! LET'S GO!
~~~~

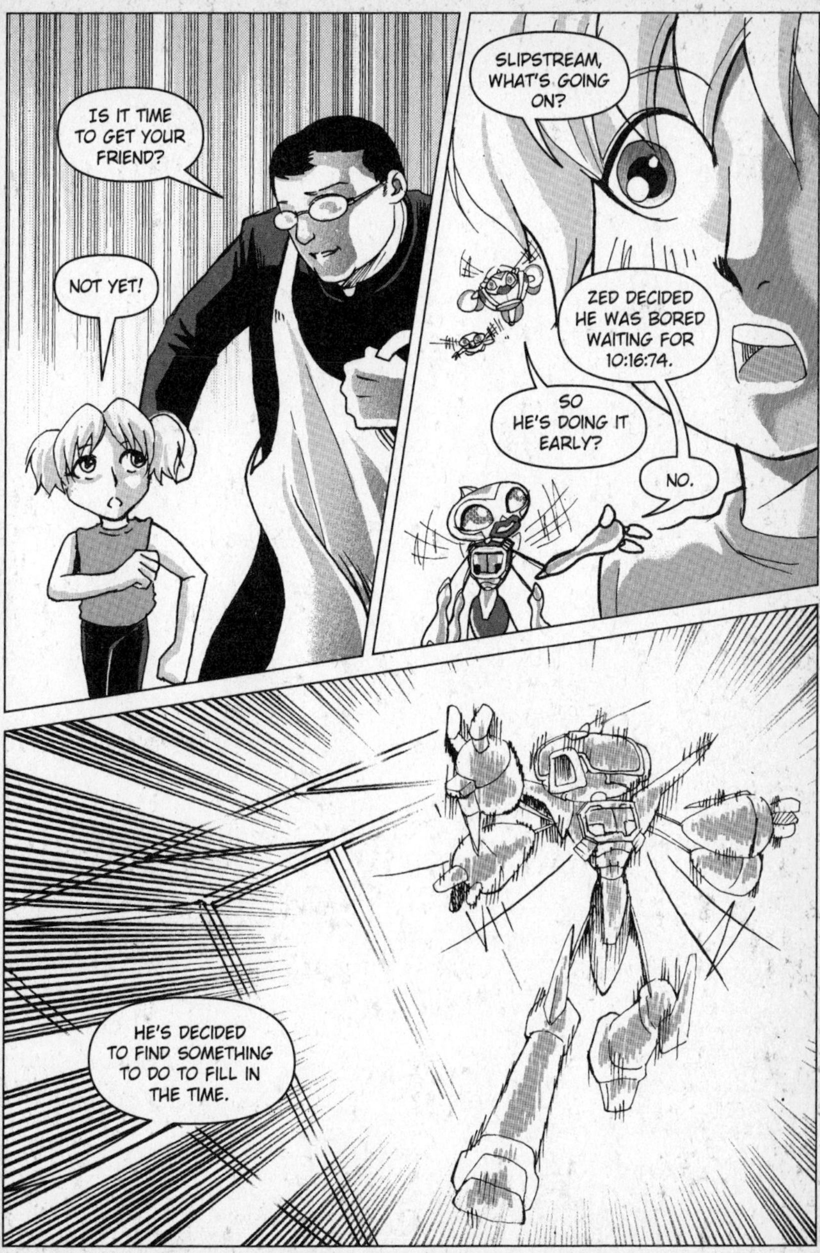
IS IT TIME TO GET YOUR FRIEND?
NOT YET!
SLIPSTREAM, WHAT'S GOING ON?
ZED DECIDED HE WAS BORED WAITING FOR 10:16:74.
SO HE'S DOING IT EARLY?
NO.
HE'S DECIDED TO FIND SOMETHING TO DO TO FILL IN THE TIME.

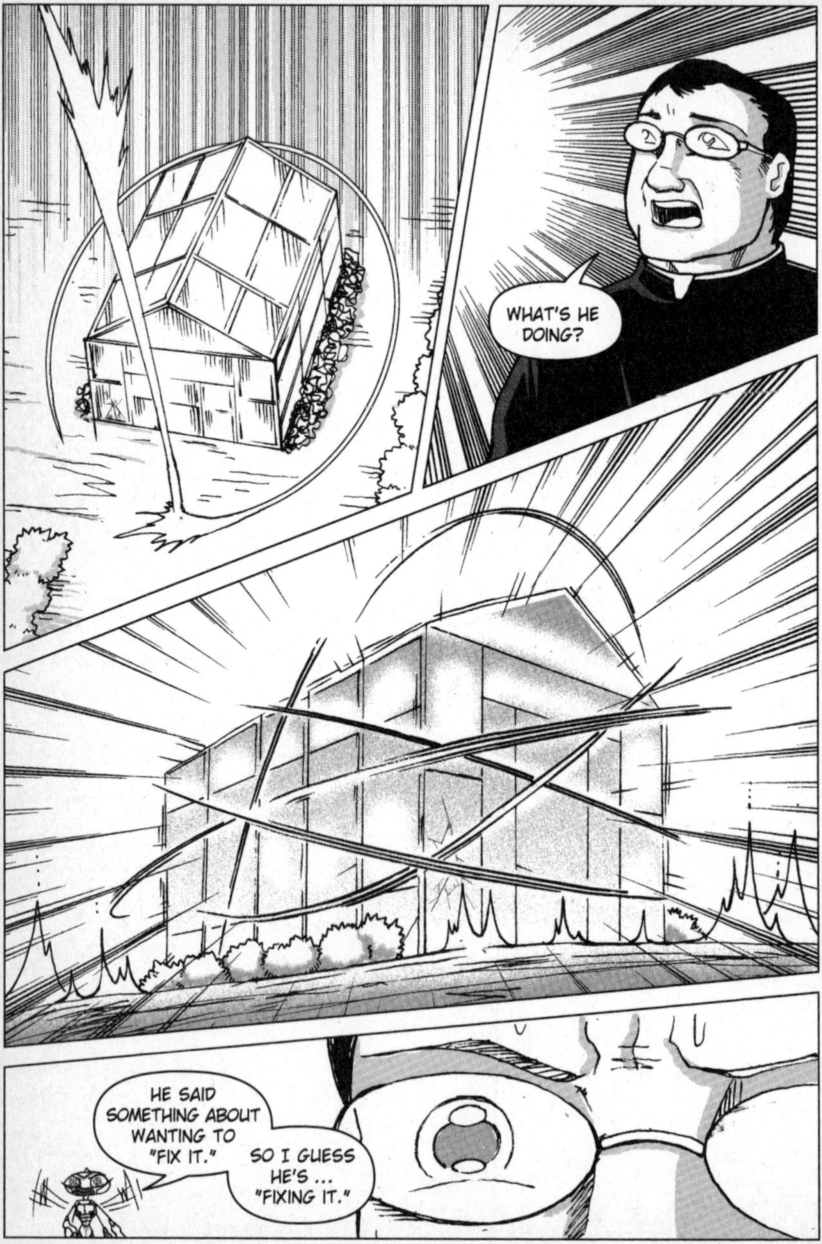
WHAT'S HE DOING?
HE SAID SOMETHING ABOUT WANTING TO "FIX IT."
SO I GUESS HE'S ... "FIXING IT."

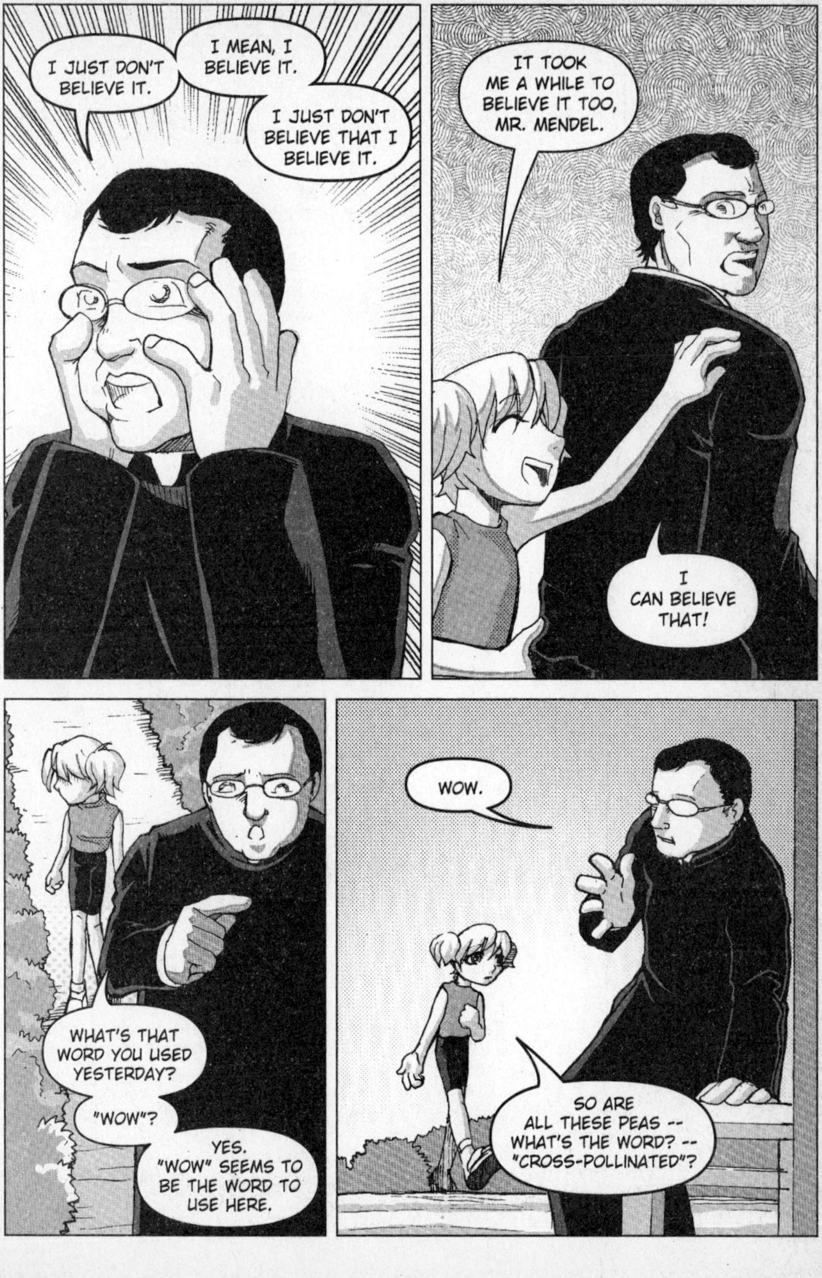
I JUST DON'T BELIEVE IT.
I MEAN, I BELIEVE IT.
I JUST DON'T BELIEVE THAT I BELIEVE IT.
IT TOOK ME A WHILE TO BELIEVE IT TOO, MR. MENDEL.
I CAN BELIEVE THAT!
WHAT'S THAT WORD YOU USED YESTERDAY?
"WOW"?
YES. "WOW" SEEMS TO BE THE WORD TO USE HERE.
WOW.
SO ARE ALL THESE PEAS -- WHAT'S THE WORD? -- "CROSS-POLLINATED"?

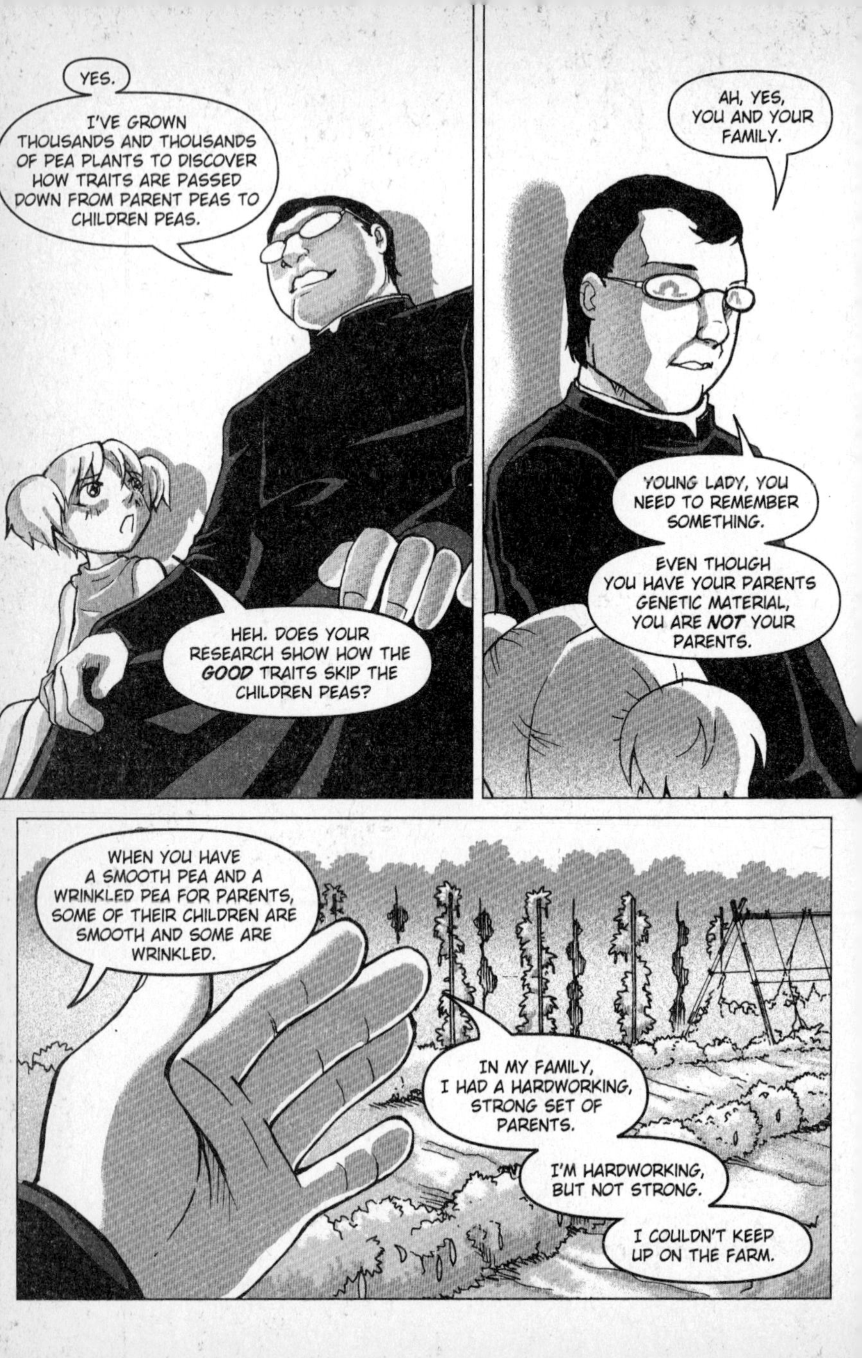
YES.
I'VE GROWN THOUSANDS AND THOUSANDS OF PEA PLANTS TO DISCOVER HOW TRAITS ARE PASSED DOWN FROM PARENT PEAS TO CHILDREN PEAS.
HEH. DOES YOUR RESEARCH SHOW HOW THE *GOOD* TRAITS SKIP THE CHILDREN PEAS?
AH, YES, YOU AND YOUR FAMILY.
YOUNG LADY, YOU NEED TO REMEMBER SOMETHING.
EVEN THOUGH YOU HAVE YOUR PARENTS GENETIC MATERIAL, YOU ARE *NOT* YOUR PARENTS.
WHEN YOU HAVE A SMOOTH PEA AND A WRINKLED PEA FOR PARENTS, SOME OF THEIR CHILDREN ARE SMOOTH AND SOME ARE WRINKLED.
IN MY FAMILY, I HAD A HARDWORKING, STRONG SET OF PARENTS.
I'M HARDWORKING, BUT NOT STRONG.
I COULDN'T KEEP UP ON THE FARM.

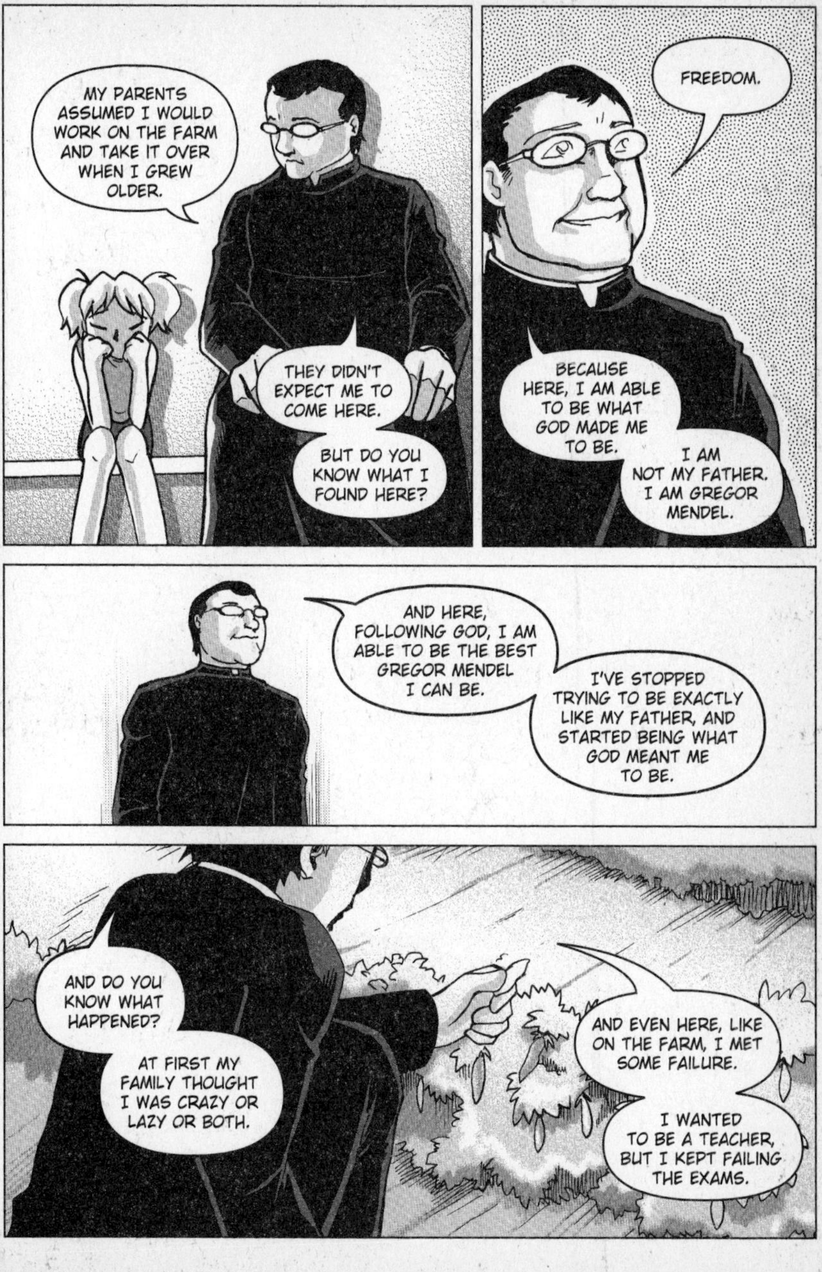
MY PARENTS ASSUMED I WOULD WORK ON THE FARM AND TAKE IT OVER WHEN I GREW OLDER.
THEY DIDN'T EXPECT ME TO COME HERE.
BUT DO YOU KNOW WHAT I FOUND HERE?
FREEDOM.
BECAUSE HERE, I AM ABLE TO BE WHAT GOD MADE ME TO BE.
I AM NOT MY FATHER. I AM GREGOR MENDEL.
AND HERE, FOLLOWING GOD, I AM ABLE TO BE THE BEST GREGOR MENDEL I CAN BE.
I'VE STOPPED TRYING TO BE EXACTLY LIKE MY FATHER, AND STARTED BEING WHAT GOD MEANT ME TO BE.
AND DO YOU KNOW WHAT HAPPENED?
AT FIRST MY FAMILY THOUGHT I WAS CRAZY OR LAZY OR BOTH.
AND EVEN HERE, LIKE ON THE FARM, I MET SOME FAILURE.
I WANTED TO BE A TEACHER, BUT I KEPT FAILING THE EXAMS.

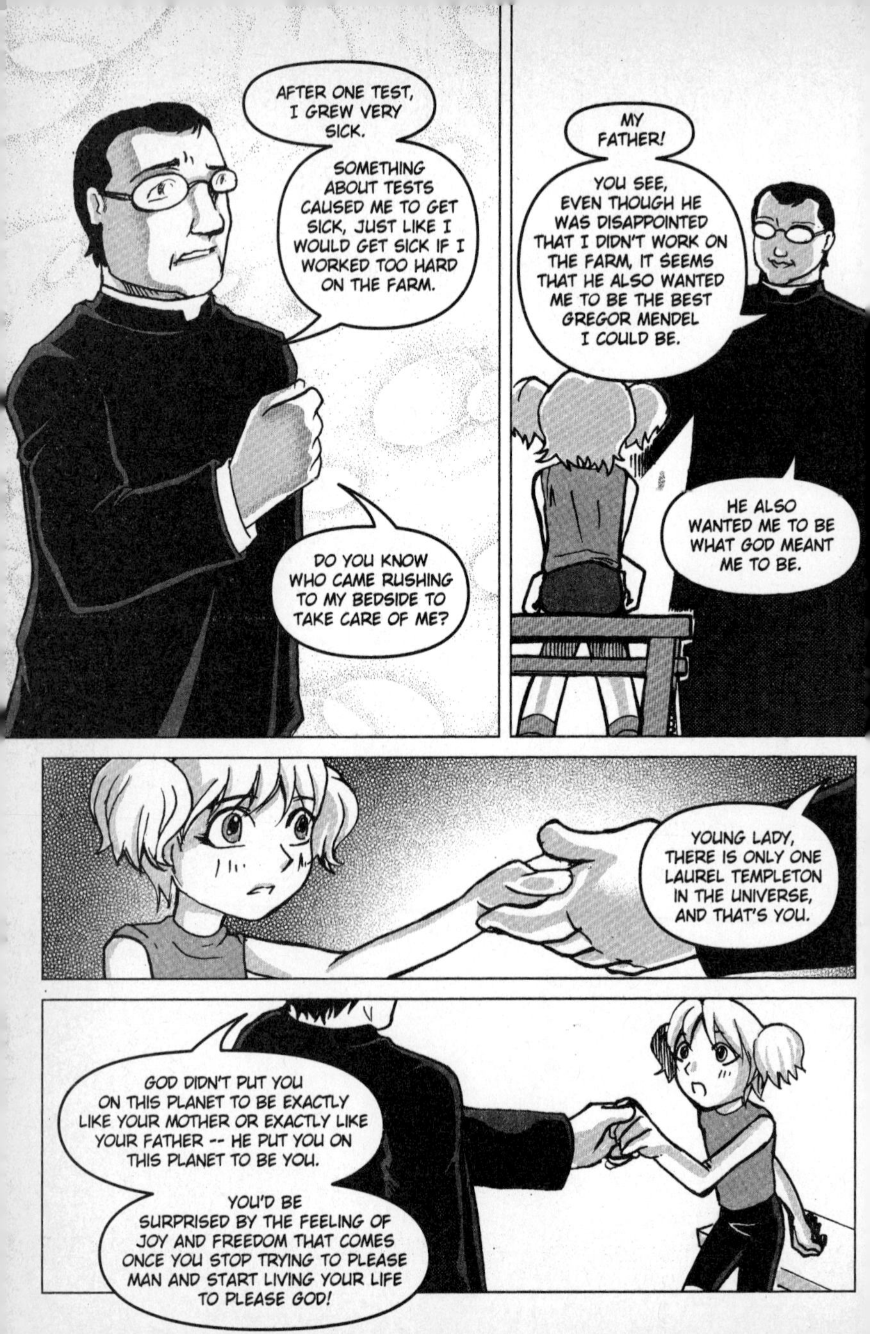
AFTER ONE TEST, I GREW VERY SICK.
SOMETHING ABOUT TESTS CAUSED ME TO GET SICK, JUST LIKE I WOULD GET SICK IF I WORKED TOO HARD ON THE FARM.
DO YOU KNOW WHO CAME RUSHING TO MY BEDSIDE TO TAKE CARE OF ME?
MY FATHER!
YOU SEE, EVEN THOUGH HE WAS DISAPPOINTED THAT I DIDN'T WORK ON THE FARM, IT SEEMS THAT HE ALSO WANTED ME TO BE THE BEST GREGOR MENDEL I COULD BE.
HE ALSO WANTED ME TO BE WHAT GOD MEANT ME TO BE.
YOUNG LADY, THERE IS ONLY ONE LAUREL TEMPLETON IN THE UNIVERSE, AND THAT'S YOU.
GOD DIDN'T PUT YOU ON THIS PLANET TO BE EXACTLY LIKE YOUR MOTHER OR EXACTLY LIKE YOUR FATHER -- HE PUT YOU ON THIS PLANET TO BE YOU.
YOU'D BE SURPRISED BY THE FEELING OF JOY AND FREEDOM THAT COMES ONCE YOU STOP TRYING TO PLEASE MAN AND START LIVING YOUR LIFE TO PLEASE GOD!

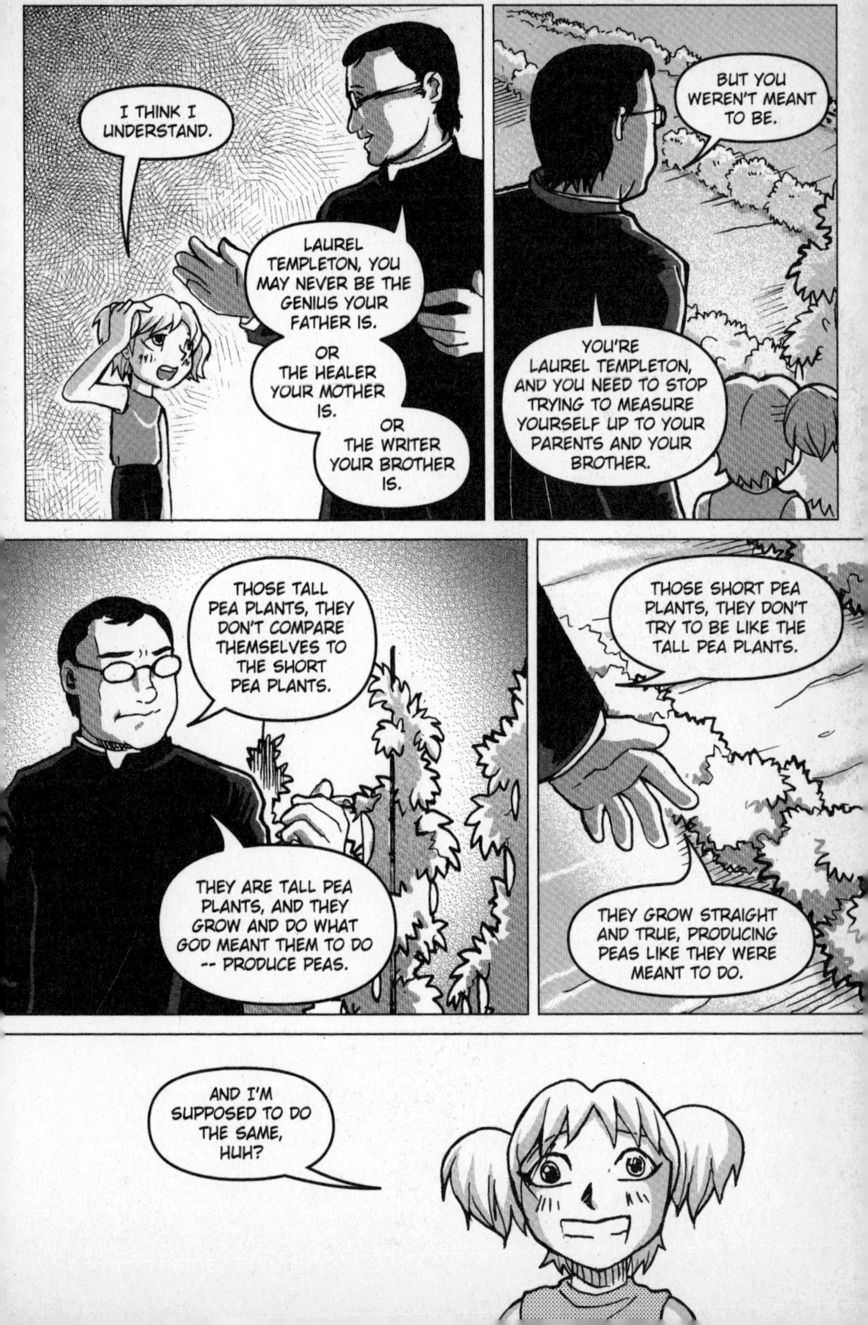
I THINK I UNDERSTAND.
LAUREL TEMPLETON, YOU MAY NEVER BE THE GENIUS YOUR FATHER IS.
OR THE HEALER YOUR MOTHER IS.
OR THE WRITER YOUR BROTHER IS.
BUT YOU WEREN'T MEANT TO BE.
YOU'RE LAUREL TEMPLETON, AND YOU NEED TO STOP TRYING TO MEASURE YOURSELF UP TO YOUR PARENTS AND YOUR BROTHER.
THOSE TALL PEA PLANTS, THEY DON'T COMPARE THEMSELVES TO THE SHORT PEA PLANTS.
THEY ARE TALL PEA PLANTS, AND THEY GROW AND DO WHAT GOD MEANT THEM TO DO -- PRODUCE PEAS.
THOSE SHORT PEA PLANTS, THEY DON'T TRY TO BE LIKE THE TALL PEA PLANTS.
THEY GROW STRAIGHT AND TRUE, PRODUCING PEAS LIKE THEY WERE MEANT TO DO.
AND I'M SUPPOSED TO DO THE SAME, HUH?

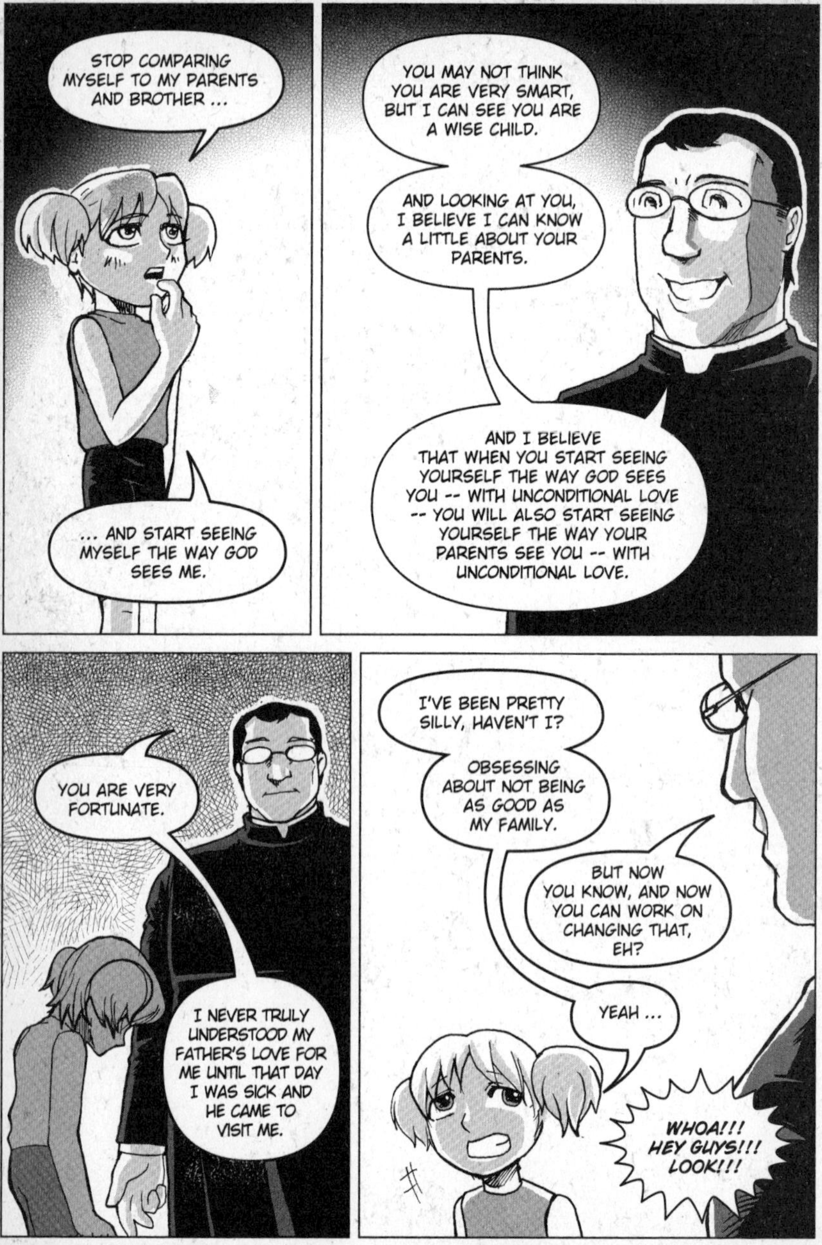
STOP COMPARING MYSELF TO MY PARENTS AND BROTHER ...
... AND START SEEING MYSELF THE WAY GOD SEES ME.
YOU MAY NOT THINK YOU ARE VERY SMART, BUT I CAN SEE YOU ARE A WISE CHILD.
AND LOOKING AT YOU, I BELIEVE I CAN KNOW A LITTLE ABOUT YOUR PARENTS.
AND I BELIEVE THAT WHEN YOU START SEEING YOURSELF THE WAY GOD SEES YOU -- WITH UNCONDITIONAL LOVE -- YOU WILL ALSO START SEEING YOURSELF THE WAY YOUR PARENTS SEE YOU -- WITH UNCONDITIONAL LOVE.
YOU ARE VERY FORTUNATE.
I NEVER TRULY UNDERSTOOD MY FATHER'S LOVE FOR ME UNTIL THAT DAY I WAS SICK AND HE CAME TO VISIT ME.
I'VE BEEN PRETTY SILLY, HAVEN'T I?
OBSESSING ABOUT NOT BEING AS GOOD AS MY FAMILY.
BUT NOW YOU KNOW, AND NOW YOU CAN WORK ON CHANGING THAT, EH?
YEAH ...
WHOA!!! HEY GUYS!!! LOOK!!!

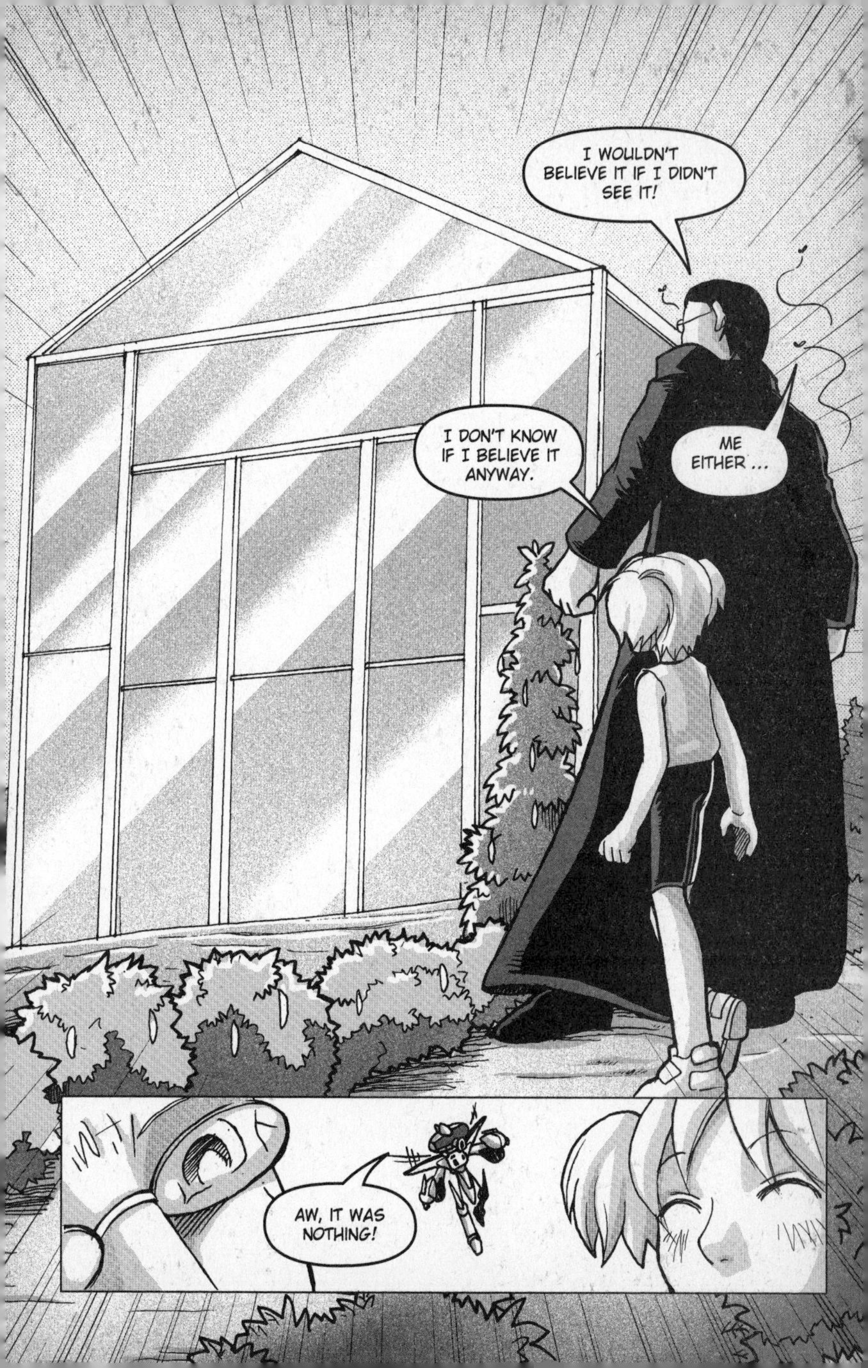
I WOULDN'T BELIEVE IT IF I DIDN'T SEE IT!
I DON'T KNOW IF I BELIEVE IT ANYWAY.
ME EITHER ...
AW, IT WAS NOTHING!

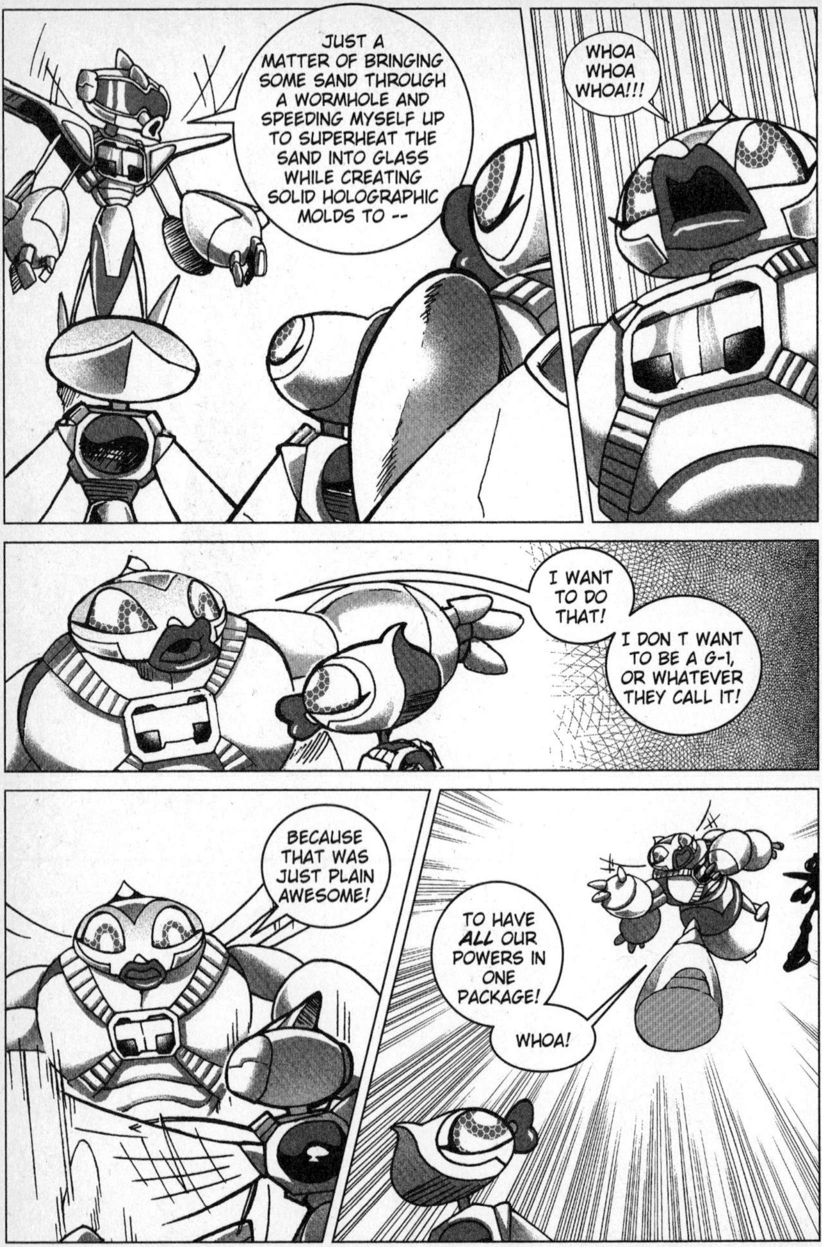
JUST A MATTER OF BRINGING SOME SAND THROUGH A WORMHOLE AND SPEEDING MYSELF UP TO SUPERHEAT THE SAND INTO GLASS WHILE CREATING SOLID HOLOGRAPHIC MOLDS TO --
WHOA WHOA WHOA!!!
I WANT TO DO THAT!
I DON T WANT TO BE A G-1, OR WHATEVER THEY CALL IT!
BECAUSE THAT WAS JUST PLAIN AWESOME!
TO HAVE ***ALL*** OUR POWERS IN ONE PACKAGE!
WHOA!

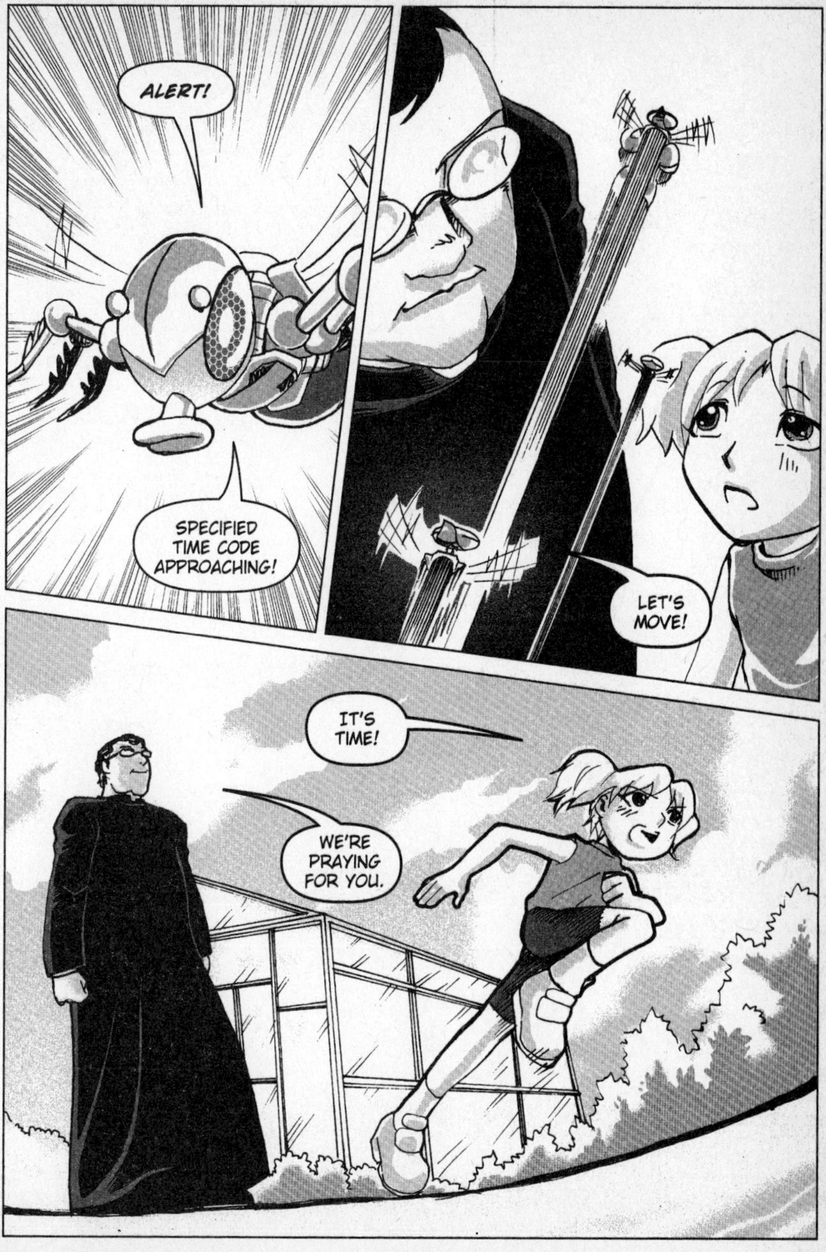
ALERT!
SPECIFIED TIME CODE APPROACHING!
LET'S MOVE!
IT'S TIME!
WE'RE PRAYING FOR YOU.

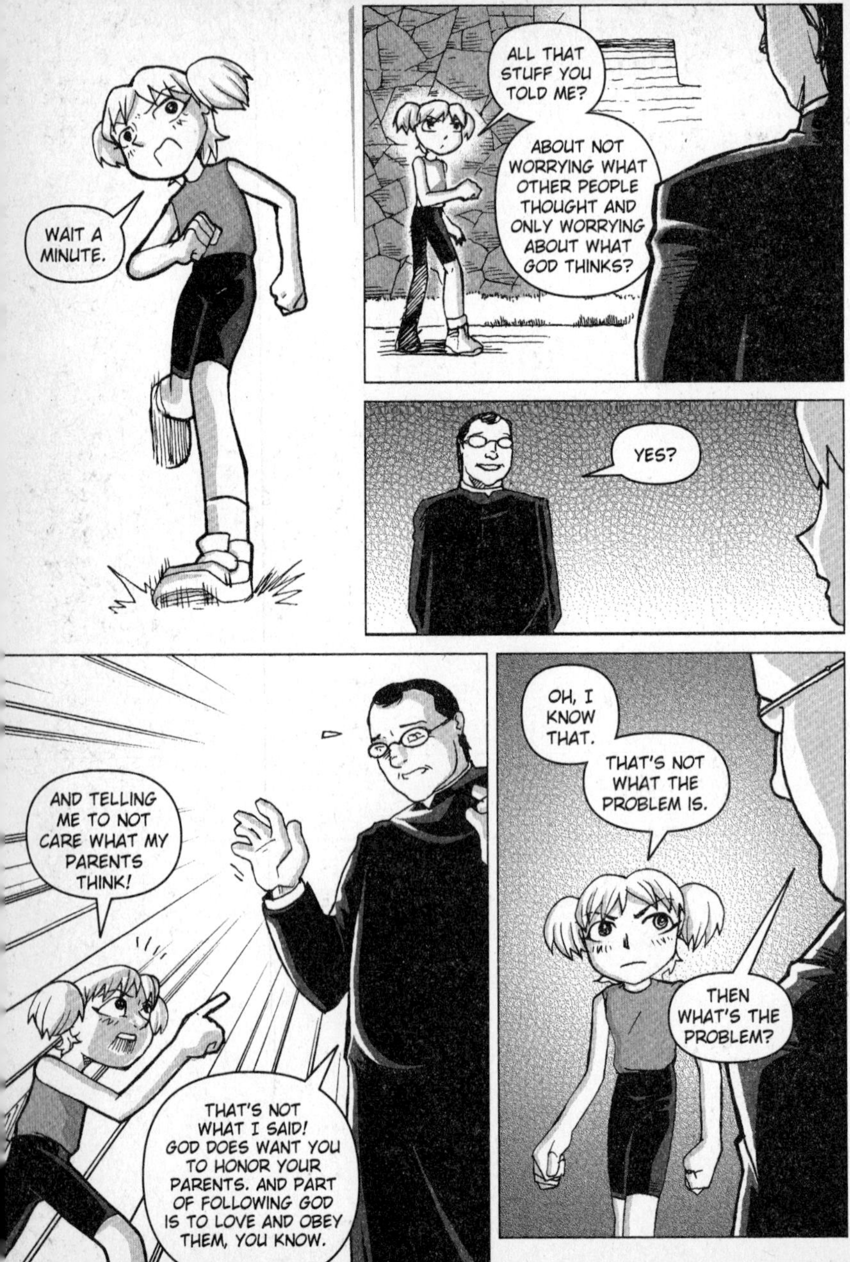
WAIT A MINUTE.
ALL THAT STUFF YOU TOLD ME?
ABOUT NOT WORRYING WHAT OTHER PEOPLE THOUGHT AND ONLY WORRYING ABOUT WHAT GOD THINKS?
YES?
AND TELLING ME TO NOT CARE WHAT MY PARENTS THINK!
THAT'S NOT WHAT I SAID! GOD DOES WANT YOU TO HONOR YOUR PARENTS. AND PART OF FOLLOWING GOD IS TO LOVE AND OBEY THEM, YOU KNOW.
OH, I KNOW THAT.
THAT'S NOT WHAT THE PROBLEM IS.
THEN WHAT'S THE PROBLEM?

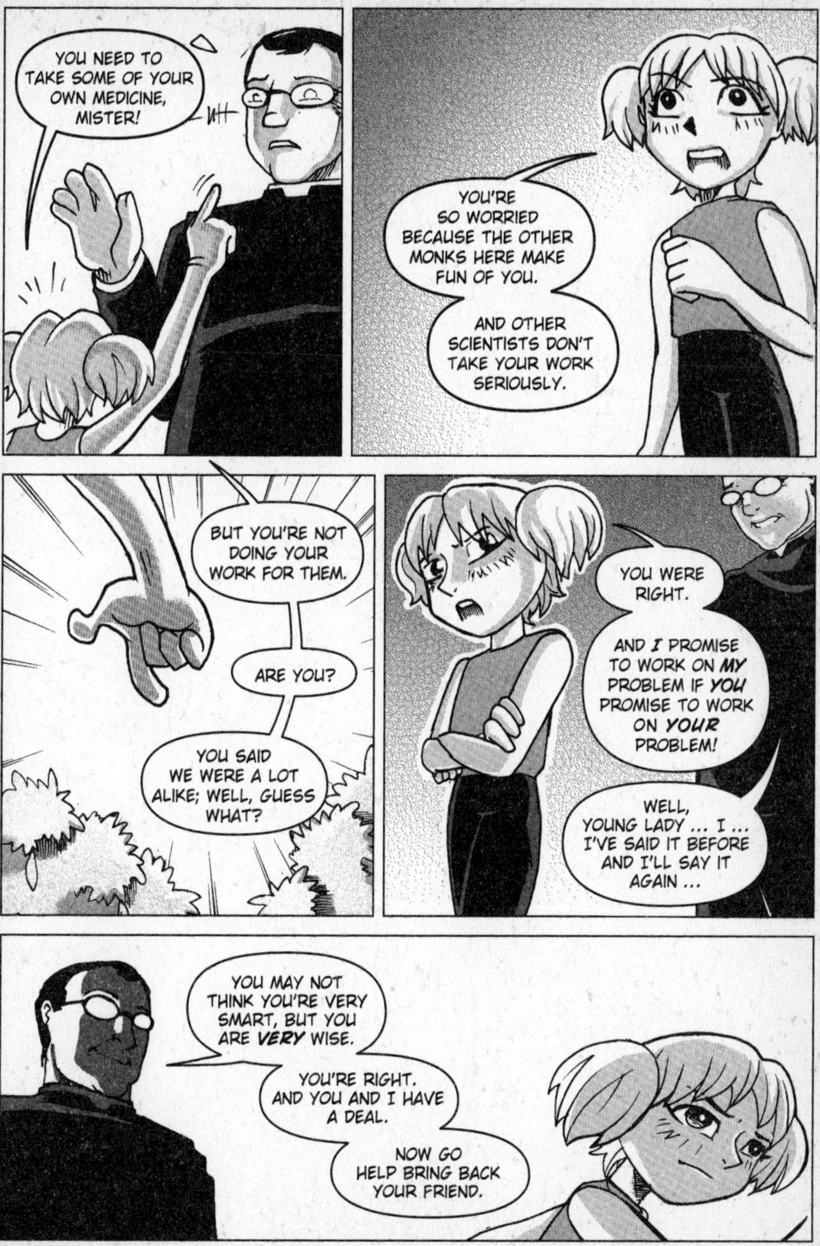
YOU NEED TO TAKE SOME OF YOUR OWN MEDICINE, MISTER!
YOU'RE SO WORRIED BECAUSE THE OTHER MONKS HERE MAKE FUN OF YOU.
AND OTHER SCIENTISTS DON'T TAKE YOUR WORK SERIOUSLY.
BUT YOU'RE NOT DOING YOUR WORK FOR THEM.
ARE YOU?
YOU SAID WE WERE A LOT ALIKE; WELL, GUESS WHAT?
YOU WERE RIGHT.
AND *I* PROMISE TO WORK ON *MY* PROBLEM IF *YOU* PROMISE TO WORK ON *YOUR* PROBLEM!
WELL, YOUNG LADY ... I ... I'VE SAID IT BEFORE AND I'LL SAY IT AGAIN ...
YOU MAY NOT THINK YOU'RE VERY SMART, BUT YOU ARE *VERY* WISE.
YOU'RE RIGHT. AND YOU AND I HAVE A DEAL.
NOW GO HELP BRING BACK YOUR FRIEND.

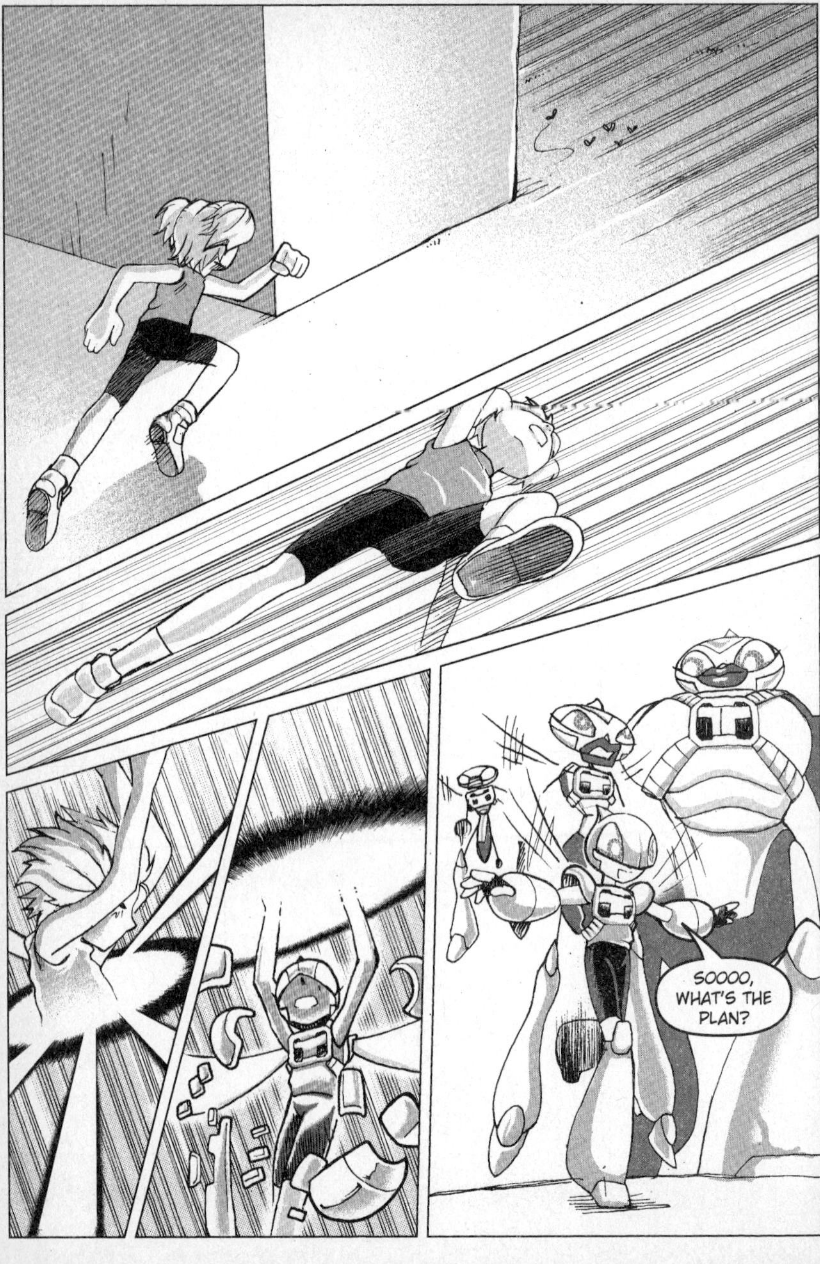
SOOOO, WHAT'S THE PLAN?

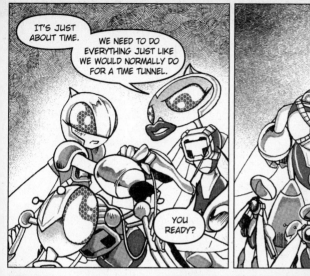

IT'S JUST ABOUT TIME.

WE NEED TO DO EVERYTHING JUST LIKE WE WOULD NORMALLY DO FOR A TIME TUNNEL.

YOU READY?

WE'RE GOING TO START OUR TIME TUNNEL TWO SECONDS BEFORE THE TIME COMES.

ZED, GIVE US A COUNTDOWN!

SEVEN.

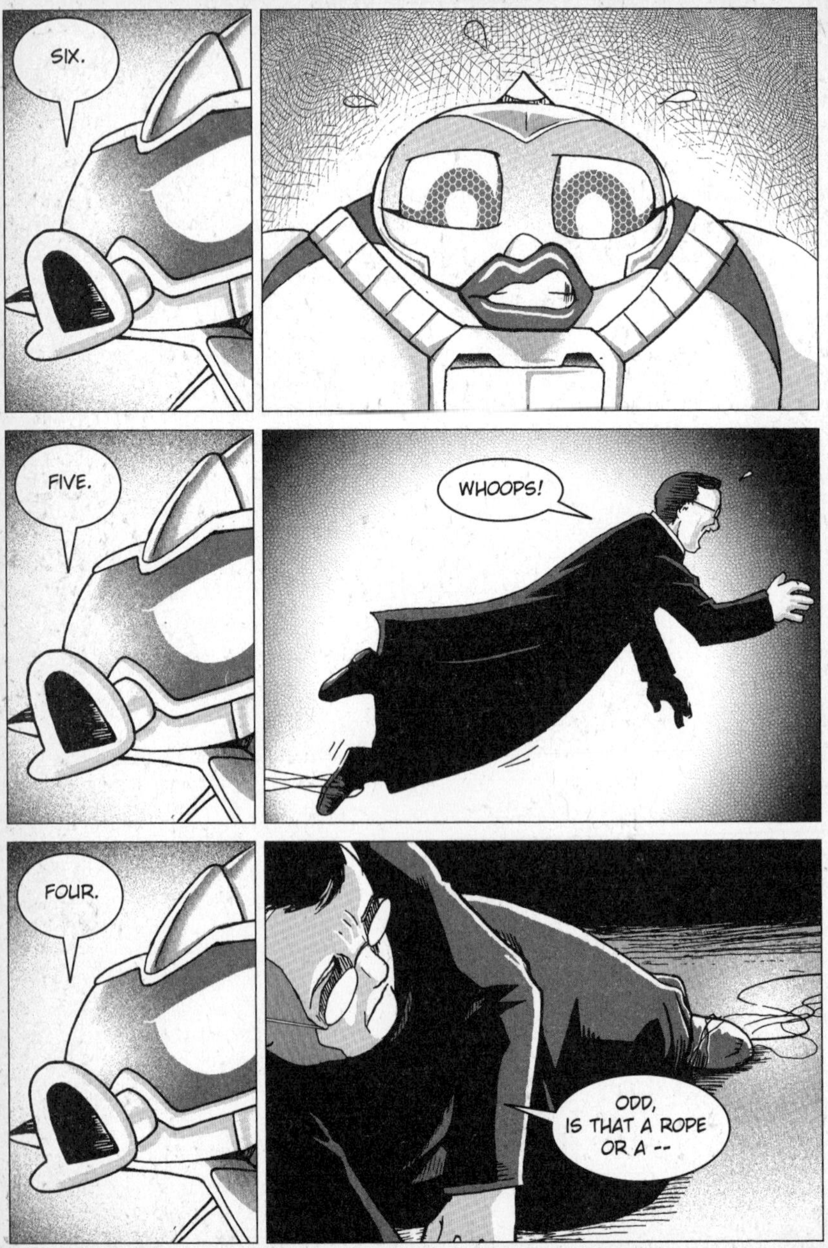
SIX.
FIVE.
WHOOPS!
FOUR.
ODD, IS THAT A ROPE OR A --

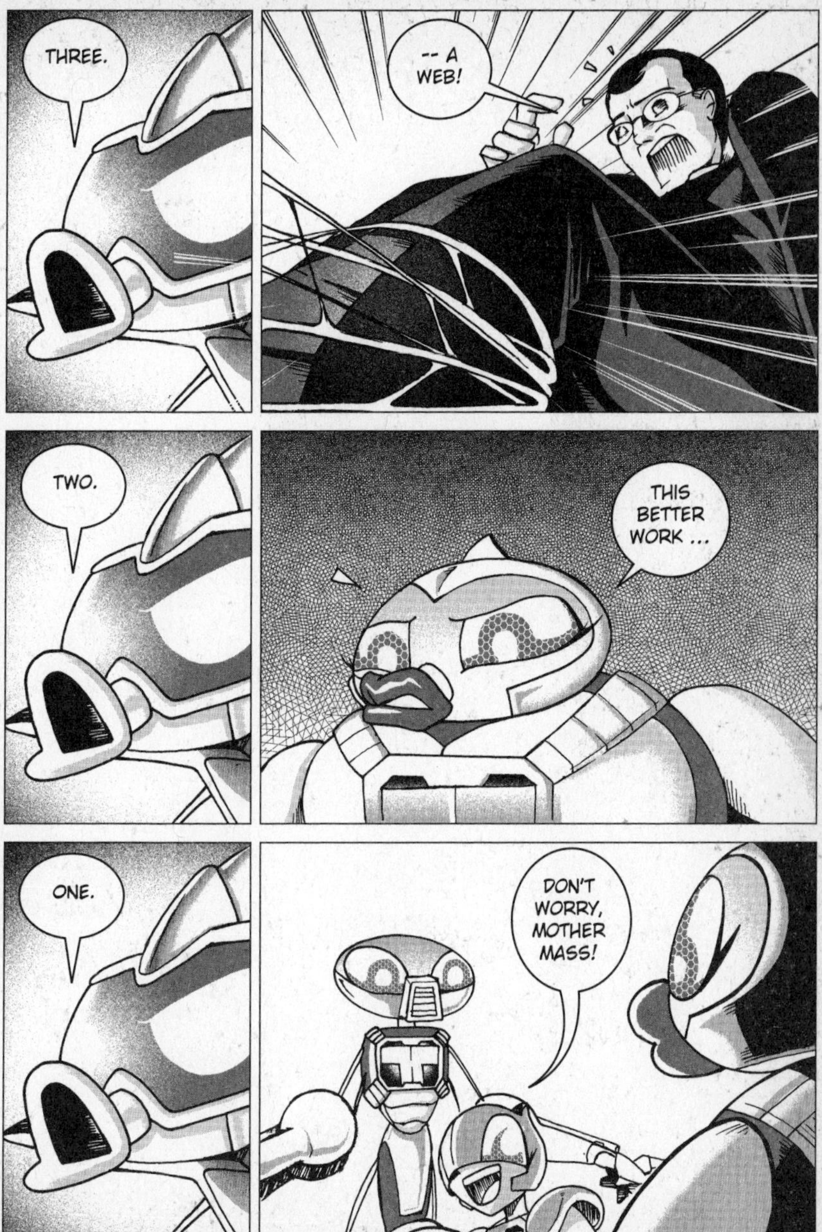
THREE.
-- A WEB!
TWO.
THIS BETTER WORK ...
ONE.
DON'T WORRY, MOTHER MASS!

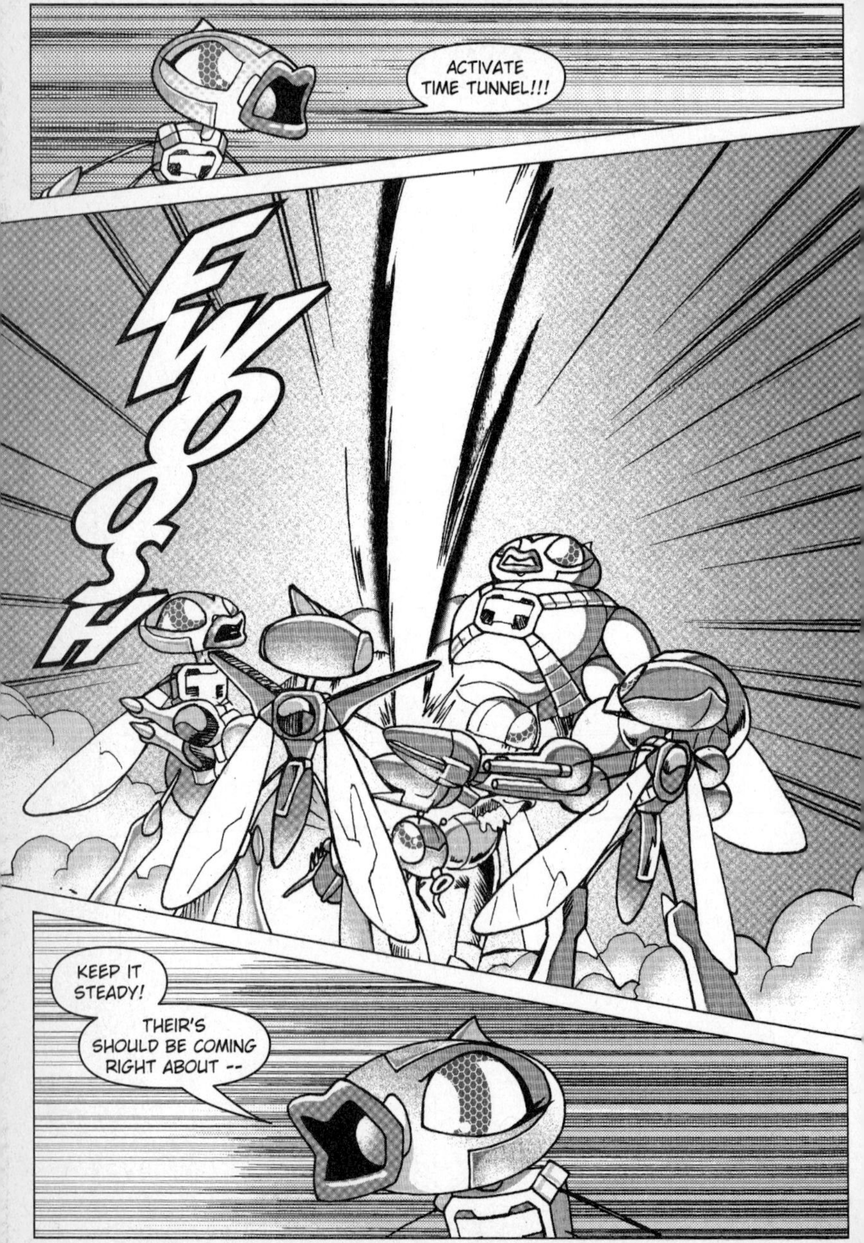
ACTIVATE TIME TUNNEL!!!
FWOOSH
KEEP IT STEADY!
THEIR'S SHOULD BE COMING RIGHT ABOUT --

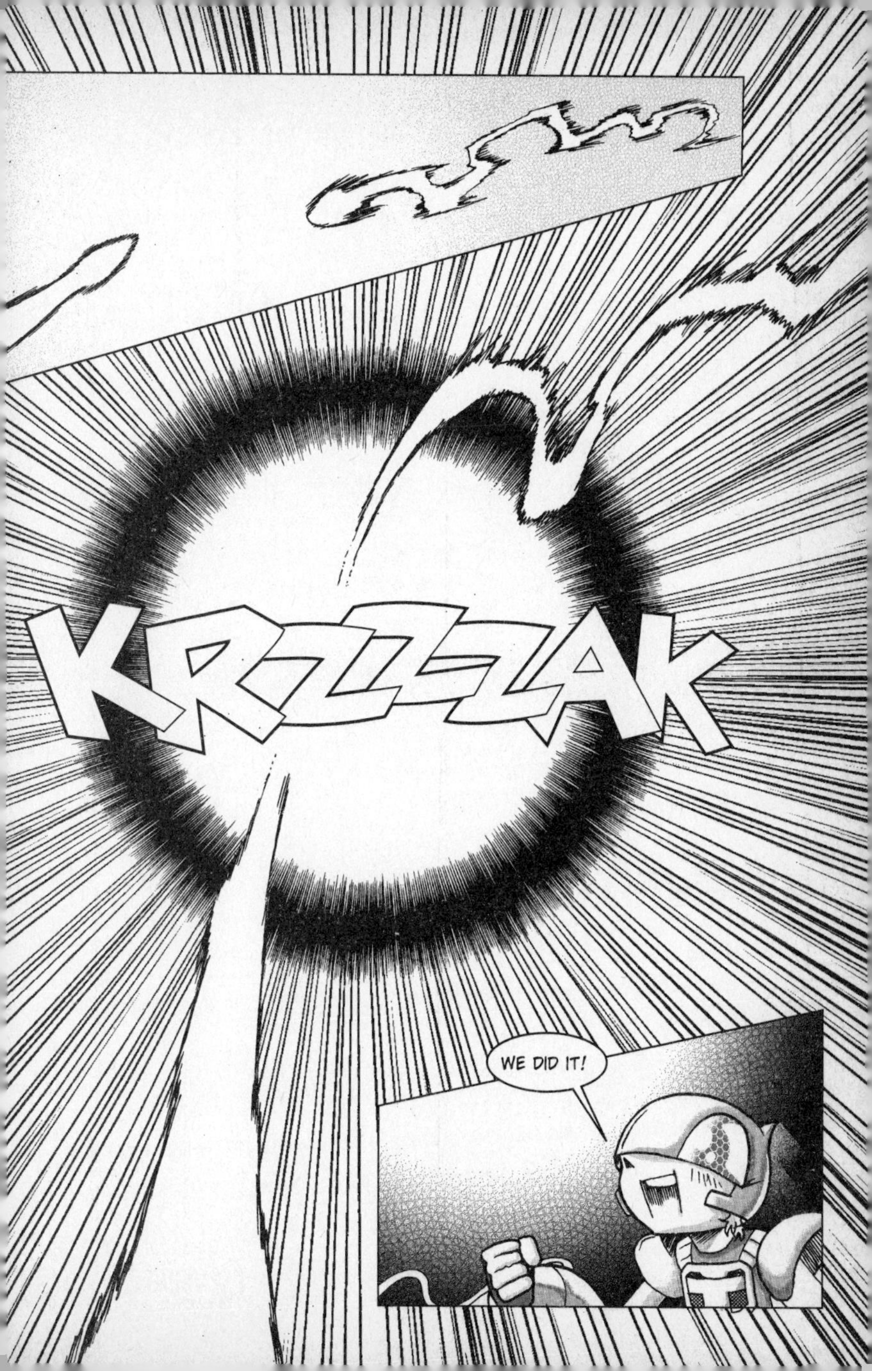
KRZZZZAK
WE DID IT!

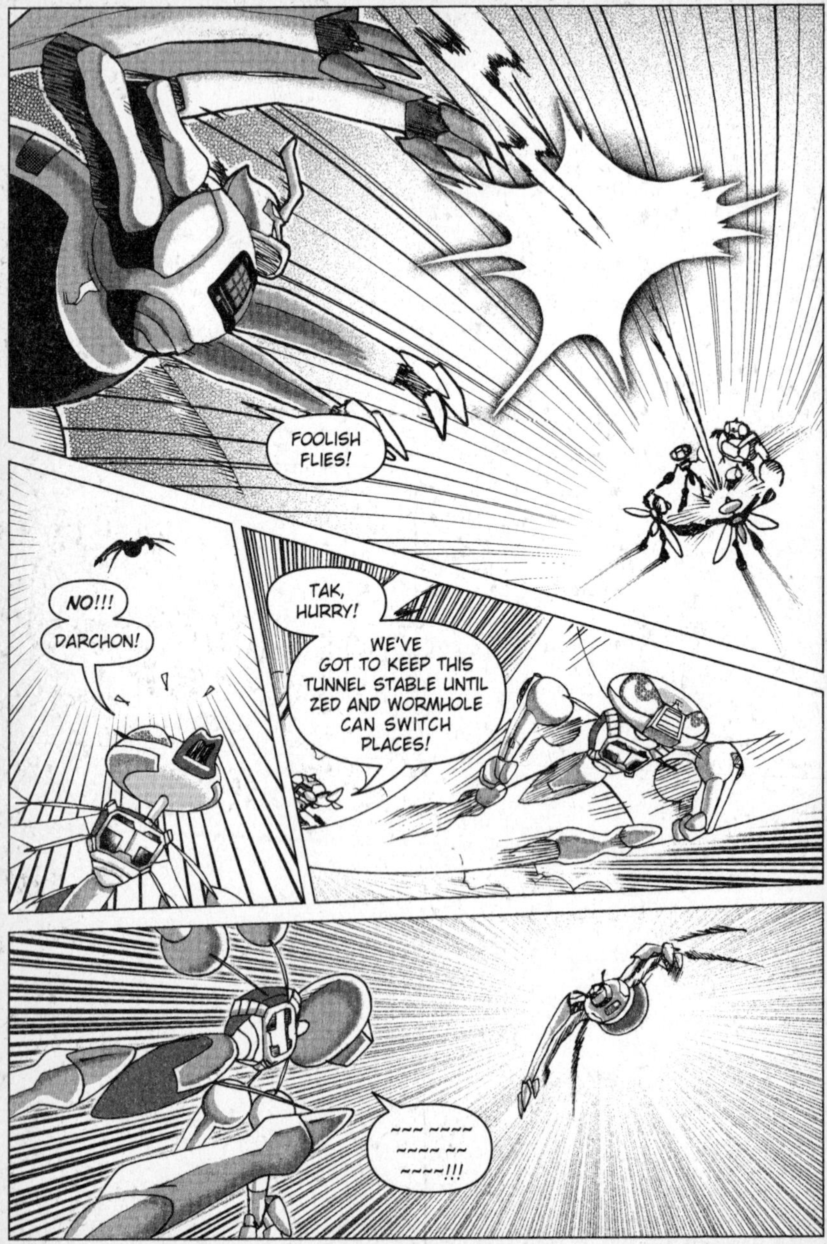
FOOLISH FLIES!
NO!!! DARCHON!
TAK, HURRY!
WE'VE GOT TO KEEP THIS TUNNEL STABLE UNTIL ZED AND WORMHOLE CAN SWITCH PLACES!
~~~ ~~~~ ~~~~ ~~ ~~~~!!!
~~~

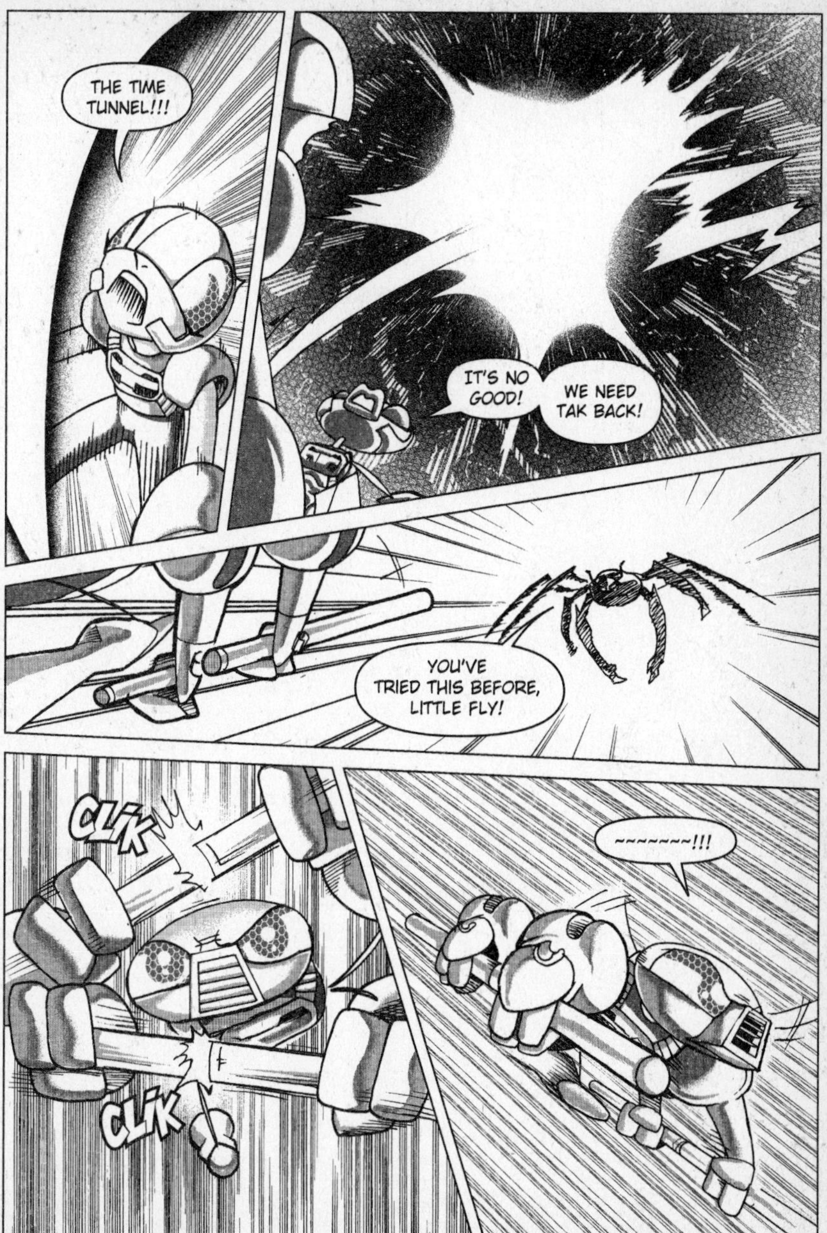
THE TIME TUNNEL!!!
IT'S NO GOOD!
WE NEED TAK BACK!
YOU'VE TRIED THIS BEFORE, LITTLE FLY!
CLIK
CLIK
~~~~~~~!!!
~~~~~~~

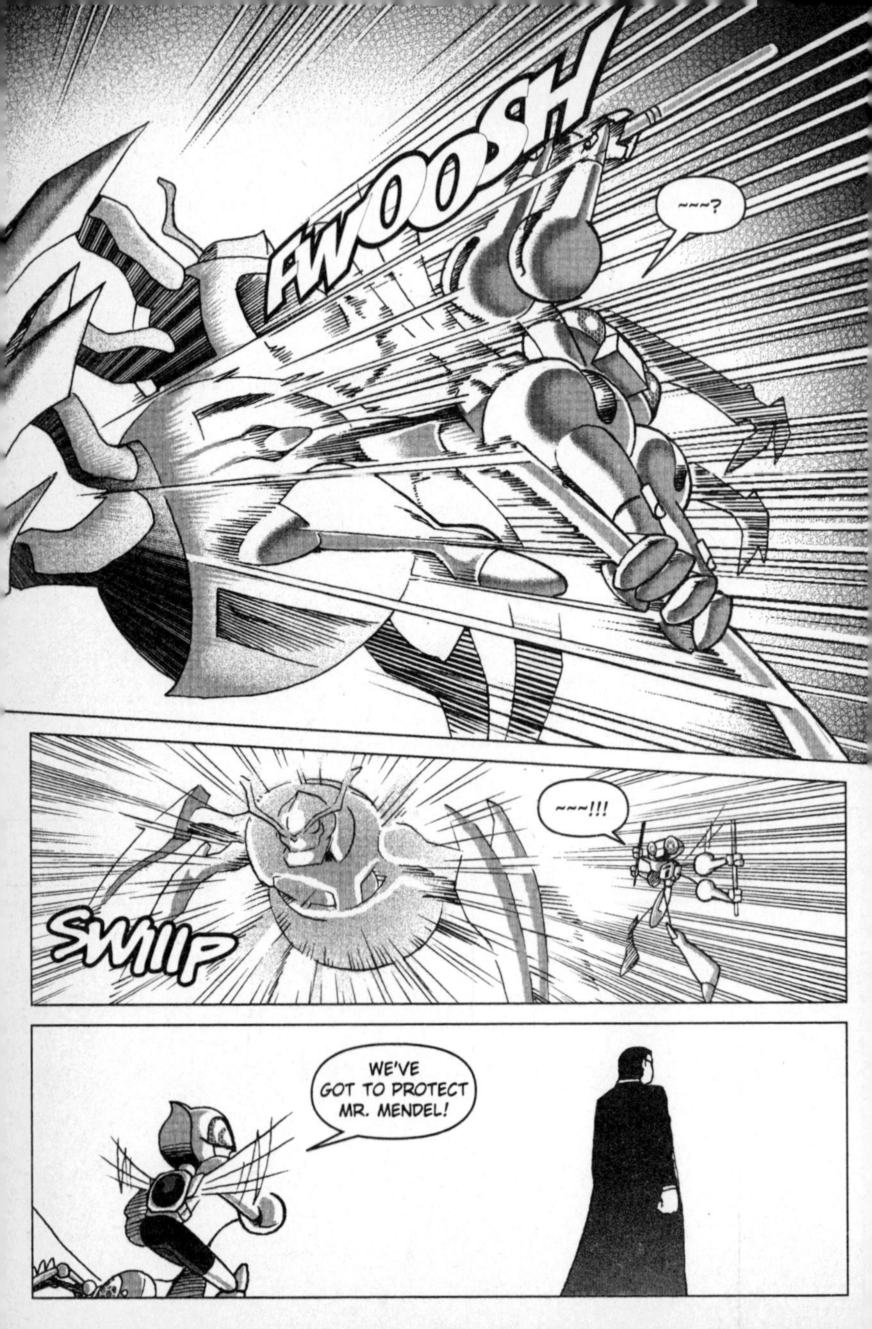
FWOOSH
~~~?
SWIIP
~~~!!!
WE'VE GOT TO PROTECT MR. MENDEL!

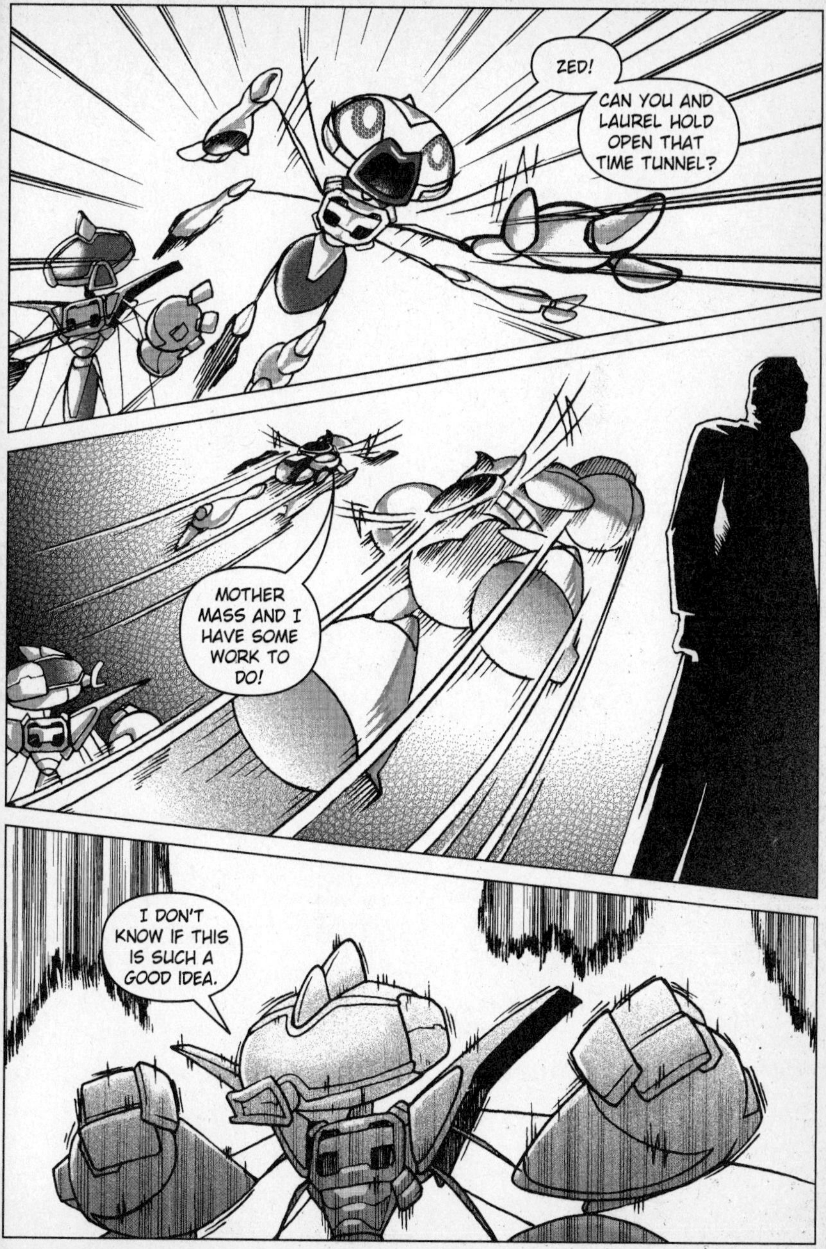
ZED!
CAN YOU AND LAUREL HOLD OPEN THAT TIME TUNNEL?
MOTHER MASS AND I HAVE SOME WORK TO DO!
I DON'T KNOW IF THIS IS SUCH A GOOD IDEA.

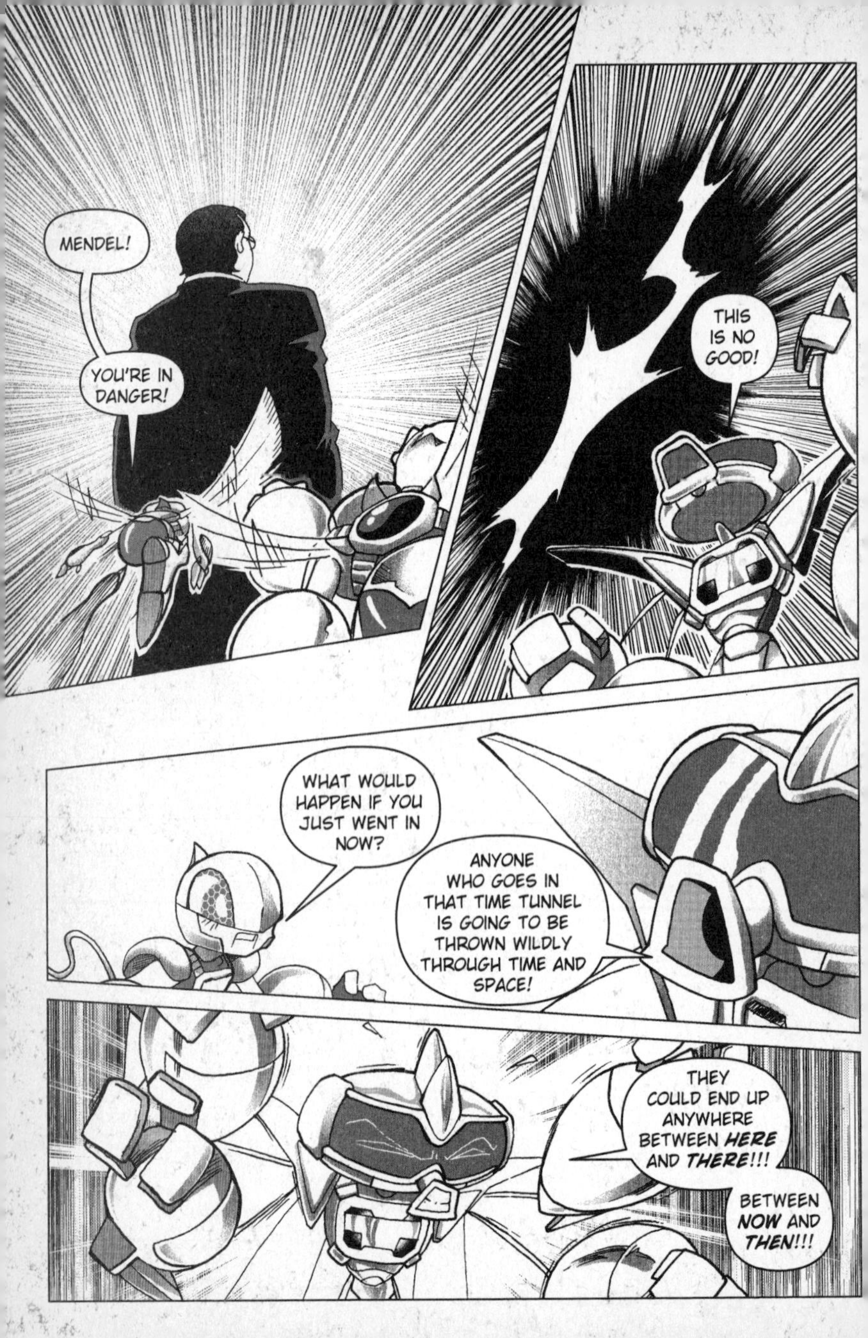
MENDEL!
YOU'RE IN DANGER!
THIS IS NO GOOD!
WHAT WOULD HAPPEN IF YOU JUST WENT IN NOW?
ANYONE WHO GOES IN THAT TIME TUNNEL IS GOING TO BE THROWN WILDLY THROUGH TIME AND SPACE!
THEY COULD END UP ANYWHERE BETWEEN ***HERE*** AND ***THERE***!!!
BETWEEN ***NOW*** AND ***THEN***!!!

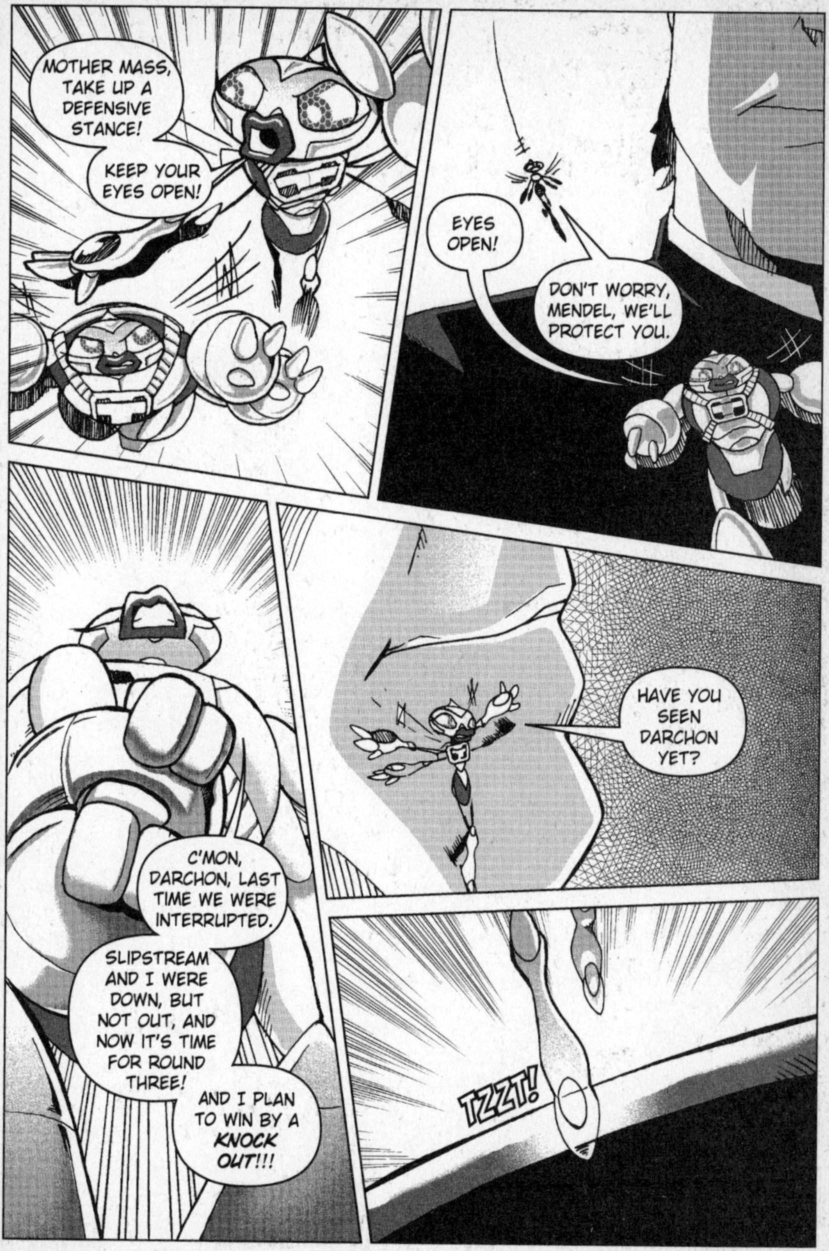
MOTHER MASS, TAKE UP A DEFENSIVE STANCE!
KEEP YOUR EYES OPEN!
EYES OPEN!
DON'T WORRY, MENDEL, WE'LL PROTECT YOU.
C'MON, DARCHON, LAST TIME WE WERE INTERRUPTED.
SLIPSTREAM AND I WERE DOWN, BUT NOT OUT, AND NOW IT'S TIME FOR ROUND THREE!
AND I PLAN TO WIN BY A ***KNOCK OUT!!!***
HAVE YOU SEEN DARCHON YET?
TZZT!

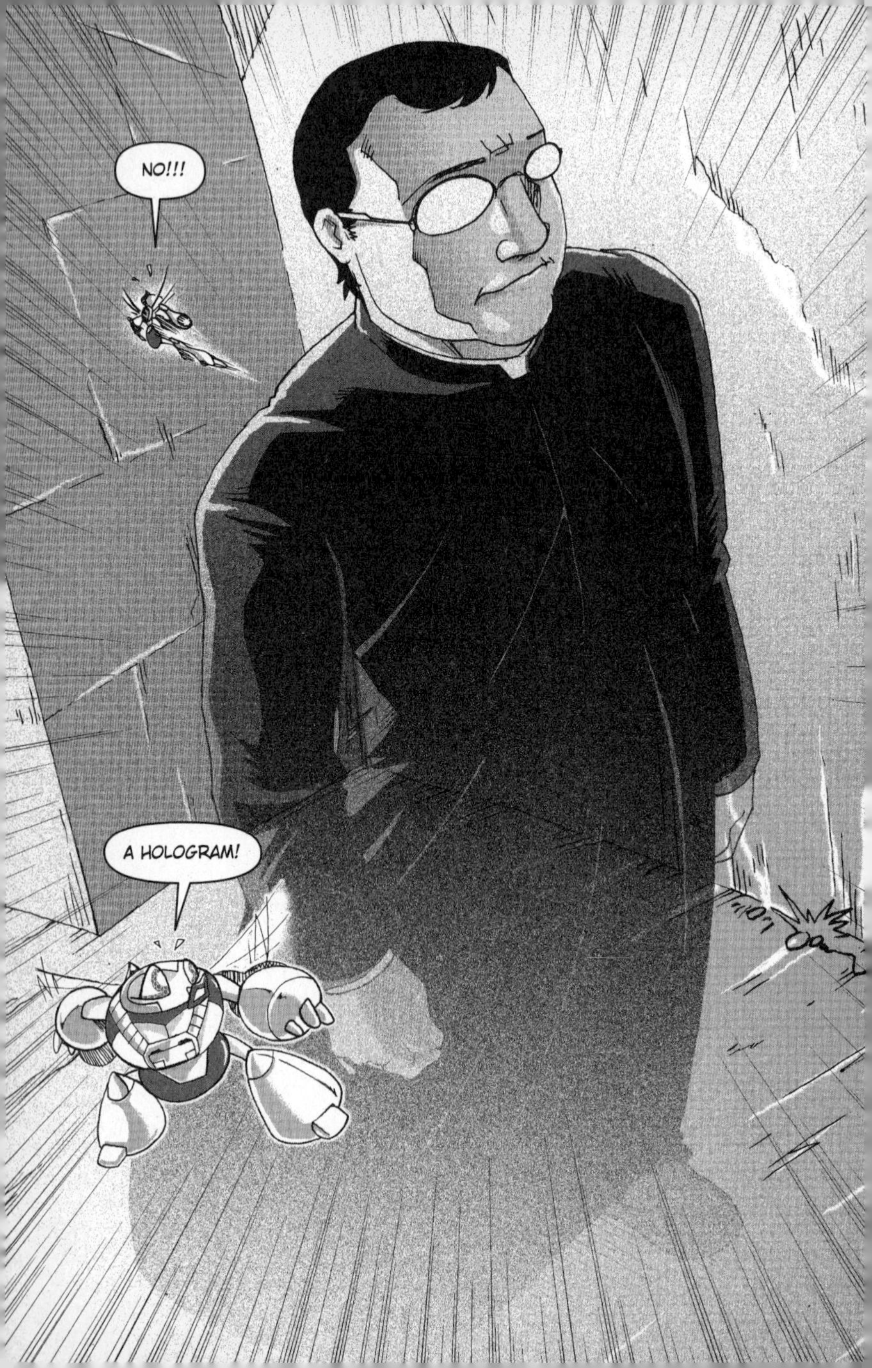
NO!!!
A HOLOGRAM!

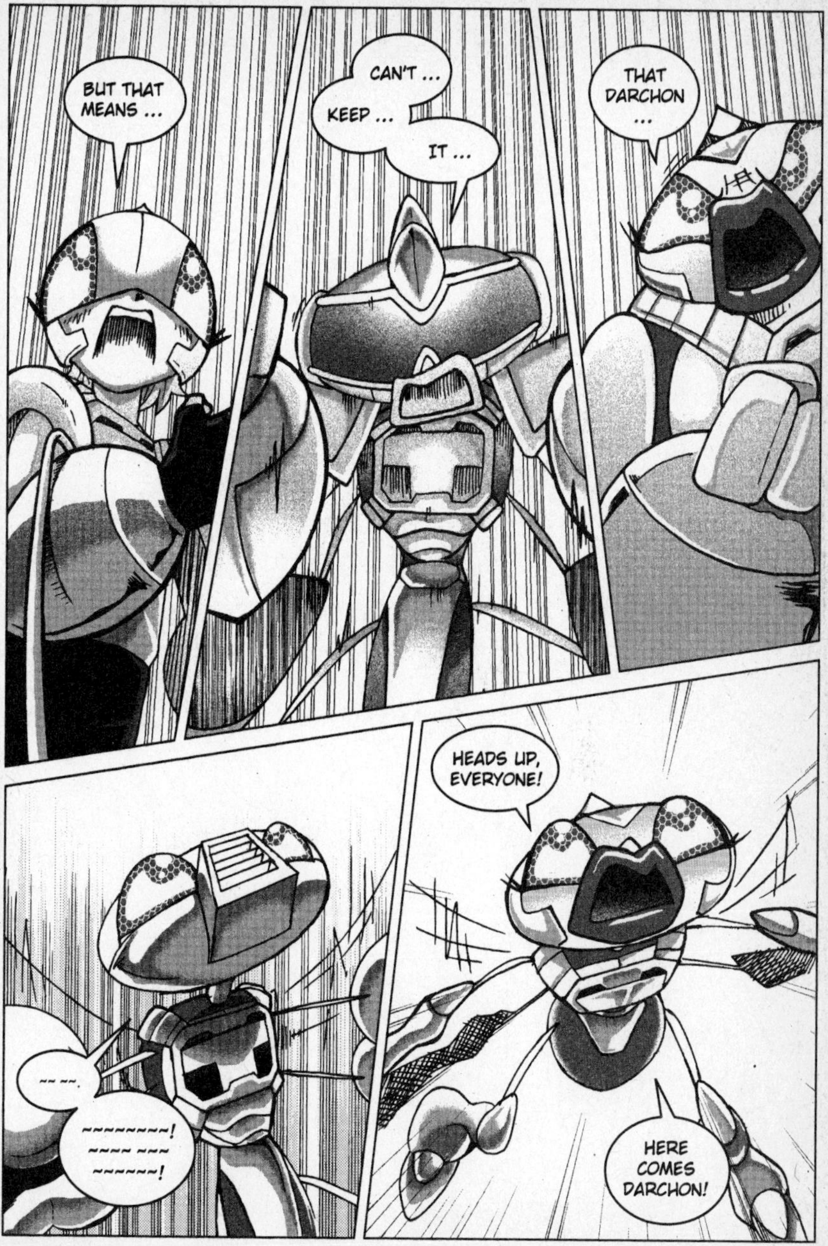
BUT THAT MEANS ...
CAN'T ...
KEEP ...
IT ...
THAT DARCHON ...
~~ ~~.
~~~~~~~~! ~~~~ ~~~ ~~~~~~!
HEADS UP, EVERYONE!
HERE COMES DARCHON!
~~~~~~~~

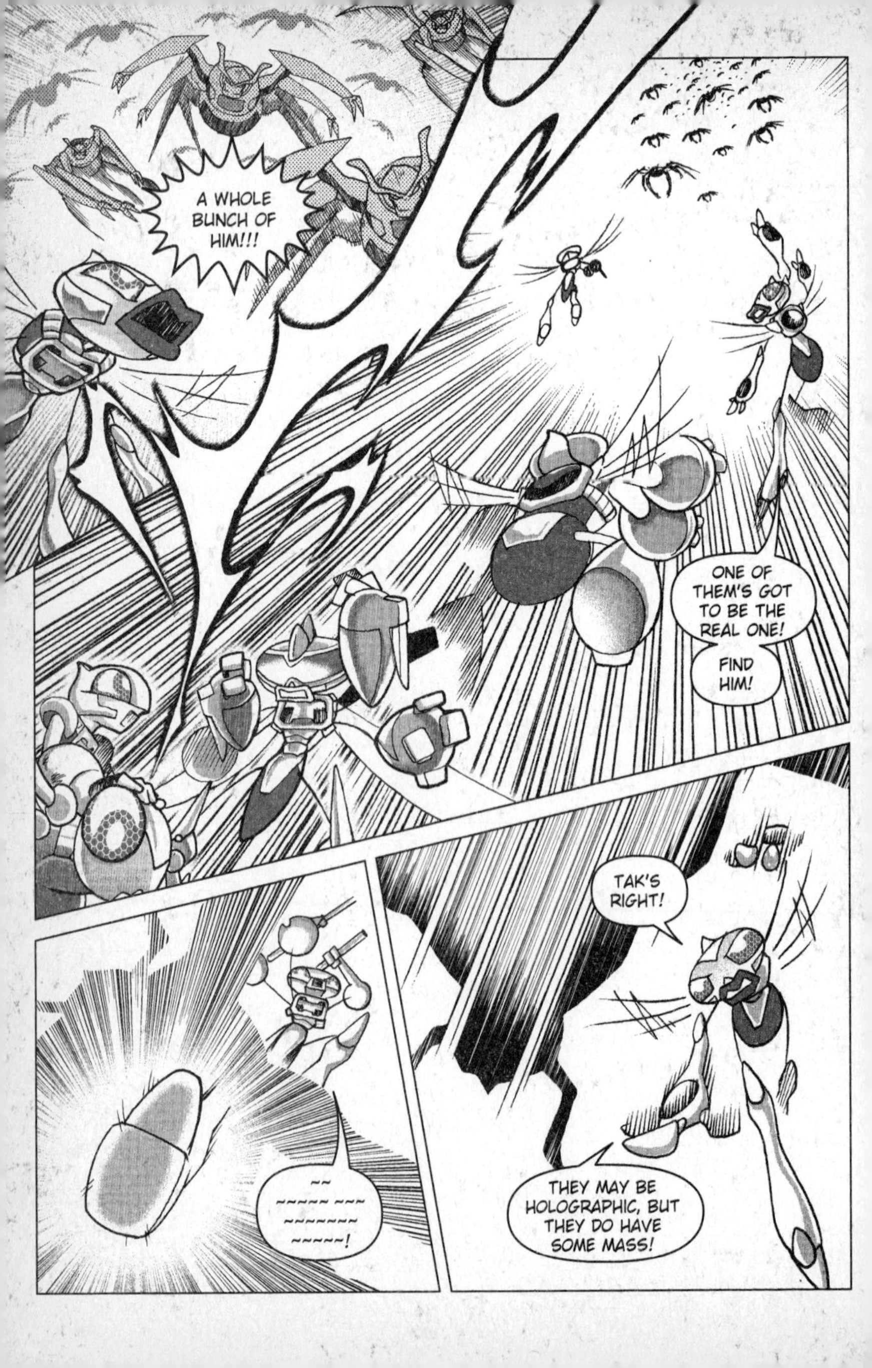
A WHOLE BUNCH OF HIM!!!
ONE OF THEM'S GOT TO BE THE REAL ONE!
FIND HIM!
~~ ~~~~~ ~~~ ~~~~~~~ ~~~~~!
TAK'S RIGHT!
THEY MAY BE HOLOGRAPHIC, BUT THEY DO HAVE SOME MASS!

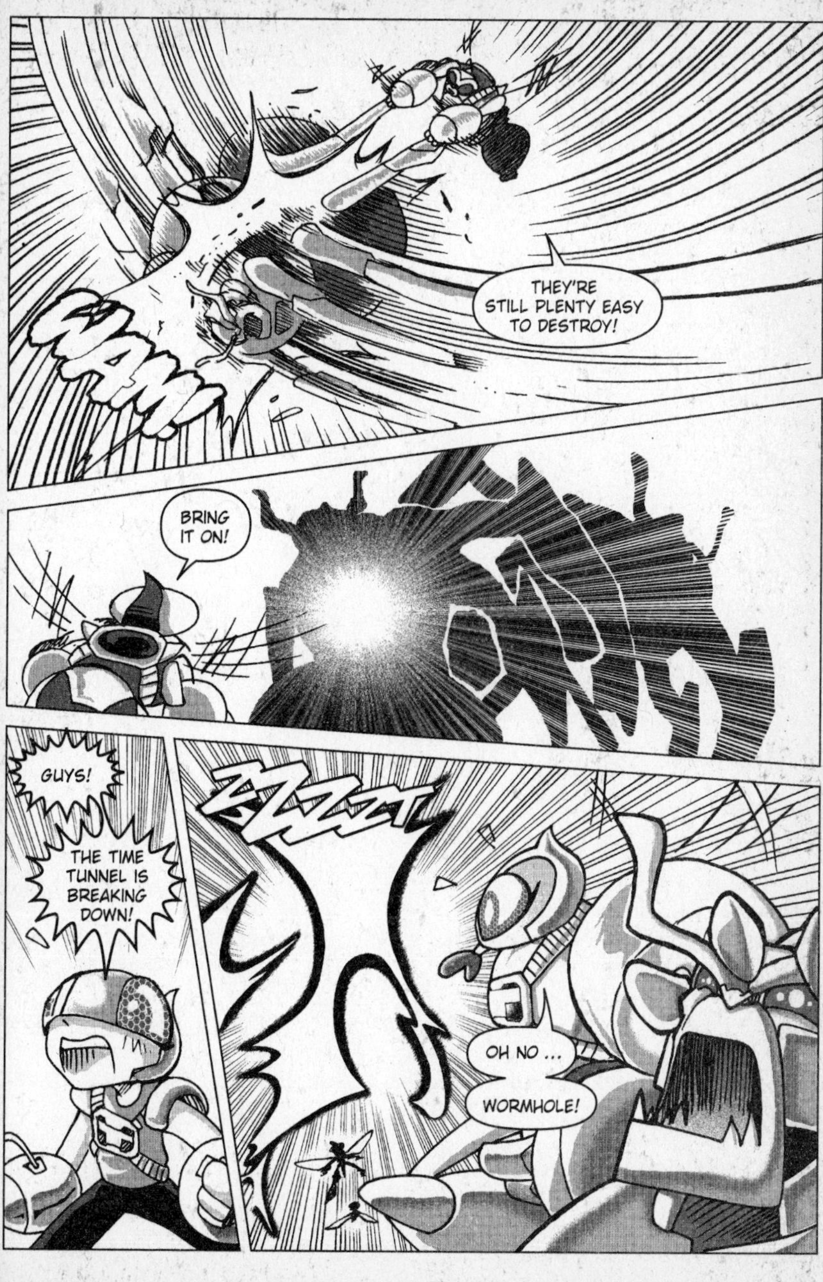
CRAM!
THEY'RE STILL PLENTY EASY TO DESTROY!
BRING IT ON!
GUYS!
THE TIME TUNNEL IS BREAKING DOWN!
ZZZZT
OH NO ...
WORMHOLE!

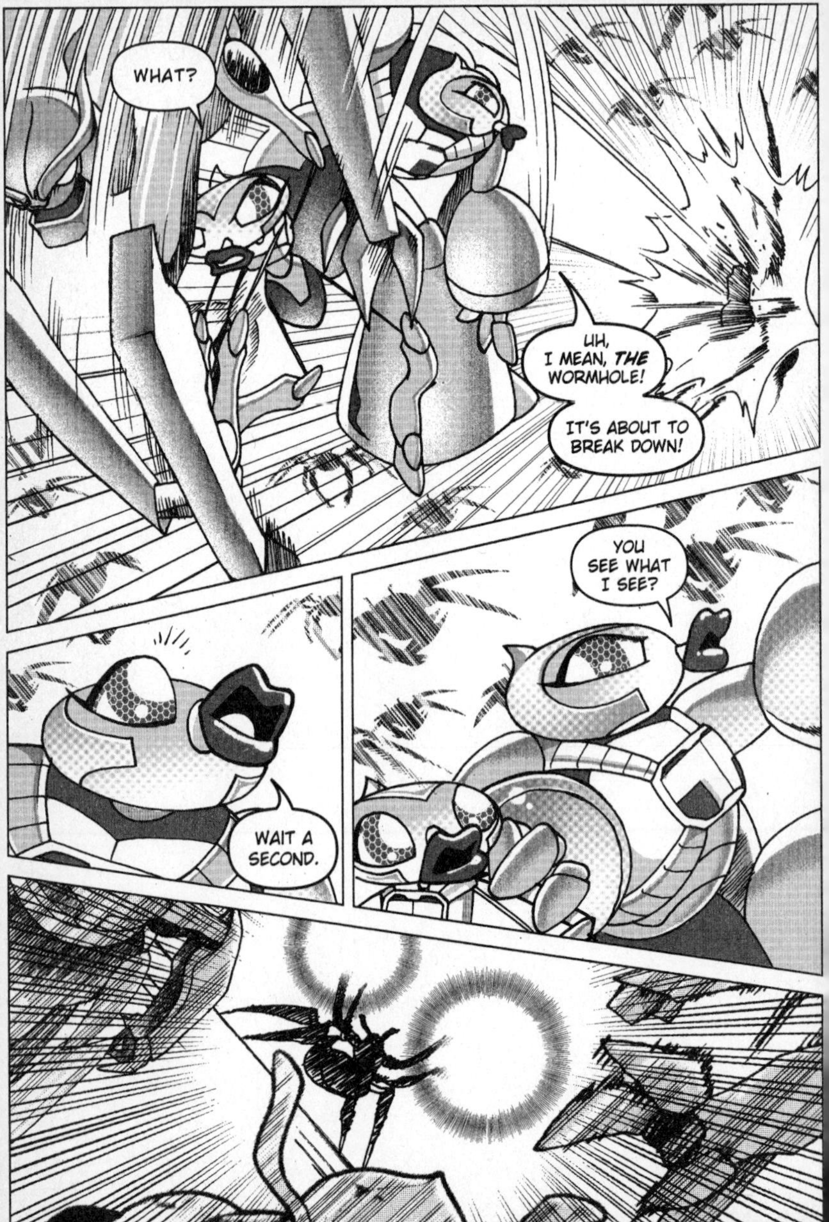
WHAT?
UH, I MEAN, ***THE*** WORMHOLE!
IT'S ABOUT TO BREAK DOWN!
WAIT A SECOND.
YOU SEE WHAT I SEE?

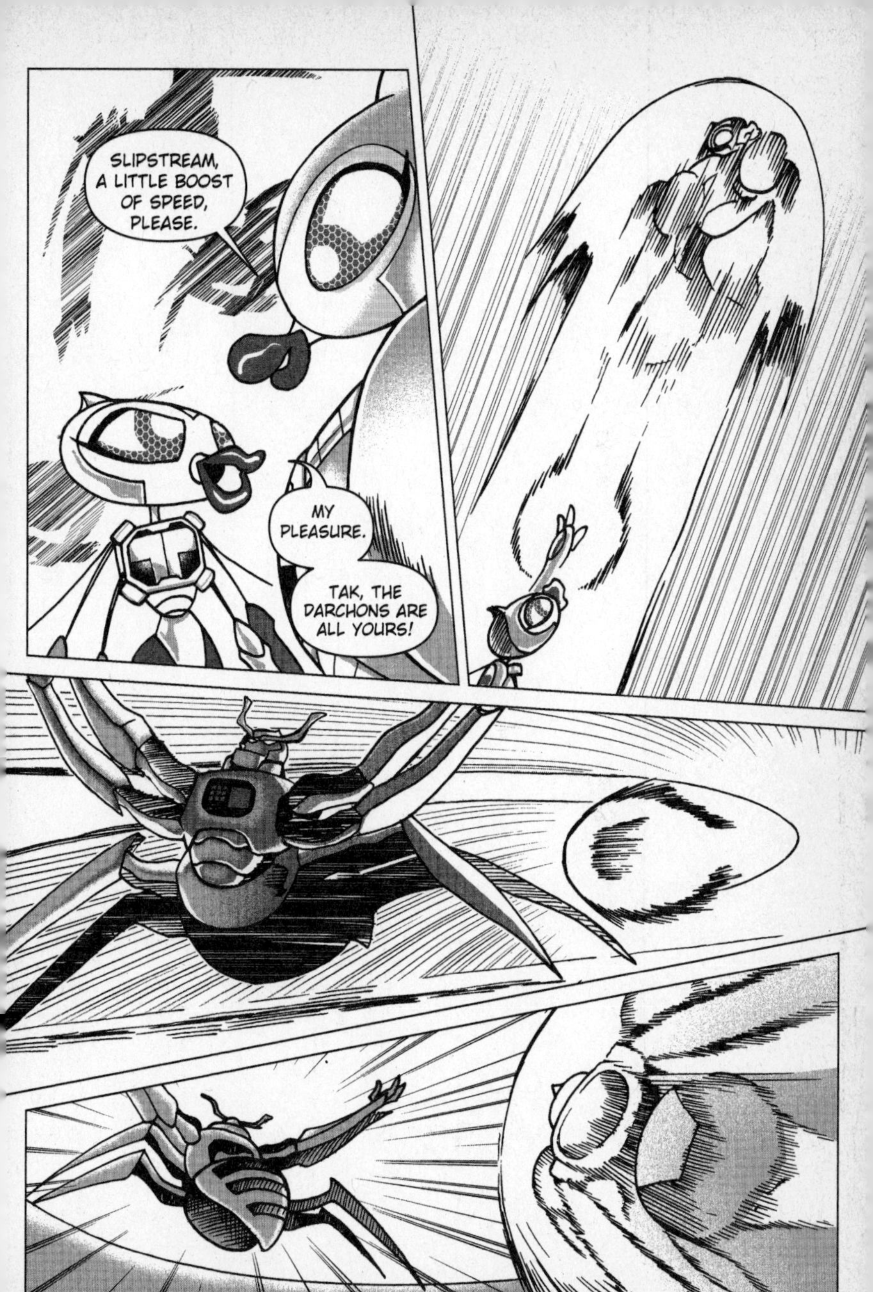
SLIPSTREAM, A LITTLE BOOST OF SPEED, PLEASE.
MY PLEASURE.
TAK, THE DARCHONS ARE ALL YOURS!

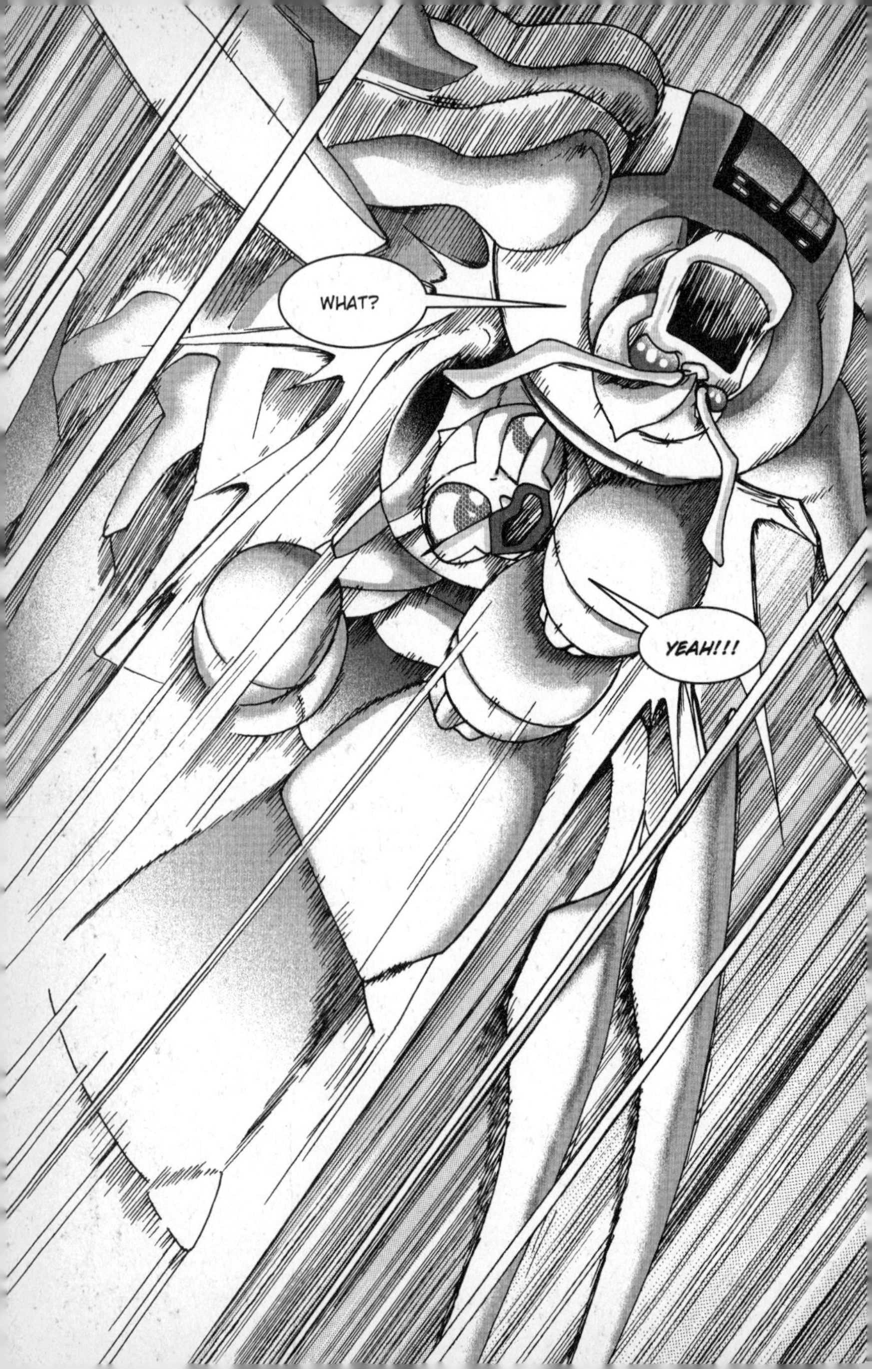
WHAT?
YEAH!!!

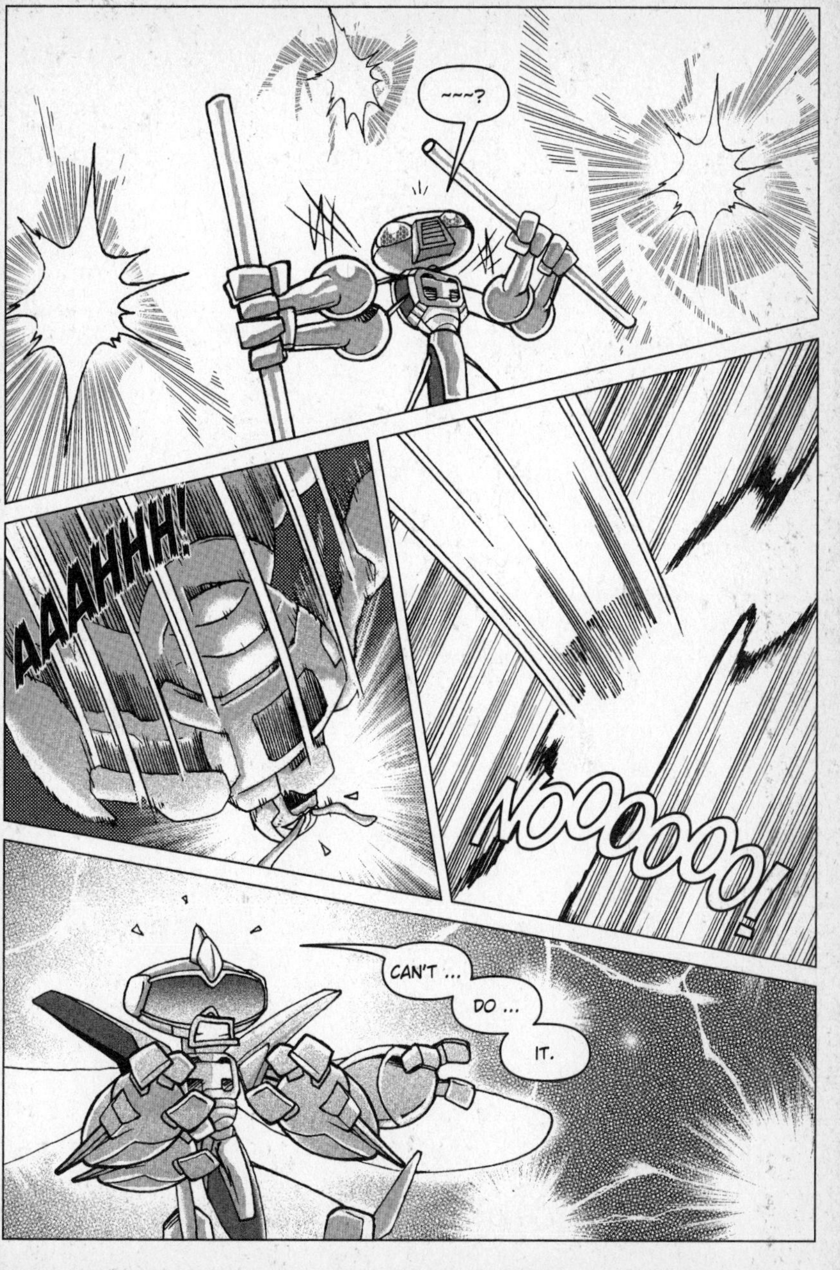

AAAHHH!
NOOOOOOO!
CAN'T ...
DO ...
IT.

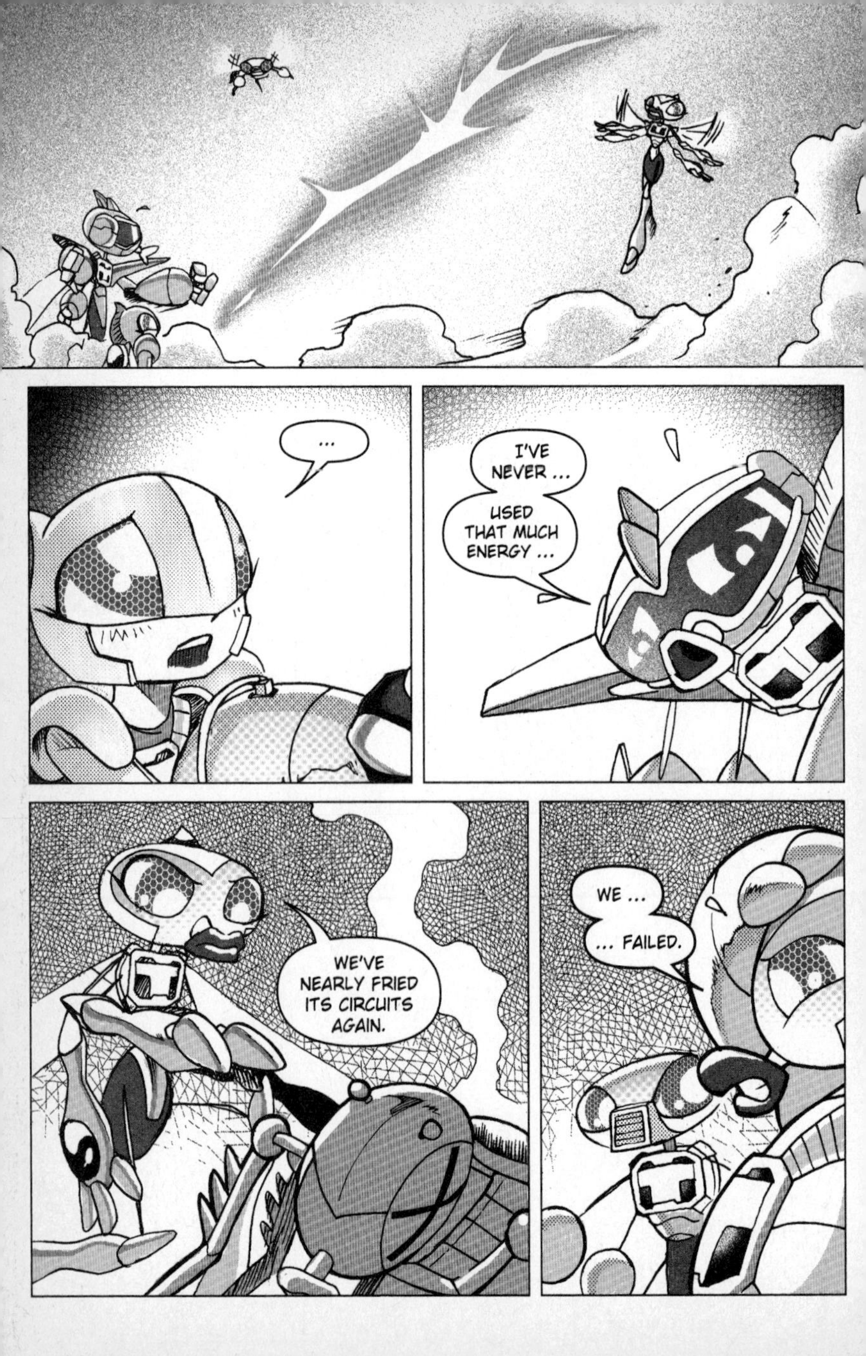
...
I'VE NEVER ...
USED THAT MUCH ENERGY ...
WE'VE NEARLY FRIED ITS CIRCUITS AGAIN.
WE ...
... FAILED.

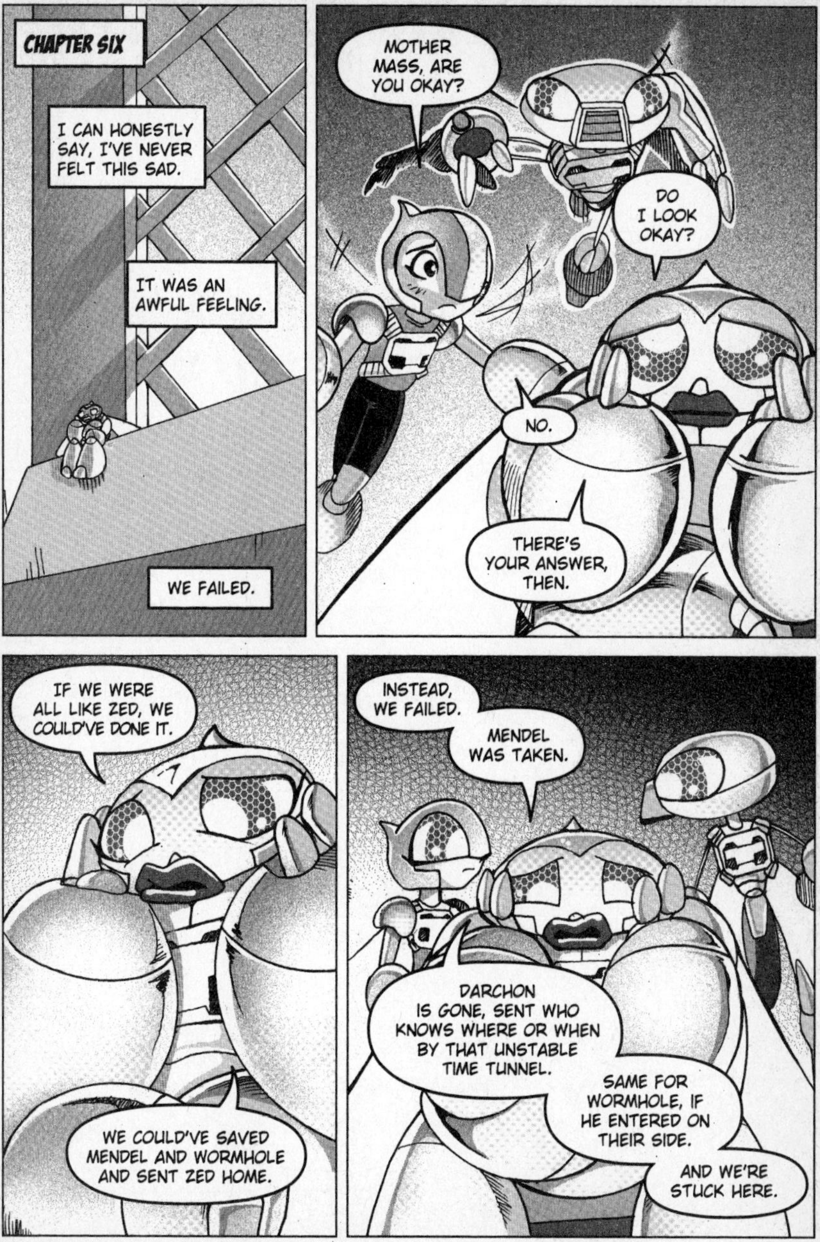
CHAPTER SIX
I CAN HONESTLY SAY, I'VE NEVER FELT THIS SAD.
IT WAS AN AWFUL FEELING.
WE FAILED.
MOTHER MASS, ARE YOU OKAY?
DO I LOOK OKAY?
NO.
THERE'S YOUR ANSWER, THEN.
IF WE WERE ALL LIKE ZED, WE COULD'VE DONE IT.
WE COULD'VE SAVED MENDEL AND WORMHOLE AND SENT ZED HOME.
INSTEAD, WE FAILED.
MENDEL WAS TAKEN.
DARCHON IS GONE, SENT WHO KNOWS WHERE OR WHEN BY THAT UNSTABLE TIME TUNNEL.
SAME FOR WORMHOLE, IF HE ENTERED ON THEIR SIDE.
AND WE'RE STUCK HERE.

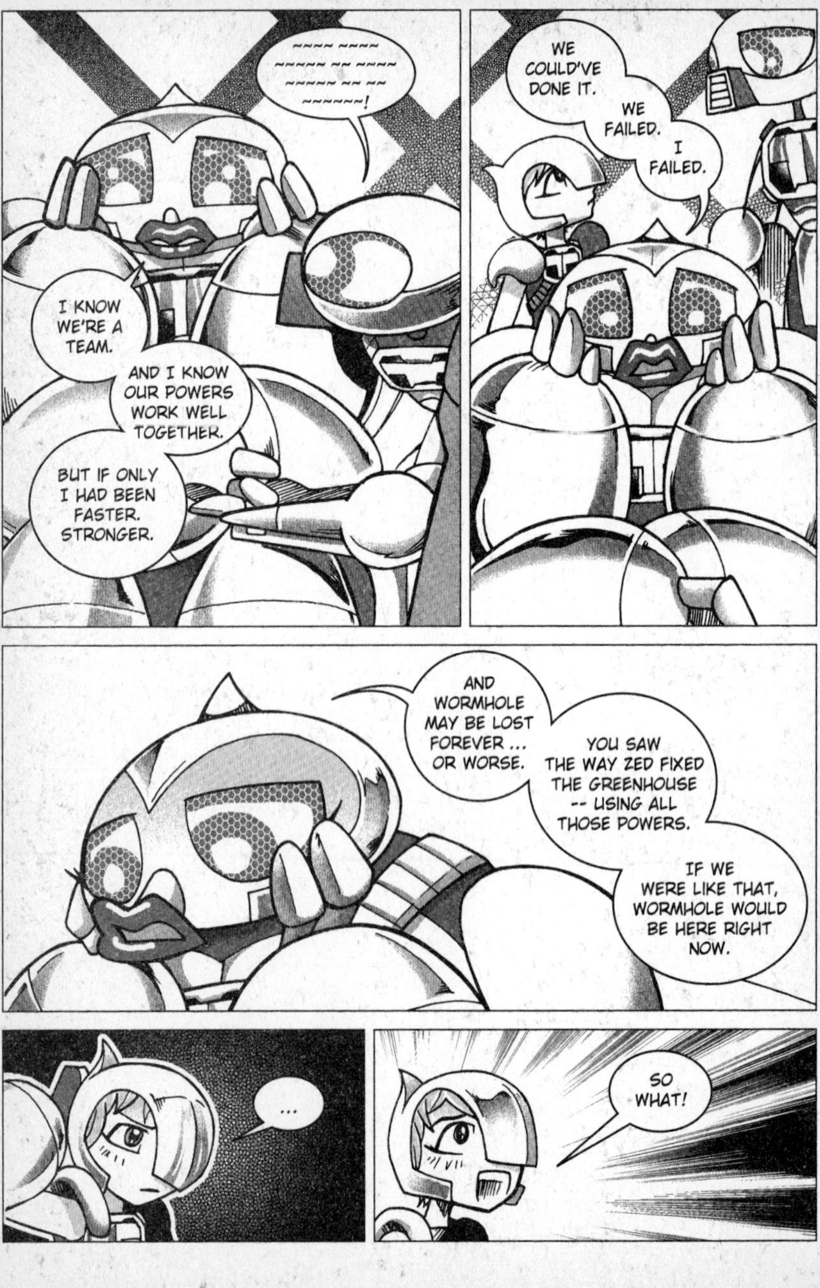

I KNOW WE'RE A TEAM.
AND I KNOW OUR POWERS WORK WELL TOGETHER.
BUT IF ONLY I HAD BEEN FASTER. STRONGER.
WE COULD'VE DONE IT.
WE FAILED.
I FAILED.
AND WORMHOLE MAY BE LOST FOREVER ... OR WORSE.
YOU SAW THE WAY ZED FIXED THE GREENHOUSE -- USING ALL THOSE POWERS.
IF WE WERE LIKE THAT, WORMHOLE WOULD BE HERE RIGHT NOW.
...
SO WHAT!

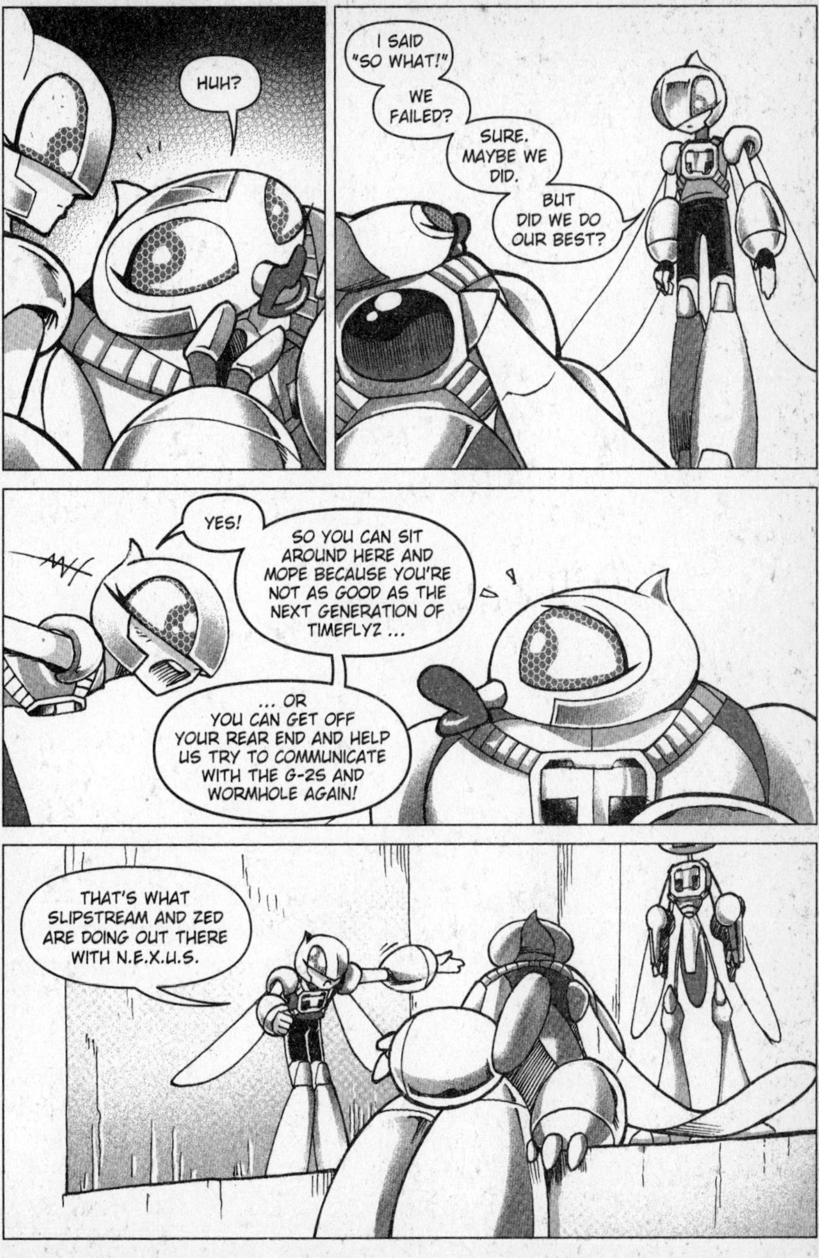
HUH?
I SAID "SO WHAT!"
WE FAILED?
SURE. MAYBE WE DID.
BUT DID WE DO OUR BEST?
YES!
SO YOU CAN SIT AROUND HERE AND MOPE BECAUSE YOU'RE NOT AS GOOD AS THE NEXT GENERATION OF TIMEFLYZ ...
... OR YOU CAN GET OFF YOUR REAR END AND HELP US TRY TO COMMUNICATE WITH THE G-2S AND WORMHOLE AGAIN!
THAT'S WHAT SLIPSTREAM AND ZED ARE DOING OUT THERE WITH N.E.X.U.S.

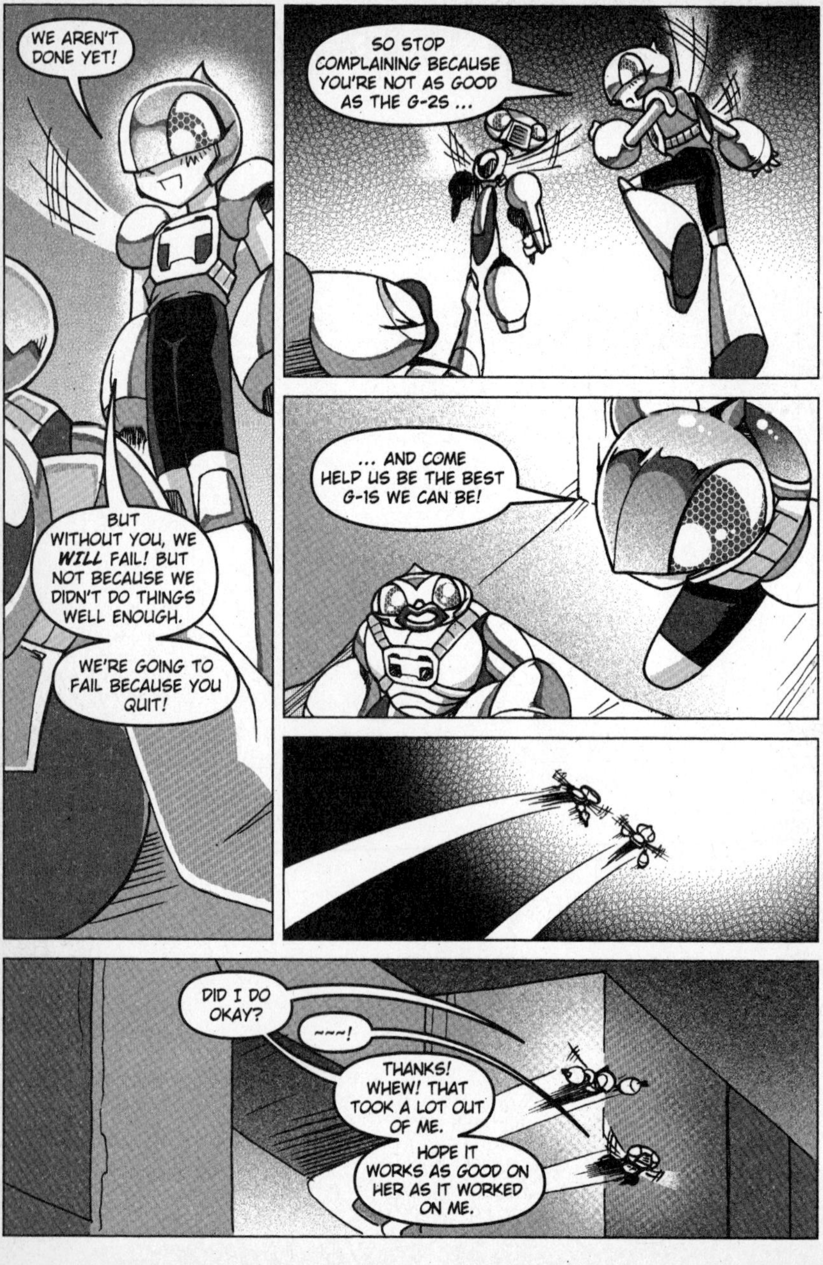
WE AREN'T DONE YET!
BUT WITHOUT YOU, WE **WILL** FAIL! BUT NOT BECAUSE WE DIDN'T DO THINGS WELL ENOUGH.
WE'RE GOING TO FAIL BECAUSE YOU QUIT!
SO STOP COMPLAINING BECAUSE YOU'RE NOT AS GOOD AS THE G-2S ...
... AND COME HELP US BE THE BEST G-1S WE CAN BE!
DID I DO OKAY?
~~~!
THANKS! WHEW! THAT TOOK A LOT OUT OF ME.
HOPE IT WORKS AS GOOD ON HER AS IT WORKED ON ME.
~~~

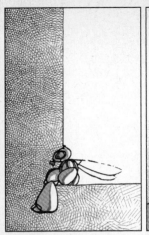

THE WORST PART OF ALL THIS ...

HMPH.

HM.

IT WASN'T WORMHOLE GETTING LOST OR DARCHON WINNING AND GETTING MENDEL OR THE PLAN TO GET WORMHOLE BACK NOT WORKING.

IT WAS THAT THE LITTLE GIRL WAS RIGHT.

I WAS BEING SILLY.

HMM?

THAT LITTLE STINKER!

LAUREL TEMPLETON REDUX

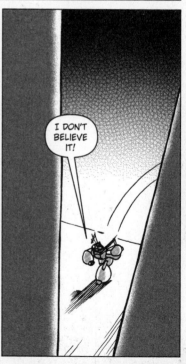

I DON'T BELIEVE IT!

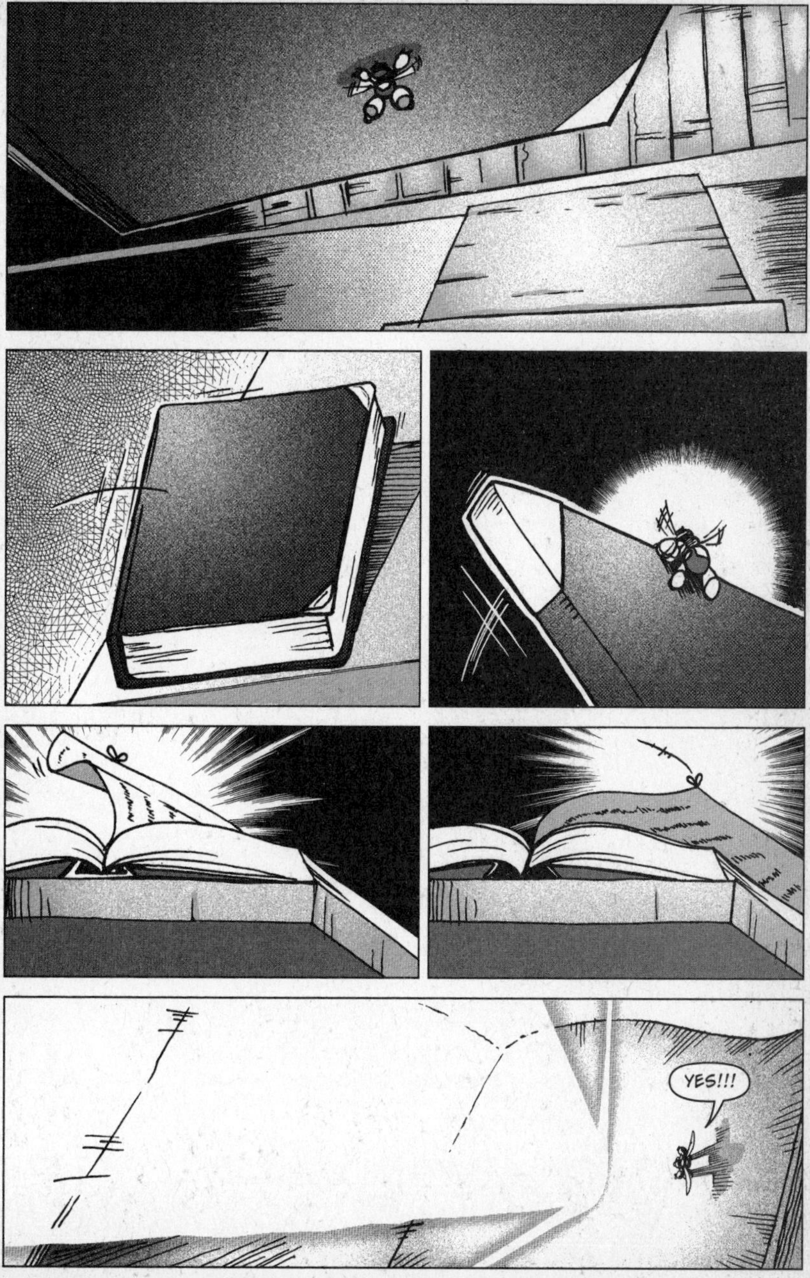
YES!!!

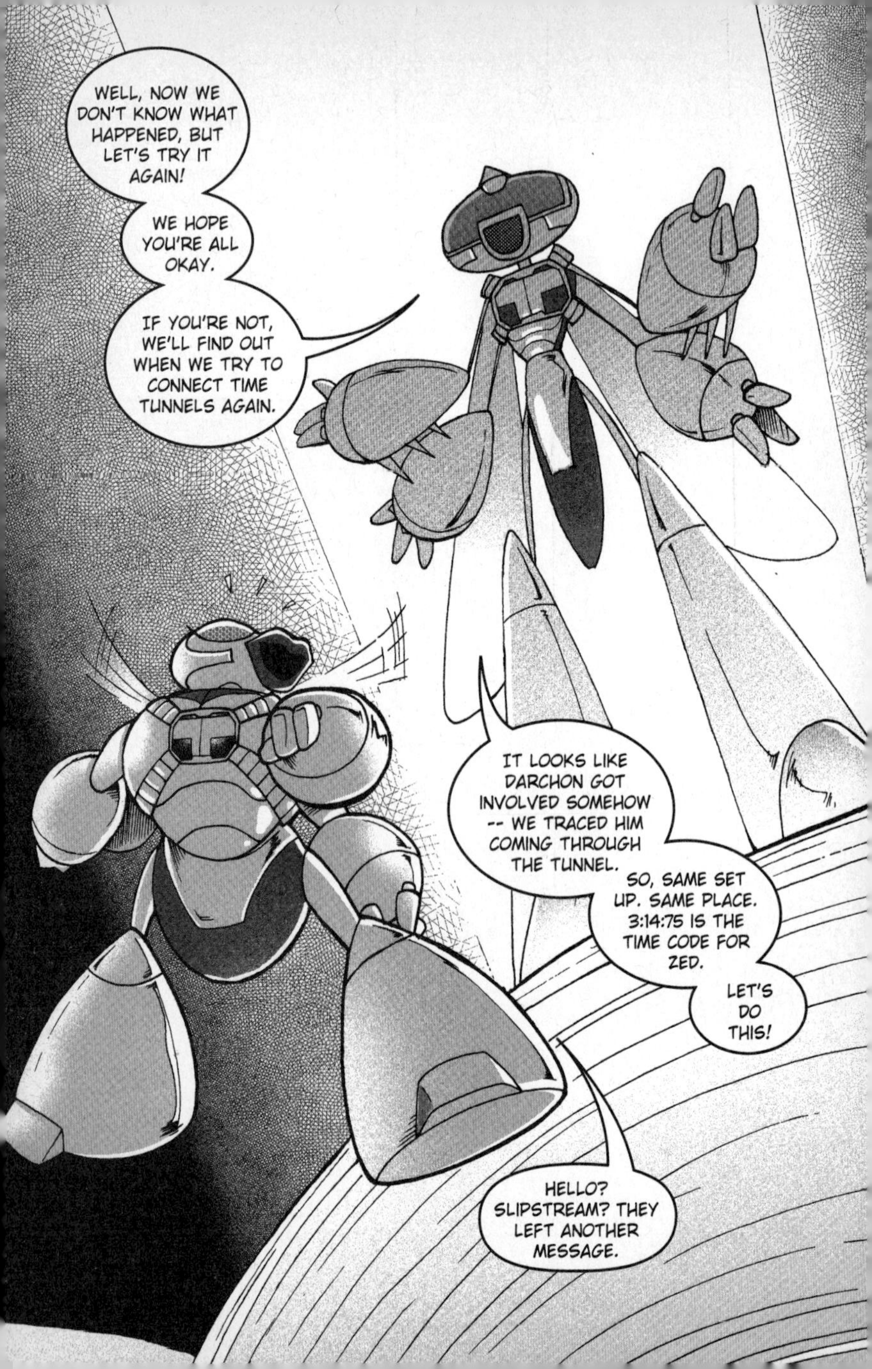
WELL, NOW WE DON'T KNOW WHAT HAPPENED, BUT LET'S TRY IT AGAIN!
WE HOPE YOU'RE ALL OKAY.
IF YOU'RE NOT, WE'LL FIND OUT WHEN WE TRY TO CONNECT TIME TUNNELS AGAIN.
IT LOOKS LIKE DARCHON GOT INVOLVED SOMEHOW -- WE TRACED HIM COMING THROUGH THE TUNNEL.
SO, SAME SET UP. SAME PLACE. 3:14:75 IS THE TIME CODE FOR ZED.
LET'S DO THIS!
HELLO? SLIPSTREAM? THEY LEFT ANOTHER MESSAGE.

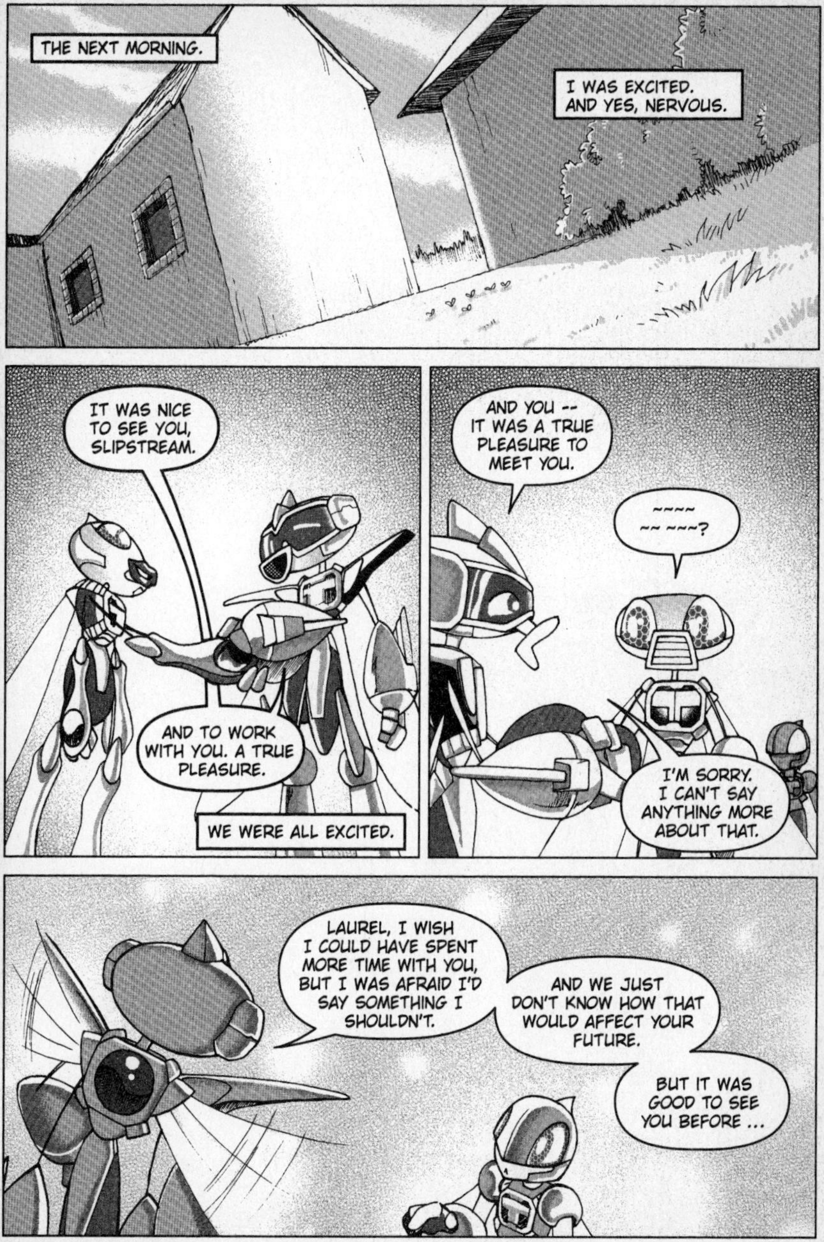
THE NEXT MORNING.
I WAS EXCITED. AND YES, NERVOUS.
IT WAS NICE TO SEE YOU, SLIPSTREAM.
AND TO WORK WITH YOU. A TRUE PLEASURE.
WE WERE ALL EXCITED.
AND YOU -- IT WAS A TRUE PLEASURE TO MEET YOU.
~~~~ ~~ ~~~?
I'M SORRY. I CAN'T SAY ANYTHING MORE ABOUT THAT.
LAUREL, I WISH I COULD HAVE SPENT MORE TIME WITH YOU, BUT I WAS AFRAID I'D SAY SOMETHING I SHOULDN'T.
AND WE JUST DON'T KNOW HOW THAT WOULD AFFECT YOUR FUTURE.
BUT IT WAS GOOD TO SEE YOU BEFORE ...
~~~~

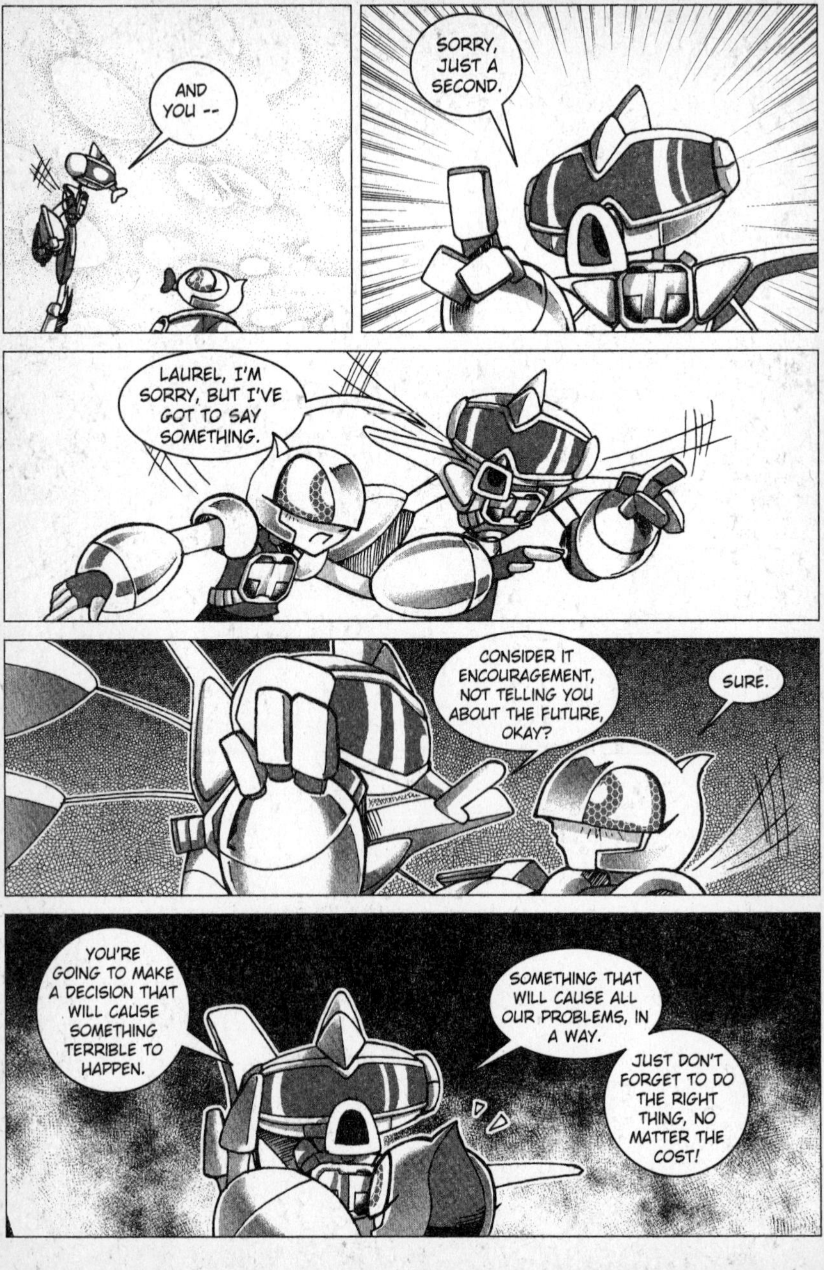
AND YOU --
SORRY, JUST A SECOND.
LAUREL, I'M SORRY, BUT I'VE GOT TO SAY SOMETHING.
CONSIDER IT ENCOURAGEMENT, NOT TELLING YOU ABOUT THE FUTURE, OKAY?
SURE.
YOU'RE GOING TO MAKE A DECISION THAT WILL CAUSE SOMETHING TERRIBLE TO HAPPEN.
SOMETHING THAT WILL CAUSE ALL OUR PROBLEMS, IN A WAY.
JUST DON'T FORGET TO DO THE RIGHT THING, NO MATTER THE COST!

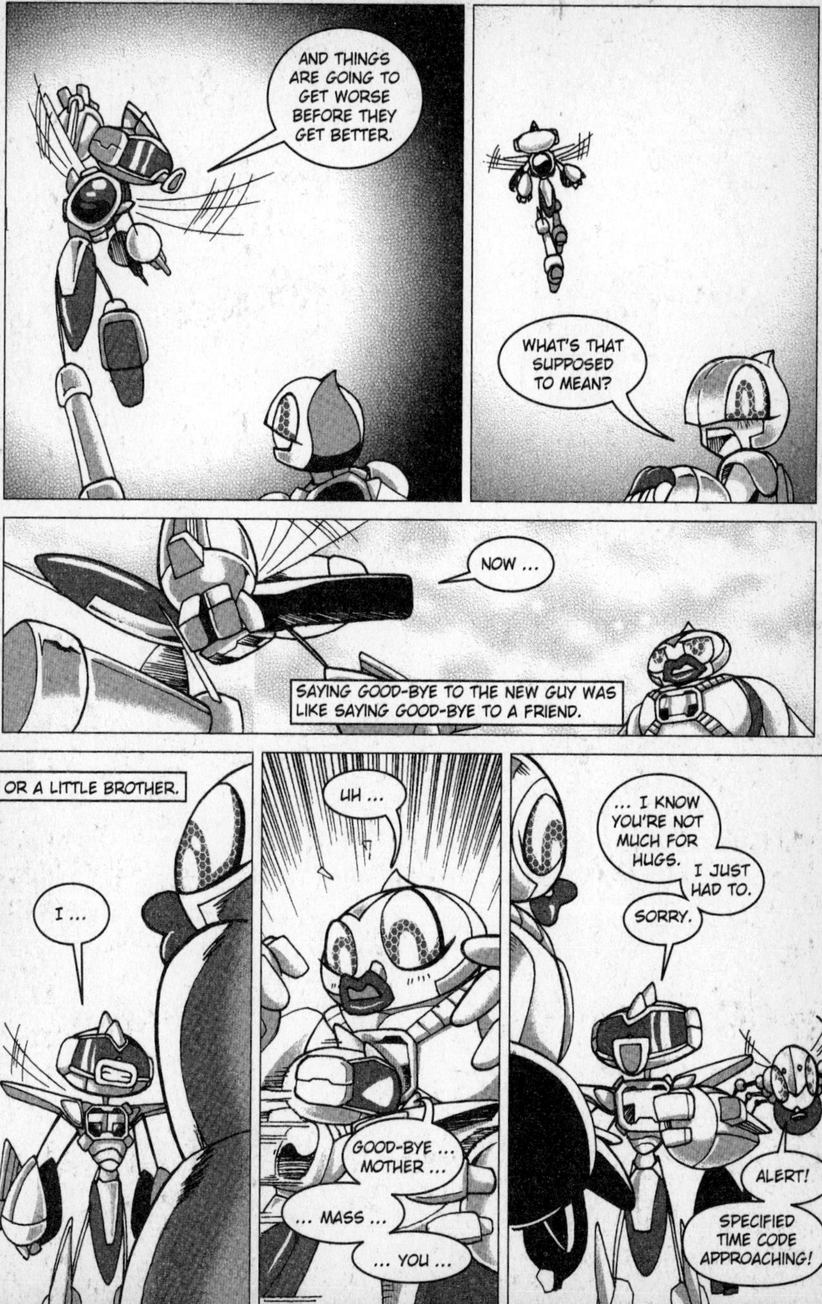
AND THINGS ARE GOING TO GET WORSE BEFORE THEY GET BETTER.
WHAT'S THAT SUPPOSED TO MEAN?
NOW ...
SAYING GOOD-BYE TO THE NEW GUY WAS LIKE SAYING GOOD-BYE TO A FRIEND.
OR A LITTLE BROTHER.
I ...
UH ...
GOOD-BYE ... MOTHER ...
... MASS ...
... YOU ...
... I KNOW YOU'RE NOT MUCH FOR HUGS.
I JUST HAD TO.
SORRY.
ALERT!
SPECIFIED TIME CODE APPROACHING!

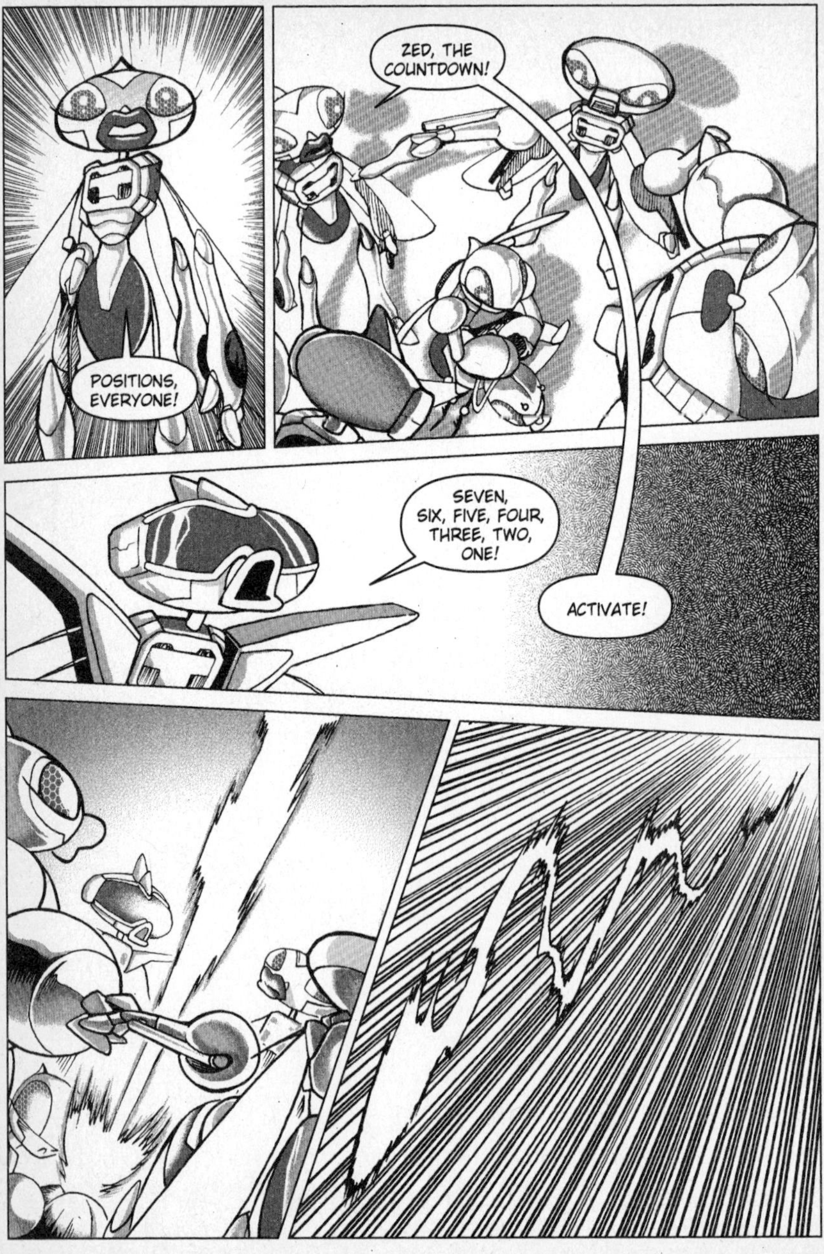
POSITIONS, EVERYONE!
ZED, THE COUNTDOWN!
SEVEN, SIX, FIVE, FOUR, THREE, TWO, ONE!
ACTIVATE!

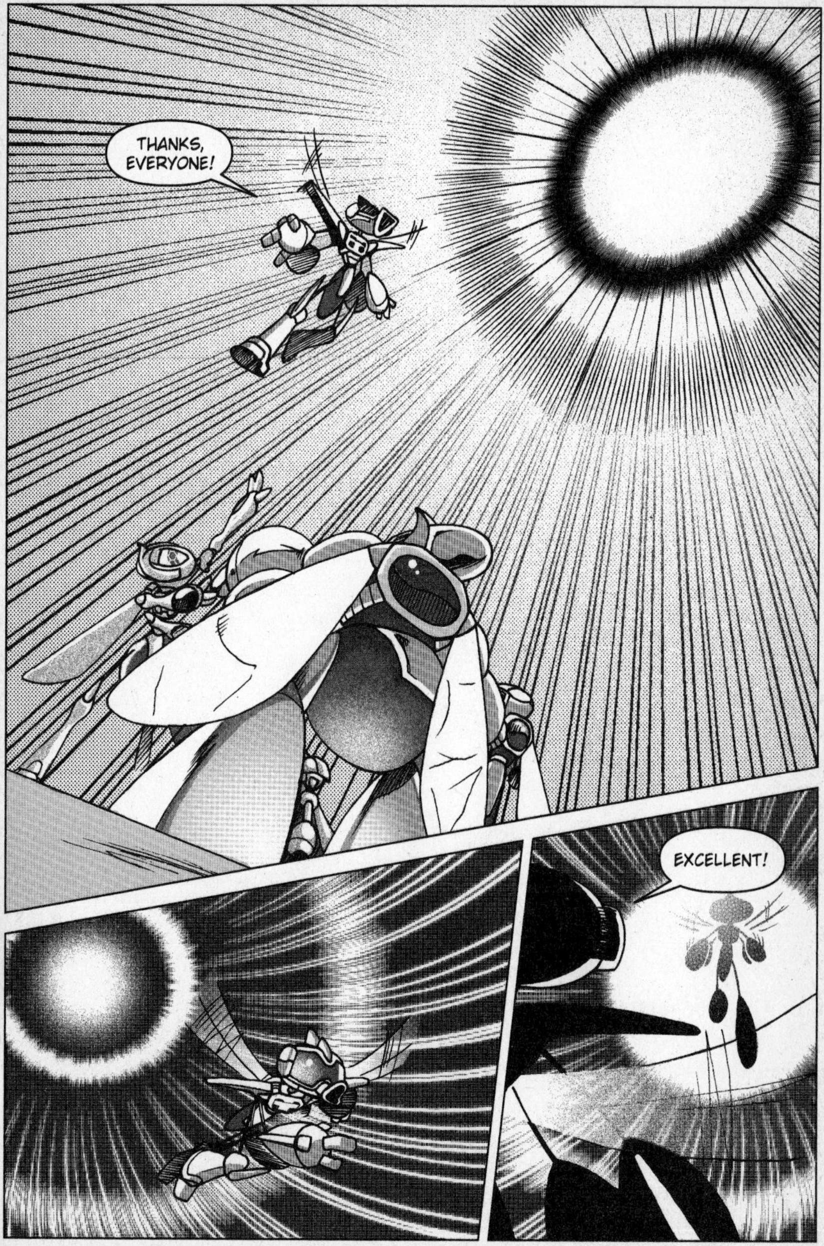
THANKS, EVERYONE!
EXCELLENT!

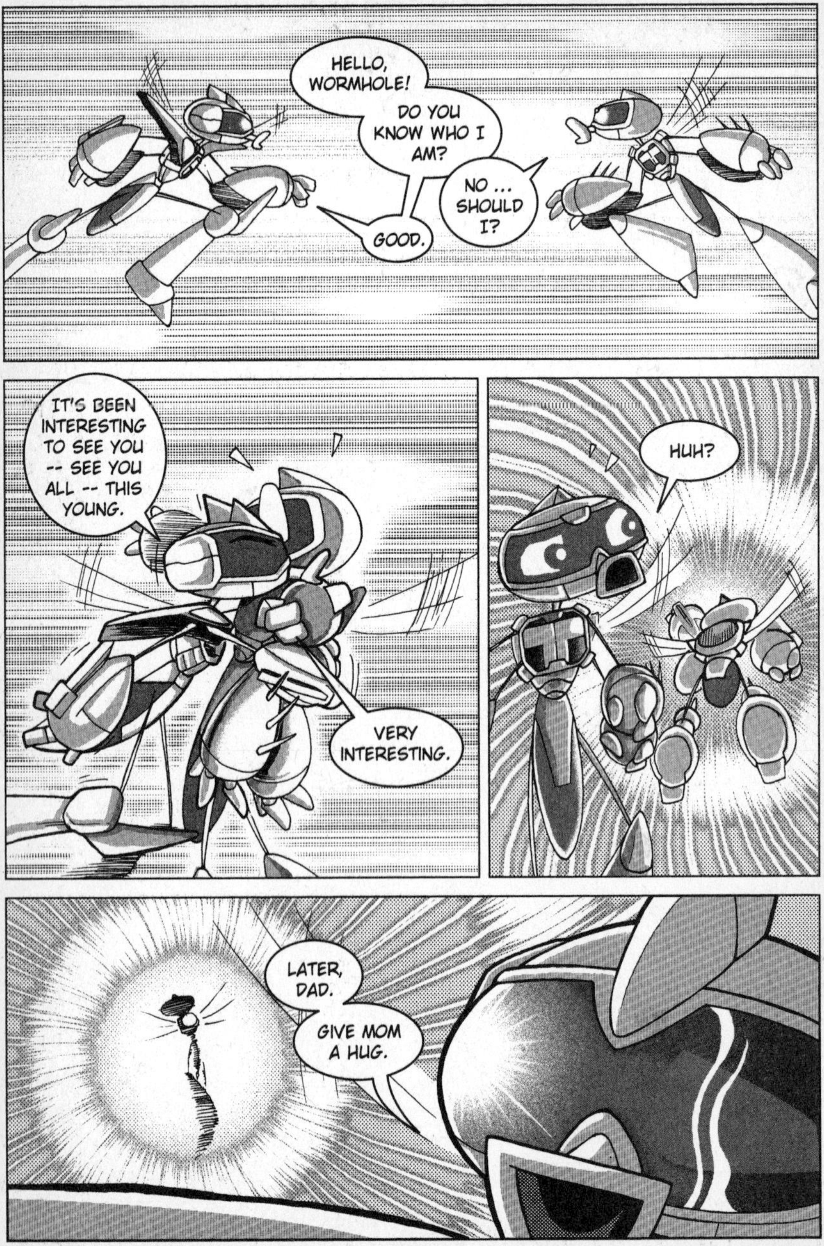
HELLO, WORMHOLE!
DO YOU KNOW WHO I AM?
NO ... SHOULD I?
GOOD.
IT'S BEEN INTERESTING TO SEE YOU -- SEE YOU ALL -- THIS YOUNG.
VERY INTERESTING.
HUH?
LATER, DAD.
GIVE MOM A HUG.

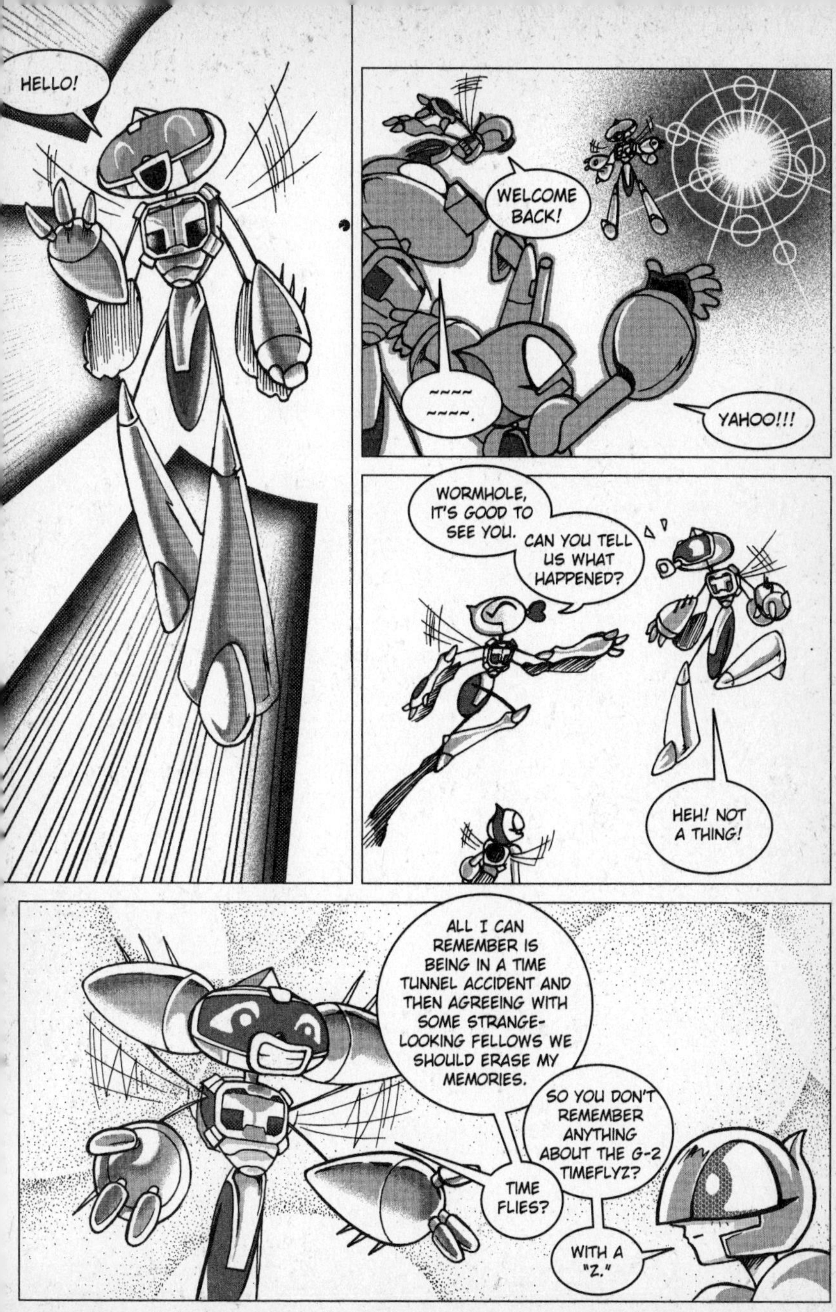
HELLO!
WELCOME BACK!
~~~~ ~~~~.
YAHOO!!!
WORMHOLE, IT'S GOOD TO SEE YOU.
CAN YOU TELL US WHAT HAPPENED?
HEH! NOT A THING!
ALL I CAN REMEMBER IS BEING IN A TIME TUNNEL ACCIDENT AND THEN AGREEING WITH SOME STRANGE-LOOKING FELLOWS WE SHOULD ERASE MY MEMORIES.
SO YOU DON'T REMEMBER ANYTHING ABOUT THE G-2 TIMEFLYZ?
TIME FLIES?
WITH A "Z."
~~~~

NOPE!

BRRRRR BRRRR?

WHAT HOLOGRAPHIC MESSAGE, TAK? SORRY, DON'T REMEMBER A THING.

OH, WAIT! I DO REMEMBER ONE THING.

I HAVE DARCHON'S COORDINATES IN TIME AND SPACE.

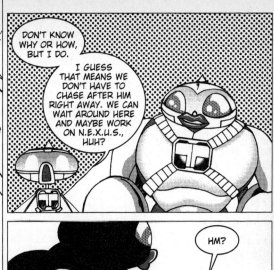

DON'T KNOW WHY OR HOW, BUT I DO.

I GUESS THAT MEANS WE DON'T HAVE TO CHASE AFTER HIM RIGHT AWAY. WE CAN WAIT AROUND HERE AND MAYBE WORK ON N.E.X.U.S., HUH?

HM?

THERE HE WAS. AND NOW I WAS ABLE TO FOLLOW THROUGH ON MY THREAT.

"WHEN I GET MY HANDS ON HIM ..."

WHAT?

I STILL DON'T QUITE KNOW WHAT'S GOING ON.

BUT I DO KNOW THIS; I'M GLAD I'M ME.

BECAUSE I GET TO BE FRIENDS WITH THEM.